'Karly Lane has a way of dragging you in and making you feel like you are a part of the story . . . It is a wonderful read.' — Beauty and Lace

'Lane vividly evokes Australian rural communities, and gives due recognition to its challenges, especially for farmers. Written with the warmth, humour and heart for which Lane's rural romances are known, *Time After Time* is an engaging read.' —Book'd Out

PRAISE FOR *A Stone's Throw Away*

'Fans will not be disappointed and new readers are likely to be converted . . . those looking for romance, suspense or contemporary novels will all find something to enjoy.' —Beauty and Lace

'With its appealing characters, well-crafted setting and layered storyline, *A Stone's Throw Away* is an entertaining read.' —Book'd Out

'Karly Lane has delivered a wonderfully immersive novel with a highly engaging plot, gripping suspense and compelling twists. *A Stone's Throw Away* is a story of courage, resilience and a passion for the truth.' —The Burgeoning Bookshelf

'I'm always highly impressed by Lane's ability to write compelling, entertaining and emotional storylines and weave some of Australia's history through her stories . . . it was an absolute treat to be back in one of her stories.' —Noveltea Corner

'There was so much emotion captured in these pages . . . Karly's novels never fail to entertain.' —Mic Loves Books

Karly Lane lives on the beautiful mid-North Coast of New South Wales, and she is the proud mum of four children and an assortment of four-legged animals.

Before becoming an author, Karly worked as a pathology collector. Now, after surviving three teenage children and with one more to go, she's confident she can add referee, hostage negotiator, law enforcer, peacekeeper, ruiner-of-social-lives, driving instructor and expert-at silently-counting-to-ten to her resume.

When she isn't at her keyboard, Karly can be found hanging out with her beloved horses and dogs, happily ignoring the housework.

Karly writes Rural and Women's Fiction set in small country towns, blending contemporary stories with historical heritage. She is a passionate advocate for rural Australia, with a focus on rural communities and current issues. She has published over twenty books with Allen & Unwin.

ALSO BY KARLY LANE

KARLY LANE

Wish You Were Here

ALLEN&UNWIN
SYDNEY · MELBOURNE · AUCKLAND · LONDON

This edition published in 2023
First published in 2022

Allen & Unwin
Cammeraygal Country
83 Alexander Street
Crows Nest NSW 2065
Australia
Phone: (61 2) 8425 0100
Email: info@allenandunwin.com
Web: www.allenandunwin.com

Allen & Unwin acknowledges the Traditional Owners of the Country on which we live and work. We pay our respects to all Aboriginal and Torres Strait Islander Elders, past and present.

 A catalogue record for this book is available from the National Library of Australia

ISBN 978 1 76147 059 2

Set in Simoncini Garamond by Bookhouse, Sydney
Printed and bound in Australia by the Opus Group

10 9 8 7 6 5 4 3 2 1

For Kaitlin,
Thank you for being the best personal
assistant, farm manager and offsider a mum
could ask for, especially since you do it for love
and not cash!

Prologue

Reggie MacLeod stared out her office window at the gloomy grey skies and watched the raindrops dribble down the windowpane, trying to remember the last time she'd seen the sun. She should be used to it by now—the UK weather—but somehow it continued to surprise her just how often it bloody rained!

The cold never bothered her here—she'd grown up in Ebor, a little village in the New England region of New South Wales in Australia on her family property, River Styx. She knew about cold. Early mornings feeding animals before school in winter were still not her favourite memories. But the summers were hot and long, and even now if she closed her eyes she could almost smell the sweet scent of wattle and eucalyptus on a warm breeze.

1

Reggie shook her head as though trying to dislodge the glum mood she was in and looked back at the computer screen in front of her. *Focus*, she instructed herself firmly.

She couldn't pinpoint the reason why she'd been feeling so miserable lately—she had no reason to be, her life was pretty much perfect. She had the job she'd always dreamed of having, an apartment in one of the most beautiful parts of London, friends and colleagues who respected her and an income that allowed her the freedom to travel and explore Europe as much as she liked, and yet this annoying melancholy kind of emptiness kept poking its head up more and more often, sapping her joy and making her long for something she couldn't quite define, which always seemed just out of reach.

Her mother was convinced all she needed a good man—although she knew her parents were secretly worried that she'd end up falling in love with an Englishman and staying in the UK forever. So far, despite the fact Reggie had an active social life, she'd never found anyone she'd been serious about. There *had* been that one Scotsman she'd spent a lovely weekend with in Edinburgh a few months ago. Too bad it turned out he was married and away on a boys' rugby trip.

She let out a frustrated sigh as she once again forced herself to concentrate. She was handling one of the firm's biggest client's new ad campaign—she should be running on a high since her boss had put so much faith in her ability to pull this thing off. It had been something she'd been working towards ever since she got here, and yet, now that she had it . . . it really was crazy, but it almost felt as though she'd lost interest. She closed her eyes briefly as the thought materialised. She could never allow herself to utter those words out loud. Ever. It was ridiculous to even be thinking it. How could she think a career she'd spent years working so hard on was suddenly . . . overrated?

Thoughts of home had been playing on her mind lately, and with each phone or video call, she missed her family more. Maybe she just needed a visit. She was homesick, that was all. Maybe once she went back, she'd recharge her batteries and find the passion for her job again. The thought cheered her up no end. As soon as she finished this presentation, she'd put in for a few weeks' holidays and go home.

Her phone rang and she gave a small chuckle when her brother's name flashed across the screen.

'Talk about ESP,' she murmured. 'Hey, great timing, Goober,' she said, wedging the phone between her neck and shoulder as an interoffice message flashed up on her screen that she needed to answer immediately. 'I've just decided I'm going to book a trip home soon.'

For a moment there was no reply on the other end of the line and Reggie frowned as she finished typing a reply on her keyboard. She pulled the phone away from her ear and put it back again. 'Brent? Are you there?'

'Yeah,' her brother's deep voice answered, as he cleared his throat quickly. 'Reg, something's happened.' His usual laidback teasing tone was missing, and instantly Reggie felt her blood freeze in her veins. 'It's Mum and Dad.'

'What's happened?' Her voice sounded hollow—empty.

'They were in a car accident. They're both in a bad way. I think you should come home as soon as you can get a flight.'

3

Reggie didn't remember much after that, just snippets of things—informing the receptionist she was leaving, muttering something about her parents, booking the plane ticket, going back to her apartment. Her neighbour, Tiffany, had answered when Reggie knocked on her door and, taking one look at Reggie's pale face, helped her organise everything.

It was Felicity, Brent's fiancé, who picked Reggie up from the airport. The city traffic blurred as they headed for the hospital where her parents had been transferred from the accident scene.

'They're going to be all right,' Felicity said to her, taking her eyes briefly from the road to give her a reassuring look. 'Ray and Peggy are two of the strongest people I know. They won't give up without a fight.'

Reggie desperately wanted to believe her, but the initial prognosis hadn't been so promising.

'How's Brent?' Reggie asked. Her eyes felt gritty and sore from the long flight and minimal sleep.

'He's doing his best to stay positive. But he's trying to do too much. Be everywhere. He wanted to pick you up himself but he had to drive back to River Styx yesterday. He'll be back tomorrow.'

'Thank you for staying here with them,' Reggie said, reaching over to squeeze her soon-to-be sister-in-law's hand. 'I know Brent couldn't have managed without you. He's lucky to have you—we all are,' she added, noticing the strange, tight smile on the other woman's face. 'Are you doing okay?'

Felicity was like a second daughter to her parents—and a sister to Reggie. She and Brent had been together since high school and was a part of the family. It couldn't have been easy trying to comfort Brent as well as deal with her own grief over her in-laws' accident.

'I . . .' Felicity started, then abruptly clamped her mouth shut, shaking her head and quickly wiping away a stray tear.

Reggie bit her lip against the threat of her own tears. She couldn't break down now—not before she went in to see her parents. She had to hold it together for them.

'I'm just really glad you're here, Reg,' Felicity finally managed.

The smell of the hospital, so clinical and alien, confronted Reggie the moment she walked through the front doors. She followed Felicity along a corridor and into an elevator, arriving at the ICU where they waited for the doctor to finish his rounds.

Her mother had what they suspected were severe spinal injuries, which would put her into a wheelchair for the rest of her life, requiring extensive physiotherapy and help with day-to-day care. Her father's leg injuries were going to require multiple operations.

Her parents were situated in two different parts of the hospital and Reggie was allowed to see each of them briefly. Her mother was still sedated—they'd put her into an induced coma until the swelling eased so the doctors could continue to assess her—but it was already obvious that her injuries were extensive. The doctors were waiting to see if there was any brain damage. Reggie felt the blood drain from her face as she lowered herself into a seat beside her mother's bed.

If it weren't for the name above the bed and the slender hands on top of the blankets, Reggie wasn't sure she'd have recognised her mother beneath all the bandages, tubes and bruising. She was so still, so quiet—nothing like the animated, happy mother Reggie knew.

'You can hold her hand,' Felicity said gently. 'They say it helps.'

Reggie reached for her mum's hand and slid her own warm ones around it, willing some of her own energy into the almost lifeless-looking body beside her. 'Please be okay, Mum. I can't lose you.' She blinked rapidly to try to disperse the gathering tears but there were too many of them and they overflowed and ran down her cheeks. Felicity put an arm around Reggie and held her tight as they sat together silently, willing the woman in the bed to come back to them.

A few floors up, her father looked almost as bad as her mother. He was covered in bruises and cuts, his eyes swollen shut and his legs . . . Reggie did her best to keep the horrified expression from her face as she took in the bulky, medieval torture devices piercing her father's lower legs—the wounds still fresh and raw from the accident.

'I look like a pig on a spit,' her dad's croaky voice sounded, making Reggie jump. She'd thought he was asleep.

'Hi Dad. How do you feel?' she asked, before rolling her eyes, and shaking her head. Dumb question.

'Like a pig on a spit would feel, I'd imagine,' he said, trying to smile, but only managing a grimace. 'Your mother?' he asked, holding her eyes.

'I've just come from seeing her. She's still . . . asleep,' Reggie decided on, as opposed to mentioning the coma.

She'd never seen her dad cry before. She'd seen him a bit teary-eyed on the odd occasion, but usually with happy or proud tears—never before had she seen Ray MacLeod truly weep. It broke her heart.

❖

Reggie had taken six weeks off work, but as the full picture of her parents' injuries became clear, she resigned herself to the fact that she wouldn't be returning to her job in London and organised for her flat to be packed up and her belongings sent back home. It was going to be months before either of her parents was allowed back to River Styx and then years of rehabilitation between them. There was no decision really to be made. She wouldn't be returning to London.

Over the next six months, Reggie and Brent worked together running the property and caring for their parents. The job was too much to take on alone, and Reggie knew that if she left there was no way Brent would be able to manage working the property as well as the accommodation and the ongoing care of her parents. So, the plan was for her to remain until her parents were able to care for themselves.

She'd decided she wouldn't return to the UK, but there would come a time when she wouldn't be needed so much on the farm, and she'd made loose plans to take a job in Sydney so she could come home whenever she needed to.

And then Brent was diagnosed with a brain tumour.

It had stunned everyone. After everything they'd been through with their parents' accident, to be hit by something so horrific had been almost impossible to comprehend. It'd been a fluke that Brent had even been diagnosed. He'd gone to the doctor with a sore leg and happened to mention the recent headaches he was having and had been sent for tests. No one had expected the results to come back with the devastating news of a tumour—and, even worse, that it was one of the more aggressive types.

He'd undergone surgery to try and remove it but there was nothing the doctors could do.

Within five months of Brent's diagnosis, he was gone.

Chapter 1

Reggie loved this time of year on River Styx. The surrounding paddocks were coloured in a wintery palette of browns, yellows and greens and the bare-limbed Chinese poplar trees lining the driveway were standing sentinel, looking cold and naked without their green leafy foliage of the spring and summer months.

She complained about the cold like most locals, but deep down she kind of wished it was winter all year round. What wasn't there to love? Thick winter jumpers to hide the annoying rolls that winter comfort food always added. Boots and more boots. Reggie was a certified bootaholic, although she justified her boot addiction with reasonable logic—they were necessary.

She had her trusty work boots, which were also her riding boots; she also had her *good* riding boots and a backup pair in a different colour. Then there were the going-out boots. She knew she'd gone a little overboard with the boot-buying lately—it didn't take a psychologist to figure out she'd been shopping for boots as a kind of coping mechanism—but it made her feel good when she opened a box and breathed in that gorgeous, new leather boot smell. For a moment she could forget all the stress and the huge upheaval she'd been dealing with. It was an escape, albeit an expensive one, which is why she'd decided not to buy any more for a while.

This morning she wore her trusty tan work boots, which were still warm from the night they'd spent drying out in front of the fire.

She opened the door and the frosty morning air hit her in the face. Okay, so maybe there were a *few* things she didn't particularly like about winter.

It was different when you could enjoy the cold from inside, in front of a fireplace or snuggled up under a mountain of doonas. But going out in the early morning to feed animals was not enjoyable in any way, no matter how many layers you had on.

The crunch of gravel beneath her boots punctuated the quiet of the yard and Reggie watched as white puffs of frosted air came out as she breathed. She exhaled and admired the magic of turning hot air into cold, the same way she had ever since she was a child, before burying her hands deeper into the pockets of her heavy jacket and making her way towards the shed outside the main house yard.

A nicker nearby brought her head up from where it had been tucked low in the collar of her coat. Five horses nodded eagerly at her as she approached.

'Morning guys,' she called, 'breakfast is coming.' The sound of her boots echoed inside the high walls of the aluminium open-sided shed. She selected the various buckets and went about making up the horses hard feed, before loading them all into a cart to drag across to the fenced-off night paddock and dish them out to the waiting horde.

The horses ranged in age from twenty-one down to seven years old. Her family had always been avid horse people, and horses had always been part of her family. Over the years they'd had many brumbies caught from the nearby Guy Fawkes National Park. They were as much part of River Styx as the land itself.

Her brother and father had broken in all of them—it'd been a time-honoured tradition passed down through the MacLeod family. Reggie had done most of her own horse handling, but she'd never had the gift her father and brother had—theirs was something special.

She stopped to watch the horses for a moment, something that always brought her a contented peace. Happy horses, doing what they did best: eating.

She listened to the munching and closed her eyes to take in the other noises around her. She often found herself amused when people visiting described the country as quiet. This morning the wind moving through the trees in the surrounding bush sounded like the roar of an ocean. The magpies—so many—sang their songs and competed for attention with the family of kookaburras nearby. It was anything but quiet. Still, she supposed, compared with traffic it would seem quieter, at least.

River Styx was primarily a beef property, but it had also become a popular New England holiday stay, with cabin accommodation that offered visitors a break from everyday life to unwind and reconnect with nature. It was three hundred and sixty hectares, surrounded by the New England National Park, with the Styx River flowing through the property, fed by many smaller streams, and a huge dam teeming with the much sought-after brown and rainbow trout; it truly felt like a piece of paradise.

The accommodation business had been her brother's idea. During one particularly bad drought season, soon after he'd started working on the farm, he'd drawn up a business plan to tap into the tourism and recreational fishing markets. Their region had so much to offer visitors, and they weren't limited to summer tourism as some locations were. Winter stays had been proving a huge trend for people who wanted to experience freezing their butts off for a change. And fishing tourism was a popular and growing sector that would work perfectly with the cabin accommodation.

With most of their beef cattle sold off and the workload around the family farm reduced, Brent had convinced their parents this was a good investment and they built three modest cabins on the property, which then grew to five.

Brent had never been a scholar. In fact, his name had become a local legend at their high school, a legend Reggie had heard endlessly repeated as she followed her brother through, waiting for the surprise to cross teachers' faces as soon as they realised she was the sister of the kid who'd sent most of them on mental-health breaks. Yes, she was *that* MacLeod, and yes, she actually enjoyed school. She hadn't had so much as one detention in her entire school life.

They'd been like chalk and cheese, Brent and Reggie.

She'd been a star pupil at school. It wasn't hard when your primary school only had twelve kids, but even in high school, an hour and a half trip either way, she was in the top classes. She always knew she wanted to leave and forge a life in the city—bright lights and excitement had been what she dreamed of—and as soon as she finished Year Twelve she'd left for university.

Brent, on the other hand, hated school and couldn't wait to get out, but Reggie's parents would only agree to let him leave school if he had a job—even though all he'd ever wanted to do was work on the farm alongside their father. Their dad had been adamant that he needed a career to fall back on. So, Brent, being Brent, had toddled off and secured a building apprenticeship the next day with a local builder. He'd worked there for close to seven years before his boss had shut down the business, and then he finally started working with their father.

Reggie, having moved to London after uni, had been sceptical about the holiday-stay and fishing venture, but she had to admit that Brent's enthusiasm was pretty persuasive, as was the business plan she'd helped him put together.

It got cold around Ebor in winter—*really* cold. Unlike Guyra and a few smaller places nearby that were a tad higher in altitude, the Ebor area didn't always snow ... it just felt bloody cold enough for it! But when it *did* snow, the sleepy little village and the highway that ran through it exploded with people heading up to see snow. At the first mention of possible snow, bookings would skyrocket as people planned spur-of-the-moment weekends away.

Then there were the romantic getaways, with couples coming to enjoy brisk bush walks and sitting in front of a roaring fire with wine and a plate of cheese and biscuits.

The surrounding national parks were a beacon for the more adventurous hiking and eco crowd. Visitors could walk a few minutes from the property into a national park and explore to their heart's content.

Meanwhile, their enormous dam, always well stocked with trout, drew New England trout fishermen from all over the country. Brent's idea to open up the accommodation and fishing side of the business was a smart move, without a doubt. With her marketing contacts and Brent's passion for the project, they launched River Styx cabin stays in every fishing, camping and outdoor living magazine across the country and the advertising paid off with a surge of bookings flooding in within the first few short weeks of opening.

But it had never been part of the plan for Reggie to run it.

No one had seen the sudden blow of losing Brent coming, and the hole he'd left behind in their family was still gaping and raw.

Chapter 2

The soft nudge of a warm nose on Reggie's leg drew her attention back to the job at hand, and she bent down to pat the ageing black and tan kelpie who'd appeared by her side. Reggie glanced up to search for her father. Rose only ventured outside in winter now when her owner did. She heard the drone of the compact two-door All Terrain Vehicle they affectionately called Glenda moments before her father came into view.

Her heart tugged at the now-familiar sight of her father hobbling across to her after climbing slowly out of Glenda. He could only manage short distances on foot and depended on the ATV or a mobility scooter for getting about in town. It still shocked her some days to remember that he wasn't as agile as he used to be—not since the accident. His fractured femur had developed an infection early on in hospital, which resulted in permanent limitations. Added to the pre-existing heart condition that had already put him on lighter work duties, it restricted what he could do work-wise around the property.

At first Reggie had fallen back into the jobs of her younger years, but as time had gone on she'd had to learn things that had always been Brent and her father's domain.

She didn't consider herself a real farmer; there were a lot of aspects of farming she didn't like and sometimes her soft heart got her into trouble. She disliked market days when they brought the cattle in to load them into trucks for the sale yards. She knew it was stupid—they were cattle, not even pet cattle, just cattle that lived and roamed the property growing and getting fat in order to fulfil their destiny as top-quality, Australian-grown beef. She felt like a bit of a hypocrite—after all, she loved a good steak—it was just sometimes a battle to harden herself to the reality of farming.

'Hey Dad,' she greeted her father with a smile.

'Bit brisk,' he replied, clapping his big, work-hardened hands together. She loved her father's hands. They were probably one of her favourite childhood memories. They had always dwarfed her own—big, meaty, dependable farmer hands. She'd seen them working machinery in a paddock, then tenderly helping a calf into the world when a cow was having trouble delivering. They'd helped her up after she'd fallen down, both figuratively and literally as she'd grown up, and they'd held her brother's hand beside a hospital bed in a firm, safe clasp that refused to let go even after Brent had passed. The memory of that pain, watching a father lose his son, still haunted her and brought a sting of hot tears to her eyes.

'It is,' she said, sniffing quickly and clearing her throat as they watched the horses eat the last of their feed.

'The cattle down in the bottom paddock need to be moved in the next day or so and I got a call from Fred Parson next door sayin' he spotted a fence down near the northeast corner. We need to get it fixed before we move the cattle closer that way. Last thing we want is bloody Parson getting a free service from our prize bull.'

'Well, if he saw it down why the hell didn't *he* fix it?' Reggie muttered. She wouldn't quite call it a feud, but Fred Parson and her father had a long-running mutual dislike of each other. Fred had been circling like a damn vulture after her parents' accident, certain he'd be able to pick up River Styx to add to the already substantial land he owned. His family had been grazing the area for generations. She couldn't stand the man, and his children were just as bad. She'd gone to school with Justine and Simon had been Brent's age—both thoroughly spoilt and full of their own self-importance. Simon in particular had been causing his parents headaches from an early age, getting himself in trouble and then getting out of it thanks to his family's influence. He and Brent had been in many a fight during their school years, until Simon had been sent away to board for the last few years of high school. He had returned home only a few years earlier after it was rumoured he'd been mixing with some dodgy businessmen and barely escaped prison when a deal he got mixed up in went sour. No one really knew for sure if this was true, but he'd come home bitter about something.

17

'I'd do it myself, but . . .' Her father left the rest unsaid, giving a frustrated sigh instead.

The northeast section of the property was probably the most remote. While her father still did a lot of maintenance for areas that he could get to in his rusty old farm ute, or on Glenda, that section of the property was far too rough for him to reach.

'It's okay, I was planning on heading over there soon to check the boundary fences anyway.' It had been a few months since she'd done it, and she'd been meaning to ever since the big winds had started. It only took one tree falling the wrong way to take down part of a fence somewhere.

'Just wanted to give you a heads-up.' Her father turned his attention back to the horses, who were now licking the sides of their buckets for the last morsel of their feed, and then he said, almost hesitantly, 'Your mother and I have been thinking about bringing someone on to help out full time.'

This wasn't a new discussion. At least once every six months they brought up the same idea.

'There's no point, Dad. The cost of paying a full-time wage would ruin any profit the cabins are making.'

'You barely take a wage as it is—it's not right,' Ray grumbled.

'Because I don't need it.' It was true, she didn't draw a full wage for herself. At first, because everything had been so up in the air, and then after Brent died she'd been too heartbroken and busy trying to hold everything together until her parents were able to take care of themselves—as much as they could at least. She didn't feel right about taking the same wage Brent had taken—for starters, she didn't do the same amount of work he had, but also, once she'd looked at the accounts, she'd realised they couldn't afford to. Brent had been an awesome farmer and builder but a lousy bookkeeper. It had taken months to sort out the farm books with Col, their accountant, and when she had, she realised there had to be some serious changes.

The cabins had been the best move the farm had ever made financially—because without that income coming in, she knew they'd be in a lot worse shape than they were.

They had their valuable breeding stock, thanks to Brent and his stubborn determination to hold on to them when a lot of others had to sell off everything during the last drought, and this had had been their other saving grace. Then again, it hadn't been part of the plan to buy an expensive bull to add to the herd of breeding heifers, but when the opportunity had come along Brent hadn't stopped to run it by her father, he simply came home with the animal out of the blue one day. It had been the first time Reggie had seen her father furious at her brother since they were teenagers, and the bull was part of the reason River Styx was in such bad shape financially . . . well, that and a few bad seasons over the years.

At the moment, cattle prices were still up, and they were slowly making their way back into the black, but hiring a full-time worker would cut into that profit again and she'd worked too hard to go backwards now.

So far they'd got by, paying a few local workers to lend a hand at busy times, and it was working well. At least it had been until the Parsons had hired their usual workers and they'd had trouble finding anyone to replace them in a hurry. She knew her father believed Fred had hired the men out of spite, managing to tie up most of the local workforce they usually depended on, but Reggie had been hearing rumours around town that Simon Parson had been hiring labourers for a few of his own projects in the district. What projects, no one really knew, he'd just suddenly been splashing money around the place left, right and centre, so it seemed a little more likely the labour shortage came from Simon's projects rather than a vendetta against the MacLeods.

'What if we look into some kind of skills training program—or a traineeship again?' she asked reluctantly.

'That didn't work out so well last time,' he reminded her.

It hadn't been a total waste—they had gotten some extra help when they'd needed it, but unfortunately as soon as the young kid they'd put on had finished his required time with them, he'd left for a mining job—leaving them back at square one again.

'Let's just think on it some more. For now, we're doing okay,' she assured him. 'I don't want you and Mum to worry about all this—especially you. You're not supposed to be stressing.'

'I'm not stressin',' he grumbled. 'You sound like your mother.'

She'd been trying her best to protect them since coming back. It was her job—they'd done their time worrying over farming and raising kids. After everything they'd been through, she didn't want them to have to stress about anything else for a while. For the most part she'd succeeded. She wasn't about to burden them with things out of their control now.

There was plenty to do first thing in the morning and Reggie kissed her father's cheek before heading inside the shed to get the chook feed sorted.

Peggy MacLeod loved her hens and ducks. Before the accident, if you couldn't find her in the kitchen, chances were, she'd be out in the garden or with her feathered friends.

The accessible pathway from the back door out to the chook yard was a work in progress, but once finished it would allow her to spend more time with her animals again. For now, though, Reggie had taken over the feeding, watering and collecting of eggs.

As she pushed open the gate, a ruckus greeted her as feathered fowl came running from all directions, squabbling and jostling for position around Reggie's feet as she tipped out the grain and layer pellets. At the rear, waddling a little slower than the others, came her mum's favourite hen, Henny Penny, who had to be at least eight years old but was still going strong.

The guinea fowl squawked and screeched and let out their annoying high-pitched noises as she threw their grain, fuelling them for their daily patrol of the paddocks and yards, scavenging for bugs and pests and keeping all the nasties at bay, the only thing the stupid things were good for. At night they roosted in the tall trees around the chook pen, but every morning they were in the yard waiting for their grain.

As she left, Reggie scooped up Henny Penny and took her out of the pen to let her have free range in the house yard as she liked to do a few times a week. This also allowed her mother to have some time with Henny Penny when she came out to sit on the verandah throughout the day.

Reggie kicked off her boots at the back door before shrugging out of her heavy coat and hanging it up on the peg inside. She paused as she passed the hall table scattered with family photos and picked up a timber-framed photo of her brother leaning against the rails of the stockyard, grinning at the camera, his eyes squinting against the afternoon glare. She put it down after a moment and picked up one of her parents, snapped laughing at something hilarious, her father's eyes gently crinkled, and the camera catching the brightness of her mother's wide smile. Reggie put the photo back and straightened. She couldn't remember the last time she'd seen either of her parents laugh like that. She was beginning to wonder if she ever would again.

Chapter 3

The aroma of the stew Reggie had put on earlier that morning was wafting through the house, luring her and her growling stomach towards the kitchen.

Her mother, in her wheelchair, was sitting at the table with her father, and they both looked up expectantly as she walked into the room.

'I guess I'm not the only hungry one?' she observed, raising an eyebrow at her parents.

'Can you come and sit down for a minute, darling?' Peggy asked, as Reggie moved to collect cutlery from the drawer and set the table.

Noticing their wary expressions, Reggie suddenly lost her appetite. Lately there had been no good news coming from a round-table that started with, 'Can you come and sit down?'

'What's happened?' she asked without preamble as she dropped into a chair across from them.

'Nothing, everything's fine,' Ray hastened to reassure her.

'But your father and I wanted to have a word with you,' her mum said quietly. 'We think that maybe it's time we thought about some options.' Her mother was rushing her words as though she were ripping off a bandaid.

'Options? For what?'

'This place,' her mother said, folding her hands in front of her.

'We already talked about all this just this morning,' Reggie said, turning her confused gaze to her father.

'We've been talking about it some more today.' Peggy shrugged. 'We wanted to discuss the possibility of putting this place on the market.'

'Selling? You can't be serious!'

'Darling, we have to do something. It's not right that you've given up your whole life to run the farm. Your father and I think it's sensible to look at some ideas.'

'Why now? Things are just getting back to normal.'

'That's the problem,' her mother said. 'This shouldn't be normal. With you running around doing everything and us . . .' She sighed with frustration.

'Is this something you both want? Or are you saying this because it's what you *think* I need?' Reggie asked. Her parents, especially her father, had always said he would never willingly leave—that they'd be carrying him out in a box—and she'd heard, on more than one occasion, her parents talking about neighbours and friends who'd sold up to go into retirement homes on the coast, to live an easier life in their old age, and how that would never be her parents' idea of a happy retirement. She knew neither of them wanted to sell.

'The accident changed everything,' her mother said sadly. 'None of us are having the life we imagined.'

Although her mother had lost the use of her legs, she'd recovered from the accident far faster than the doctors had been expecting. She was regaining her independence and learning how to take care of herself at an age when many people were seemingly happy to slow down and let others take some of the load.

They'd renovated the bathroom to accommodate her wheelchair and installed bars and seating to help make things easier, and she was doing most of her own personal care again, but she could still no longer move about as easily as she once had, and losing the ability to drive wherever and whenever she wanted was something she hadn't been handling too well. Her mother had always been a fiercely independent woman involved in lots of charity work and social events, but since the accident, she hadn't returned to any of them, which worried Reggie. At times like this, the friends her mother had made over the years would have been great to have around—but she'd withdrawn into herself while trying to adjust to her new life and had never gone back.

'Yes, it changed a lot of things. But we can't do anything about that,' Reggie said gently.

'You came home to help when we needed you—and your dad and I can never tell you how much that meant to us,' her mother said softly, 'but then . . . Brent . . .'

Reggie saw her mother stop and force her son's name out before closing her eyes against the wave of pain that followed. Reggie knew how that felt—it still caught her off guard whenever she made the mistake of mentioning his name out loud.

'You've lost a lot to be here,' her mother said sadly.

'I lost nothing I didn't want to, Mum,' Reggie said in a tight voice. 'If I truly missed my old life, I would have gone back to it.'

'But you've given up your life for close to two years now. It was only supposed to be for a little while. This was never something you wanted,' her mother said, waving a hand around the house.

'It wasn't originally, that's true, but things change. And anyway, the plan was always going to be that once you both couldn't or didn't want to run this place anymore, you'd be able to stay here, with family, living onsite.'

'That was when your brother would have been here—raising his own family. Living *his* life doing what *he* loved doing. This isn't what *you* love doing—your job was your calling. But instead you're caring for your parents and working the farm. You won't ever meet anyone stuck out here,' her father said gruffly. 'We won't be the reason you end up an old spinster with no family of your own.'

'If I end up an old spinster, it'll be because it was *my* choice. Not because I'm stuck anywhere doing anything I didn't want to be doing. You never worried about Brent.'

'Brent had Felicity,' her mother said.

'And look how well that went,' Reggie snapped. She didn't mean to sound so bitter, but she hadn't forgiven Felicity for leaving Brent when he'd needed her the most.

'The point your mother's trying to make is that Brent had the chance to meet the person he was going to make a future with—regardless of how that turned out,' her added quickly. 'You, on the other hand, haven't. And working as hard as you do, you don't have the chance to find anyone.'

'Dad, I'm hardly over the hill yet,' she complained. 'I have plenty of time to meet someone.'

'When?' Peggy asked bluntly.

'Pardon?' Reggie said, blinking.

'When are you going to meet someone? Where have you been to meet someone? Into town? To the sales? Out doing groceries?'

Okay, well, she supposed that was a fair enough question. There *were* actually very limited places she went regularly, and the number of eligible men was seriously low once you ruled out the married ones, the unfaithful ones and the downright no-way-no-how ones.

'We think that it's only fair to you that we consider selling up so we can buy a place in town somewhere and let you go back to your life.'

The idea of leaving to return to her old life should have filled her with excitement, or at least some kind of hope, and yet it didn't. Reggie had lost contact with most of her old workmates and the friends she did stay in touch with couldn't relate to her life now. They didn't understand cattle prices or the importance of long-term weather forecasts and they had no real desire to come down and visit—a stay out in the country wasn't exactly their idea of a fun holiday.

But even thinking about her job suddenly filled her with anxiety. She'd been out of the game for so long now that everything would have changed. The idea of building up her portfolio from scratch filled her with dread. She wasn't sure of the exact moment she had stopped missing her old life and considered this as her future, but that's what had happened. She didn't want to do anything else. This was her home.

'I understand if you both *want* to start somewhere else—but can we at least explore some other options? I can't afford to buy you out, but I have my savings and my superannuation, and I think if we sat down with Col we might even work out a way I could get finance and buy a house wherever you want to live in exchange for me working this place and living here.'

'We're not taking your savings,' her father said. 'Besides, you'll end up with this place after we're both gone anyway, but we'd rather give you a solid foundation with cash from sellin' than the debt that's still hangin' on to the business.'

'I don't believe you really want to leave River Styx. In fact, I'm convinced you don't. I mean, Brent's here . . . and *you've* both already planned to have your ashes scattered here—so why would you want to sell it? I don't *want* cash. I want my family in one place on the farm where I grew up. I'm perfectly happy with the way things are. And you're right, farming was never something I thought I'd be doing, but I am . . . and I like it. I think I've been doing an okay job?' she said, searching her parents' eyes.

'Of course you have,' her mother said, jumping in.

'You said options,' Reggie went on, reminding them. 'What are the others?'

'We could look at putting on a manager,' her mother said.

'Replacing me with someone,' she said in a deadpan tone, as she switched her gaze between them.

'Not replacing you. Taking some of the pressure off,' her father said.

'We can't afford to do that now.'

'Perhaps we can look into it down the track, once we are in a position to do it,' her mother said.

Reggie saw that as a small win. If they took selling the place off the table, she could push the whole manager idea away for now and worry about it later.

'Okay,' she said, trying for a calm tone, 'and if I ever get to the point where I'm unhappy—' her breath caught slightly '—I promise I'll let you know,' she finished once she'd regained control of herself. She couldn't do that. Crying didn't change anything, and it didn't make you feel better—no matter what anyone said. All it did was make you vulnerable and sad and she was sick of feeling both of those things.

'All right. I suppose we can live with that compromise. Once we're in a better place financially, we'll sit down and discuss it again,' her mother said.

Reggie gave a nod before standing up to finish setting the table. She sensed her mother's worried gaze upon her but refused to look up. There was no way she was going to let her parents sell this place just because they were worried about her finding a husband. As if she even needed one of those. The last thing she wanted right now was a relationship to complicate her life. She had enough to deal with here, simply holding everything together, without any of that kind of nonsense.

Chapter 4

Reggie whistled at the two dogs sitting quietly in their warm kennels and watched them jump into the ute. She scruffed them affectionately, smiling at their lolling tongues and big, faithful brown eyes as they waited to start the day.

Jack and Tess had been Brent's dogs; he'd raised them from pups and trained them as cattle dogs, and she knew they had felt his passing deeply. The day she'd driven Brent to hospital—the last time—both dogs had howled as she drove away. She could still hear their mournful cries. Somehow they'd known it would be the last time they'd see their master. She wasn't sure how they'd known, and *she* certainly hadn't been expecting it. It was supposed to be a trip to the emergency room to have some fluid drained, which had happened multiple times before, but this time he'd deteriorated rapidly and by the next morning he'd passed.

She drove along the dirt tracks worn down by tyres and thousands of cattle hooves over the years. The main track led past their huge dam—now used for farm-stay visitors to fish from—and on through the gully that led out to the wide flat pasture beyond.

As they reached the mob of cattle, grazing happily and oblivious to the icy wind that raced across the plains and swept into the surrounding treetops, the dogs jumped from the tray of the ute to start work.

Reggie couldn't whistle the way Brent had trained the dogs to respond to—but luckily, being the intelligent animals kelpies are, they figured out what she asked of them. Or more likely, they understood what to do because they'd been doing the job their entire lives and didn't actually *need* her direction. They could practically do the job on their own—she'd already reached the conclusion she was really only needed out here to open gates. Reggie was okay being the assistant.

Her gaze fell on the bull in the centre of the paddock. He'd lifted his massive head when she'd appeared, chewing slowly as he watched her. He was an impressive animal by anyone's standards, but Reggie knew he was extra special: the product of twenty years of careful breeding. The original bull had been imported from Norfolk Island, a massive Norfolk Blue, and mixed with a carefully selected line of Belgium Blue and Angus Short Horn breeds to create this brand new breed. And River Styx was the only stud in the Southern Hemisphere to breed them.

The mob of cattle were a beautiful colour, having a distinctive dark blue-grey coat with a speckle of white on their rump, some in the oddly distinctive shape of the southern cross, which contributed to their name: True Blue Southern Cross. The males were muscular and well-tempered. Their meat had the desirable marbling in demand from restaurants and butchers, and they did well feeding off pasture without the need of feed lotting to fatten up. With the genes for fast growth and adaptability to conditions passed down from the Angus Shorthorn, and the Belgium Blue's ability to turn feed into lean muscle, the resulting breed was a remarkable animal.

This bull had been the key to her brother's new venture—the new bloodline Brent had registered and planned to continue breeding. The beast was known locally as Big Wally, named after his original owner Jock Wallace, although his official breeding name was River Styx Jock's Dream, and he was famous for the distinctive size of his scrotum. In this case, size *did* matter and also would also prove profitable since this season's pregnancy rate was ninety-seven percent.

Reggie moved the cattle into the new paddock and closed the gates behind them, watching as they waddled with their huge pregnant bellies. The first of the cattle had started to drop their calves only a few days earlier and this group would be due any day now.

A familiar sadness swept through her at the idea. *Brent should be here*, she thought as she watched the cattle grazing happily.

The first few weeks after the calves' birth were the most dangerous around here—with the threat from predators a constant worry. The worst was wild dogs. There had been a spike in numbers after a particularly good season and there'd been growing concern in the farming community about how brazen the packs had become.

Cows were great protectors, though, and their young stood a better chance than other stock, such as sheep, which were smaller and far easier targets for not only wild dogs but also large birds of prey such as eagles and even crows—who found newborn lambs that had been left alone while their mothers grazed particularly easy to attack. Nature was cruel. There were no two ways about it, and her job as a farmer was to protect the livestock she'd been entrusted with to the best of her ability. It was a responsibility she and every farmer took seriously.

Reggie had no qualms about shooting vermin. She never hunted for the fun of it but, when it came to dealing with wild dogs hell-bent on ripping apart calves or crows ready to peck out newborns' eyes, she was more than ready to do what she had to in order to protect them.

On the ridge above, she spotted a movement and strained her eyes to focus. Jack and Tess had already located it, and let out low, threatening growls as a howl echoed through the cutting. She reached for the gun under the seat in the ute and pulled it out, looking through the scope.

The dog was large with a black coat. It looked like it might have Alsatian or something similar in its breeding, but with a more muscular body. The problem with wild dogs was they bred themselves into some of the most ferocious mixed breeds imaginable; survival of the fittest was nowhere more apparent than in wild dogs. The weak weren't part of the blood line.

Unlike her brumbies, these wild animals were dangerous—life threatening, even. Not only to stock, but they were becoming a problem for humans as well. Local bushwalkers had reported recent close encounters with a wild dog, but so far there hadn't been any attacks.

That said, not long ago a local farmer had been found mauled in his driveway. The coroner couldn't say if he'd had a heart attack prior to wild dogs coming across him or if the dogs had attacked him and then he'd had a heart attack, but the fact was they found large bite marks on his skin that were not from any of his own dogs, and one of his kelpies had been found a few days later, savaged and lying in the bushes nearby.

'Easy, guys,' Reggie soothed, although she felt like growling alongside them. *Bloody wild dogs.* This one was too far away up on the ridge to try for a shot.

She knew what she'd be doing for the next couple of nights now: coming out here to check on stock. She couldn't wait—there was nothing she wanted to be doing more than sitting out here in the dead of winter, with a freezing wind ripping through her, to ward off feral dogs instead of being tucked up in bed under her warm blanket.

Tim Warbois stared into the campfire, watching the flames dance and crackle. His long legs were stretched out before him, his boots absorbing the warmth of the fire as he burrowed down into his heavy jacket against the chill of the frosty night air.

The cold didn't really bother him. He'd been much colder than this before.

His tent, pitched on the banks of a wide river, was a long way from anywhere. Just the way he wanted it. Three days he'd been here and he hadn't seen a single other person.

His mind briefly touched on Alicia and he felt a ripple of guilt. He needed to call and tell her he was okay. She'd probably been trying to get a hold of him and would worry when she couldn't. He didn't mean to be such a dick, but when he'd left Sydney he hadn't been capable of anything except getting the hell out. Grief and panic had been clawing their way through his chest. He couldn't hear the voice of reason over the roar of pain that echoed through his head.

Dean was gone. Each time he thought about it, the wound inside him reopened.

They'd made a deal . . . Dean was supposed to reach out if he ever felt that low.

He tried, a little voice reminded him bitterly, *and you weren't there.*

They were all gone now. He was the only one left.

His chest felt hollow, as though everything inside had been ripped out, leaving him numb and empty. What was he supposed to do now? How was he supposed to go on living when everyone he cared about was dead? Where did that leave *him*? Alone—that's where. There was nothing left to keep him in Sydney. Who would even notice if he just . . . disappeared? *It would be so easy*, he thought. It was the same thought he'd been having for days now. What was the point of going on when everyone else had left? It was peaceful here with just the bush and the river to keep him company. He wouldn't be found for weeks, maybe even months, and when they did find him, they'd work out who he was and put him down as just another statistic. A faceless, nameless veteran. They would sweep it under the rug, just like they had with the others.

A breeze suddenly picked up, and the fire leaped to life, throwing sparks of yellow and orange high into the air. He tilted his head back and stared into the vast blanket of darkness above as memories of long nights huddled around a fire, staring at the stars, replayed on an endless loop in his mind. A lifetime ago now. If he closed his eyes he could be back there; he could almost hear the familiar voices beside him, the sounds of the desert around them, foreign yet familiar. He could picture the grinning faces and hear the quiet murmur of conversation—tall stories and good-natured jabs. The warmth of the fire touched his face as he felt a smile tug at his mouth. God, he missed them. He opened his eyes, half-expecting to see them all there. The pain of his isolation went through him in waves and the tears he'd been trying not to give into finally fell. This wasn't the plan. They were all supposed to be here—just like they'd always promised . . . But they were all gone and he was alone.

Chapter 5

Reggie locked the door and gave the verandah one last look. She'd just finished making up the cabin after its last guests departed, ready for the next lot to arrive tomorrow. It wasn't an overly demanding job—in fact, she kind of liked it, or the end result at least. It gave her a quiet pride to walk out of a clean, freshly made-up cabin that looked inviting, warm and friendly. The little touches like the scented candles and the fresh native foliage she liked to put inside had been *her* contribution to the business.

While Brent and her father had built the cabins, her mother had played an important role in helping pick the furniture and design the layout, as well as naming them. They were all named after tree species found on the property—a mixture of both native and introduced.

The first two cabins were named after the trees located either beside or behind the cabins: Jacaranda cabin and

Flame Tree cabin, distinctive with their striking purple- and red-flowering canopies in summer. Ribbon Gum cabin had a massive fifty-metre gum tree visible from the bedroom window and Tree Fern cabin was set off to one side and overlooked a small stream surrounded by tree ferns and moss-covered rocks. The Wattle cabin boasted a stunning display of bright yellow flowers during spring.

She looked out at the empty sixth cabin at the very end of the track and a familiar wave of melancholy washed over her. She knew it would annoy Brent no end that the cabin remained unfinished. He'd started it before being diagnosed and hadn't completed it in time. Now it sat there as a constant reminder that you weren't guaranteed the opportunity to tie up loose ends before fate stepped in and handed you a grenade.

Reggie gave a long sigh as she pushed herself away from the railing and walked down the three steps from the Jacaranda verandah. There was always something on the to-do list. That unfinished cabin was at the extreme end of the list and she hadn't been able to justify spending the money on it before. And even though they were doing better now, she really didn't think the time and effort involved would make that much of a difference. It was more a constant reminder that she hadn't finished what Brent had started, and it continued to niggle at her.

Priorities over sentimentality, she told herself firmly, and she could almost hear their accountant's voice congratulating her for being so strong.

Tim sat in his car with his hands on the wheel, staring straight ahead as the intersection loomed in front of him. He'd been driving on dirt roads for the last few days with no destination in mind but he had eventually found himself back near a main road. He wasn't sure he was ready to face the world just yet, but he was in need of supplies. Maybe a detour into civilisation wouldn't be such a bad thing.

He wound down his window as he cruised to a stop at the intersection and a cold blast of air hit his face. The trees outside were being blown about like those inflatable tube men that flailed their limbs in front of car yards, and the fresh air helped clear his head.

Well, Deano, mate . . . which way should I go? he asked silently, looking slowly in both directions as he weighed up his options.

On the passenger seat beside him, the pages of a fishing magazine he'd had sitting there for the last few months flipped crazily as the wind filled the inside of the cabin. Tim reluctantly closed his window against the bluster and as the pages settled he glanced down and saw a photo of a serene dam. The ad read, 'River Styx Cabins. Fish. Stay. Play.'

A tingle ran down his spine and for a moment he wondered if he should believe in messages from the beyond and all that other bullshit, but he shook it off. There was nothing on the other side. That stuff was just stories made up to ease the pain of loved ones left behind.

He checked the address at the bottom of the ad and let out a slow breath. *Good a place as any*, he thought as he put his car into gear and pulled out onto the road.

There was something about cattle. Reggie didn't love them the way she loved horses, but she did have a soft spot for them—unless of course you counted the days when mustering went wrong. Baby *anythings* were always cute, but calves were extra cute with their fluffy little bodies and long, wobbly legs and wide, shiny black noses. She loved spotting the new babies sticking close to their mothers each time she came to check on them. She called the dogs and worked the mothers and calves into the yards, briefly managing to separate the young to weigh and tag them.

'Yes, I know,' she said out loud as the cows jostled and cried out from where they were locked away. 'You can have your baby back in just a few minutes, I promise.' On a stud, calves had to be weighed as soon as possible after birth in order to maintain accurate records for the stud books, but it was sometimes a risky task because cows were super-protective of their young. She chuckled as she remembered a childhood incident with a stroppy old cow who had turned into a monster each time she calved. Despite her father's warning, Brent had turned his back on her for a minute and narrowly missed having a horn up his clacker—then he'd scaled the stockyard fence faster than a rat up a drainpipe, as their father had put it.

Thankfully, the True Blues were a much calmer breed. There was no way the stud would keep an animal with temperament issues in their breeding stock program. Still, no mother enjoyed being separated from their newborn, so Reggie could forgive a bit of noise.

She jotted down the numbers and tags and made a mental note of how many cows were yet to calve. She was hoping for a bumper year this season. With many people having sold off cattle during the last drought, sale prices were still high, and they needed to make a good profit while they could. Farming was always a gamble. Good years came and went and all you could do was try your hardest to be prepared.

She opened the gate and released the last calf. 'There you go, back safe and sound,' Reggie said, watching to make sure all the calves found their mothers before letting them all back out into the paddock.

As she sat in the grass, listening to the stillness afterwards, a sudden howl broke the silence and Reggie felt the hairs on the back of her neck stand up.

Wild dogs. Again.

Another howl sounded and the cattle also stopped to listen.

She eyed the treeline ahead and frowned. She hated that about them—the lurking. It gave her the creeps. The dogs hung back in the shadows, watching. She could hear them now, the yelps and the howls as the strategically positioned pack communicated, ready to launch into action at a moment's notice, hunting as one with swift, brutal precision.

The big black dog she'd spotted the other day emerged from the bush slowly. His walk was slow and deliberate as he held Reggie's eye.

'You arrogant bastard,' she murmured softly, standing and moving towards the ute. She reached for the gun where it was usually stored, only to find the spot empty. Her father must have taken it out sometime over the past few days. She quickly returned her gaze to the dog. It was as if he knew she was unarmed. If dogs could have a human expression then this one was wearing a smug grin.

Jack and Tess were both on high alert, their tails straight and eyes glued to the other animal as they emitted low, ferocious growls. 'Stop,' Reggie ordered, in the tone she used to make sure they listened to her, and the growling ceased, but they remained tense and poised to launch into an attack at the first opportunity they got. 'Into the car—now!' She opened the cab door and they reluctantly entered as she slid in behind them, keeping half an eye on the black dog.

The animal tilted its head slightly as it observed her, its yellow gaze never leaving hers for a moment. The intensity of that stare sent a chill down her spine.

The cattle needed to be moved, but she wasn't letting the dogs out. They'd head straight for the black dog, and she knew that's what he was hoping for—to lure them to him before the rest of his pack came out of hiding to ambush them. It was such a strategic, almost-human move that it truly frightened her. She'd heard of it happening before—men going out bush with dogs trained to kill wild pigs, thinking wild dogs would be no match for their trained animals . . . But they rarely returned home with them alive.

Her two wouldn't stand a chance.

Putting the ute into gear, she floored the accelerator and bounced across the paddock at speed, blasting the horn when she got closer and making a small, satisfied sound in her throat as the dog finally scurried away. She was fairly sure it wouldn't be enough to scare him off for good, but at least for now he was gone. She'd been putting off mentioning the dog situation to her father. He wasn't supposed to be stressed because of his heart, despite the fact that for years his doctor had everything under control. But it was also the principle of the matter. She was supposed to be in charge out here. She needed to be able to deal with this without worrying her dad about it.

She was worried enough for the both of them that the dogs had come this far off the ridge and—worse yet—shown themselves. They were normally far more covert than that, doing their best to avoid human contact, especially in daylight hours. This was not good. She'd need to move the cattle again and do something about these dogs.

Chapter 6

Reggie glanced up at the sound of a vehicle slowing down. She looked out the office window and saw a white, four-wheel drive ute turn into the dirt driveway and head up towards the house.

This would be the guest who'd booked into the Jacaranda cabin, she thought, taking the key from the hook behind her and heading outside to meet them.

Since it was early in the afternoon, Reggie decided to show them to the cabin herself. After hours or when the office was unattended, guests had the option of getting the key from the small key-safe at the front of each cabin using a pin number supplied via email, but today she needed an excuse to leave the accounts and stretch her legs. So, she put on a welcoming smile and opened the door just as a tall man climbed out of his vehicle.

'Hello, you must be Mr Warbois,' she said, checking the printed receipt she had ready to hand over to him. He was dressed in a pair of faded jeans and a long-sleeve shirt with the sleeves rolled up to his elbows. He appeared in need of a haircut—his shaggy hair, the shade of bronze-brown gumnuts, almost covered his eyes and he kept brushing it aside with his fingers. His beard, the same shade as his hair but with some lighter flecks through it, made her think of a yuppie barista from East London, only she had a feeling he wouldn't be caught dead using any kind of product on it like they would.

'Tim,' he said. His voice was deep, almost a little rusty, as though he hadn't used it in a while.

'Hi Tim, I'm Reggie. This is the main house so if you need anything during your stay, just bang on the door and someone will be here. If you want to follow me in your car, I'll show you the cabin you'll be staying in.'

'I can find it,' he said abruptly before adding a quick, 'thanks' on the end and something that looked like a wince but that she thought was supposed to be a smile.

'Well, here's the key. You need to turn on the fridge, and the hot water switch is inside the main bedroom. There's split wood around the back of the cabin for the fire, and if you need some more, there's plenty in the shed over there,' she said, pointing to the silver shed across from them. 'If you need anything, just give me a yell,' she added, dropping the key into his hand and sliding her hands into her back pockets. She watched him clamp his fingers closed around the key and give her a nod before climbing back into his vehicle.

'I won't be needing anything,' he assured her.

Reggie stared after the car and gave a small, surprised chuff. *Well, there you go—a self-sufficient man who doesn't need anything from anyone*, she thought. That suited her just fine; she didn't have time to be running after grumpy, lumberjack-looking men anyway.

The sun had managed to poke its head out between the grey clouds and Reggie tipped her head back to soak up the gentle warmth. In summer there would be days when the sun was unbearable—but during winter, it was divine.

She loaded the last of the shopping into the car and ticked off another job on her list. She'd done a rubbish-tip run and dropped off all the recycling from the cabins, which was a tidy little earner considering most guests tended to pack a considerable amount of alcohol, leaving behind lots of cans and glass bottles.

She'd restocked all the consumables for the cabins and delivered more brochures to the tourist centre before dropping into the post office to collect the mail, noting the new delivery of magazines that would need to go into the cabins when she got home.

'Regina!'

She turned at her name and smiled as a woman hurried across the street towards her. 'Hello Mrs Nelson.' Birdie Nelson was the president of the local Country Women's Association branch and had been among a number of people who'd been there to lend a hand when her parents had their accident. The woman was a veritable force of nature, organising a roster of hospital visitors and dropping off food and supplies to Brent and Reggie as they readjusted to life with their parents back home. Reggie was sure they wouldn't have coped as well as they had without her.

'I'm so glad I caught you. I've been meaning to have a chat. It's about your mother,' Birdie said, looking worried.

'What's the matter?'

'I've just been a little concerned. I've been trying to encourage her to come along to a meeting, but she seems reluctant. I mean—after everything she's been through, I totally understand it would take a while to get back to normal . . . but if she got out of the house and was able to be with her friends again . . .'

Reggie sighed. She understood exactly what Birdie Nelson was saying, and she'd been trying her best to get her mum to go back to some of the things she'd enjoyed before the accident. 'I wish she would too, but every time I suggest it, she seems to withdraw. I think it's just a matter of letting her do things in her own time.'

'Of course, dear,' Birdie said, touching Reggie's arm lightly. 'But please let her know that we're all so looking forward to seeing her return and if there's anything she needs we're always here.'

'Thank you, Mrs Nelson, I'll tell her. And thank you, for everything you and the other ladies have been doing. We really can't thank you enough.'

'That's what we do. We're a community—a family. Peggy would have been first in line to help any of us. Maybe remind her of that,' Birdie said sternly, and then she followed it up with a soft smile. 'Send her our love.'

'I will,' Reggie said as she waved goodbye.

As she turned back to the car, she caught sight of a blonde-haired woman who'd been about to walk past her on the sidewalk. They both froze automatically, before Reggie shook herself out of her stupor and pulled her door open with more force than was necessary.

'Reggie, wait!' the woman said, stepping forward hesitantly.

Reggie paused, wondering what Felicity could possibly want to say to her.

'How are your mum and dad going?'

'As if you care,' Reggie snapped.

'I do. Of course I care.'

For the briefest of moments Reggie felt a twang of compassion for the hurt look on Felicity's face, before she remembered how she'd broken her brother's heart. She steeled herself once more. 'Why don't you call or visit them yourself if you're so concerned?'

Immediately a flicker of alarm replaced the hurt expression, and Felicity swallowed and took a step back.

'Yeah, I didn't think so. You'd have to finally face them and explain why the hell you dumped their son at the lowest point of his entire life and didn't even come to his funeral.'

'I couldn't . . .' she said. Her voice had a husky edge to it as her eyes filled with tears. 'I wanted to go . . . but I just . . .'

Reggie gave a disappointed shake of her head. 'It was best you didn't anyway. It was for family and friends—you know, people who genuinely cared about him.'

'I loved him,' Felicity said defiantly, more defiantly than Reggie had ever seen her act before. 'You didn't understand anything about our relationship . . . You were living on the other side of the world. You had no idea what was going on between us at the time.'

'Not once did either of you mention things weren't going okay,' Reggie pointed out.

'We'd been drifting apart for ages—before the accident happened. When he got sick I just . . . couldn't . . .'

'You're right. I don't understand. And I don't want to. It's over. You're free to move on now. Oh wait. I forgot—you already did. Straight into Simon Parson's arms before Brent was even in the ground.' She didn't wait for a reply—she couldn't stand there a single moment longer. Reggie wasn't normally a cruel person, but when it came to Felicity and the way she'd abandoned her brother, the man she'd been planning to marry, when he'd needed her most—abandoned all of them really—she felt a burning rage inside her. It shouldn't still hurt this much, but it did. She'd never forgive Felicity for that. Ever.

Chapter 7

'Good boy,' Reggie murmured as she tightened the girth strap on her saddle. She gave Clancy a pat before leading him over to the mounting block. Usually it was easier to take the quad bike or ute to check on cattle and fences, but today she decided to ride.

In the past, it had been a regular thing for the MacLeods to muster cattle on horseback. When she was younger it had been just another weekend chore they did as a family. She and Brent had spent most of their childhood on horseback in one form or another: pony club and pony camps during school holidays, then campdrafting and team roping when she was in her teens. They'd been an unstoppable team in the show events for a few years—except for the couple of years in her early teens when it had suddenly become uncool to ride horses at the show with your brother. But she'd quickly outgrown that phase and got back in the ring doing what she loved, until she left home and pretty much stopped riding altogether.

The good old days, she thought now as she listened to the gentle clip-clop of Clancy's hooves on the hard-packed dirt track below. Nowadays she liked to plod, not race. Maybe it was getting older that suddenly made her realise there was a limit to how much danger you should put yourself in—she'd never thought twice about jumping something or racing Brent home when she was a kid. Now, though, the ground suddenly looked a lot harder and bones took a lot longer to mend. She didn't have the luxury of taking a few months off work while something healed—more than ever before, she needed to be able-bodied. There wasn't anyone else to do the work.

And yet there was still something so soul-satisfying about being on the back of a horse. The creak of the leather beneath her provided a soothing backdrop to the sounds of mother nature as she cut through the paddock and the scattered bush that separated the house paddocks from the rest of the property.

The property was made up of a mix of terrain, ranging from fenced pasture and grazing land to dense bushland that rubbed shoulders with national park. There were gullies of rainforest, crisscrossed by part of the Styx River system, that cut off a portion of the property, only crossable by fording the shallowest point. The back of the property was probably the most stunning part—just as it had been since before white settlement in the district. She and Brent had spent hours exploring and playing in the bush—swimming in the cold, clear water, fishing and catching tadpoles and bugs and riding their horses. It had been the most idyllic childhood any kid could dream of. A pang of longing passed through her and she closed her eyes briefly at the pain. *God, I miss you, Brent.*

The sound of water trickling grew steadily louder as she approached the river. Further upstream and downstream, the banks, edged with rock and stone, stood a distance of sixty metres or more apart with deep spots that dropped away in the centre and made crossing difficult. Here, however, the river narrowed and wasn't any more than a foot or so deep in the centre. They called this place The Crossing and it was where they brought the cattle through when they let them out into the back block to forage during summer.

Today she needed to check on the boundary fences. While one section was new—thanks to the last fire season burning through them and being replaced—a substantial part of the fencing was on its last leg and, with the cattle due to be moved our here soon, she needed to make sure it was okay.

The trees grew thicker over this side of the creek. They shaded the dirt track from above and large boulders dotted the landscape like marbles dropped by a giant toddler having a tantrum, creating gullies and caves on the hillsides. Reggie found herself thinking about the people who'd lived here before her, the Aboriginal peoples and early settlers. It still bewildered her how people had managed to live in this beautiful yet unforgiving bush.

It was difficult to imagine being an early settler woman out here, raising children, *having* children. The thought of being pregnant and giving birth in what would have been remote and inaccessible country before the advent of cars and hospitals terrified Reggie. *How* had those women coped? Even now, it seemed as though she was in the middle of nowhere—the only person on earth. The only company she had was the gentle sound of Clancy's breath and the creak of her saddle.

Suddenly Clancy's ears moved forward and he stopped abruptly. Reggie searched the bushland in front of them as she murmured softly to the horse, patting his neck with one hand. 'What is it boy?'

The horse moved sideways, and his eyes widened as he blew out a loud snort. A dark form slowly stepped out from the shadows.

Reggie's heart stopped and a short, sharp curse echoed inside her head. The huge black dog stood there, head held high, its unnerving gaze holding hers with almost human-like arrogance.

'Go on—get!' she yelled, using her most intimidating tone. But it had little effect on the animal before her. *Why isn't it scared of me?* she wondered with growing concern. Wild dogs were notoriously flighty, fleeing at the first glimpse of a human . . . but not this one. She urged Clancy forward and gave another loud yell, waving her hand for good measure, but instead of running, the dog lowered its head and bared its teeth with a low growl.

Reggie felt her body tense and was aware of Clancy's unease beneath her, but before she could figure out her next move, the dog ceased its growling, turned and disappeared back into the bush.

As Reggie stared at the now empty track ahead of her, a rush of air left her lungs and she forced herself to calmly lean forward and comfort her horse. 'Good boy, Clance. We're okay,' she said, more to convince herself than the horse. The reverberations of that menacing growl still hung in the air as Reggie turned Clancy around and headed home. The fences could wait till she came back with the ute.

The feeling of being watched remained with her the whole way back to the crossing and Clancy's ears twitched in every direction as he moved much more urgently than earlier that day. Reggie never carried a rifle when she rode—she didn't have a scabbard for one thing, because this wasn't the wild west after all, and she found it too cumbersome to try to ride with one. Today was the first time she'd wished she had.

Once they'd crossed the creek, she felt Clancy begin to calm and let her own shoulders relax a little. She hadn't been aware of how tense she'd been until she felt the weight lift. That dog was getting a little too close for comfort. Something would need to be done about it.

Early the next morning, Reggie spotted their guest already down at the dam, fishing. It was bitterly cold and a sharp wind had blown up. She didn't get fishing—especially fly fishing. It was so . . . boring. She didn't have the patience to stand in the water and continuously cast for hours on end, waiting for a stupid fish to fall for the fake fly on the end of a hook. But there were a lot of people who loved it, and lots of the people who rented cabins came to do just that.

The previous year they'd released close to two hundred trout into the big dam for the sporting fisherman to catch.

For most of the year it was strictly catch and release, and only during trout season were guests allowed to keep any.

She went about feeding the horses and chooks before throwing into the back of the ute the gear she'd need to fix the broken fence her dad had mentioned was near the back northeastern corner of the property. A small repair job she could handle, but if it was a big one she'd need to call in someone to give her a hand. She hoped it was something she could do on her own—she didn't want to waste a day ringing around looking for a fencer.

'Have any luck?' Reggie called as Tim walked towards her on the way back from the dam later that morning.

'Not really. Are you sure there are trout in that dam?' he asked.

'Yep, saw them go in with my own eyes.' She grinned, placing the gun case in the back seat.

He gave a doubtful grunt and pulled his sunglasses off his face, hooking them onto the front of his shirt. 'I'm thinking you have the right idea—maybe shooting them would be easier,' he said, nodding towards the back of the vehicle where she'd just stored the rifle.

Reggie gave a smirk. 'You reckon that would help?'

'Probably not,' he agreed lightly. 'What are you hunting?'

'Wild dogs. There's been one lurking around lately.'

He held her eyes with a serious kind of intensity. There was something commanding about it. Was he weighing up whether she was qualified to be walking around with a weapon? It immediately irritated her.

'There are a few other places you can try your luck for trout. A short walk that way and you'll find the river,' she said, pointing beyond his shoulder in an attempt to distract him from his brooding.

He turned his head in the direction she'd indicated then looked back at her. 'Is that bull safe to walk past?'

Reggie followed his gaze and smiled. 'That's Wally. He won't bother you if you walk through the paddock.'

'He'd be a good security dog. Looks mean enough.'

'Nah, he's a gentle giant . . . unless you wear hi-vis around him,' she added as an afterthought.

'How's that?' Tim frowned.

'Apparently, when he was younger, he had a bad experience with a truck driver loading him at night—he freaks out at hi-vis glow strips.'

'Right. Don't wear hi-vis. Got it,' he said.

In the brighter light Reggie took the opportunity to look Tim up and down properly. His skin was tanned, and he had faint squint lines around his eyes—she noticed these more often on people who spent a lot of their time working outside in the sun. His face and neck were red from the cold wind that had been relentlessly blowing for the last couple of days. He'd be feeling the wind burn later tonight. Without his sunglasses she saw his eyes were a deep blue, like the middle of the dam under a blue summer sky. She never swam in that part—Brent had loved telling her scary stories when they were kids about the monsters that lived in the centre of the dam. *Dangerous blue*, she thought, and gave a silent scoff.

'So, you're fairly new to fly fishing?' she asked.

'How could you tell?' he asked, with an endearingly embarrassed grin that threw her for a minute.

'The price tag's still on your tackle box.'

'Oh. Yeah. I only picked this stuff up on the way here. I was always gonna try it one day.' He shrugged. 'Decided now was the time.'

'Good a time as any,' she agreed. 'My dad's been fly fishing all his life. He's semi-retired from farming now, but he often gives guests a few lessons to get them started if you're interested.'

'I'll see how I go tomorrow. I might be selling this stuff on the side of the road by then,' he said, and then nodded to her as he returned to his cabin.

She watched him walk away before getting back to work. She still had to fix that fence. Not everyone was here on a holiday.

Chapter 8

Tim resisted the urge to look back over his shoulder at the woman he was becoming way too curious about. It hadn't started out that way. The first day, when he'd checked in, he hadn't really given her a second thought, but, having noticed her running back and forth over the last few days, he'd started to take notice. The woman didn't stop. One minute she'd be driving a rusted-out old ute somewhere, next minute she'd be in a tractor heading someplace else, then he'd see her riding a bloody horse!

He was getting tired just watching her. Although, truth be told, after watching her riding that horse yesterday, he was pretty sure he'd *never* get tired of that. He hadn't even realised he had a thing for cowgirls until that moment. The fact she'd somehow managed to stir a spark of interest inside him was a small miracle—over the last few months he'd been unable to feel any kind of emotion, unless you counted anger and grief.

The gun had thrown him momentarily. It was weird how sometimes the smallest thing could trigger a memory, or in this case a feeling. He'd immediately gone onto high alert until his rational side had kicked in and reassured him everything was fine. Battle instincts never quite switched off.

His thoughts returned to their conversation about fishing. He didn't have a bloody clue what he was doing—fly fishing had been Dean's dream, not his. He was already beginning to regret the stupid promise he'd made; this whole thing had turned out to be harder than he'd been anticipating. More than once today, as he stood on the bank of the dam, he'd decided to pack up and keep driving and yet, he was still here. *You made a promise, knob head,* he heard Deano say, almost as if he were standing right beside him.

Only, when Tim had made that promise he hadn't thought he'd be here fishing on his own. *You were supposed to be here too, dickhead.* The familiar sadness descended once more, and he thought back to the day of the funeral—watching Alicia as she sobbed between her parents while the celebrant read poems about being at peace now and the end of the battle. Anger stirred in the pit of his belly at the memory. There was no end to the battle, that was the whole damn point. It was the battles, every single one of them, that continued to rip away at his soul—at all of our souls. Every. Single. Day.

You were supposed to hang on! You all were! Simmo and Fitzy too, but they were all gone. Tim took the bottle of Scotch from the kitchen bench and headed over to the table. He was tired of remembering, tired of turning the 'why's' over in his head all day long and never coming up with any answers. He took a long drink and let it burn down the back of his throat. He didn't want to think about it anymore. He just wanted to sleep.

Reggie finished picking up the garbage bins—all empty, thank goodness—from behind the cabins on her way back from fixing the fencing. She'd noticed a few had blown over earlier when she'd been on her way out; the wind had been particularly savage that morning, the kind that whipped up out of nowhere and snatched your breath away. She always felt on edge when it was windy.

When she reached the last cabin, by the glen, she continued walking. It'd been a while since she'd visited her special place.

The fairy glen had been her second home as a child. Even now, as an adult, it still held as much wonder and delight each time she saw it as it had back then. A grove of trees and ferns surrounded a trickling creek, barely a metre wide, creating a miniature forest where it was all too easy to believe in the fairytales of her youth.

Her family ties to her Scottish heritage were still strong, despite more than five generations of MacLeods having lived in Australia. She'd grown up on the stories of her ancestors who'd lived, loved, fought and died on the Isle of Skye. The MacLeods had had a castle called Dunvegan and had been the guardians of an ancient relic known as the Fairy Flag, which was said to have magical powers of protection. The story went that a clan chief married a fairy who, after a time, had to leave him but left the flag behind to protect the clan.

Here in the fairy glen, Reggie and Brent had played for hours. Brent built a little wooden bridge for the fairies to cross when he was seven, and it was still there, surviving all this time and becoming part of the landscape. Here, the moss grew on trees and rocks, and long, wispy Spanish moss, or Old Man's Beard as her mother called it, hung off branches and gently floated in the breeze. If ever magic existed, it was right here in this special place. Over the years, Reggie had added ceramic red-and-white toadstools and fairy doors at the bottom of tree trunks, as well as a village of fairy houses. The visiting children loved it, and Reggie always got a smile when she occasionally found letters to the fairies and tiny fairy rings made with pebbles left behind. She'd like to say she only continued decorating this place for the kids, but she'd be lying because she loved it just as much now as she had when she'd been a child.

The gentle babble of water as it trickled and fell over the rocks soothed her as she sat on a log and closed her eyes. Once, she used to talk to her fairy friends, but now she found this was the place she always felt most connected to Brent. Maybe because the glen was so quiet that it was easier to listen to your thoughts. Or maybe it was just one of the places that held so many wonderful memories of when they were kids— she didn't know for sure, but it was different here. She could always hear his voice when she sat here for a while.

Hearing a small splash, she opened her eyes and searched for the source, almost holding her breath so she didn't scare it off. In the water nearby, just downstream of the fairy bridge, she caught the slithering, dark shape of one of their resident platypus. It was fitting that they lived in the fairy glen—they were just as shy and almost as elusive as the fabled fairy, and the protected glen offered them a safe home in the banks beside the creek. The flat, duck-like bill poked up above the water, its sleek body swimming along the surface for a few moments before diving back under the water and digging through the rocks and dirt as it searched for insects and worms to eat.

Change is coming sis, she thought she heard as above her the breeze blew through the treetops. It didn't even scare her anymore. It was probably just her own imagination craving a connection to the brother she still missed, but it gave her comfort to imagine him sitting there beside her watching the platypus and listening to the trees rustling.

She wasn't keen for change. There'd already been more than enough—she wasn't sure her family could take much more.

A sudden thump and crack of sticks startled her as a small wallaby bounded into the glen. When the wallaby noticed Reggie, it did an abrupt zig-zag, bounding over the fence and jumping off into the bush beyond. *I need to get back to work anyway*, she thought, reluctantly getting to her feet. With a final glance around, she said a quiet goodbye and stepped back out into the real world—away from the fairies.

Chapter 9

That night when Reggie came home, dinner was already on the table.

'Surprise!' her mother said triumphantly.

For the first time in too long, her mum's smile had returned, and, despite her private worry about the wild dogs, Reggie couldn't help but smile back. 'You cooked dinner?'

The recent renovation to the kitchen, adding a lower bench that stepped down from the original so that her mother could reach it comfortably, and creating better access to the fridge to accommodate her chair, was paying off. Since the accident, her mum had barely been back in the kitchen, which had been her domain and happy place for as long as Reggie could remember. It hadn't seemed like the same kitchen without her mum baking and humming as she put the final touches on a roast dinner or bagged up delicious biscuits for some fete or bake stall she was organising. Reggie hoped the renovation might be a fresh start for her mum's cooking, something familiar her mum could find joy in again after so much pain.

'It's only a pie,' Peggy said, almost shyly, but she couldn't hide the shine of pride in her eyes.

'It looks great, Mum,' Reggie said, blinking back happy tears. This was so much more than a shepherd's pie. It was a major achievement. It almost felt like a normal, happy dinner. There was a lightness in the kitchen that had been missing for a long time.

'What do ya reckon about the new bull's calves? Cows seem to be calving them okay,' her father said, sitting down across from her at the table and making conversation. It'd been difficult for her dad to talk to her like this—about farm matters. She knew it wasn't anything to do with her being a girl; she suspected it was because these were the conversations he used to share each evening with Brent.

Since coming back home and taking Brent's place, she always felt like a bit of a disappointment. She knew she was a poor substitute for the son who'd been able to sit and converse about cattle and breeding and feed and crops with him as an equal. Reggie knew only the bare basics—stuff she'd grown up listening to but not really taking that much notice of— until she'd been thrown back into it a couple of years ago. She was learning slowly, but sometimes she feared it was too slow. Still, it always gave her a little glow of pride when her father asked her opinion about something.

And this was important. The bull had been Brent's big gamble. It had been an even bigger gamble than building the cabins. Their only chance to get back on top of the debt he'd accrued would be if this bull lived up to all the hype and produced calves of exceptional quality. If he turned out to be a dud, they would be screwed.

'Yeah, so far so good. They all seem to be a good size.'

'I had a yarn with that new stock agent fella this morning,' her dad started, and Reggie paused from loading up her fork to glance at her father.

'He reckons there's been a lot of interest in our steers since the last sales. Said he has a few interested clients. Apparently, he wants to do a write-up in *Rural Today* magazine and a few of the papers, to get a bit of interest.'

Reggie felt her interest pique at this bit of news.

'Of course, he's just trying to butter us up so we'll sell through him at auction. I told him we'd come and see him a bit later and go over a few things. Once we've got all the weights and tagging done, we'll have more of an idea what we're working with.'

'That sounds like a plan,' Reggie agreed, and a happy little bubble floated up inside her at being included in the farm's future plans. Not that she would actually get to make the decisions, she thought. Her dad was the one really driving this whole thing, but she would be there alongside him, and that was pretty special.

'I reckon it's safe to say your brother was on the right track after all,' Ray said with a hint of pride in his voice.

'I reckon he might have been.'

Conversation moved to her mother's garden and the seedlings she was hoping to put in, and Reggie was glad it was something her parents could do together that got them out of the house and back into some kind of normalcy again.

'I meant to tell you, Mum, I bumped into Mrs Nelson the other day in town. Everyone's eager to see you back at the meetings.'

Reggie watched her mother's face carefully for any signs of shutting down the conversation but was encouraged when the usual reluctance wasn't there.

'Birdie's been a godsend,' Peggy said, smiling fondly.

'Do you think you'd like to go to the next one?'

'Oh, I don't know . . . we'll see.'

That was her mum's standard fall-back for 'don't bother me with this right now'. Reggie didn't want to press her mother on the subject—she'd had to learn when to push and when to back off since coming home. There was a fine line between encouragement and getting your head bitten off. They'd all had to adjust to this new way of life, and it hadn't been easy for anyone. Her mother had had the biggest adjustments to make. When she lost her mobility she lost so much of her identity. She was always the no-fuss, practical one who calmly fixed everyone else's problems and got on with it. Suddenly now she was the one who had to be taken care of, and needing to depend on others was something Peggy MacLeod hadn't done in a very long time.

'Were the evil stepsisters there with her?' Ray asked.

Reggie bit back a smile. He was referring to Bertha Cravet and Marge Biswell who were also heavily involved in the local CWA. This was not the time to encourage him, but it *had* been a source of family entertainment for years, the rivalry between her father and the two women he'd known all his life and gone to school with. 'No. They weren't.'

He gave an unimpressed harrumph, and Reggie caught her mother's eye, swapping an exasperated eyeroll.

'Dad, I was thinking, if you see our guest from Jacaranda cabin down at the dam,' Reggie said, 'you might like to wander by? He's brought all the fly-fishing gear, but I'm not so sure he knows what he's doing.'

'I saw him down there today,' her father said, nodding in between forkfuls of pie. 'He looked more like a contemplator to me. I'm not sure he's really there for the fish.'

'Maybe if you happened to be down there, you could lend a hand?'

'Yeah, I might take a wander down tomorrow, if I see him around,' he said.

Her dad also needed purpose, Reggie had realised. She worried that he still tried to do too much around the place, especially things his doctor had warned him not to do. If she could find something to keep him occupied—that he loved doing—then maybe he wouldn't feel as though he should be doing *more*.

'I heard wild dogs this morning,' he continued, and Reggie frowned. She'd had no luck when she'd gone out looking for the black dog earlier.

'Yeah, I saw them the other day—well, one of them. A big black thing.'

'Where?'

'Just past the crossing.' She wasn't about to reveal how close she'd got to it or how unsettling the whole thing had been. 'I was surprised to see them down this close.'

'That *is* close,' he said, frowning at his plate before looking up. 'What did it look like?'

A memory of the sharp teeth it had bared flashed through her mind and she quickly pushed it away. 'Like a cross between an Alsatian and a werewolf,' she said. 'I went out after it, but I didn't have any luck.'

Her father gave her a heavy stare. 'I don't want you goin' back out after it alone. It's too dangerous. I'll make some calls and see if I can get someone to come out—maybe Dougie Dwyer or one of the Geerling boys from up the road.'

'I can handle it, Dad,' she said, trying to stay calm.

'You are not going out there lookin' for this thing,' Ray said, using the tone of voice that both she and Brent knew not to argue with as kids. That annoyed her more than anything—the fact her father was using that tone on her now, as an adult.

She glanced across at her mother, who had been watching the exchange with a frown. Reggie pushed her annoyance aside with considerable effort and nodded. Truthfully, she had no desire to meet that thing alone again either, she just wished she could have handled it without anyone else's help. How was she supposed to prove herself if her father kept calling in help every time things got a bit difficult?

Chapter 10

The wind had finally settled and the difference was remarkable. Tim could actually feel the warmth of the sun on his face as he looked up to the blue sky above. The sound of a vehicle approaching made him lower his head and he shielded his eyes to see the same rusted old ute he'd seen Reggie driving. For a moment he was caught off guard by the thud of his heart-rate picking up. But then the door opened and a stocky man dressed in moleskin pants, a checked shirt and a wide-brimmed hat struggled out of the car. Tim watched as he took out a fishing rod and small tackle box before making his way over to him.

'G'day,' the man said, adjusting his hat as he came to a stop at the fence line. 'You must be Tim.'

'That's me,' he answered, thinking this had to be Reggie's father.

'Nice to meet ya. I'm Ray. Hope you don't mind some company.'

Fact was, he kind of did mind, but there wasn't much he could do about it. 'It's your dam,' he said, shrugging.

The older man hobbled over to a spot a little further up and set down his box.

Tim tried to focus on dragging the line in and out of the water and ignored the fact the guy next to him was probably wondering what the hell he was doing. In his peripheral vision, he watched Ray send his line in an elegant arc above his head that floated through the air and landed in a perfectly straight line on the water in front of him.

Why couldn't he get his line to do that? Every time he tried, it ended up getting caught in the wind and blown downstream or tangled in a clump of grass behind him somewhere—not even making it into the bloody water at all.

'You want to remember fly fishing is about convincing the fish that he's about to eat something he'd normally eat. You gotta make your fly land on top of the water as smoothly as possible, like a big juicy dragonfly.'

Tim's previous attempts had been nothing like that . . . at all. Taking a deep breath, he tried his best to copy the man's cast, adjusting his hand on the rod and pointing it down from his waist. With the line extended in front of him, keeping his wrist straight, he lifted his arm and rotated it backwards

'Bring your rod out a bit to about two o'clock,' Ray said, his eyes still focused on his own rod—seemingly not even watching Tim's progress. 'Now pause and wait for the line to form a loop behind you. Good. Now bring the line forward to about the ten o'clock position.'

Tim couldn't believe it—the damn thing was almost dead straight in front of him.

'Now slowly lower your arm, so it gently lays the line on the water. You don't want to do anything that's going to scare the fish—remember it's all about trickin' him into thinkin' he's all alone in nature. Good job,' Ray said, and gave a decisive nod—still not even glancing in Tim's direction.

It barely felt like he'd been given a lesson in fly fishing for dummies.

Tim cautiously tried the technique again and felt a stupid self-satisfied smile fill his face when he nailed it. Nothing to it really, once you knew how.

The two men settled into a companionable silence. The gentle trickle of the water as it tripped and fell into a smaller stream behind them provided a relaxing backdrop to the occasional bellow of a cow or craw of a crow somewhere in the distance.

After a while, Tim watched Ray pull his line back and a smile cracked Ray's weathered face as he bent down and held up a silvery slithering trout.

Son of a bit—

'Thought I might be losin' my touch there for a minute,' Ray said and gave a wheezy chuckle as he removed the hook then lowered the fish back into the water and let it swim away.

Losing his touch? He'd barely been there half an hour before he'd caught one.

'Mind if I sit here a spell?' Ray asked, easing down onto a log on the bank. 'Legs not what they used to be since the accident. Can't stand up too long anymore.'

'Go right ahead,' Tim said, returning to his casting with renewed determination. At least he knew there were fish in here now—although they'd won the award for the best fucking hide-and-seek champions of the year. He hadn't seen a glimpse of the bloody things before now. 'Was it a farming accident?' Tim asked after a moment.

'Nah. The wife and I were in a prang. Some idiot high on drugs came around the bend on the wrong side of the road. Didn't think either of us would make it for a while.'

'Sorry to hear that,' Tim said with a wince.

'This is a good place to heal,' Ray said with a kind of certainty that made Tim eye him a little warily—unsure if he were speaking about himself or . . .

'Once you get you get the hang of that, there's a few good spots further up you should try.'

'I'm not really set up with all the gear—it was a spur of the moment kind of thing to try it,' Tim said, before having a strange urge to add, 'It was my mate's thing, fly fishing. Something he always wanted to do.'

Ray gave a thoughtful nod of his head as he stared out across the dam. 'I take it he isn't around anymore?' he said almost gently, or in as gentle a manner a tough old farmer could manage. The words poked at Tim's bruised heart.

'No. He, ah, passed a few weeks ago. We were always talking about taking it up—fly fishing,' he added quickly, then swallowed down a lump in his throat. 'Just never got around to it.' Why the hell was he saying any of this?

The old bloke nodded. 'Yeah, I know a thing or two about that. We always think we got forever.'

The sound of the bubbling water somehow felt soothing as the quiet settled between them once more.

'We used to talk about heading bush for a few weeks, all the boys, once we got back home. It was something that got us through some pretty dark days while we were overseas.'

'You were in Afghanistan then?'

'Yeah. Did a couple of tours. A while back now.'

'My older brother was in Vietnam. I missed out . . . luckily,' Ray added with a grunt. 'He spent some time out bush for a while when he came back. Lost his share of good mates both over there and when he got home too. It's a terrible thing, war,' he said, shaking his head slowly. 'Terrible thing.'

Tim couldn't argue there.

'We lost our son a few years back,' Ray went on. 'Left a lot of things unsaid . . . unfinished. Sometimes it's important to finish them.'

Tim eyed the man and soaked in his words. That's what he was doing, finishing the dream they'd always talked about but never got around to. Anger tried to stir once more as it usually did whenever he thought too much about Deano and the others, and he immediately felt bad. He was constantly fighting a war within himself when it came to his mates. Grief was the loudest emotion—but it was always closely followed by anger. Why didn't they fight harder? Why didn't they tell him how close they'd been to making a decision so brutally final? Why would they leave him to continue fighting this fucking endless loop of pain? They were supposed to be in this together, watching each other's backs the way they always had, except that when they came home, somehow, everything just fell apart. They'd had to learn how to deal with life again; families and nine-to-five jobs. Everything was different and none of them fit in anywhere anymore.

In a way Tim was luckier than the others. He hadn't had a family to come back to. Most people wouldn't consider that lucky, but he was convinced in this case it was. He'd watched the others struggle to go back to the men they were before they'd left, to be the fathers and husbands and sons they'd once been. He saw the toll that took on them mentally. He didn't have anyone hovering over him—depending on him to return to *normal*, whatever that was now—and maybe that's why he was still alive. But that didn't make much sense, because if anyone was going to give up, surely it should have been him, the one with no one who would really care if he was here or not. Not the three men who'd had everything to live for and families who would have done anything to help them get better.

None of it made any sense. But still . . . here he was, trying.

'Yep, this is a good place to heal,' Ray said again with a long sigh. He rose slowly and moved past Tim on his way back to the ute. 'You stay as long as you need.'

Tim was unsure if he meant at the dam or here in general. But, either way, being here didn't seem like such a bad idea.

Chapter 11

There wasn't a lot of maintenance to do in winter, mostly because the grass grew more slowly, but Reggie liked to make sure the area around the cabins always looked neat and tidy, so she watered the grass year-round. There were no flowerbeds or special plantings around the place, which kept the work down. Reggie had never had her mother's green thumb and couldn't be trusted to keep a house plant alive. Instead, they made use of the native trees that they'd planted in neat rows along the driveway and in front of the cabins. In summer, the lush green leaves provided welcome shade, but in autumn their beautiful foliage made postcard-perfect backdrops with the gold, red and yellow leaves that Reggie adored.

At the moment though, in the middle of winter, all those glorious, coloured leaves had dropped and were now crunchy mounds of brown underfoot. Families with young kids loved playing in the deep piles of leaves, and she remembered fondly the days when she and Brent had spent hours covering themselves in leaf blankets.

Reggie stopped the ride-on mower at the corner of the last cabin when she spotted Tim walking towards her.

'Hey,' she said, cutting the engine and eyeing him curiously. She hadn't seen him for a whole day and was surprised he was seeking her out.

'I'm hoping to extend my stay a few days,' he said, getting straight to the point as he stood with his hands shoved deep into the pockets of his fleece-lined flannel jacket.

'I'll double check the bookings, but I'm pretty sure it's free since it's mid-week.'

'Great. Thanks.'

'No worries,' she said, reaching for the key to start the mower, but paused when he didn't move to walk away.

'You manage all this on your own?' he asked, looking at mower before returning his gaze to her face.

'Yeah. Well, Mum and Dad help out with bookings and the paperwork side of things occasionally, and Dad does some of the lighter work.'

'But you don't have any other staff?'

'Nope. Just me.'

'Seems like a lot of work for one person.'

Reggie shrugged. 'We get by.'

'I met your dad this morning. Gave me a few pointers on fly fishing,' he said, gently kicking the toe of one boot into the ground as he spoke.

'That's good. Did it help?'

'Nah, still couldn't catch anything.' He grinned briefly—the change in his face was immediate and unexpected, but it was quickly replaced by the guarded, neutral expression he usually wore. 'He mentioned the car accident he and your mother were in . . . that had to be tough.'

Reggie felt one eyebrow raise slightly as she wondered how this conversation had come about—neither her dad nor this man seemed like the chatty types.

'Anyway, I just wanted to say thanks . . . for asking him to give me a hand. I figured you must have had something to do with it.'

'I'm glad he could help. He doesn't get a chance to talk fishing very often, so he would have really enjoyed it.'

'Well, I better let you get back to it,' he said, when a small silence began to grow between them. She wasn't altogether sure if he wanted to stay and chat or if he was just being polite. He always seemed so standoffish, like he simply enjoyed his own company, and yet, there was also something lonely about him. Lost even. She reached for the key again. She had enough of her own problems to deal with without borrowing anyone else's.

'I'll let you know if there's any issue with extending your booking, otherwise, it's all good.'

He gave a nod and small wave, taking a step back as she moved forwards. She replayed their conversation in her head as she parked the mower in the shed and headed inside the office to change his booking.

She wondered what his plans were. This was the perfect place to stay to get away from it all, and families often came here to reconnect with their kids—the cabins had no wi-fi and phone reception was so dodgy that it may as well have been non-existent. They'd even had the odd writers' retreat here, the peace and quiet providing the inspiration many writers craved. But she was curious why *he'd* come here.

She probably wasn't the best personality type for working in this industry, where guests expected a non-judgmental, non-interfering attitude, but she'd always been curious about people's stories. She usually restrained herself from asking a hundred-and-one questions of people when they booked in, but it didn't stop her imagination running overtime and she often found herself guessing people's backstories. Some were here on a secret rendezvous—meeting up away from spying eyes for a romantic weekend. Others were escaping the city hustle and bustle to live out a childhood fantasy of enjoying the country life. Most families, she assumed, were just seeking some quality time in a place without the usual distractions that came with the hectic pace of living nowadays. Here there was nothing but open space, fresh air and a clarity that came with being able to hear your own thoughts again.

In the office, she opened the laptop and logged into their website back-end, pulling up the bookings page. It was a quiet few weeks across all the cabins, with only two other couples booked in on the weekend. She was happy Tim wanted to extend his stay. *Purely because it's good for business*, she thought when she found herself surprisingly excited by the news. She wasn't *excited*, she scolded herself. She was just happy she could provide a guest with a satisfactory outcome. That was it. She ignored the little scoff she heard inside her head and closed the laptop.

❖

Tim watched the jaunty swing of Reggie's ponytail poking out the back of the pink baseball cap she wore and bit back a smile. She'd been popping up in his thoughts all day.

Ever since meeting Ray earlier, something seemed to be shifting inside him. Maybe it was simply that he'd had a chance to talk about Dean and the others out loud—instead of it going round and round inside his head like a stuck record. Not that he'd said a lot, but it had been more than he'd said to anyone in the last few weeks.

Whatever it was, it made Tim realise he wasn't ready to leave just yet.

He'd seen a fancy SUV pull up in front of the cabin next door to him late the day before and felt a small twinge of annoyance—he'd enjoyed having the place to himself—but so far he hadn't seen or heard any movement. Perhaps the other guests were here for a romantic getaway and staying indoors in front of the fireplace.

He followed the road in front of his cabin and decided to keep walking. He hadn't come up this way before and the cool air on his face made him feel alive. The other cabins along here were similar to his own, with verandahs at the front and chimneys poking up through the tin roofs. Unlike his, though, most of these chimneys weren't puffing out white smoke, as they were empty of guests at the moment. He'd been relieved to hear there weren't any other guests expected for the next few days when he'd spoken to Reggie. It was selfish of him, he supposed, but he'd been enjoying the quiet and was loath to give it up.

The cabins were a good distance apart, he noticed, each with their own view of something—the dam, the paddock, some trees and a mountain, and none of them looked in on another.

When he reached the last cabin, he noticed a path leading into the thick trees behind it. A timber post stuck out of the ground where the path reached the trees and had a sign nailed to it that said, 'The Fairy Glen'. With nothing else to do, he decided to follow it. Where the rest of the paddocks and landscape surrounding the property were shrouded in winter hues of golds, browns and oranges, this area was lush and so green it almost hurt his eyes to look at. The moment he stepped into the shade, there was an immediate sense of stillness. It was quiet, not really in an eerie way, but as though he'd stepped inside a room and closed a door.

A small creek ran through a gully. Moss-covered logs lay where they'd fallen years ago, slowly decaying but creating natural bridges across the water. Large ferns and native grasses grew with abandon between the rocks and trees, which were draped in long strands of pale green moss, like grass icicles.

Further along he noticed that someone had placed tiny cottages no bigger than his hand in a clearing, complete with little signs saying, 'Fairy crossing' and 'Please tread carefully, fairies play here'. It looked like a kid's paradise—if kids were into fairies.

He sat down on a log and closed his eyes, listening to the sound of the running water.

You're pretty shit at this fly fishin' stuff, Warie. He could hear Dean's voice and chuckle in his head. *It didn't look that hard on YouTube.*

Yeah, well, it's taking a bit of practice, Tim admitted.

You'll get there, mate. Out of all of us, you were always the one who strived for perfection.

That familiar hollow feeling gaped inside Tim. Christ, he missed Dean's voice.

I know you're hurtin', mate. But you've gotta let it go now.

Let it go? Are you fucking kidding me? I've lost everyone. You all left me! I just don't understand—

It wasn't about you. That's the point. It wasn't about Alicia or the kids or my dad. It wasn't about anyone except me. It was my choice—one I can't explain.

Well, that's really fucking selfish.

For a moment there was silence before Dean's voice came again, weary. *Yeah, it is. But it's the choice I made for me. It's not anyone else's guilt to carry. Just mine.*

The wind in the trees above almost sounded like it was singing a song, momentarily distracting Tim from the pain that clutched at his heart like a giant hand, squeezing tightly.

It was hard coming back, he heard Dean say. *It was fuckin' exhausting, mate. You didn't have to pretend you were fine every single day so you didn't worry your wife. You didn't yell at your kids and see the fear on their faces. I was a tickin' time bomb, Warie. My nerves were shot . . . I could hide the drugs for a long time, but Alicia was beginning to see through it all. I was just too tired to keep fightin'.*

Tim opened his eyes and felt the air leave his lungs as he looked around, positive that he'd find his best friend right there beside him. But there was nothing. Just the gentle trickle of the water and the soft rustle of the leaves. Was he losing his mind? Maybe he'd spent too much time alone with his grief and pain—clearly he had, if he thought he'd been having a conversation with his dead mate.

He gave a strangled kind of groan as he lowered his head and stared at the dirt and grass beneath his feet. He shouldn't be freaking out—hadn't he been wishing for just one more chance to see Dean, so he could shake him? Christ, punch him maybe, or hug him, and find out *why?* To have the opportunity to find out what the hell he'd been thinking. Tim thought that if he had the chance to stand before Dean once more he'd have been able to make sense out of everything somehow. If only he could turn back time and do everything differently. How far back would he go to change things? After they got home? Before they went to Afghanistan? Before they joined the army? How far back did everything start going to shit? And could he ever really have stopped it? Or no matter what he'd done, would they still have ended up here?

Maybe Dean had been right—maybe this was all about him and nobody else was supposed to be taking on the blame and guilt. But it didn't make it hurt any less and he couldn't help feeling like there had to have been some other way. Tim knew he'd never be able to understand Dean's choice, and he also knew that he couldn't continue to run away from life and stay this angry anymore either. But letting go felt like losing his best friend all over again. And it bloody hurt.

Chapter 12

Tim sat on the verandah the next morning, drinking his coffee as he soaked in the view of the dam before him. Mist swirled up from the water and rose into the air like the dam was the stage of a magician's trick. It was cold, but the coffee was hot and he had on enough layers to resemble the Michelin man, so it didn't bother him.

Birds dipped their beaks in the edges of the waterways, while wild ducks bobbed about on the dam surface before diving under to catch breakfast. Kangaroos and wallabies bounded about, their alert heads moving this way and that as they chewed grass, watching for the slightest movement that might signal danger.

He tossed the dregs of his coffee over the railing and stood up. He could relate to the roos' constant vigilance—he'd lived like that himself. It was a hard habit to break and one that he'd never completely gotten rid of. To this day he found it difficult to sit with his back to a door and any kind of car driving slowly instantly set him on high alert.

Today he planned on taking one of the tracks Ray had pointed out to him and practise throwing his line out in the stream further up. He shrugged on his backpack and grabbed his fishing gear, then headed off across the paddock towards the track.

He could have driven, but he'd been missing exercise. He needed to get out and breathe; to smell the fresh air and feel the blood pump through his veins again. He'd done a lot of sitting, thinking, sleeping and drinking over the last few weeks—all the stuff that for him only perpetuated the cycle of misery and frustration. What he needed now was to clear his head.

It wasn't a difficult hike to reach the next stream, which, he'd discovered after reading through some information booklets in the cabin, was a smaller arm of the Styx River that broke off into lots of little tributaries along the way, crisscrossing the property.

He walked downstream, searching for a spot to set up, and eventually found a place where he could get down onto the rocks and walk out into the water before it dropped off into a deeper part. There were some nice logs along the far edge of the water—good places for fish to hide—so he set down his pack and got out his line.

This part of the river was sheltered from the wind, but there was no escaping its noise. It blew through the tall treetops nearby like the roar of an ocean—and, if he hadn't known better, he could have sworn there was a beach just behind the treeline somewhere.

He'd gone to bed the night before thinking about the glen and trying to come to some kind of logical explanation for the conversation with Dean. Eventually he put his mind at ease by deciding his subconscious had just taken over.

He wasn't into anything spiritual or otherworldly. He'd dated a woman once who wouldn't start the day before she'd read her horoscope. Unsurprisingly, it hadn't worked out. She told him it was because their star signs were incompatible, but he thought it was more that she was a bit of a fruitcake. Besides, she didn't like coffee, and if *that* wasn't a red flag, he didn't know what was.

Whatever yesterday had been, or hadn't been, it seemed to have lifted a bit of the weight from his shoulders and today he felt more optimistic than he had in a long time.

He watched the crystal-clear water running through the green reeds and moss on the riverbed and tried to imagine how peaceful it must be under the water. Birds flew down and drank from the river, some staying to catch bugs that were floating nearby before fluttering off to do whatever the hell birds did all day.

The sun had burned off any of the earlier traces of mist and the sky was a bright, fathomless blue that stretched as far as he could see without a single white cloud. He breathed in deeply and tilted his head back so the warmth of the sun fell on his face.

Wouldn't be dead for quids.

The words echoed through his head, as clear as the whip bird that called out somewhere deep in the dense bushland across the river, and it caught him off guard before a small, reluctant grin tugged at his lips. Anyone else would probably have been appalled at the thought, but dark humour was how they'd coped with a lot of the daily crap that went on in military life, and that was exactly what Simmo or Dean would have said if they were standing right here next to him.

The four of them had been inseparable from basic training right through to selection for the SAS. They'd endured some of the most gruelling preparation and operations imaginable and been sent into places no one in their right mind would ever voluntarily go. They were a little crazy—surely you had to be to love doing the job they did. It was a lonely one. They had each other, but it was often at the expense of relationships and family. They could be gone for months on end, with no contact with loved ones. And when they were home it was almost as bad—none of them could talk about their work to anyone. It made their bond even tighter, because they only had each other to depend on and there was no one else who really understood what they did. Sometimes it wasn't pretty. They were the guys who were sent in to do what no one else wanted to do. They were highly trained, completely professional—and totally dispensable if the shit hit the fan.

There was no other life like it and, as hard as it was for anyone else to understand, it was almost impossible to let go of it.

'You know, if you guys want to do something useful—help me catch a bloody fish,' Tim muttered, taking his sunglasses from the front of his shirt and putting them on to cut through the glare off the water.

'Typical,' he mumbled after a while with no sign of a nibble.

Ray's words from the day before came back to him as he concentrated on making the fly fall to the surface of the water as gently as possible. *Make the fish think it's a real insect,* he repeated to himself.

Suddenly he felt a tug so small that for a moment he didn't react, then another, firmer this time, which made him leap into action, muttering a curse as he moved. *Pull or be pulled* came to his mind from something he'd read in the cabin. Either the trout was pulling or you were—it should never reach a stalemate. *Okay,* Tim thought, *he's certainly pulling, so that's a good start.* The river here wasn't very deep, so Tim could see the fish on his line and swore as the slippery rocks beneath his boots almost up-ended him a few times. Eventually, though, he managed to manoeuvre his net under the fish and secure the catch.

The rainbow trout slithered and twisted, the spots and distinctive pink stripes along its sides glistening. Tim quickly removed the fly from its wide mouth and carefully took it from the net, feeling its slippery body fighting to escape. Even if it hadn't been strictly catch and release here, he would have let it go anyway. The truth was he didn't much like eating fish.

He sat back on his heels and watched the fish vanish into the depths of the water, making for the shelter of the logs and rocks on the other side of the river. *So that was that,* he thought, unsure how to interpret the emotion he was feeling. His aim had been to learn how to fly fish and catch a trout.

Catching any more really didn't appeal to him, but the method was incredibly soothing. He reached for his rod and continued to stand and cast out his line, again and again, listening to the leaves as they rustled in the wind and soaking up the warm sunshine.

Chapter 13

Reggie arrived home from town and noticed the ATV missing from the shed. She gave a cursory glance around but couldn't see any sign of her dad and couldn't think of anything that he needed to be doing. She was still frowning as she walked into the kitchen and found her mother at the window, where she had just lowered the phone to her lap.

'Mum? Is everything okay?'

'I've been trying to get hold of your father. He's been gone a while.'

Reggie's stomach clenched. 'Where did he go?'

'He said he thought he heard the cattle making a bit of noise, so he went for a drive to take a look.'

That shouldn't have been anything to worry about, but Reggie couldn't seem to shake the feeling that something wasn't right. She summoned a confident smile for her mother and gave her a quick hug. 'You know Dad, his phone is probably flat. I'll go and find him. He's probably already on his way back.' Her smile faded as she climbed back into the ute and headed towards the paddock they'd moved the cattle into.

She quickly spotted the ATV in the far corner, but there was no sign of her father. Pulling up beside it, she pushed open the door and scrambled out, calling to her dad. In the distance she noticed movement and shaded her eyes from the sun. Two men were making their way slowly towards the vehicle.

As realisation set in, Reggie uttered a low curse before running across the paddock towards Tim, who was supporting her father's limping weight.

'Dad! What happened?'

'That bloody dog. The cattle were goin' crazy, and I spotted an injured calf. I was on my way across to it when I lost my balance and fell over. Must have knocked myself out for a minute. When I came to, I sat up and heard growlin', and there it was—that flamin' black mongrel dog.'

'Did it attack you?' she asked, her gaze searching him for signs of ripped clothing or blood.

'Wanted to. I couldn't reach the bloody gun, but I threw some dirt clods at it, kept it away a bit, then this bloke suddenly appeared and chased it off.'

'How did you know he was out here?'

'I was heading back from fishing in the stream your dad told me about,' Tim said, tossing his head in the direction of one of the small tributaries that ran across the property. 'Heard the commotion and came over.'

'Lucky he did. That bastard is getting braver by the day.'

'Can you get Dad back to the house?' she asked Tim. 'I need to go and find the calf.'

'No point,' her father said. 'It's dead.'

Reggie felt the air rush from her lungs. 'I'll bring the cattle up to the front paddock—we can't afford to let that dog pick off any more calves.'

'Yeah, probably a good idea,' Ray said, and Reggie noticed he was looking a little pale.

'Come on, we need to get you checked out.'

'Don't fuss,' he said, waving her off as they approached the ute. 'I'll be right after I sit down for a bit.'

'Dad—'

Her father sent her a look that, even now, as a grown adult, made her stop talking.

'Fine!' she said, throwing her hands in the air. 'It's not like you have a heart condition or anything,' she muttered as she crossed to get in Glenda so Tim could drive her ute.

As she called the dogs and moved the cattle slowly back towards the homestead, she kept her eyes on the old ute that led the way. She was still annoyed at her father's refusal to take his heart issue seriously. There was a time and place for being stoic and soldiering on—but immediately after a stressful encounter with a wild dog was *not* the time. The doctor explicitly said he should avoid stress. 'Bloody stubborn men,' she said, clenching the steering wheel tighter. Maybe her mother could talk some sense into him.

After the dogs pushed the last of the stragglers through the gate that Tim had left open for them, she closed it and took a moment to survey the open paddocks behind her—looking for any kind of movement—but the wild dog had vanished. It had had its fun and slipped back into the safety of the dense bushland that surrounded the property. For now, the cattle would be safe, up in the paddocks closer to the house. There was normally no need to bring them up this far—most years, dog attacks weren't much of a threat—and it was usually reserved for the horses and locked up to rest over winter. She'd sort out a better solution later, but for tonight, at least, they should be okay.

At the house, Reggie found her mother on the verandah, looking relieved.

'I'll be back in a second with the car, Ray,' Tim said, already turning to jog up the road towards the cabins.

'What's he doing?' Reggie asked.

'He offered to take me to the hospital,' her father said.

'So, you *are* going to go and get checked out?' she asked slowly.

'I'd only have to put up with you two watchin' me all night like a flamin' hawks if I don't.'

Reggie sent her mother a surprised look as Peggy wheeled her chair backwards. 'I was just on my way to get a few things together . . . in case they want to keep you overnight.'

'I'm not bloody stayin' overnight in hospital.'

'It's just in case,' Peggy called from inside the house.

Reggie was still trying to process the fact her father had changed his mind about a check-up when they heard the sound of an engine starting up at the cabin.

'He's a good fella, that Tim,' Ray said gruffly.

'It was lucky he was out there and heard the commotion. We're going to have to do something—we can't afford to lose another calf.'

'Dwyer was going to get back to me about comin' out,' Ray muttered. 'I'll give him another call. That black dog's a crafty bugger. I reckon it's the same one we had trouble with a few years back. Your brother and I tried to track it and couldn't catch the bastard. I reckon it's back—and lookin' for some easy pickin's.'

'That's what I don't get. There should be plenty of food around—the kangaroos and wallabies are everywhere. I don't understand why it's attacking livestock. They aren't even eating it all, so it's not because they're starving.'

'Nah,' her father said, his eyes narrowing out towards the ridge in the distance. 'He just likes the hunt, I reckon. I tell ya, Reg, I was worried there for a minute when I ran out of things to throw. He wasn't scared.'

The fact her father was admitting he was concerned made Reggie even more certain that something had to be done about the animal. What if next time one of them was out alone and something happened? 'Well, he won't be getting any more calves now they're up here. They won't come this close to the house.'

'Yeah. I think that's the safest bet for now. Keep that rifle with you, when you go out,' Ray said as Tim pulled up beside them.

'I will. He'll be long gone by now though.'

She stood back as her dad climbed slowly into the big four-wheel drive. 'Thanks for this, Tim . . . but are you sure? I can run him in. You're supposed to be here relaxing,' she said.

'I don't mind. Besides, it's easier if I go. You've got stuff to do here and wouldn't get finished till late if you went in.'

Reggie blinked. That was true, and the fact he'd considered this surprised her. 'I don't know how you made him change his mind—but thanks.'

'It's a guy thing,' Tim said, sending her a crooked grin that had the effect of a swift kick to her chest. He turned before she could reply and she busied herself taking the overnight bag from her mother as she came back out onto the verandah.

As the dust trail slowly faded, Reggie squeezed her mother's shoulder gently and smiled. 'You know he's only going to come back and say he told us so when the doctor clears him, don't you?'

'Let's hope so,' Peg said.

'He'll be fine, Mum. He's a tough old bugger. He's not done with telling us how much we fuss over him too much, yet.'

'He just gets so frustrated when he can't do the things he's always done.'

'I know. It must be hard.'

'It wouldn't be so bad if it'd just been me who'd lost my mobility, but your father . . .' she said, trailing off. 'You know he can't sit still for more than two minutes. I worry he's going to try and do things out of sheer bloody-mindedness and really hurt himself.'

'We'll just have to find things to keep him occupied. Maybe we can do more fishing-based things, offer school-holiday programmes or something? Or look into organising some kind of fishing group . . . there must be lots of retired men who like to fish and would jump at the chance to meet up with other fishermen.'

'That sounds like something he might enjoy,' her mother said, tilting her head slightly as she considered the idea. 'I'll do a ring around and see if any of the CWA girls have some ideas.'

'Okey-dokey.' Reggie smiled, glad that her mum had something to concentrate on for a little while. She kissed her mother's cheek before heading over to the ute. There was unfinished farm business to attend to.

When she returned at the end of the day, she kicked off her boots and heard her mother saying goodbye on the phone.

'Oh, there you are, that was your father. They're keeping him in. Apparently the ECG they did wasn't as steady as the doctor would have liked.'

'Oh no,' Reggie said, wincing. 'Bet he wasn't happy about that.'

'No. Not particularly.'

'Oh well. Better that he's in there under observation than out here if there's something going on. It can't be too much of a concern, though, or they'd have sent him to a specialist. Probably just being cautious.'

'Oh, yes.' Peg nodded. 'It was probably the shock of it all that's put everything out. I'm sure it'll settle.'

Reggie watched her mother as she checked on dinner. She could do with a little bit of a settle herself. It had been an exhausting day all around. She'd gone back out looking for the dog as soon as she'd seen her dad off. She figured what her father didn't know wouldn't hurt him, but as usual she hadn't been able to spot the black dog. The damn thing had simply vanished. But its days were definitely numbered. There was no way, after today's near miss, she was going to allow that thing to stay alive.

Chapter 14

Reggie was just getting the plates out for dinner when she heard Tim's car pull up outside. She set the plates on the table and walked across to the door. It had become dark in the last half hour, making it seem later than it really was.

'Come on in,' she told him, holding the screen door open as he approached.

'I don't want to interrupt,' he said quickly, eyeing the kitchen table.

'You're not,' she said, waiting for him to wipe his boots on the mat before he walked past. 'Mum,' she called, 'Tim's back.'

'I thought I'd drop in and let you know he's okay. I'm guessing he rang to tell you he was staying in,' Tim said, looking slightly uncomfortable as he shoved his hands into the pockets of his jacket.

'He did. I imagine that went down well.'

'He wasn't happy.'

'Oh, Tim. Hello, love,' Peg greeted him warmly as she wheeled herself out from the bedroom. 'Thank you so much for everything you've done today.'

'No worries. I'm just glad I was in the right place at the right time.'

'Will you stay for dinner? We were just about to sit down.'

'Oh . . . no,' he said. 'I didn't mean to hold you up from eating. Just wanted to let you know he's okay.'

'You're not holding us up,' Peg said. 'Reggie, set another place for Tim. It's the least we can do after you drove all the way into the hospital and back. Go and sit down,' she ordered Tim in her no-nonsense way, handing him serving bowls of creamy mashed potatoes and steamed vegetables to carry.

Reggie bit back a grin as he obediently crossed to the table. Clearly he was used to taking orders. She picked up the cast-iron casserole dish of beef and gravy stew and followed. 'Dig in,' she told him, handing over a ladle.

'This looks amazing,' Tim said, staring down at his plate as he waited for Reggie and Peg to serve their meals.

'Don't wait for us, eat before it gets cold,' Peg instructed with a warm smile. 'There's plenty more once you get through that lot.'

If there was one thing her mother loved most, it was to cook for her family, especially the *men* in her family. Nothing satisfied her nurturing instinct more than the male appetite, and Brent used to eat like a horse. Reggie's heart caught a little. It had been a long time since there'd been another male at the table besides her father.

'Are you enjoying your stay?' Peg asked, buttering a slice of bread as she watched Tim devouring his meal.

He paused, dabbing his mouth with a paper napkin before nodding. 'Yeah. It's just what I was looking for.'

'Oh? What's that?' Peg asked.

'Some peace and quiet. Somewhere to get away to.'

'Whereabouts did you grow up?' Peg probed. While Reggie's first instinct was to jump in and save Tim from her mother's inquisition, she was kind of curious to find out more about this man.

'All over the place,' he said, shrugging, and Reggie thought that was all he was prepared to say, until he lowered his fork and finished chewing. 'When I was in the army I was stationed up and down the east coast and over in Western Australia. The last few years I've been working around Sydney.'

'What kind of work do you do?' Peg continued, as she delicately sliced through a piece of beef then popped it in her mouth. Reggie took a sip of water, trying to look as though she wasn't also keen to find out.

'I'm a builder by trade.'

Reggie choked on her water and went into a coughing fit. 'Sorry,' she managed after a moment, looking up and seeing the alarm on Tim's face. She raised a hand to reassure her mother and their guest she was okay. 'Went down the wrong way,' she croaked, feeling her cheeks heat up as she dabbed at the water on her shirt.

'My son used to be a builder,' Peg said softly as she smiled at Tim across the table.

Tim nodded, his eyes not leaving hers. 'Ray told me about him the other day when we were fishing. I'm sorry for your loss.'

Peg managed a brief smile before clearing her throat. 'Thank you. We miss him terribly.'

'I can imagine,' he murmured, then lowered his gaze and took another mouthful.

The silence was broken by her mother's cheerful announcement that there was apple pie and cream for dessert, and she wheeled away from the table into the kitchen to check on the oven.

'I didn't mean to upset anyone by bringing up your brother,' Tim said quietly to Reggie after her mother left.

'You didn't. It's just that it's still hard to talk about him without getting sad sometimes,' she explained.

'Yeah. I get it.'

The way he said it made Reggie look up. 'You've lost someone too?'

He twisted his lips before pushing his empty plate away. 'A few someones.'

Avoiding her curious gaze, he lowered his own and stared at the tablecloth. 'I've lost a couple of close mates over the last few years . . . and one just recently.'

'I'm sorry,' she said softly.

'Yeah.' His abrupt reply spoke volumes. She heard the pain, lingering not far from the surface. 'I just needed some time alone for a while—to get my head around it all, I suppose.'

'That's fair enough.' This explained the moody, reserved personality, Reggie thought, feeling a little bad for assuming he was just being difficult.

'Dessert!' Peg announced.

As Reggie reached across to take his empty plate, Tim put a hand on her arm to stop her. The action made her gaze dart to his as the skin beneath his hand began to heat. 'Let me do something,' he said, releasing her arm then collecting both plates and leaving the table. Reggie didn't realise she'd been holding her breath until it escaped in a rush when Tim left the room.

For the remainder of the meal they stuck to general topics—Tim asked about the area and the history of the property, and Reggie was happy for her mother to tell him all about it. She kept glancing at her arm, resisting the urge to yank up her sleeve and inspect it, as she could still somehow feel the warmth where his hand had touched her. That was completely ridiculous and yet . . .

'Coffee?' her mother asked after they'd all finished eating.

'Not for me, thanks Mrs MacLeod,' Tim said, rubbing his stomach. 'I can't remember the last time I ate so much. That meal was the best I've had in years.'

Reggie watched her calm, sensible mother beam at the man before her and did a double take—was her mother *blushing?*

'You're most welcome. I hope we can have you over again soon.'

'Thank you,' he said again, helping to collect the dishes and carry them over to the bench.

Reggie took in her mother's drawn features—her eyes were looking a little dark underneath and she'd become less animated. 'I can do this Mum, you cooked.'

'Actually, I might head to bed. Watch a bit of telly before I go to sleep.'

'Are you okay?' Reggie asked, suddenly concerned.

'I'm just a little tired—I think I might have done a bit too much today.'

'Just be careful,' Reggie warned gently. 'I don't need both of you out of action.'

'I'll be fine after a sleep. I hope your father manages to get some rest—you know how he is, he doesn't like hospitals.'

'I'm sure the nurses will knock him out if he gets too obnoxious,' Reggie laughed, but she was only half joking.

'Good night, Mrs MacLeod,' Tim said as Peg kissed Reggie goodnight and prepared to leave the room.

'It's Peg,' she said and smiled. 'And thank you again for all your help today.'

'It was no problem.'

When her mother left the room a moment of awkward silence followed, and Reggie found herself wiping imaginary crumbs from the benchtop, unsure what to do with her hands all of a sudden. 'Well, thanks again . . .' she said, thinking he was probably just as uncomfortable as she was. He was likely trying to think of a polite way to leave.

'I don't mind helping,' he said.

'You were a huge help—I'd still be out there bringing in the cattle if I'd had to take Dad into the hospital.'

'I meant . . . I don't mind helping clean up . . . the kitchen,' he said, gesturing towards the dirty plates on the bench.

'Oh,' Reggie gasped, feeling like an idiot. *Of course he wasn't asking for validation about how helpful he'd been today, dumb arse.* 'Oh, no,' she said, quickly coming to her senses. 'This won't take long to clear up.'

Instead of listening, he stepped forward and continued packing the plates into the dishwasher.

For a moment Reggie wasn't sure what to do, but then she decided to just let him help, and they worked in a companionable kind of silence as all the dirty dishes were packed away. Reggie closed the dishwasher door and turned it on.

'If you need a hand while your dad's out of action, I don't mind helping out there too,' Tim offered, leaning back against the counter as she wiped down the benches.

'You're supposed to be on holiday.'

'It's not exactly a holiday.' He shuffled his feet a little before continuing. 'I've been in a bit of a down mood—after I got the news about Deano, my mate. Then, about two weeks ago, I just suddenly had enough. I quit my job, packed up my flat, got in the car and . . . headed north. I had no real destination in mind—I just needed some space.'

'So, how'd you find this place?' she asked, resting her hip against the counter opposite him.

'I saw an ad in a fishing magazine. When I looked the place up, you were nearby. So, I decided to come and check it out.'

'Lucky for us,' she said, meaning for it to come off as light-hearted. Somehow it ended up sounding more intense.

For a moment the silence between them felt palpable. There was something about this man that Reggie felt drawn to— it was more than simple curiosity. She'd been trying to deny it, getting angry each time her heart would skip a beat when she spotted him in the distance. She was too sensible—not to mention *busy*—for this kind of schoolgirl crush behaviour, and she'd be mortified if he ever suspected it. He was just a guest and he'd be leaving soon, never to be seen again.

'I should let you get to bed,' he said, clearing his throat abruptly and snapping her out of her thoughts.

'Thanks again,' she said, following him to the door.

'Let me know if you need a hand tomorrow,' he reminded her before turning away and heading out of the house and up the track that led to his cabin.

She rubbed her hands against the chill outside and turned her glance towards the nearby paddock, just able to make out the darker shapes of the cattle in the moonlight. At least she'd sleep better tonight. A medley of howls started up almost as if on cue, and Reggie's jaw clenched tightly. Her eyes narrowed as she looked off into the distance. They were still out there, lurking in the dense bushland and roaming through the endless miles of national park. With the cattle gone, she hoped it might encourage them to move on somewhere else. A shiver ran through her as the wind picked up and she stepped back inside and closed the door, shutting out the cold and the lurking danger.

Chapter 15

Reggie sat up in bed, her heart racing as she tried to work out what had just awoken her. A loud whinny sounded and she tossed back her blankets, pulling on a large knitted jumper from the bottom of the bed and hurrying to investigate.

She made a quick detour to the gun cabinet and grabbed the rifle—she wasn't taking any chances after what happened today. At the back door she tugged on her boots, hearing the dogs barking from where they were locked up in their overnight kennels. She grabbed the torch that was kept on the shelf beside the door and slipped outside into the harsh cold.

It had started raining during the night, judging from the wet ground that squelched beneath her boots, and the moonlight was now hidden behind heavy cloud-cover, making it hard to pick anything out. She followed the beam of torchlight bobbing along in front of her. She could hear the horses pacing as she approached the fence, the torchlight picking up the glow of their eyes as she moved it across the paddock to count them.

'What's going on, guys?' she murmured softly, sliding between the gate rails and walking steadily towards them. It wasn't like them to be so agitated. They moved about, circling and snorting, and Reggie grew more concerned. She reached up and touched the neck of her gelding, gently stroking him as she ran the light over the rest of his body, searching for injuries. There wasn't a scratch on him, so she continued the process with the others until she was satisfied that she could rule out any kind of paddock injury. Gradually their pacing eased and they stood uneasily but far more quietly, and Reggie moved the light around the paddock boundary.

The dogs had stopped their incessant barking and now only the occasional low growl sounded from the row of kennels. She called out to settle them back down. Nothing appeared to explain what had set the animals off but, satisfied that none of them had been hurt and that there was no visible threat, she made her way back towards the house. Tomorrow, in daylight, she'd see if she could solve the mystery. It could have been anything from a kangaroo to a wild deer deciding to go for a run a bit too close to the house, and she was irritated that it had dragged her from her warm bed late at night.

Early the next morning she woke to the sound of kookaburras laughing in the big gum tree outside the house and let out a small groan that it was time to get up. She didn't need an alarm clock around this place—nature was more than happy to provide a wake-up service.

Reggie smothered a yawn as she crossed the kitchen to fill the kettle, her gaze falling on the paddocks outside the window and roaming across the dew-dropped cobwebs in the grass. The rising sun lit up the browns and yellows of the winter pasture, dripping everything in golden light, and she watched the fog rising from the dam as the sun slowly began to chase away the brittle cold of the night.

'Morning, love,' her mother said as she wheeled herself into the room.

'Morning,' Reggie answered, automatically taking down the tea pot and scooping in the tea leaves of her mother's favourite brew.

'I heard a commotion last night,' said Peg, tucking her faded red dressing gown across her lap. It was the same dressing gown that had covered Reggie and her brother on the lounge whenever they were home sick. 'I heard you go out, but I must have fallen asleep before you got back in. Was everything all right?'

'Yeah. I don't know what they were going off at. I couldn't see anything. I'll take another look this morning, but it was probably just a roo or something.'

'They've been getting into my flower beds again,' Peg grumbled. 'Damn things.'

Reggie set a cup of tea beside her mother and sat down with her coffee and toast.

'Wasn't last night lovely,' her mother said after a sip of her tea.

Reggie paused between bites of her toast. 'Yeah. It was nice.' She crammed another bite in quickly, hoping to avoid any further comment on the subject of last night.

'He seems like a nice boy,' Peg continued.

'He's not exactly a boy, Mum,' Reggie said with a chuckle.

'Oh, so you noticed then?' Peg asked, innocently peering over the top of her cup at her daughter.

'Noticed what?'

She saw her mother roll her eyes. 'Honestly, Regina. This is why I worry about you being stuck out here working so hard.'

'I'm not stuck anywhere I don't want to be,' Reggie said calmly.

'So you keep saying.'

'Mum, I'm serious.'

'Yes,' she sighed, 'I know. But when fate drops something in your path, you need to pay attention.'

'Meaning Tim?'

'Maybe,' she said. 'Or maybe someone else, who knows. All I'm saying is considering you don't get out much, if someone happens to turn up on your doorstep—maybe you should take notice.'

'He's a guest,' Reggie pointed out, offended by her mother's blunt assessment. 'I'm pretty sure cracking onto the guests is frowned upon in the tourism industry.'

'He's single,' Peg replied, using a tone that reminded Reggie of the one she sometimes used to coax Clancy into his halter when the vet was coming.

'How do you even know that?' she asked, frowning.

'I asked him when you went to wash your hands last night.'

'You asked him if he was single,' Reggie repeated in a deadpan tone. 'Oh my God, Mum!'

'What?'

'You may as well have just told the guy I'm a desperate loser who needs their mother to try and set them up on a date or something.'

'Oh rubbish. I was just making conversation with him.'

'Right.'

'Stop being so defensive. Besides, there's nothing wrong with getting a little bit of intel.'

'Okay, Agent Bond,' Reggie muttered, getting up from the table to take her plate to the sink. 'Do you need anything before I go out?'

'Nope, I'll be fine, thanks.'

Reggie kissed her mum's cheek and left the house, still horrified that Tim may have seen through her mother's subtle attempt at reconnaissance. She'd keep a low profile today and hope that she didn't bump into him. After all, he was only here to fish and find some peace and quiet. He'd be gone in a few days.

Tim stared at his reflection in the bathroom mirror and realised he barely recognised the person staring back at him. He ran a hand over the bushy beard that had thickened up over the last month or so and the shaggy hair that hadn't had a decent cut in who knew how long. He heaved a resigned sigh. He'd lost enthusiasm for life months ago and had been letting a lot of stuff slide—even before everything with Dean happened. Was he heading down the same path as the rest of them? Three mates in the last six years—all dead.

He'd let them down.

Simmo had been the first casualty, and it had come only a year after they'd returned home. Tim had still been in the army then, happy to continue doing what he'd always done, but the others were all married or had partners who wanted a normal life with their men home more often, and one by one they'd started leaving the army for civilian jobs and lives.

They'd vowed to stay in contact—after all, they were more like brothers than colleagues. They'd shared experiences not many other people could really understand. But somehow, once they all returned home, get-togethers became more of a reminder of things they all wanted to forget, and slowly the barbeques and nights out stretched further apart until they barely even spoke on the phone.

Seeing the others at Simmo's funeral drove home how messed up their lives had become. His death had shocked all of them, and yet, it also hadn't. Somewhere deep inside they all knew they'd contemplated the same thing at least once since returning home. They'd gathered after his funeral and promised each other that if anyone was ever feeling that low, they would reach out. Fitzy had been next, and the weight of guilt inside Tim began to grow. *Why didn't he call? Why didn't he say something?* he'd asked himself a thousand times after hearing the news.

But then a voice would bite back: *Why didn't you call him? Why didn't you check how he was doing?*

He and Deano had sat side by side, drinking in silence on the back steps of the old hall where Fitzy had been married only a year earlier. There wasn't much to say.

They had talked about the fishing trip again, and had made plans to head off in the new year. But the new year had come and gone, and Dean got a job with his father-in-law and had to work, so the fishing trip was shelved again. *I should have followed it up.*

Then, a week before he died, Tim had a missed call on his phone. He'd tried to call back, but it rang out and Dean hadn't called again.

In the cabin bathroom, he sighed. He didn't like this angry stranger who was glaring at him in the mirror. It was time to get rid of him once and for all.

Chapter 16

Reggie put the horses' feed out and fed the dogs, checking inside the shed for anything that may have been disturbed through the night, but she couldn't see anything. She needed to refill the cabins' wood supplies before the next visitors arrived, something she'd been putting off for a few days.

They were lucky there was a never-ending supply of timber on River Styx. Bad weather often knocked down trees and they could always be used to keep the woodsheds for the cabins well stocked. It was her father's job, usually, to split and stack the wood—and something that, thanks to chainsaws and log splitters, was a lot easier to do now than in the past. Reggie started up the log splitter and then threw the freshly split timber into the trailer attached to the quad bike.

She'd noticed Tim's car heading off property earlier and breathed a sigh of relief that at least she wouldn't be bumping into him unexpectedly for a while. This whole thing had thrown her slightly off balance. She didn't want to find him attractive—she wasn't even sure she did. Okay, so he *was* attractive, in a hairy, man-who'd-been-living-in-the-Canadian-wilderness-for-a-year kind of way. But still . . . she didn't want to feel like this. What was the point? Once he left, she'd only be moping about feeling sad, and she didn't have time for that crap! She'd rather not have any kind of interest in anyone and just work.

She parked the bike behind the first cabin and began stacking the split wood neatly into the little woodshed. It was kind of relaxing, this monotonous type of chore. The physical side of it helped her take her frustrations out on something, while the fact she didn't need to think too hard allowed her brain time to switch off from thinking about the books and numbers for a while. Once she'd finished, she placed a few of the pieces on a wide, flat stump and began splitting them into kindling-sized pieces with a small axe.

Suddenly, she caught movement out of the corner of her eye and swung around, swearing.

'Sorry. Didn't mean to startle you,' Tim said, eyeing her warily.

For a moment Reggie simply stared. It seemed he'd had a haircut while he'd been in town, and a shave. The change was . . . unsettling. Gone was the wild facial hair, leaving just a tad more than a five o'clock shadow beard in its place. His hair had been shaved up the sides and trimmed on top, and he looked . . . *like he'd stepped out of the pages of an outdoor camping magazine,* an awed little voice in her head said. *All fit and clean-cut and . . . sexy. Wait!* She did not just think that.

'Didn't anyone ever tell you never to sneak up on someone holding an axe?' she snapped as she desperately tried to regather her composure.

'Can't say it's ever really come up in conversation before, no,' he said, crossing his arms. 'Does your mother know you swear like that?'

Reggie gave him a look before wiping her arm across her forehead and tucking a stray strand of hair behind her ear. 'Is there something you need?' she asked, belatedly realising she'd failed at her usual friendly, nothing-is-too-much-trouble, host voice.

'I was coming over to ask if I could maybe do the rest of that for you?'

Reggie followed his gaze to the axe in her hand with a frown.

'I could actually use the exercise,' he added quickly. 'Seriously, it's going against everything in me to sit on that verandah and listen to you chopping wood while I'm doing nothing.'

'It's my job,' she told him. 'You don't need to feel guilty.'

'Do you really want to risk a shit review on TripAdvisor because you ruined my holiday by allowing me to be stressed?'

'Are you really going to threaten me with a bad review unless I let you?'

'Absolutely. It would be a one-star for sure.'

Reggie bit back a smile. She hadn't expected a sense of humour from Mister Tall-Broody-and-Silent. Maybe all that hair and beard had been smothering it. 'Okay then,' she said, handing over the axe and stepping back. 'If you insist.'

'I do,' he said firmly, taking the axe and removing his outer jacket.

'You only need enough kindling to fill that,' she said, nodding at the large silver pail by his feet. 'Then just sit it on top of the wood in there.'

'No worries.'

Reggie hesitated. This was so weird. What on earth was this guy playing at?

'Okay, I've got it. You can go and do whatever else you need to do,' he said, waiting for her to go.

'Okay. Knock yourself out . . . Actually, try *not* to knock yourself out. I don't need any more paperwork.' God only knew this was probably already a massive lawsuit waiting to happen. She just wouldn't think about it, she decided as she walked away to start her next chore.

'So, what do you think of the new bloke?' her dad asked out of the blue on their drive home from the hospital later that day.

'What new bloke?'

'Tim.'

'Tim's the new bloke?' she asked dryly. 'Funny, 'cause I thought he was a paying guest?'

'So, you like him, huh?' Ray chuckled, which turned into a coughing fit and ended on a low curse.

'Are you sure the doctor discharged you?' Reggie asked, glancing sideways at her father.

'Course he flamin' did. Stop tryin' to change the subject.'

'I'm not try—' Reggie gave an inpatient huff and frowned at the road ahead.

'You wouldn't be so prickly if you didn't like him.'

'Oh, for goodness sake! He's a nice guy, okay? Happy? I don't know him, though, so he could potentially be a serial killer or have a wife and set of kids back home somewhere,' she said. *Or be on the run from the police,* her fertile imagination delighted in adding.

'Aren't you supposed to be the gruff, suspicious father who doesn't let anyone date their daughter?'

'That was when you were sixteen and had all those bloody tomcats from around the district sniffin' about.'

'Delightful,' Reggie muttered with a shake of her head.

'He's comin' for dinner tonight,' her dad added as he gazed out the window at the passing paddocks of brown and gold.

'What? Why?'

'I don't know, your mother invited him.'

'Since when do we suddenly start inviting the guests home for dinner?'

'There's something about this one,' Ray said after a moment of silence. 'Reminds me of your Uncle Ted.'

Reggie's brow furrowed at that. She didn't really remember her dad's older brother very well; he'd died when she was about four or five in a motorbike accident. There was a photo of him in the loungeroom, taken when he'd been a soldier heading off to Vietnam. There were only a few others of him in the yellowing family photo album, usually with him holding up a fish or drinking a beer. She knew her dad got sad whenever he thought about Uncle Ted, and she suspected there was a story there.

'He's got the same demons, I reckon.'

Demons definitely didn't sound good. 'What do you mean?' Reggie asked, curious now despite herself.

'Nothing,' Ray said, seemingly shaking himself from his moment of reflection. 'Like I said, he just reminds me of Ted a bit. I guess your mother senses something about him too—you know what she's like,' he added gruffly.

Yes. She did. Always taking in strays. However, this was the first full-grown, male stray she'd brought home. 'Well, I just hope you and Mum remember that he'll be gone soon—so don't get too attached.' She couldn't believe she was having this conversation with her parent! What was going on? Had everyone lost their senses?

By the time Tim's knock came on the back door, Reggie had managed to work herself into a frenzy of nerves and was praying for some kind of emergency to give her an excuse to leave. Of course, there was little chance of that happening—she had everything too well under control, didn't she!

She watched as Tim shook her father's hand and nodded to her mother, handing over a bottle of wine before looking across at her. 'Reggie.'

'Hello, Tim. Thank you for your help today,' she said somewhat stiffly.

'Was there a problem?' her father asked, lifting an eyebrow. He was probably thinking she'd deliberately left him out of it so he wouldn't worry.

'No. Tim just offered to chop some kindling for me today for the cabins.'

'Oh, well wasn't that nice of him.' Her mother beamed across at Tim.

'It seriously wasn't a big deal. I didn't have anything else to do.'

How lovely, Reggie thought, feeling slightly miffed. *Imagine having so little to do all day that you went looking for work.*

'Well, I'm sure Reggie really appreciated it—she works too hard,' her mother said.

'I really don't,' Reggie protested uncomfortably.

'I'm happy to lend a hand any time.'

'So how long are you planning on staying, Tim?' Peg asked a few moments later as they sat down with a drink before dinner.

'Actually, I was going to see if I could extend again.'

'I don't know,' Reggie said as she tried to mentally flip through the bookings schedule in her head for the week following his departure date. 'I think we've got a group booking coming in pretty soon.'

'You know,' her father said, 'I've been thinking.' Reggie immediately tensed. All her dad's great ideas started with those very words. 'Maybe we can come up with a solution that helps everyone.'

Tim, to his credit, didn't look immediately alarmed, merely curious. Reggie, on the other hand, was having heart palpitations as she feared what could come out of her father's mouth: an arranged marriage . . . adoption into the family . . . replacement of her entirely?

'We've been looking for an extra set of hands around the place,' her father said. 'Despite what my daughter thinks, she can't do everything on her own,' he added pointedly.

'Dad,' Reggie warned, then lowered her voice. 'We discussed this and decided the budget couldn't stretch that far at the moment.'

'Which is why,' Ray said calmly, 'I'm suggesting a food and board proposition in exchange for some labour. Peg tells me you're a builder by trade,' he said, turning his attention back to Tim.

'That's right.'

'We've got a cabin that needs finishing and, if you'd be open to lending a hand around the place in between building, we'd be happy to put you up in here.'

In the house? What the fu—

'Or there's the shed,' Ray added.

'It's not really a shed,' her mother said quickly. 'Our son used to live in there—it's really quite cosy and has its own bathroom and fireplace.'

This is not happening.

'Well, I don't want to get in anyone's way,' Tim started, eyeing her stunned face uncertainly.

'Rubbish. You'd be doing us a favour,' Ray said, dismissing his concern immediately. 'Shed only gets used when the relatives visit, so it's sittin' out there empty at the moment.'

'Are you okay with this?' Tim asked Reggie, turning to face her.

What could she possibly say to that? *No, I'm not, because you make me all tingly and stupid?* 'I guess,' she said, then shrugged. As if she had any say in it. 'I mean—only if you'd rather work than be on holiday,' she added doubtfully.

'I'm not really on holiday,' he said again. 'I'd probably have to start looking for work soon anyway,' he said, sounding a little uncertain himself.

'Well,' Ray jumped in, 'no need to answer right now— offer's there.'

'Thanks.' Tim nodded. 'I'll definitely think about it.'

Unbelievable. Reggie shot her parents a look that clearly asked if they'd lost their freaking minds, but they just smiled.

'Let's eat,' Peg said, ending any further discussion of the matter.

Chapter 17

Tim had been surprised by the dinner invitation but found himself looking forward to it. He tried to tell himself it was simply because nobody in their right mind would turn down a home-cooked meal. They were few and far between for him.

He wasn't close with his family. He grew up without a dad and when he'd left school and joined the army his mother had made it clear she'd done her time raising a kid she'd never really wanted.

It hadn't mattered so much once he settled into army life—*they* had become his family, and he'd fitted in better there than he'd ever done at home.

But a sneaking suspicion began to niggle inside him that maybe—just maybe—some of his eagerness to accept the invitation to dinner had been because he'd have an excuse to see Reggie again. She'd disappeared after the kindling incident earlier and he was surprised by how much he'd been looking forward to catching a glimpse of her again.

Apparently, her father's idea about staying on to work hadn't been run by her first, if the look on her face was anything to go by. And he had to admit that her expression hadn't exactly been morale boosting. Still, he did like being here, and the idea of staying on for a bit and working, well, it was actually starting to sound like a good plan. He didn't need much in the way of pay for now—he had savings and wouldn't have any expenses to worry about, and he'd been curious about that cabin at the end of the track. He'd taken a stickybeak through the window the other day and wondered what the story was. It looked like nothing had been done to it in a while.

'So, Tim,' Peg said, after they were all seated and had begun to eat. 'How's your holiday going? Are you missing the city?'

He gave up trying to explain that it wasn't a holiday. 'Not terribly. I've been wanting to get out of the city for a while.'

'We get lots of people doing that up here. Whereabouts are your family?'

'I don't really have any,' he said matter-of-factly, before glancing over and catching the shock on her face. He sometimes forgot normal people didn't react well to his dysfunctional family state. 'I mean, I'm not close to my mother, and she wasn't close with the rest of her family, so I don't really know them.'

'Oh. How sad.'

He'd never really thought too much about it—except on the odd occasion when he'd gone home with army mates at Christmas and realised what a normal family life looked like. As a kid he'd often thought about other families and how big and noisy they were, but he'd been lucky, living in a street where there were heaps of other kids. He'd spent most of his time out playing with them instead of sitting at home alone. Later, he kind of liked that he had so much freedom compared with his mates, who had to follow rules and be home at a certain time. His mum was rarely home when he was a teenager, and he had been free to do whatever he liked.

'It's okay—you don't really miss what you never had.'

He caught Reggie watching him quietly from across the table and saw a flicker of sympathy run across her face. He shifted uncomfortably.

'How long since any work was done on the cabin?' he asked, mainly to deflect the sudden interest in his lack of family life.

He glanced up at the strange silence that followed his question.

'Almost two years,' Reggie finally answered. 'Brent was building it before he got his diagnosis.'

Oh. Great way to kill the mood. 'Right.'

Peg gave him a bright smile. 'He and Ray built all the cabins.'

'The cabins were his idea,' Reggie added.

'Don't mind tellin' you, I had my doubts about the whole thing at the start,' Ray said in his usual gruff manner. 'But once that kid got an idea in his head . . .' he said, leaving the sentence unfinished.

'Turned out he was right,' Reggie said with a smile.

'That he was,' Ray said, nodding.

On his way in, Tim had noticed the collection of family photos on the wall in the lounge room and had studied a photo of a stocky man in a dusty Akubra sitting on a horse, grinning at the camera. He didn't need to be told it was Brent MacLeod. His similarity to Ray gave it away. The pain of his death had left a huge hole in these people's lives, and it was clear that he was sorely missed. Brent was a lucky guy. Tim was shaken by a sudden thought: if he died, there'd be no one left to mourn him at all. Who would miss him? Who would even care?

'Tim, dear?' Peg was asking, and he turned his head towards her quickly.

'Sorry?'

'I was just wondering if you'd ever been to the UK?' she asked. 'We were just discussing my nephew and his wife who'd moved over there recently.'

'Oh. Sorry,' he apologised. 'Yeah, I was there briefly—mainly just a stopover.'

'Have you done much overseas travelling?' Peg continued, picking at her meal delicately. 'Regina spent three years over in London with her work—didn't you, darling?'

He followed the woman's gaze across to her daughter, who looked uncomfortable about being drawn into the conversation. He wasn't sure if it was because of him, or if she was always this standoffish with people. Somehow, he suspected he was the problem.

'Yep. I did.'

'Why don't you tell Tim about it—I'm sure he'd be interested,' Peg prompted.

'I'm sure he wouldn't be.'

'What kind of work did you do?' Tim asked, jumping in to save the situation getting even more uncomfortable than it already was. Clearly Reggie was getting tired of being prodded by her mother.

'I worked in marketing for an advertising company.'

'She was good too,' her mother added proudly.

'Mum . . .' Reggie groaned. He watched on with a hint of amusement at the way her parents were so open about how proud they were of her and her brother. Every time they mentioned their children there was a bright spark of pride colouring their words, almost making him wish he could do something half as great to earn that kind of parental glow.

'She could have been running that office by now,' Peg said wistfully, and he saw Reggie's expression change from embarrassed to something else entirely—he couldn't work out exactly what it was, but the mood at the table suddenly changed.

'Well, I'm not doing that anymore, am I?' Reggie said tightly. 'That was in the past.'

Around the table, he saw Peggy lower her gaze to her plate and Ray frown into his beer. Clearly this was a bone of contention within the family.

'I've been to a few places overseas—but none that most people want to go to for a holiday. The army's not big on sending you to a nice tropical island.'

'Oh,' Peg said, nodding. 'No, I suppose they aren't. Those deserts don't look much fun.'

'Actually, Afghanistan and a lot of the places over there aren't always the dry, desert-like places you see on TV,' he told her. 'There are parts of the country that are really beautiful. The mountains are amazing.'

'We actually watched a documentary on that not long ago, didn't we, Ray,' Peg said, nodding at her husband. 'About this young American tourist riding a yak.'

'Crazy Yanks,' her father said.

'Yak trekking,' Reggie said thoughtfully, and the tension in the room relaxed.

'Don't even think about it,' Ray grumbled. 'We've got our hands full around here at the moment.'

'I'd like it noted that I'm planning on tabling this idea in the future.'

'Noted, darling,' Peg said cheerfully. 'Wouldn't that be fun.'

'No, it bloody wouldn't be,' Ray sighed. 'Where would you even get a yak from around here?'

'I can find out,' Reggie said, reaching for her phone.

Her father looked at her sternly and she grinned.

'I think they live a long time—' Tim offered up as conversation '—like thirty years or something.' For the next few minutes, he found himself listening to Reggie rattle off a further list of interesting yak facts from Google and came to the conclusion that he wouldn't care if she were talking about yaks or the price of eggs, he could sit and watch her light up as she spoke, just like this, all night.

'We're still not getting a yak,' Ray said, squelching the idea firmly as they finished their meal.

'Darling, why don't you and Tim go on out and sit by the firepit? It's a lovely night for it,' Peg suggested after dinner, and Tim sent a covert glance across at Reggie to gauge her reaction to the not-so-subtle attempt her mother was making to orchestrate some time alone for them. He almost felt sorry for her when he clocked her embarrassed expression, but not sorry enough to turn down the offer.

'I'd never turn down an invitation to sit around a fire. It beats staring at a wall by myself,' he added for good measure.

He couldn't be sure, but he thought he heard her mutter something rather unladylike under her breath as she rose from the table. But she covered it up quickly with a smile, which looked more like a toothy snarl than an actual smile.

'Help yourself to some timber next to the house,' Ray said, taking his time to stand. 'I'm off to bed. Too much excitement for this old fella to handle,' he said. 'Night all.'

'Night, Dad,' Reggie said, then narrowed her eyes at her mother when she also said her farewells.

'I'll let you off the hook if you really don't feel like sitting around a fire tonight,' Tim said in a low tone after her parents left the room.

'Like you said, it's better than staring at a wall.'

He tried not to take her lack of enthusiasm personally. 'Righto . . . I'll go start the fire then.'

'I'll bring out the coffee.' She moved into the kitchen and let him see himself out the back door. As he collected the kindling and some larger bits of wood, he let his mind wonder at his weird reactions to Reggie MacLeod. What was it about her? Sure, she was attractive—but not in the way the women he used to date had been. There'd been a certain type of women who hung around military men; they were always outgoing and ready to party. At least that's how it had been back in his younger days. Now he tended to swipe his phone screen to find a date when the mood hit—which, if he was being completely honest, hadn't been in a long while. Reggie didn't seem like the kind of woman who would have been hanging around in the local pubs and night clubs of Perth and Sydney.

She had a wholesomeness about her—she didn't need makeup and manicured nails. Her blue eyes could catch his attention without needing the fake eyelashes and heavy eyeshadow he'd seen some women wearing. He had no real idea about women and makeup, but he did know which look he preferred.

It was more than her looks though. It was the way she had stepped up for her family; the life she'd taken on when her brother had died and her parents had been injured. She had a kind heart and a work ethic to put half the men he knew to shame. She was a confusing mix of dirt and laughter, sunshine and soap, with a dash of the salt of the earth. She was unlike anyone he'd ever met before.

Chapter 18

With the fire roaring and the fold-out chairs from the verandah at the ready, he was seated and waiting by the time Reggie came outside carrying two mugs of coffee and a bag of marshmallows.

She saw his double-take at the marshmallows and grinned with a shrug. 'You can't sit at a campfire without toasting marshmallows.'

'That's what I always said to my mates,' Tim said, picturing the kind of response he would have got and smiling despite a sharp stab in his chest.

'You miss them a lot,' she said, after she'd settled into her seat.

'Yeah. I do. This trip was supposed to be with all of us.'

'Those are the hardest things,' she said, and when he glanced across, he saw pain in the depths of her eyes. 'Remembering all the things you were supposed to be doing with them,' she added softly.

In that instant he knew they shared a common bond—grief. For a while they sat side by side in silence, staring into the flames as the hypnotic shapes danced. Then Tim started telling her about his mates and the things he missed most, and, gradually, he started in on their stories. Before long, they were laughing over something stupid Dean had done and he felt a tiny bit more of the weight he carried begin to shift.

'So, being a marketing guru is a bit different to being a farmer.' He hadn't wanted to broach the subject again, but he'd been curious ever since her mother had brought it up.

He saw her hesitate as she stared into the fire. 'Yeah, I guess.'

'You gave it up to help out here then?'

'Yep,' she said, without elaborating. He'd had the occasional girlfriend tell him it was like pulling teeth to get him to make conversation at times, and now he was on the other side. He recognised the signs of someone who didn't want to talk about something—it didn't take a rocket scientist. But something pushed him to continue. He didn't know why it was so important to him, it just was.

'Do you miss it?'

'Not really.'

'Yeah? Sounds like you were on your way to big things—must have been a big decision to give all that up for this.'

He felt the weight of her gaze as she lifted it from the fire to hold his. 'It wasn't. My parents needed me and then my brother died. There *was* no decision.'

Even a complete stranger would be able to tell she was giving him *all* the warning signs to back off now, but he was still curious. 'Do you think you'll even go back to it?'

'No. That was another life.'

'Your dad mentioned the other day on the trip into the hospital that you'd given up a lot to stay here . . . that's a pretty impressive thing to do for your family.'

'I haven't given up anything,' Reggie said, sounding frustrated. 'I wish they'd just stop feeling so guilty. I'm where I want to be—doing what I want to do. I just don't know what else I can say to make them understand that.'

'That's the thing about guilt—it's good at making you think *it's* right.'

'I get why they think I'm just saying what they want to hear—it was a big step to go from a job in London to farming in Ebor,' she said. 'But sometimes it takes a shake-up to remove the blinders, you know?' She looked up, searching his eyes.

Oh, yeah. He knew all about shake-ups.

'Maybe I'd achieved everything I set out to do,' she said with a shrug of her shoulders. 'Sure, I loved my job, but I was never heartbroken about leaving it—I don't know . . . I kind of feel that if that's what I'd wanted to do it would have been a much harder decision to make . . . and it honestly wasn't,' she said with a small chuckle. 'If you'd tried to tell me before I left school that one day I'd be back here being a farmer, I'd have been horrified. It never crossed my mind—Brent was the farmer, like Dad.' She smiled fondly. 'But now . . . every time I've tried to imagine going back to what I was doing—I can't,' she said simply. 'I came home, and it just felt *right*. This is where I want to be. I just don't know how to convince my parents that this is enough, and they haven't ruined my life. If anything, I think they saved it.'

'They'll come around—I've never been a parent, but I reckon they must only want you to be happy.'

'And I am. Doing this. What about your parents? You said you aren't close with your mum . . . does that mean you don't see her?'

'Pretty much.' He picked up his mug and examined it. 'I left home to join the army . . . sent her an invite to my passing out parade, but she didn't come and that was pretty much that.'

'What about your dad?'

'Never knew him. He wasn't around when I was a kid. His name's on my birth certificate—but I've never gone looking for him.'

'Do you think you will one day?'

'Probably not. If he wanted anything to do with me, he's had the last thirty-two years to do it.'

'That must be really lonely for you . . . no brothers or sisters?' she asked.

'Not that I know of—but the old man probably managed to knock up someone else at some point, so chances are there could be some out there somewhere.' He saw her sad look and gave a small, dark chuckle. 'Don't go feeling sorry for me— seriously. I came to terms with it a long time ago. Joining the army was the best thing I ever did. It was like a fresh start. The people I met became more of a family than I'd had before.'

'That's why you miss your friends so much—the ones you've lost. They were like your brothers.'

The comment momentarily stole his breath and he swallowed hard to regain his composure. 'Yeah. Something like that, I suppose.'

The fire was warm before them, cracking and popping as yellow and orange flames devoured the log he had thrown on earlier. They didn't speak for a while, and he took the opportunity to observe her from the corner of his eye as she stared into the fire.

Tonight, she wore her hair down and it was longer than he'd imagined—it was the first time she didn't have it pulled back or covered with a woollen beanie. It fell just below her chin at the front and gradually got longer towards the back. She *really* wasn't anything like the women he'd dated in the past. Their idea of a fun weekend was spending it in a shopping centre or getting their nails done. He couldn't imagine any of them sitting by a fire on a freezing cold winter night, drinking coffee and toasting marshmallows.

'Do you think you'll take Mum and Dad up on their offer to stay?' she asked, jolting him from his thoughts.

'Do *you* want me to take them up on it?' he replied curiously.

'It's got nothing to do with me,' she said, glancing across at him before turning her gaze back to the fire.

'You didn't exactly seem thrilled by the idea earlier.'

'I wasn't expecting it, that's all.'

'I won't take it if you'd rather I didn't.'

'Doesn't bother me,' she said, sitting forward in her chair and reaching her hands out to warm them.

'It's not like I have any other plans right now, I suppose.' The truth was—he had no plans. He hadn't thought past getting here the other day, but, now that he was here, he didn't want to move on just yet. There was something inexplicably soothing here. It was peaceful, almost as though the moment you stepped foot through the front gate you were inside a bubble. The cold air had cleared his head of the thick fog that had been lingering for the last few months, and now when he was alone with his thoughts they weren't so jumbled and confusing.

'If you start this cabin job,' Reggie said, breaking into his thoughts, 'you have to finish it before you decide to leave.' She looked away from the glow of the fire to hold his gaze. 'None of us could stand to see it sitting there—half done and locked up again. We need to move on.'

'I get it,' he said quietly.

'Do you?'

'Yeah. I do. It's part of your brother. It links him to your family. It's important.'

'He used to tell Mum and Dad, "Don't worry—I can't go yet—the cabin's not finished,"' she said, and her breath hitched a little. 'I don't know if he really believed that, or if he was just using it to keep Mum and Dad positive. I know *I* thought he had more time than he did. It all happened too fast. None of us were ready to say goodbye.'

'I don't know if anyone is ever really ready.'

'Probably not. Maybe I was just trying to ignore the inevitable.'

'Sudden or drawn out—it still hurts like a bitch,' Tim said, tipping the last of the coffee down his throat.

'Were your friends' deaths sudden?' she asked quietly, after a few moments.

Tim let out a slow breath. 'On the surface, I guess they were pretty sudden . . . But deep down I think it'd been coming ever since we got home.'

'Were they all . . . did all of them take their own lives?' she asked hesitantly.

He couldn't blame her for not wanting to say the S word. Even today it still felt taboo to come out and call it suicide. 'Pretty much. One was a car accident . . . but he was over the alcohol limit and managed to hit the only tree around for miles—without any skid marks. The other two were gun related.'

'I'm really sorry, Tim,' Reggie said gently, and he gave her a small smile in return.

'I could have stopped all of them. I wasn't good enough at checking in on everyone. I tried to move on and forget the past and I left them behind in the process.'

'It doesn't seem very fair to take on all that blame yourself. I'm sure they had family and friends around them who they could have turned to, even if you weren't there.'

'No one who knew what was going on in their heads— really knew, I mean,' he said, holding her concerned gaze. 'It's hard to explain to people who weren't over there.' He caught her chewing at her bottom lip and tried to shake off the dark mood. 'It's okay—it is what it is. I didn't mean to put a damper on the night.'

'No, it's fine . . . I just don't know the right words to say to all that,' she said, sounding helpless.

'I honestly don't think there are words. But it's good to just hear it out loud instead of mulling it over in my head endlessly—it's just depressing as a conversation,' he added with a twist of his lips.

'Then you should say it out loud whenever you need to,' Reggie said, giving him a decisive nod.

'So, I guess that means I'm sticking around to finish this cabin, then?'

She took a moment to answer, as though coming to terms with something inside herself. 'I guess you are.'

Chapter 19

Reggie collapsed onto her office chair and let out a long, weary breath. Today had been hectic. It'd started with making sure all the cabins were ready for the group booking due to arrive. Tim had moved into the shed the day before and she'd done a last-minute mow and tidy up of the area in preparation for their fifteen new guests.

The arrival of the minibus should have been a forewarning that the weekend was about to get a little wild: Reggie could hear music blaring before it had even turned into the driveway, and when it did it was decorated with pink streamers like something out of the movie *The Adventures of Priscilla, Queen of the Desert*.

It appeared their fifteen guests were here for a hens' weekend.

A vivacious red-head in her late forties walked through the door a few moments after the bus came to a stop, accompanied by two other women. One seemed as though she'd started the party on the bus and the other was a little more sedate—Reggie realised she had been the designated driver.

'We made it!' the red-head announced.

'You did,' Reggie agreed. 'Where have you come from?'

'Tamworth,' the driver said wearily. It wasn't that far to drive, but Reggie figured a bus full of tipsy women might make it *feel* a lot further.

'My fiancé made the booking. He and his mates stayed here fishing one time,' the red-head said, then leaned closer, lowering her voice. 'He thinks sending me into the back of beyond will stop us getting into any trouble.' She giggled as she straightened back up.

'Silly boy,' her brunette friend added, examining her blood-red and lethal-looking manicured nails.

Reggie glanced down at her own short, dirty, broken nails and surreptitiously slid her hands into her pockets as she tried to remember the last time she'd had a manicure.

She wasn't sure if she should take offence at the fact that these women clearly wouldn't have picked River Styx for their hens' weekend given a choice, but was suitably impressed that, despite this, they weren't letting it ruin their fun.

'Well, I'm sure you'll all have a great weekend,' Reggie said, standing up from her chair. 'I'll show you to the cabins.'

It was bedlam. They unloaded the bus, with more food and alcohol than she'd ever seen at the cabins—and that was saying a lot considering some of the fishing parties who had stayed here. There was a chaotic rush of laughing, stumbling women deciding which cabins they were each staying in, and way too many bags for a two-night stay. Leaving them to it, Reggie headed back to the office.

Later, once someone had managed to sort out sleeping arrangements, the music started and the party began.

'How long is that bloody racket going to go on for?' Ray grumbled, standing out on the verandah later that evening as the sound of laughter and music echoed down towards them.

'I don't think it'll be an early night.'

'Well, this is gonna be a bloody lovely weekend . . .'

Normally, when guests were being this loud too late in the evening, they did something about it. There had only been two occasions when it had been necessary—both times Brent had handled it, and thankfully it had only ever been followed by a bit of good-natured protesting. However, since the women were all from the one party, there were really no other guests being impacted by the noise and it didn't seem worth trying to do something about it.

'Oh, let them have their fun, Ray. They aren't hurting anyone,' Peg said.

'Some of us have to sleep you know.'

'You could sleep through a cyclone.'

'I'm sure they'll wind down soon,' Reggie said, looking up at the bright cabins with shadowy figures moving about inside. After all, they'd been drinking before they'd even arrived. Surely they'd have to sleep soon.

Reggie made her way through the morning feed and was just coming out of the chook pen when she glanced up to find Tim by the gate.

'Morning,' she greeted him. Her eyes felt gritty and sore. 'Did you get much sleep last night?' she asked.

'A bit. You got yourself some lively ones there,' he said, jerking his chin towards the cabins.

Reggie sighed. 'Yeah. Sorry about the noise.'

'It's fine. I used to live next to a house full of uni students. I can handle a bit of party noise.'

Technically he wasn't a guest anymore, so she didn't have to worry about his comfort, but it still worried her a little that he was also having to put up with all the racket. 'Hopefully they'll be all partied out after last night.'

'Hopefully. Yell out if you need me to do anything—I'll be up at the cabin,' he said, starting to turn away.

'You're not supposed to be working on weekends,' she said, and he swung back to face her.

'Unless you have anything else you need me to do, I figured I'd get a start on the clean-up.'

'Seriously, you don't have to work on a weekend. That wasn't the deal. Go and explore or something.'

'Only if you come with me,' he said. His gaze suddenly lost all its earlier friendly-guy-next-door vibe and was something a lot, well, *more*.

'I . . . ah, don't think I should leave that lot unsupervised, to be honest,' she stammered, as she fought to hide her reaction.

'Oh well, call me if you need anything then,' he said, stepping back to let her pass him. She caught a whiff of something warm and clean and a little spicy.

'Sure,' she said, ducking her head and hurrying away before she did something stupid, like sniff him.

As Reggie bounced along in the tractor on her way to drop off another round bale of hay for the cattle, her phone rang. Glancing at the screen, she frowned, automatically alert as soon as she saw her mother's name.

'Mum. Everything okay?' One day she'd be able to answer the phone without worrying there was an emergency.

'Everything's fine,' her mum assured her. *Bless her cotton socks,* Reggie thought. Her mum understood why she panicked, but she never got cranky like her dad sometimes did when she hovered or worried, instead Peg just reassured her and went on as though nothing had happened. 'I just had one of the girls from the cabins come down to ask if someone could help them make a fire in the fire pit. Should I ask Tim to go over?'

Reggie glanced at her watch and realised it'd still be a while before she could get back there. 'Yeah, that's probably the best idea.'

'Okay, darling. See you when you get back.'

Well, that should be interesting, Reggie thought as she pictured Tim being ogled by this bunch of women. She tried not to identify the tiny flash of emotion the thought sparked. It certainly wasn't jealousy. At all. what could she possibly be jealous of?

❖

Tim put the hammer back in his tool belt as he answered the call from Peggy and straightened up. 'Yeah, no trouble at all. I'll head over there now,' he said, after she'd asked if he could light a fire for the guests. He was relieved that the first thing any of the MacLeod's had asked him to do was something he actually *knew* how to do. Farming related stuff he was fairly confident he could figure it out with a bit of help, as long as it wasn't anything to do with a cow on his own. But building a fire? That he could do with his eyes closed.

As he neared the large fire pit surrounded by several benches in front of the cabins, he could hear the party starting up for its second night. He was surprised to realise it was already starting to get dark as the late afternoon settled in.

He headed up the small set of steps and knocked on the door of the nearest cabin to check it wasn't too early and that they were ready for him to light the fire. Instantly the noise inside ceased before a loud chorus of cheers and laughter went up. The door was flung open and he came face to face with a woman in a clingy dress, wearing a feather boa around her neck.

Her eyes widened as she gave him a once over. 'I ordered the policeman, but oh well. A dirty construction worker will do,' she said with a predatory grin.

A what now? There was no time to ask questions as the woman grabbed the front of his shirt and dragged him inside the cabin.

He was too stunned by the sea of faces before him to react, until a loud cheer went up and music started playing.

Someone dragged a chair forward and a red-head wearing a crown with an inflatable penis on top was pushed into it and the women began to chant.

Tim found himself frozen to the spot. Never, even in all his crazy army days—and there'd been many a crazy moment— had he *ever* found himself in this particular position: alone in a room full of drunk, over-stimulated, horny women.

'Take it off! Take it off!' they chanted.

Instantly Tim's brain snapped back into gear. *Oh. Hell. No.* He held up a hand and tried to take a step back, but the woman who'd greeted him at the door grabbed hold of him again and started undoing his shirt buttons. *What the actual hell?* 'There's been some kind of mistake,' he managed. 'I'm just here to light the fire.'

'Oh baby, you can light my fire any time,' a woman nearby called out as he pried his shirt away from the woman with the busy hands.

'I love a man with a big *tool* . . . belt,' another yelled, and he cursed inwardly as yet another set of hands fumbled with the toolbelt at his waist. How the hell had he got himself into this mess? And, even more concerning . . . how the hell could he get himself out of it?

Chapter 20

Reggie parked the tractor and climbed down onto the gravel driveway. As she'd driven up, she'd noticed the outdoor fire pit was still dark. Maybe her mum hadn't been able to get on to Tim after she'd called earlier.

With a tired sigh, she headed up the road. She'd been picturing a nice hot shower when she got home, but that would have to wait until after she lit the stupid fire.

Any thoughts of the hens enjoying a quieter night tonight were soon dashed as she heard the loud laughter and . . . *screaming*. Not horrified screams, more like over-excited-women-at-a-concert type screaming. Reggie wondered what the hell they were doing, then thought, *Not my monkey, not my circus*. That was, until the door of a cabin opened and a figure stumbled out, cursing, followed by women spilling out onto the verandah, their hands waving . . . *cash?*

As the half-naked figure on the verandah turned, Reggie found herself staring at a tousled-looking . . . *'Tim?'*

'Thank fuck, Reggie! Would you *tell* them!'

Reggie found her stunned gaze switching between Tim and the women in complete bewilderment. 'Tell them *what*, exactly?'

'That I'm not the bloody stripper!'

Of all the things that had been running through Reggie's mind, *that* had not been one of them.

As a chorus of frantic 'take-it-off's started up, Reggie shook her head and headed up the stairs. 'Ladies,' she said, raising her voice over the ruckus. 'I'm sorry to disappoint, but there seems to have been some kind of mix-up. This is my builder, not a stripper.'

The silence that followed was deafening, and for a moment Reggie thought the women were mortified, but then they burst into sudden, uproarious laughter.

'Yes, yes,' Tim nodded. 'It's hilarious,' he muttered, holding up his tool-belt with one hand and pulling his unbuttoned shirt back over his torso with the other as he brushed past Reggie and headed down the steps.

Reggie bit her lip to stop the grin that threatened to spread across her face and forced herself to remain professional. 'I'm sure it was an honest mistake,' she said, facing the women who were in hysterics, holding each other up as they tried to speak.

'I think I'm going to pee my pants,' one woman managed between guffaws, while two more were wiping actual tears from their eyes as they sat on the verandah, howling.

'Oookay,' Reggie said, deciding to leave them to it and go light the fire pit. Rounding the corner to get some firewood, she almost bumped into Tim, who'd beat her to it—his arms were stacked with timber and his clothing was all back in order. 'Are you okay?' she asked, stepping aside to allow him to pass.

'Just dandy.'

Biting her lip again, Reggie hesitated before following him to the fire pit. 'What happened?'

'I came over to make a fire like your mother asked me to, but before I could open my mouth, they dragged me inside.'

A giggle threatened to escape before she firmly pushed it down. 'I'm sorry. That must have been . . . a shock.'

'I wasn't expecting to get mauled.'

'Did you get hurt?' she asked, suddenly wondering if maybe this was more serious than just funny, but he eyed her sideways and shook his head.

'Just my dignity. That was crazy,' he muttered, shaking his head.

Loud talking and music had replaced the laughter as Reggie glanced back at the cabin. 'They do seem a little . . . excitable.'

'The army needs to send in a bunch of women at a hens' night as the first wave of shock and awe in future. I can guarantee that'll scare the crap out of the enemy.'

A small chuckle did escape her then. Here was a big, strong army guy—battle hardened—who'd been traumatised by a bunch of alcohol-infused, randy women. 'Sorry,' she said, when he gave her a disgruntled look. 'You don't have to do this, let me finish up,' she said, reaching for the firewood.

'I've got it,' he said. 'Although I'm not so sure it's a smart move letting them near a fire.'

Reggie looked at the cabin once more and frowned. 'They'll probably be too drunk to come outside. Maybe just make it a small fire to be on the safe side,' she added.

'You don't have to stay,' he said as he began stacking up the timber.

'I think I'd better.'

'I'm kind of relieved you said that, to be honest,' he said, as his lips twitched a little. 'I think I need a bodyguard.'

A memory of him standing on the verandah flashed though her mind and she was about to smile, until she recalled the bare skin of his chest and felt a tiny flush wash over her. It was no wonder those women were going crazy. It *was* a rather nice chest. 'In all seriousness,' she said, clearing her throat, 'I *am* really sorry you had to go through that.'

He knelt down on one knee as he balanced the wood in his arms, continuing to build the fire. 'You know, every guy fantasises about being able to please a bunch of women, but after that experience . . .'

'That's a real fantasy?' she asked.

'Well, maybe not *quite* like that,' he said, shuddering as he looked back at the cabin.

'You know, if this was turned around . . . if I'd been the one who knocked on that door and a bunch of guys thought I was stripper and did that,' she said, suddenly serious, 'I would have been terrified.'

Tim looked up and frowned. 'I hope you don't knock on cabin doors alone when a bunch of guys are staying here.'

She didn't. But it kind of irked her that he felt a need to ask. 'I'm not *that* stupid,' she said calmly. 'All I was getting at was it probably shouldn't be funny just because it was this way around.'

'Yeah well, I think the fact that a man in that situation wouldn't be in as much danger as a female is *why* it's funny. Still . . . they were not taking no for an answer,' he said, shaking his head.

After a few minutes, he got a decent fire going and started placing the larger logs on top.

'Nice fire.'

'I'm better at building fires than I am at stripping,' he said, and shrugged.

Reggie grinned. 'It's lucky we aren't hiring you as a stripper then, isn't it?'

'Technically, you aren't hiring me,' he pointed out. 'And I won't lie, I thought about taking that cash they were waving around for a minute there.'

'I'm sure if you knocked on the door they'd take you back,' she said. They both looked up as a car slowly headed up the driveway towards them and a young, well-built guy climbed out, dressed in a police uniform . . . of sorts.

'Is this the hens' party?' he asked, stopping in front of them.

Reggie and Tim both pointed towards the cabin, swapping glances and smiles after he left.

'I think you just lost your chance at making some easy cash.'

'That poor, poor bastard,' Tim said. 'He'll earn every cent.'

Chapter 21

Tim had never been so relieved as when he saw the dust trail following the bus-load of women down the driveway. He'd declined Reggie's offer of dinner at her parents' following the whole stripper ordeal, and instead spent the night watching a game of football and drinking beer in the hope of fortifying the manhood he'd almost lost.

Apparently Reggie had not shared the recent events with her parents, thank God. Or if she had, no one mentioned it the next day, for which he was eternally grateful.

The echo of horse hooves clopping on the hard-packed dirt of the open-ended shed sounded and Tim carried his cuppa to the sliding door that opened up into the spacious area, spotting Reggie leading a dark-coloured horse inside.

'Morning,' he said, watching the way she ran her hands down the animal's sleek neck and rubbed her face against its nose.

She gave a small start before returning his greeting.

'Sorry, I didn't mean to scare you.'

'All good,' she said with a brief smile. 'It's just going to take some time to get used to anyone being here again. Everything okay?'

'Yeah,' he said, leaning his shoulder against the wall. 'It's fine. Thanks.' It was better than fine; he had a self-contained bachelor pad complete with wide-screen TV, and it even had a bar set up in the back corner. He stood there as she moved around the horse, placing a blanket across its back before disappearing into the tack shed nearby to bring out a saddle and lift it up and onto the animal's back.

'That's a well-trained horse,' he said, watching as it stood docilely while she went about getting it ready. It wasn't even tied up.

'She'd want to be—she was trained by the best.' Reggie smiled, giving the horse a fond pat. 'Dad and Brent trained all our horses. People used to line up to have their horses broken in by them. Do you ride?' she asked as she fastened a strap around the horse's stomach.

'Nah, I prefer horsepower with an engine . . . and a brake,' he added.

'These have a brake. It's called "Whoa",' she said with a grin.

He quietly took in her dress code of long-sleeved work shirt, aqua vest and tight jeans. Her coffee-caramel hair was tied in a ponytail and pulled through the back of a baseball cap, and her ever-present brown cowboy boots made her look as though she'd stepped out of a glossy country workwear brochure.

He finished his coffee and tossed out the dregs on the grass outside. 'Where're you headed off to?'

'Just taking Tilly here for a ride to check on the cattle. She hasn't been out for a while.'

'Do you ride all of them?'

'I try to—although Banjo and Waratah are pretty much in retirement nowadays. They were Mum and Dad's horses. But I still try and keep Clancy, Henry and Matilda in work as much as possible—they're too young to be paddock ornaments just yet. What are your plans today?'

'I need to have a chat with your dad. I've got that list of supplies that I need to make a start on the cabins.'

'That's good,' she said, turning to face him, now that her horse was sorted.

'I, ah, wasn't sure if you wanted to be at the meeting as well?' So far she'd been absent whenever anything to do with the cabins came up, and he wasn't sure if that was by choice or just bad timing.

'I'm sure between you and Dad you'll be able to get it all sorted,' she said lightly, before making a kissing sound and waiting for the horse to back itself up beside a set of mounting steps. Tim couldn't help but admire the easy way she swung her leg over the saddle and settled herself on the big animal. He'd never realised what a pair of jeans and set of boots could do for his libido before now.

'No worries. I'll see you around,' he said, stepping out of the way as she wheeled the horse around and headed out of the shed. *I'm here to work*, he reminded himself as she rode out of view. It was just an added bonus that he got to see Reggie first thing in the morning to kickstart his day.

He'd pretty much come to terms with the fact he was developing a bit of a crush on the woman who was now effectively one of his bosses. Did grown men even *get* crushes? He'd never really been in this predicament before. If he was attracted to a woman, he just went with it, but this was different. He hadn't been looking for anything—he still wasn't looking for anything. Currently with no job, no fixed address and no real idea what he wanted to do in the future, he was a disaster. Throwing a woman into the mix now probably wasn't the smartest idea. Still, he knew Reggie wasn't just some woman he found attractive. He genuinely liked and admired her. He'd never met a woman like her before, and the worst thing was he couldn't read her—at all. He had no idea if she felt the same way about him. He sensed he made her a little jumpy but he wasn't sure if that was in a good or bad way. She was a hard one to read.

Every time he managed to talk some sense into himself and get his head straight about it all, she would appear by the shed and all his resolutions to avoid any romantic ideas would fly straight out the door.

As if he didn't have enough to think about without the added pressure of trying to impress a woman who could handle a five- or six-hundred kilo horse, fix a fence and drive a tractor. He had a feeling it would take a lot to impress Reggie MacLeod.

Chapter 22

Reggie fought the urge to look back over her shoulder at the man standing in the shed doorway. He distracted her. He didn't even have to try—he just had to stand there and look all manly and self-assured.

She'd been so distracted thinking about him this morning she hadn't even noticed when he'd suddenly walked out the door and surprised her. She'd become all thumbs as she tried to focus on tacking up Tilly and prayed he didn't notice how nervous he made her.

Ever since the night they'd spent by the fire, her feelings had shifted from merely curious to suddenly *interested*. She didn't want to be, though. That was just plain dumb. Sure, for now he was more than a guest—he was more or less an employee and he'd be sticking around longer—but the same problem remained. He'd be moving on once the cabin was finished; he wasn't here permanently. Maybe if she'd had a fling with him when he'd been a mere guest staying a handful of days she'd have got it out her system, moped about for a bit once he left and then moved on—but now that he was here longer, the one-night-stand thing couldn't apply. It'd be an awkward case of trying to avoid each other if it somehow didn't turn out well and that wouldn't help anyone.

Besides, she wasn't looking for a relationship—long-term or otherwise!

Tilly tossed her head a little and Reggie let out a slow breath, loosening her reins. 'Sorry, girl,' she apologised. Horses picked up on everything and clearly Tilly had sensed her unsettled mood. 'We don't need a man, do we, girl,' she murmured. 'They just complicate everything.'

As she approached the paddock, she manoeuvred the horse so she could lean down and open and then close the gate behind them, then skirted the mob of cattle, doing a head count and checking for any new calves.

Yesterday she'd noticed one of the cows had an extremely tight-looking belly held very high, and Reggie had been keeping an eye on her as she'd started to lose condition. Her father had been warning her that she'd quite likely be dropping twins, and Reggie was a little anxious. For good reason, as it turned out—as she circled the mob on Tilly, she spotted the cow lying down and quickly delivering a calf. Reggie grabbed the radio and called the house to let her father know, sure that he'd want to come down and gloat about having told her so, but her mother informed her that Ray had just left for town.

Reggie watched the cow get to her feet and moments later lie back down as labour started again.

But after a few minutes, Reggie felt a sinking feeling. A head and only part of one leg appeared. She really didn't want to have to get involved, but with only one leg presenting instead of two, she was beginning to suspect it was stuck.

Of all the bloody times for her father not to be here.

Reggie brushed the sweat from underneath the brim of her hat. If she left it too long, the calf would suffocate. *Don't panic,* she told herself, striving for a calmness she didn't feel.

She tried her father's number, the whole time watching the cow unsuccessfully pushing, and swore as she got the 'unable to connect' signal, indicating her father was out of reception. Fan-bloody-tastic.

Stay. Calm.

She ran over her options: she needed to run the cow into the cattle yards, but they were some distance away and Reggie knew the mother wouldn't want to leave the first calf behind—making it near impossible to try to herd her in fast enough. *Shit.*

Her gaze fell on the first calf, who at least looked fine and was sitting up.

She was going to have to intervene or they'd lose the second calf. Time was running out.

Reggie slid down from Tilly and slowly made her way towards the labouring cow.

She might be able to grab the leg while the mother was still down, but as she drew nearer the cow struggled and kicked wildly, ending that idea abruptly.

Don't panic!

She could ride back to the shed and grab the calving chains and ute, but that would take too long.

At that moment, Reggie heard the sound of a car approaching and she glanced up sharply, sighing in relief as her father's old ute pulled up.

She barely had time to register the fact that Tim was driving.

'Your mum sent me in case you needed . . . help,' he said, eyeing the calf blinking at him with its torso still inside its mother.

Yes! This could work. 'I do. Get in and drive,' she said, bending to scoop the slippery, still-covered-in-birthing-fluid first calf into her arms and racing to the rear of the ute. 'Head to the cattle yards,' she called, climbing onto the back of the ute tray and balancing her precious cargo on her lap. She watched with a great deal of sympathy as the mother struggled to her feet, calling for her first baby.

As they reached the yards, Reggie placed the calf near the crush and whistled for Tilly who obediently trotted towards her.

'I need to bring the mother up into the crush, so stay there and block her escape,' she told Tim who, to his credit, didn't waste time asking questions about what the hell she was doing.

'Come on, girl, I know this sucks but we're going to lose that calf if you don't move *now*,' she said, forcing the cow forward. She had to get her into the yards so she could turn the calf.

But the cow was moving so slowly!

Don't. Panic.

'Come on, girl!' Reggie waved her arms and whistled loudly, wishing she had the dogs with her.

Eventually, she managed to get her into the race, reaching for the length of rope her dad kept in the back of the ute on her way past, before sliding the bar behind the labouring cow and locking her into position.

'I'm sorry, girl, I really am,' she murmured, giving the cow a gentle rub, but there was no time for more coddling. Surely they'd already taken too long?

Reggie allowed a small shaky breath to escape her as she went around to the rear of the cow and saw that the calf's head had dropped back inside slightly and labour seemed to have paused for the moment.

That's exactly what they needed—a tiny breather to get her nerves back under control and for her to Calm. The. Fuck. Down. She could feel Tim watching her closely, waiting quietly for her next instructions.

Reggie carefully pushed the calf's head backwards, remembering with relief that the advantage of twins was that they were typically smaller than a single calf, making them easier to move around inside the cow's pelvis.

Focusing on what she could feel, she realised the second leg was bent and gently moved it into the correct position. She secured the rope around the two outstretched legs, but it was barely even needed as the cow gave one big push and calf number two came catapulting out into Reggie's arms.

She quickly placed the slimy bundle of long legs onto the ground and realised it was barely breathing.

Shit, shit, shit! Don't. Panic.

'Grab me some of that grass,' she said, reaching an urgent hand towards Tim. He glanced briefly at where she was pointing and snatched a handful. Reggie plucked a long, straggly piece from the bunch and tickled the calf's nostril, praying that her father's old stories were right. The cutest little sneeze followed, and she gave a small chuckle as she watched the calf's tiny chest expand as its lungs filled with air.

She looked up at Tim standing beside her and couldn't help the grin that stretched across her face.

'We did it!'

'*You* did it. *I'm* still trying to catch up on what the hell I just witnessed,' Tim said, and Reggie noticed he was looking pale. She glanced down at herself and realised she was covered in cow goop and poo. It normally wouldn't matter. She wasn't sure why it should matter now, in front of Tim.

'I need to get these two weighed for the registration book. Could you give me a hand?' she asked a little gruffly.

'Sure,' he said, sliding a hand into his back pocket and looking uncertain as he waited for instructions.

'Can you lift the bigger one up and put it into the basket for me?' she asked, nodding at the metal cage-type basket that was attached to the rear of the tractor.

'Why do you have to weigh them?'

'It's part of being a stud. You need to keep records for pretty much everything.' Reggie pulled the record book from the waterproof envelope attached to the weighing cage and waited for Tim to deposit the first calf onto the scales. 'Great. Now for the little one,' she said, moving across to help scoop it up. While he was smaller than his brother, he wasn't a bad weight and he was looking more alert by the minute. 'Okay, we can let Mum out now to do her thing. You might want to stand back,' she cautioned. She moved across to the cow, who was still locked in the race and beginning to get agitated. She slowly eased the rail aside and the cow gingerly backed out then hastily crossed to the two calves on the ground, nosing at them and tending to their clean up.

'Will they be okay?' Tim asked, as she stopped beside him.

'Yeah, I think so. I'll ask Dad to come and check her out when he gets home. I really wish he hadn't left to go into town when he did.'

'He wouldn't have done it any better than you did. That was pretty cool.'

'It's not exactly my favourite job—I try to avoid it if possible.'

'I can see why. It's pretty gross . . . but still kind of amazing.'

'Well,' she said, screwing her nose up as she caught a whiff of herself. 'I'm heading back for a shower.'

'Thank God. You stink,' he said, then chuckled.

Maybe it was the adrenalin high—or just pure, bloody relief—but suddenly she felt lighter. '*I* stink?' she said, feigning outrage. Without thinking twice, she stepped close and threw her arms around him, squashing her gunk-stained shirt against his. 'Now *you* stink, too!' She was so busy laughing at his wide-eyed, horrified expression that she didn't see it swiftly replaced by something else entirely until she glanced up and caught the simmering look in his eye. Her hands were still holding onto his forearms, and they suddenly felt on fire against the heat of his skin as she realised that they were standing chest to chest.

It should have horrified her that she was covered in birth fluid and blood and stank like something from a sewer pipe, but the only thing that registered was the fact she could feel his body against her own and it felt . . . good.

She watched his head lower slowly and she felt his breath hover against her lips for the slightest moment before they touched hers and the world tilted beneath her feet. Her hands tightened around his arms as she fought to hold herself upright, and his grip on her waist, steady and secure, held her in place.

She had no idea how long they kissed for—it could have been hours, though she was fairly sure it wasn't—but when he eased back she found herself breathing unsteadily and her pulse fluttering.

'I really need to go and wash this stink off me,' she heard herself saying, and she closed her eyes, mortified. *Awesome Reggie—your mastery of words is truly inspirational.* 'The cow I mean . . .' she added quickly.

'Yeah—I figured,' he said.

Clearing her throat, Reggie let go of his arms and took a step back, immediately missing the warmth of his hands at her waist. 'Well, thanks again for your help,' she said as she crossed to Tilly and heaved herself up into the saddle.

'Happy to help—chopping wood, birthing partner, moral support . . . You name it, I'm there.'

She returned his warm smile for a moment longer before shaking her head and turning Tilly towards home. Everything had changed between them and she should be regretting that kiss, but somehow the smile was still on her face when she reached the shed and started unsaddling her horse.

Chapter 23

'Reckon we'll keep that cow in the yards for a few more days and feed her up a bit before we let her out. Put a bit of the condition she lost back on,' her father said that afternoon when Reggie spotted him by the yards after returning from cleaning the cabins.

'Yeah, I thought you might say that. How are they?'

'Doin' well. You did a good job,' he said gruffly, and Reggie smiled as a bubble of pride filled her chest. 'First set of twins we've had in a while.'

'You were right.'

'Course I was—you doubtin' your old man?'

'Never.'

'Good. How'd young Tim go?'

She chuckled and then remembered the kiss and sobered quickly. 'Good. I was glad he brought the ute down when he did.'

'Reckon we'll be able to make a farmer out of him?'

Reggie frowned a little as she looked over at her father. 'A farmer? Since when was Tim going to be farming?'

'You never know.'

'Dad, I really think you and Mum are forgetting that he's only here until the cabin's finished.'

'He doesn't seem to have any other plans and we could use a hand around the place.'

'You can't expect him to work for room and board indefinitely,' she countered.

''Course not. But I reckon we could take a look at the books again down the track and find a bit of spare money somewhere.'

'Sure, Dad,' Reggie said wearily. There was no way Tim was going to want to work here as a farm hand—he was a builder. This little sojourn was only temporary, something he needed while he collected his thoughts and came to terms with his grief. Why did her parents not understand this? She would have to be the sensible one—and keep a tight rein on whatever the hell that thing had been between them.

The next morning Reggie went in search of her father, following the noise coming from the unfinished cabin and spotting Glenda the ATV parked outside.

'Hello?' she called, poking her head in through the doorway and finding Tim and Ray deep in conversation as they looked over a plan of some kind. Her father glanced up and waved her over. She could feel Tim's gaze on her as she stepped inside, but she avoided eye contact. She hadn't seen him since the post-calving celebration—and that's all it had been: just two people hyped up on adrenalin.

'Tim's made a few suggestions about the layout here,' her father said, pointing a stout, calloused finger at some lines on the drawing.

'What's wrong with the original layout?' she asked, lifting her eyes to meet Tim's briefly, before switching to her father's.

'Nothing's wrong with it,' Tim replied calmly. 'You'd just have more space in the kitchen area if we swung this whole design around the other way.'

'I reckon he's got a point,' Ray said.

'Does it really make that much difference?'

'Depends,' Tim said with a shrug, leaning back against the wall with his arms folded across his chest. 'Do you want your guests to have a bit more room to spread out in?'

'Will it cost any more to change it?'

'Not that I can see.' There shouldn't have been anything the least bit stimulating about the conversation they were having and yet her insides were starting to do that stupid fluttery thing again. For one crazy moment she swore her lips began to tingle as she recalled their kiss the day before.

'Doesn't bother me then,' she said with as much indifference as she could muster, eager to escape. 'I was just looking for you to let you know I need to go into the feed store and grab some stuff. Do you have any scripts you need picked up from the chemist while I'm in town?'

'No, the doc sent me home with enough pills to sink a ship. I should be right for a while,' Ray said. 'But Tim was just sayin' he needed to go into the hardware store today too. No point takin' two vehicles. You should go in with missy, here.'

'If you don't mind,' Tim said, looking at Reggie warily.

''Course she wouldn't mind—why would you mind?' her father asked Reggie, sounding confused.

'I wouldn't . . . I don't,' she said irritably, 'but I was planning on going now . . . how long do you think it'll be until you're ready?'

'I'm ready whenever you are,' Tim said, pushing away from the wall.

'That's settled then,' Ray said, nodding. 'Get Jefferies to put whatever Tim needs on our account, Reggie,' her dad instructed as they all made to leave the room.

Reggie nodded, stepping aside as her dad climbed back into Glenda. She waited as Tim slid the glass door shut behind them.

'I don't mind driving myself in if it's a problem,' Tim said as they walked along the track towards the shed.

'It's not,' she told him, suddenly feeling bad about her reaction.

'Is this about yesterday?' he asked.

She really liked this guy better when he'd first come here and didn't like to talk. 'No.'

'Okay.'

Now she felt even worse. 'It's . . . I don't know . . . yesterday was just . . . an accident.'

'I'm pretty sure you don't accidentally kiss someone.'

'We got caught up in a moment—that's all.'

'We were covered in something slimy and gross—fairly sure accidentally kissing you wouldn't have been my first instinct unless I'd wanted to do it *on purpose*,' he said.

'Do we really need to talk about it?' she asked as they reached the shed and walked towards the four-wheel drive.

'I guess not,' he said, opening the passenger door and eyeing her through the vehicle.

Good. She closed the door and reached for the key in the ignition, ignoring how small the cabin felt with the two of them inside. It was going to be a long drive into town.

As the engine started, a loud burst of Slim Dusty bellowed through the speakers, making Reggie reach for the volume dial and turn it down quickly. 'Sorry. Dad must have been driving this last.' She ejected the CD and reached across to the glove box, brushing her arm on his as she did so. 'Sorry,' she stammered. 'I . . . could you . . .'

He opened the glove box in front of him and pulled out a handful of CDs then passed them to her.

Reggie hesitated before selecting one. 'Do you like the Dixie Chicks?'

She saw the slightest movement around his eyes as he fought a full-blown wince. She sighed. 'What about ABBA?'

'I'm just along for the ride,' he said diplomatically, but she could have sworn she *felt* his testosterone levels quiver a little and she bit back a grin.

'Adele?'

He turned his head towards her. 'Okay now you're just messing with me,' he said, and she chuckled despite herself, shaking her head as she selected a silver disc and inserted it into the player.

As the first strains of 'Flame Trees' sounded and Jimmy Barnes' gravelly voice filled the car, relief flooded his face. 'Cold Chisel I can do,' he said gratefully.

For the first few kilometres they simply listened to the music. The lyrics always took her back to when she'd first listened to them. School discos, university—road trips into town with Brent. In fact, this was his CD. She hadn't listened to it since she'd been back home. She was a creature of habit and could listen to the same CD on repeat without ever growing tired of it.

'This song always reminds me of a night out in Townsville,' Tim said as 'Khe Sanh' played.

She glanced across at him, a little alarmed that she'd been having similar thoughts. 'Reminds *me* of a night I should have said no to a fourth tequila sunrise,' she said.

His deep chuckle set off some more of those pesky flutters. 'Funny how music can take you back to a certain time and place, instantly,' she added.

'Yeah. Happens to me all the time.'

'I reckon this whole album is responsible for sending people back in time to nights that included a lot of alcohol and some poor decisions,' she said.

'I think you might be right. Good times though.' He turned his head to look out the window and she wondered if he was thinking about his mates who'd died.

'If you'd let me play Adele, you could have a whole new set of memories,' she said, hoping to lighten the mood.

'I don't need music to remember you,' he said, without turning away from the window.

Reggie swallowed and tightened her grip on the steering wheel. The grey clouds that had been hovering in the distance crept lower and within a few minutes fat drops of rain started hitting the windscreen.

Armaglen was a bustling regional centre with a bit over twenty-five thousand people. It boasted a university as well as a number of private schools and colleges. Reggie had always loved the old architecture and the stunning cathedrals that were tucked away in meticulously tended gardens and parks.

Reggie pulled up in the carpark outside the hardware store and followed Tim inside. While he went to find the things he needed, she made small talk with the owners, who were long-time friends of her parents.

'Got yourself a new fella?' Allen Jefferies commented as he followed Tim's movements around the store.

'He's helping out at River Styx,' Reggie corrected him quickly. 'Finishing the cabins.'

'Ahh,' Allen said, nodding with a flash of sympathy. 'It'll be good to get that last one done.' Allen had spent a lot of time with Brent as he'd planned and put his dream together. If anyone understood the significance of this project, it would be him.

'Seems like a capable enough bloke,' he added, nodding towards Tim's direction. 'How'd you find him? Isn't from here?'

'He was a guest and Dad got chatting to him . . . one thing led to another and here we are,' Reggie said, picking up a colourful torch from a display on the counter beside her.

'Hmm,' Allen said, nodding again. 'Serendipitous.'

'Is that the word of the week from book club?' Reggie teased. Allen and his wife had started a local book club to, in their words, add a little more culture to their lives, and had been trying to get her to come along to a meeting for months.

'It does seem fitting,' he said, lifting a bushy grey eyebrow in a wise old owl kind of way.

Tim walked back to them carrying a basket of bits and pieces and placed it on the counter, ending any further discussion. Allen's remark lingered in her ear. Tim's arrival had been serendipitous, but she stopped short of describing it as anything fate-like. It was just a very lucky coincidence that he had arrived at River Styx when they needed his help.

Chapter 24

The Feed Shed was one of a couple of places in town that supplied locals with all their livestock needs and, while slightly smaller than some of its competitors, Reggie liked that the owners were local farmers too and could help solve the problems people came to them with.

They'd also started stocking a mind-blowing range of boots and clothing as a side trade and Reggie always liked to check out any new arrivals.

'Reggie!' Carol, one of the owners, smiled as Reggie climbed out of the four-wheel drive in the drive-through area and lowered the tailgate in preparation for loading it with feed.

'Hi Carol.'

'Your boot senses must have been tingling,' she said, as Reggie reached her. 'We just finished unpacking a new shipment.'

Reggie groaned. 'Noooo. I told you, I've bought too many pairs this year.'

'Rubbish,' Carol said, waving the notion away. 'There's no such thing as too many boots.'

Tim came to a stop beside her, and she saw Carol's blue eyes light up. 'Carol, this is Tim. He's . . . doing some work on River Styx.'

'Oh, well, nice to meet you, Tim,' she said warmly.

'Likewise,' he said, nodding and standing with his hands shoved deeply in his pockets.

'How are you enjoying the place?' she continued, tilting her blonde head like a little sparrow as she waited for his answer.

'It's great. There's some really beautiful country up around here.'

'Have you been to the falls yet? You really need to get out and see them.'

'It's on my list.'

'Well, don't you go and work him too hard,' Carol said, turning to Reggie.

Glaring sternly at the older woman, Reggie quickly started rattling off her order, putting an end to any further embarrassment. Tim earned more brownie points when he jumped in and began loading the big bags of feed into the car, and Reggie gave a small start as she realised both she and Carol had momentarily become distracted watching him work.

'So, should I add a pair of boots to the order?' Carol asked, mock-innocent.

'Not today, Carol. I'm being strong.'

'But you haven't even looked at them,' she protested.

'I'm not in a hurry, if that's what you're worried about,' Tim said, coming back over.

'It's not. I'm just resisting the urge to buy more boots.'

Carol disappeared, only to return carrying a box that she set down on the counter. 'Oh, look! And they just so happen to be size sevens,' she said, pretending to be surprised.

The pale green leather with delicate sunflowers embroidered across them literally made Reggie's mouth drop open. They were stunning.

'I thought of you the moment I spotted these in the catalogue. Try them on,' Carol said, handing a boot across to her.

Reggie took a step back, almost too afraid to touch them in case her credit card flew out of her wallet to the card reader on the desk. She had to be sensible. She'd just been giving her parents a stern talk about budgeting for the property . . . How was she supposed to look them in the eye if she dipped into her savings to buy a pair of boots that she didn't even need? 'No thanks, Carol. Not this time. I've got to watch what I spend for a while,' she muttered, hating that Tim was standing beside her watching all of this with a slightly bemused expression.

'Well, that's a first,' Carol said, looking bewildered. 'Okay, that's fine. I'll just leave them under the counter here for a couple of days in case you change your mind.'

'Thanks, Carol. That's all for today,' Reggie said with a bright smile as she paid for the feed.

❖

'She really wanted you to buy those boots,' Tim commented as they headed out.

'Yeah. That's probably my fault.'

'That she's pushy?' he asked doubtfully.

'I've been a pushover where boots are concerned ever since I came home. I think she was just in shock.'

'A boot fetish, huh?' he said, smiling when Reggie scoffed. He liked when she forgot to be so serious and worried all the time. Admittedly, she'd tried to be open and friendly when he'd first arrived and *he'd* been the one to shut down any conversation, but that was before. Before River Styx had started working whatever magic shit it had been working on him.

Ray had been right—it was a good place to heal. Not that he was suddenly cured of his grief and guilt by any means, but he did feel different since he'd been here. Something had begun to change and the fog of pain he'd arrived with had started to clear—at least enough to notice Reggie MacLeod. Only problem was, while he was tentatively opening up, she was determinedly shutting down and he wasn't quite sure why.

'Some people spend a fortune on drugs—my addiction is boots,' she said simply.

'Well, I guess it's not the worst thing to be addicted to.'

'So, what's yours?'

'My addiction?' he asked.

'Yeah.'

'I don't have one.'

'Come on—we all have that one thing we just can't say no to. There has to be something.'

For a moment he heard Alicia's words replay through his mind, from the day of the funeral.

They'd been standing at the graveside—just the two of them, after most of the crowd had walked away—staring at the gaping hole with the shiny black coffin at the bottom.

'You know it wasn't the gun that killed him,' she'd said softly, her eyes fixed on the hole where her husband now lay.

'What do you mean?' he'd asked.

He watched her eyes flutter, almost as though the effort to move them towards him was painful. 'It was the same with the others—with all of you,' she added, holding his eyes with her sad, tear-filled gaze. 'Their addiction to danger is what killed them—it's what drives you all. There was nothing to fill that void after they left the army, and I watched Dean struggle every day, trying to find something that could replace it. You're all addicted to the rush that danger gives you and I hope to God you can find a way to get over it, Tim, because I can't go to another funeral for someone I care about. I can't do this anymore,' she'd said. Tears ran down her face and she turned away, leaving him alone.

Tim cleared his throat roughly and pushed the memory away. 'Nah. Can't think of anything.'

'What a saint,' Reggie muttered.

Yeah, that's me, he scoffed at himself, *I'm a real saint.* 'So where to now?'

'We can't come back from town without stopping at the bakery,' she explained, pulling up in a section of the main street that looked older than the part of town they had just driven through. The store had an old timber awning out the front and a pair of swinging screen doors. 'Dad's been going to this bakery since he was a kid,' she said, undoing her seat belt.

As they went inside, a tiny bell sound tinkled and Tim's mouth instantly started salivating at the smell of freshly baked bread and pastries.

'Well, hello there, Reggie,' a friendly, round-faced woman said as she came out from the back of the store, her mousy-brown and grey hair pulled back by a headband. 'Haven't seen you in a while.'

'Hi Meryl.' Reggie smiled back. 'I've been pretty busy lately, haven't been into town in ages.'

'How're Mum and Dad?'

'They're doing great. Mum's improving by leaps and bounds every day. We have to slow her down from doing too much,' Reggie said with a grin.

'Oh, that's so good to hear.'

'She's even back in the kitchen now.'

'So that's why you haven't been in lately . . . I've got to compete with Peggy's baking again,' the older woman said, rolling her eyes good-naturedly.

'No one can compete with your pies, Meryl,' Reggie said. When the woman glanced across at Tim, he jumped in quickly before Reggie could introduce him as the hired help once more.

'I'm Tim,' he said. 'I'm working out at River Styx.'

'Oh?' Meryl said, her eyes widening a little. 'Last time I heard, the Parsons had nabbed all the local workers.'

'Tim isn't from around here,' Reggie explained, and the women shared a look.

'Well, that explains it then,' Meryl said with a brief chuckle. 'Nice to meet you, Tim. So, what can I get you today?' she asked, looking back at Reggie.

'The usual, thanks,' Reggie said, and then turned to Tim. 'What kind of pie would you like?'

He looked up at the impressive chalkboard on the wall and felt a little intimidated by the choice. How were you supposed to pick just one? 'The Ned Kelly special looks good,' he said, ordering it more out of curiosity than anything else—how the hell did they manage to fit an egg, bacon, hash brown and beef into a single pie?

He moved to take out his wallet, but Reggie shook her head and stepped in front of him. 'My treat,' she said, before handing him the collection of white paper bags Meryl slid across the glass countertop.

They walked back outside into the sunshine, and Tim wondered if he'd ever get used to the sudden shock of cold air that hit him each time. The blue skies and sunshine belied the chill of the air.

He followed Reggie to a brown picnic table beside the bakery and sat down across from her, placing the bags between them.

'They're better eaten straight away,' she told him, taking hers out and sliding his bag across to him.

He took his pie out and observed it with interest. It was bigger and taller than the usual meat pie, and the pastry looked golden and flaky. He could feel his mouth start to water once more.

'Are you going to eat it, or ask it to marry you?' Reggie said with a smirk as she watched him.

'I don't know yet,' he said, picking it up and biting into it. Instantly a riot of flavours exploded inside his mouth—the slightly salty hit of the bacon, a warm egg, the crunch of a crispy hash brown and warm, rich gravy and mince all coming together in one near-orgasmic bite.

'Holy sh—'

'Good, huh?' She grinned across at him, cutting into his expletive.

'This is amazing.'

'Right?' She took another bite of her own pie and brushed off a few crumbs around her mouth.

'No wonder your dad's been coming here forever.'

'Now you know where the bakery is, if you come into town, don't come home without a pie,' she warned, and he knew she wasn't kidding.

They ate in silence for a few moments, watching the odd car drive past. While a lot of the cars were sedans and city-type vehicles, more often they were four-wheel drives and utes. Even in the city it seemed just about everyone had a four-wheel drive nowadays but, unlike their city cousins, these were the real deal—complete with dust, dogs and the occasional load of hay bales.

'Who're the Parsons?' Tim asked, breaking the silence as he recalled the conversation in the bakery.

'Mum and Dad's next-door neighbours,' Reggie said around her next bite.

'The place with the fancy big gates and stone wall a few kays before your place?'

'That's them.'

'What's the deal with the local workers?'

She shrugged. 'They got in early and hired the guys we usually get in for some seasonal work. Dad wasn't too happy about it. There's not a great deal of love lost between the Parsons and the MacLeods,' she added dryly.

'A modern-day feud?'

'I don't think anyone really remembers what the original issue was between our families, but no doubt it had to do with a Parson being an arrogant jerk. Dad always said they're lucky we live here and not back in Scotland. Dad's ancestors once chased his neighbour's whole village into a cave and lit a fire outside, killing them all by smoke inhalation.'

'Brutal,' Tim said.

'Well, in their defence, they were retaliating against the neighbours burning a hundred or so MacLeods to death by locking them inside a church then setting it alight, so . . .'

'I'll make a note not to piss your father off in case he calls in his Scottish relatives.'

'If he was going to do it, he would have done it years ago for the Parsons,' Reggie said airily.

She stood up and dusted the remaining crumbs from the pie off her lap, then waited for him to toss the rubbish in the nearby bin before heading back to the car.

Throughout the morning he'd found himself getting distracted by her mouth—he'd been preoccupied back at the feed shed, watching her. He wanted to talk about the kiss. God only knew why—he'd never been big on the whole 'talk about your feelings' thing—but damned if he didn't want to now.

He'd been in the house fixing a leaking tap for her mother when Reggie had called on the radio for her dad. Peggy had known straight away there might be trouble and asked him to head over and see if she needed some help. He had had no idea how he'd be able to help—he didn't know the first thing about cows, especially ones about to give birth.

Then he'd watched Reggie deal with the situation in her usual calm, unflappable way and he'd realised that in an emergency she'd be the person he'd want around. He'd seen that she was scared, but she'd worked through that and came up with a solution to each and every problem along the way. He may not have been aware of exactly what dangers she was facing, but he had known that she'd been under a great deal of stress and she had still remained calm and dealt with it.

When she'd looked over at him after delivering the tiniest cow he'd ever seen in his life, his breath had caught at her beaming smile. She was . . . beautiful. He'd always thought the term *glowing* was the stupidest thing he'd ever heard, but right at that moment her smile had lit up the distance between them and she had truly glowed. She'd taken his breath away.

When she'd teased him about his squeamishness afterwards, he hadn't been expecting the instant electricity that had sparked between them when her body pressed against his own. It hadn't mattered that they were separated by layers of clothing—the current was strong and the instant his lips had touched hers he had been lost in the sensation. It was just a kiss—it shouldn't have been earth-shattering, and he'd had plenty of kisses before—but nothing had prepared him for it and it had been plaguing his thoughts ever since.

Now he wasn't sure what to think. She'd made it clear earlier she didn't want to discuss it. Was it because she'd found it too horrible to think about? Or could it be that it had thrown her for a loop as well and she was just as confused about it as he was? He really wanted to bring it up again, but something told him if he did, he'd risk the fragile truce they'd been sharing since leaving River Styx.

As they drove home, Cold Chisel continued to take them both on a trip down memory lane, and he realised this was the happiest he'd been in a long while. Who would have thought? A trip into town, some old tunes and a meat pie was all it took. Possibly the woman beside him had a part to play in it as well. She just didn't know it.

Chapter 25

'Stop frownin', we'll be fine,' her father said as Reggie helped load the suitcase in his the car. 'It's just a specialist check-up.'

'I know, but I think it would save a lot of stress if you didn't have to drive. I said I was happy to take you.'

'Save a lot of stress? Drivin' in Sydney with you last time pretty much gave me a bloody ulcer.'

'Okay, fair point,' she had to concede. She was a terrible city driver.

'Besides, we're only driving as far as Duncan's place, and they'll be taking me in to the specialist.' Her dad's younger brother and his family had been lifesavers during the first scary weeks after the accident. They lived near Newcastle, so they'd been on hand to help with travelling to and from hospitals and rehab stays. 'Your mother wanted to try a trip away. We've been trying to get her back out and about and this seems like a good place to start.'

'Yeah, I know. It's great she wants to leave home for a bit. I just hope it's not too much.'

'Stop bloody mollycoddling us,' Ray grumbled, and instantly Reggie felt contrite.

'Sorry,' she sighed. She knew how hard it had been for them but she also understood how difficult it must be for a parent who'd always taken care of their child to suddenly have their child taking care of them—especially when that transition felt premature.

'Look,' her father said, softening his tone as he turned towards her, 'I know there're a lot of things we can't do anymore and we just have to accept that, but the things we *can* do, well . . . we need to keep doin' them while we still can. Aunty Mary will take care of your mum and they'll have a nice catch-up, so she won't be stuck in the car any longer than she has to be. And I won't be under any stress drivin' through the city because Duncan will take me to my specialist visit. So, see? It's all under control.'

Reggie summoned a smile and gave her father a hug. 'Okay, I'll stop worrying.'

When her mother came out, Reggie helped settle her into the car and stepped back, waving as they drove off. *It* will *be good for them to get away for a few days,* she thought as the last of the dust settled back on the dirt driveway and the car disappeared from sight. But she knew she'd still be worrying until they got back home again.

'Hey,' Tim's deep voice came from behind her and she jumped, swinging around with a curse. 'Sorry, I thought you heard me coming.'

'No, I didn't. You scared the hell out of me,' she snapped. She took a breath and gave him an apologetic smile. 'Sorry. I must have been a million miles away.'

'Your parents going away?'

'Yeah—just for a couple of days. Dad's got a specialist appointment in Sydney.'

'I could have taken them down if they needed,' Tim said, looking down the driveway.

'Nope. I tried. Dad wants to get Mum away for a few days.'

'Well, that's good, though, isn't it?'

'Yeah, it is,' she said, nodding. 'I guess this is what it felt like when they had to let me go out into the big scary world and do stuff on my own.'

'I'm pretty sure they'll be fine.'

'How's the cabin going? You got everything you need?' she asked, changing the subject.

'Actually, that's what I was coming down to see you about. I'm going to head into Armaglen and grab a couple more boxes of screws to finish off the deck. You need anything while I'm in there?'

'Oh. Okay, I'll grab you the credit card.'

'Nah, don't worry, I'll get them.'

'No, you won't. If it's part of the cabin construction, we'll buy it.'

'They aren't that expensive. It's not a big deal.'

'Actually, if you feel like company, I might just come in with you. I've only got paperwork waiting for me in the office and I do *not* want to do that right now.'

'Sure. Give me a yell when you're ready,' he said, turning to head back to the shed with a wave.

She told herself that she simply didn't feel like sitting inside today, but the truth was that a few hours stuck in a car with Tim seemed like a much better offer.

Tim's day was looking up. He'd been wondering how he would manage to swing another road trip with Reggie and the opportunity had just dropped into his lap. He wasn't about to turn down the offer of spending some time alone with her for the sake of an argument over who paid for a few lousy boxes of screws.

Over the last week Reggie had kept her distance, and for the first time in a long time when it came to a woman, he wasn't sure how to proceed.

The fact that Reggie didn't seem to be falling over herself to be around him wasn't exactly encouraging, and he probably should be taking that as a sign she wasn't interested. Still, on the occasions they'd found themselves together, usually at her parents' place for dinner, he picked up on that weird electric current that continued to run between them.

He'd accepted her distance and given her space, figuring if she wanted to take that kiss further, she'd come looking for him. So far that plan hadn't been working out too well.

But he knew she wasn't completely unaffected. Two days earlier, he'd arrived back at the shed and found her trying to reach a box that was stored on a shelf just out of her reach and had gone over to help. He hadn't meant it in any way other than being helpful, but as he had reached above her he had smelt the citrus scent of her hair beneath his chin and had sensed the warmth of her body in front of his own and they'd both stood frozen there like a pair of stunned statues for a moment before he'd cleared his throat and stepped away.

'Thanks,' she'd said, lowering her gaze and taking a sudden, overly keen interest in the box she held.

As he'd watched her walk away, he couldn't help but notice the little grin that had appeared on her face. He was certain she wasn't as indifferent to this thing between them as she was making out. He just had no idea what to do about it.

Today as they drove, though, she seemed more relaxed. Less guarded. They talked about a lot of things. She asked more about his past, and he found himself telling her stories about Deano and the boys that he hadn't thought about in years—the fun times, before all the sadness took over. It felt good to remember their younger years. There'd been a lot of great things about his career; more good than bad, to be honest. It was just that the bad things had been really bad— enough to overshadow any of the good for so long.

'I know you were in the army, but what part of the army were you in?' she asked. 'What did you actually do?'

For a moment, Tim didn't answer, but he felt her watching him.

At that moment he saw the bakery up ahead and pulled in to park at the curb with a relieved sigh. He didn't want to talk about the past and answer the questions most people wanted to know. Not that he begrudged Reggie wondering about his life in the army, but he'd been in a good place lately and he didn't want to dwell on the darker parts of it, no matter how innocently the questions might be asked. 'I missed breakfast this morning,' he said. 'I'm starving.'

'Sounds good to me,' she said, seemingly happy enough to go with the change of topic. She followed him out of the car. 'You save us the table, I'll get these ones,' he said, walking away before she could object. When he returned, they sat in companionable silence and devoured their pies.

As they were finishing, two women walked up to the table and stopped to say hello.

'I thought that was you, Regina,' the first woman said, nodding across at her companion. 'Didn't I say, Marge? I think that's Regina.'

'Yes, you did, Bertha. That's what you said.'

Tim looked at the two women curiously. They were complete opposites in every way. Marge was short but built like a stick, with a long dour face and short grey hair, while Bertha was unmistakably round. She was the roundest person he'd ever seen. Her face was oval and she didn't appear to have a waist—her dress seemed to fall from an enormous bosom straight to her knees, and she had a set of shoulders that a rugby front rower would envy.

'How's your mother, dear?' Bertha asked, and her gaze darted across to Tim.

'She's doing great. She and Dad have gone away for a few days. Dad's got a check-up with his heart specialist.'

The woman's eyes whipped back across to Reggie's with the accuracy of a guided missile. 'Well, they won't find anything. The man *has* no heart,' she snapped.

'No heart at all,' Marge echoed with a frown.

'I just don't understand how such a wonderful woman like your mother ended up with a man like Ray MacLeod.'

Tim gave a small cough as a stray flake of pastry lodged in his airway. *That was a bit harsh,* he thought, wondering how Reggie was so calm about the way these women were ripping into her father.

'You know he doesn't mean half the things he says,' Reggie told them lightly.

'That man is evil. He was evil as a child, and he's even worse as a grown man,' Bertha said. 'Do you know what he said to me just the other day?' she demanded, placing her hands on her hips, reminding Tim a little of Humpy Dumpty. 'I was minding my own business, standing in line at the grocery store, and he says, "Bertha, you're ageing like a fine banana." The hide of the man!'

Tim heard Reggie clear her throat before giving an appropriately sympathetic murmur of disapproval, then she stood up from the table and eyed him meaningfully. 'It was nice to see you both, but we've got a bit on today, so we'd better get moving.'

'You send our best to your mother, dear,' Bertha said, and Reggie nodded solemnly as they turned for the car.

'Wow,' Tim said, sitting in the driver's seat and watching as the two women walked inside the bakery.

'Yeah. Wow.'

'Doesn't seem to be much love lost between your dad and Bertha.'

'It drives Mum nuts,' Reggie said with a low moan. 'They're like two stray cats whenever they see each other—the fur stands on end and they practically start hissing at each other. They've known each other all their lives and apparently it's always been the same,' she explained, sounding exasperated. 'It's not funny,' she added, frowning when he couldn't hide the smirk on his face at the thought of Ray and Bertha trading insults.

'Kind of sounds hilarious.'

'In the age of political correctness, my father is a walking lawsuit.'

Tim did laugh at that. Political correctness had gone completely off the deep end lately in his view, and he wasn't sure he was the poster boy for it any more than Ray was.

After picking up what he needed at the hardware store, they were making their way back to the car when Reggie gave a small groan. Tim glanced down to see her turn towards him abruptly. Before he could ask what was wrong, a tall, lean guy a few years younger than him walked past and did a double take.

'Reggie MacLeod. Just the person I needed to speak to.'

Tim surveyed the man. Even if Reggie hadn't already indicated she didn't like this fella, he'd still have come to the conclusion that he was an arrogant dick. He had the kind of face that made you want to punch it—just to make it a little less perfect. No one had the right to have a nose that freaking straight.

'Simon.'

A woman appeared at his shoulder and hovered slightly behind him, looking at Reggie warily. 'Hello, Reggie,' she said quietly.

Chapter 26

'Felicity.'

Tim felt Reggie stiffen where she stood. Her arm was just brushing his, and her tone was cold. Her voice had a steely edge he hadn't heard from her before—not even with him.

'There's a feral dog roaming around—it needs to be dealt with,' Simon said.

'We know.'

'It's been doing the rounds of properties and taking calves. It needs to be dealt with.'

'Agreed. We've had issues with it too.'

'Yeah, well, we have pure blood lines to protect . . . not some made up line like your brother decided to go into,' Simon said in a prim tone that had Tim's fist itching. 'I almost had it this morning. It headed up the back of your property.'

'So, you missed it?' Reggie asked pointedly, and Tim controlled a sudden grin as Simon's face tightened at her not-so-subtle stab at his shooting skill.

'I didn't get a good enough shot—it was from a distance.'

'Ah-ha,' she drawled, not bothering to hide her amusement.

'I didn't *miss*,' he told her with a scowl. 'I hit it—but it managed to get away.'

'You *wounded* it?' she said, suddenly turning serious.

'It probably won't last the night, but I don't want to see it on our property again, so go make sure I got it, will you?' he asked, adding on the last bit as though it were an afterthought.

'Why the hell would you wound an animal and not make sure you finished it off?'

'Because it went onto *your* property.'

'It's still out there wounded.'

'It's not my problem anymore, is it?' He shrugged.

'Clearly not,' Reggie said bitterly. 'Where did it cross over?'

'Last I saw it, it was headed through that section of fence you attempted to fix the other day,' he threw back. 'But don't worry, it's fixed properly this time—you're welcome.'

'Well it was probably your bloody cattle who broke it in the first place,' she muttered, turning her back on the couple.

Throughout the exchange, Tim had been trying to work out who this guy was and finally reached the conclusion that he must be one of the Parsons. He wasn't sure who this Felicity woman was, but there was obviously some kind of history there—Reggie was always polite and friendly to everyone who said hello when they were in town, even Bertha.

He gave the guy a hard look before turning to follow Reggie. He could almost feel the anger radiating from her as she walked.

'What was all that about?'

'I have to go out and look for the dog,' she said.

'What? Now?' It was already getting on to lunchtime and they still had the trip home ahead of them.

'I went out looking for it after the whole thing with Dad the other day, but I couldn't find any trace of it. It needs to be dealt with—especially if it's wounded.'

He heard the steel in her tone and realised she wasn't in a reasonable, let's-talk-about-it kind of mood right now. 'Okay. I'll come with you.' Maybe they'd locate the dog easily and be back before it got dark. But he knew from previous experience that whenever it came to making an impulsive decision like this it rarely went smoothly. Then again, even some of the best planned operations they'd practised for months had occasionally gone tits-up.

Reggie was quiet on the way home, clearly distracted, and he couldn't help but wonder if it was more than just an injured dog on her mind.

'So that was your neighbour?' he said, trying to prise out some conversation.

'Hmm.'

'He seems like a bit of a dick,' Tim said.

'He is.'

'Who was that Felicity chick he was with?'

'His fiancé,' she practically spat out.

'Is there some sort of history there?' he asked.

She looked across at him with a frown. 'History? Between Simon and me?'

'Well, no, I meant with Felicity.' *But* was *there something going on with Simon?* Maybe he'd misread the situation.

'She was engaged to Brent before he got sick.'

'Oh.'

'They'd been together for years and then Mum and Dad's accident happened, and Brent was snowed under with all the stress and the extra workload.' She turned to look out the window. 'Then he found out he was sick . . . She couldn't cope with it all and broke up with him. Didn't even tell him face to face . . . left him a note to find when he got out of hospital the first time.'

'Nice.'

'Gutless,' Reggie said, then huffed.

Well, at least that explained the animosity. It didn't seem like a particularly nice way to break up with a guy, especially when he'd just found out he had a serious disease. However, Tim wasn't going to get in the middle of this family history—it really wasn't any of his business.

They got back to the house and Reggie went inside, emerging a few minutes later with the same gun he'd seen her with before and some ammunition that she shoved into a canvas bag as she headed across to him. He'd grabbed his thick coat while she'd been inside and tossed it into the back of his four-wheel drive. 'We can take my car if you want.'

'Okay. If you're sure? This isn't exactly in your job description,' she added, pausing with her hand on the door.

'Neither was an assistant midwife to a cow,' he said with a shrug.

'This is true.' She placed the bag on the back seat and then swung herself into the front.

'Where to?' he asked from the driver's seat.

She pointed straight ahead, and he glanced up at the ridge in the distance. 'Just head that way until we can't go any further.'

It was almost two and the sun that had been shining earlier had been covered by clouds. The temperature had dropped at least a couple of degrees in the last half an hour.

Reggie scanned the countryside outside the window vigilantly as Tim drove along the track. He'd walked out this way during his first couple of days and, though he'd acknowledged the different landscapes, he hadn't been in the right frame of mind to properly appreciate them. The open pasture and scattered trees eventually gave way to bushland. Once they crossed the creek, it changed again as the trees grew thicker and the canopy closed over, creating the perfect conditions for an inland, subtropical rainforest.

'Just up ahead is the spot Simon reckons he saw it,' Reggie said, pointing, and he brought the car to a stop. They both got out and walked along the fence line, searching for any evidence of an injured animal having come through.

'There,' she said, after about fifty metres, kneeling down. 'Blood.' She pointed at the long grass and looked over her shoulder towards the base of the ridge.

'We'll have to leave the car here and go the rest of the way on foot,' she said, looking over at another small creek crossing. 'Are you okay with that?'

'Sure.'

She stood up, and they headed back to the car. Tim went to the rear of the vehicle and rummaged under the gear he kept stored in the back, taking out a long, soft-sided black bag and hoisting it onto his shoulder before grabbing his backpack and jacket. He reached the front of the vehicle and found Reggie waiting with the canvas bag containing her rifle.

'Are you planning on staying out here for a week?' she asked, pulling on her thick coat as he shrugged on the backpack.

'Doesn't hurt to be prepared.' It was habit more than anything—years of training had made it second nature.

'I didn't know you had a rifle,' she commented as they headed into the dense bushland ahead.

'I've got a licence for it, in case you're worried.'

'I'm not worried. It's not some big He-man assault rifle from your army days, is it?' she added warily.

He wanted to chuckle at the description but also felt a tiny bit insulted. 'No. The army doesn't let you take your assault weapons home when you leave.'

'Do you hunt?' she asked curiously.

'I used to—mainly just shooting on a mate's property years ago. I haven't used it in a while.' The twenty-two Hornet had once belonged to Deano's dad. Tim had used it whenever he spent holidays with the Johnsons in the early days. After Dean's death, his father had given it to him—the pain on the farmer's weathered old face had broken Tim's already cracked heart.

'I want you to have this—it would have gone to Dean eventually,' he'd said, his watery eyes dull with pain. 'But you should have it now.' The deep mahogany brown timber and craftmanship of the old rifle brought back memories of better times. He'd give anything to get them back—and then try to delay the future from unfolding before them. God, they'd thought they were ready to take on anything back then.

'What about you?' Tim asked, observing the easy way she handled her own rifle. 'Other than wild dogs, I mean.'

'No. I've never liked it. Still don't,' she added. 'I don't even particularly like guns, but they're a necessary evil in situations when an animal is suffering. I'd rather know I helped ease something's pain quickly than allow it to die slowly, frightened and in agony.'

'Like this dog?'

For a moment the compassion in her eyes hardened and he wondered if she was thinking about how close this particular dog had come to attacking her father. Then she gave an impatient sigh. 'Yeah. Even this stupid dog.'

'Not that I disagree with you—about not letting something suffer—but if the dog's injured, why not just let it die? It's been killing your cattle.'

'Because it's a wild animal doing what wild animals do. If the wound didn't kill it outright and it came across another person it might make it even more aggressive. Not to mention the fact that Simon bloody Parson, who clearly couldn't hit the side of a barn, just left it out there to die and that irritates the living hell out of me.'

He supposed that was as good a reason as any.

'Here,' she said, stopping again as she found more blood on a low branch and, this time, footprints in the dirt. 'He's probably heading for his den around here somewhere.'

'Your dad mentioned that he and your brother had tried to catch this one before?'

'Apparently. It was before I came home,' she said, her gaze scanning the area carefully. 'They haven't been spotted around here in a long while. The pack moves about a bit if their food source is compromised so chances are they have a huge territory. Makes it hard to track them. I've tried finding them a few times lately and haven't had any luck. I guess lucky for us this time that we've got blood to follow.'

He looked at the thick bushland around them—the trail had ended a while back and they were now picking their way through the trees. 'How are we going to follow a blood trail?' he asked. 'Should we go back and bring the dogs?'

'Nope. I'm not risking them getting hurt. Wild dogs are cunning as. Our dogs aren't trained hunting animals—they're no match for a pack of wild dogs. We'll just have to look for tracks and hopefully find a den.'

'Like a cave or something?' he asked.

'Possibly—there are hundreds of caves around this place, but sometimes it's just a hollow in the ground—like under those kinds of big rocks.' She pointed to a stack of large boulders and rocks that had landed in an untidy heap after being been tossed in the air hundreds of thousands of years ago when volcanoes in the area erupted and sent out a cascade of debris—like a toddler throwing a handful of blocks. The rocks were in precariously balanced stacks in some places and in deep layers across rock faces and gullies elsewhere.

'They tend to stick to dry creek beds, tree lines and fire trails when they travel. If we just stick to these tracks the cattle have made, we should hopefully come across more blood.'

'Considering he's still leaving a blood trail, he's probably got a hell of a wound,' Tim said, wondering if they'd come across it lying on a track somewhere up ahead.

'And he'll likely be extremely pissed off, to boot,' Reggie added.

Sure enough, not too far up ahead, they came across more tracks—Tim was suitably impressed by Reggie's tracking skills. She continued to confuse him, this feisty powder keg of a woman. If anyone listed her skills on paper, he'd have gotten the impression she was some butch, tobacco-chewing redneck—a bit overly colourful. If she were in a line up, she wouldn't be the one he'd pick as being tough enough to handle half the crap she did around the place.

'Where'd you learn all this stuff?' he asked as they worked their way up the incline.

'Brent and Dad,' she said. 'But mostly Brent when we were younger. We used to come up here and track all kinds of things. Not to shoot. Just for fun. Boring country kids' stuff,' she said, chuckling softly.

'Not at all. Sounds like a great life.'

'I'm sorry, Tim. I wasn't thinking before I said that,' she said, looking across at him with a worried frown on her face. 'I know you didn't have a great childhood.'

'Nah. It's okay. I mean it sure as hell wasn't as great as yours—but there were a lot of kids who had a worse one than me.'

They settled back into silence again with only the sound of their boots on the uneven ground marking their progress. It was getting late, and he noticed the clouds had an ominous look about them—dark and low.

He tightened his grip on his rifle case as they trudged on.

Chapter 27

Reggie heard herself breathing heavily as they walked up the gradual incline. She wasn't used to so much physical activity—not like this. Beside her, Tim seemed barely out of breath.

She should have just stayed home and tackled the business activity statements that were due soon. When would she learn that putting things off was never the answer? Then she would never have run into Simon and found herself out here looking for an injured dog with a growing weather event looming.

'I think I've lost him,' she admitted eventually, feeling annoyed. She couldn't see any more tracks and the bush was getting denser.

'What do you want to do?' Tim asked, coming up beside her.

She wanted to go home and get out of this cold, but she was torn between that and finishing what she started. 'Maybe we can split up and see if we can pick up the trail again? Might be quicker.'

Tim hesitated, then nodded, moving carefully in the opposite direction as she continued forward. There had to be something around here somewhere. The dog would be tiring by now with his injury, but there was no more blood to be seen.

Then she heard it, the slight rustle of leaves. She paused. Something black moved up ahead, and Reggie lifted her weapon, holding her breath as she waited, her eye against the rifle sight. Then from behind her came a low, menacing growl that made the hairs on her arms stand up.

Before she had a chance to swing her gun around, the loud echo of a gunshot rang out and she heard the thud of something heavy fall. For what seemed like hours, she couldn't move. She turned, sank to the ground and stared at the dark shape just beyond the trees behind her. The sound of heavy footsteps running towards her broke through her shock and she looked up to find Tim crouching beside her, his worried gaze probing hers intently.

'Are you all right?'

She managed a jerky nod, as a rush of comprehension quickly began to flow through her. She'd been watching the wrong animal. The dog she'd spotted briefly hadn't been the injured one. While she'd been distracted, the injured alpha had been stalking *her*.

A chill ran through her at the thought. If she'd been out here alone . . .

'I'll be right back,' Tim said, cutting through the horrible images her mind had been conjuring up.

She watched as he slowly picked his way through the scrub to where the big dog had fallen. He bent down, then straightened shortly after. 'It's okay.'

'Did you get him?' she asked, and hated that her voice seemed to shake.

'Yeah.'

Easing to her feet, she walked over and stared down at the dog now lying on its side at Tim's feet. If she hadn't known any better, she'd swear it was just snoozing on the ground.

She quickly swiped at a stray tear and gave a small, frustrated groan of embarrassment as she realised her fingers were shaking.

'It's okay. It's just the shock and adrenalin wearing off,' Tim said quietly from beside her.

'*You're* not crying,' she pointed out irritably.

'I wasn't the one who was almost eaten by a bloody wolf,' he said. 'He was a big one.'

It was an ugly looking animal, clearly a result of cross breeding somewhere along the line, as most of the feral dogs around the area were—larger than a dingo but with the same shorter stout jaw.

'Come on, let's get out of here,' Tim said, taking a step back so she could pass by him.

It was almost dark now—dark enough to need the torch Tim was holding, and Reggie realised that making it back to the car was going to be a lot slower going. The wind had picked up once more and the chill took her breath away when it came in sudden gusts. When she stumbled a second time within a few minutes, Tim stopped abruptly and turned to her. 'This is stupid. One of us is going to break a leg before we make it back to the car and neither of us can afford time off work for that.'

'Well I'm not staying out here without any shelter—we'd both probably die of exposure.'

'We're not making much progress in the dark and we won't be without shelter,' he said, swinging his pack off his back and dropping it to the ground.

'What are you talking about?' she asked, confused.

'I reckon we should set up camp and stay put until first light.'

'Set up camp? With what?' she asked, imagining him going full survival mode on her and chopping down saplings to build a gunya.

'With a tent,' he said simply.

'You brought along a tent?' she asked, eyeing the pack doubtfully.

'I told you, I'm always prepared. Look, I know staying out here probably doesn't hold much appeal, but I really am getting worried about the conditions.'

He was probably right. It was frustrating that technically they were only a few kilometres from the car, but they'd lost the light and it was getting bloody cold. She hated to admit it, but he was also right about one of them getting hurt—the last thing she needed was to be laid up with an injury.

'I guess it would be safer to at least wait out this wind somewhere.'

'Those rocks over there should offer some protection against it,' he said, walking a short distance away and digging out a small cylinder only slightly longer than his hand from his bag.

'That's a tent?' she gaped.

He flashed her a grin as he took it out of the drawstring bag and unfolded it, attaching a rope through the centre and tying it to two nearby trees before pegging it down at the corners. 'Ta-da!' He gave a small wave towards the bright orange tent.

Reggie shook her head and chuckled despite the sudden exhaustion she felt wash over her—yet another after-effect of shock, she guessed. 'That's pretty impressive.'

'You think that's impressive?' he said, giving a cocky scoff before taking out another small drawstring bag. 'Emergency sleeping bag,' he announced, shaking it open.

'It looks like a giant garbage bag,' she said suspiciously.

'Yeah, well it's not exactly luxury—but if you were lost on a mountain top in the Himalayas it'd stop you freezing to death.'

'I'm pretty sure we're not at the Himalayan stage here.'

'And,' he said, ignoring her tone, 'we even have food.' After a quick rummage, he brought out two silver packets, holding them up like a TV game-show host for her viewing pleasure. 'MREs,' he said. Seeing her confused expression, he elaborated. 'Meals Ready to Eat. We'll make a fire, and dinner will be ready in a jiffy.'

Reggie rubbed her hands along her arms and looked up as something wet landed on her cheek. 'Oh crap,' she said, 'I think that was rain.' So much for a nice, warm fire.

'No worries—the shelter's waterproof and we don't need a fire to warm up dinner, so we're all good,' he told her, handing her the torch and packets to hold as he crouched down and dug through his backpack of magic tricks.

'Freeze-dried, grass-fed lamb with mint and rosemary,' she read out. 'Sounds delicious. Are these what you used to eat in the army?' she asked as he pulled out two tall sealed pouches.

'Our MREs were a little less gourmet than this. They've come a long way since my army days.'

'So, we're going to eat them cold?' she asked doubtfully.

'No, Miss Impatient,' he said lightly, tearing the tops off the pouches. 'We're going to put them inside these.' He tipped out a small sealed sachet from each, ripped off their outer packaging and dropped them back into the pouches. He added water to each pouch from his drink bottle and then slipped the MRE packs inside and sealed them up, propping them against a nearby stone. 'Now we wait for the magic to happen,' he said, standing up.

'What are they?' she asked curiously.

'Flameless ration heaters. Uses a chemical reaction to create heat. Comes in handy when you can't have a fire. I use them hiking and camping a fair bit.'

'Not from your army days?'

'Nah, we used the good old hexi-tab stoves. Still use one sometimes when I camp—but this is a lot easier.'

A few minutes later, their meal was ready. Reggie hesitantly accepted the bag Tim handed her, glancing down at the green chunky contents. 'Is that green stuff avocado?' she asked in alarm.

'It looks a bit gnarly,' he said, 'but just try it.'

She gave the packet a sniff and was surprised to find it smelled really good. She took the small fork he handed her and dug out a chunk of the lamb, tentatively putting it in her mouth. Much to her astonishment, it tasted just like a real lamb dinner, with a kick of mint and rosemary and, despite her misgivings, even with the chunks of avocado in there, she found herself digging in for more.

To his credit, Tim didn't say 'I told you so', he just happily ripped open his own packet and sat down across from her to eat.

She huddled into her coat a little deeper as she ate and, by the time they'd finished, she felt warmer and strangely content. Moments later a few more drops hit her face, and they scampered inside the small orange shelter.

Chapter 28

Tim had chuckled at the disgusted look on Reggie's face as she'd inspected the MRE. He remembered receiving his first ration pack during basic training—he'd been cold, wet and tired and it had been the best meal he'd ever had. It hadn't been grass-fed lamb with mint and rosemary, but after marching twenty kilometres with a full pack for the first time, it had tasted better than a meal from any five-star restaurant.

When the first drops of rain hit, he scooped up his pack and made a dash for the tent, realising too late there was going to be a small problem with his shelter solution. Despite being a 'two-man' tent, it was a tight fit with two bodies inside—despite being a two-man tent.

When she followed him inside he could feel the heat of her body. There wasn't going to be any problem with hypothermia tonight, he thought, swallowing down a lump in his throat. Holy shit, his body had been acting like an overstimulated teenager for the last few days—ever since that bloody kiss. He was still feeling very confused, because while he was sure she'd been just as into it as him she'd scampered away like a frightened mouse and avoided him ever since—only they kept getting thrown into close proximity and it was seriously messing with his mind.

The one thing that had managed to clear his head, though, had been this afternoon and her close encounter with that wild dog. The memory sobered him up faster than any cold shower ever could.

The bloody dog had been smart—he had to give it that much. The more he thought about it, the more the knowledge chilled him. If it hadn't been hurt and its reaction time slower, he was positive it would have reached Reggie before Tim could have taken the shot.

Thank Christ he hadn't lost *all* his skills since leaving the army. It'd been a long time since he'd been in a situation like that and, now that he had time to think on it, he realised he'd fallen back into it without a second thought. His instincts had been on high alert as they'd picked their way through the bush. Moments before he'd registered that low growl, he'd already been turning to check his back, his sixth sense registering unseen danger. That sensation had saved his arse more times than he cared to remember, and it'd been there again today.

A chorus of howls sounded and he felt Reggie shiver beside him. 'They're probably just regrouping to figure out where everyone is,' he said, trying to reassure her.

'There's a second black one and he only looked slightly smaller than the one you shot,' she said, staring out the door flap. 'I'm hoping they decide to move on, but I don't know . . .' She looked over at him. 'I'm glad you were there.'

He felt his throat tighten up and pushed away the threatening images that were forming in his head of what might have happened if he hadn't been nearby. 'I'm glad I was too.'

He expected her to turn away, but when she didn't he held his breath and waited, his heart in his throat. Finally, she leaned in and he slowly met her halfway. He didn't deepen the kiss, despite everything inside him urging him to—he wasn't going to do anything that might scare her off again.

When Reggie eased away, he fought the crush of disappointment that surged through him, but he didn't move.

'I'm sorry about before . . . the other day,' she said, stumbling over her words and lowering her gaze to the groundsheet beneath them. 'I know you wanted to talk about it—we should have, I was just . . . I'm not exactly sure what it meant.'

'I think it was something that'd been building for a while.'

'I guess so,' she said, picking at the silver tarp lining. 'It's just that, I'm not sure some kind of casual fling is a smart thing. I mean . . .' She gave a small, frustrated sigh. 'My parents think you're the best thing since sliced bread,' she said, lifting her gaze.

'I think your parents are great too.' And he did. He could admit he liked Peggy fussing over him and worrying if he was eating enough. He hadn't had much in the way of a maternal figure in his life and some lonely, empty part of his heart craved it. As for Ray—he reminded Tim of Deano's father. A big, tough, no-nonsense bloke who believed in hard work and honesty. Maybe it was the fact they'd both lost sons that made them seem so similar. It was hard to mask that kind of pain, and he saw the toll it had taken on both of them.

'The thing is,' she said, not looking at him again as she picked her words carefully, 'I don't want them to get their hopes up.'

'About?' he prodded, unsure where this was going.

'About you and me. They've got this thing in their head about me becoming some bitter, old spinster because I gave up on relationships and a chance at a "normal" life,' she said, her hands forming quotation marks pointedly. 'If they suspect there's anything going on between us, they're only going to get excited and start planning a wedding by the end of the month.' She pulled a face that was probably meant to be droll but instead twisted at the end in a way that made his heart stutter. 'I don't think it's wise to get involved with you when you'll be up and leaving as soon as you finish the cabin. I can't handle seeing their disappointment.'

He hadn't been sure what to expect, but it wasn't the blunt honesty she just gave him. All his head heard was *wedding* and *leaving*. He hadn't been thinking any further than his attraction to her, because his future hadn't been something he'd been giving much thought to. Before he arrived here, it had been looking kind of bleak. Now, though . . . dare he actually think about it? Suddenly there was a sliver of light in the dark chasm inside him and he saw a glimpse of sunshine trying to peek in. He almost scoffed at how melodramatic he was being, but something had definitely changed and—he didn't mind admitting—it kind of blew his mind.

'Maybe I don't have to leave after the cabin,' he said slowly.

She did look up at him then, but it wasn't exactly encouraging. 'We can't afford to pay you a full-time wage,' she said sadly. 'I mean, yes, we could use a second set of hands about the place some days, but there's not enough work to justify hiring someone full-time, and on-call, part-time isn't really a great option for workers.'

'Maybe I could look for a job somewhere locally.'

She studied him for a few moments before asking, 'Why would you want to stay around here?'

'I like it,' he said, then shrugged, unwilling to reveal too much in case it came out sounding dumb. 'Your parents have been really good to me and I'm not in any hurry to leave. I'm pretty low maintenance—I don't have debt or many bills. I've got a couple of investments, so money's not an issue for me right now. There's nowhere else I have to be.'

'The longer you stay, the harder it will be for Mum and Dad to say goodbye, and they've already lost so much.'

'What about you?'

'What *about* me?' she asked warily.

'Will it be hard for you to say goodbye too?'

'Of course it will,' she said, looking down.

'Well, if I stick around, I won't have to say goodbye, will I?'

'It's one thing to be on holiday, but it's another to actually live and work here. You might get sick of not being in a city where everything's at your fingertips and you don't have to travel for hours to get to a store.'

'I'm sure I'll cope,' he said. 'Would it change your mind about me if you knew I was planning on staying around?'

'Well . . . I guess . . . I mean, I don't know,' Reggie said, sounding a little flustered. He really didn't want to put her on the spot like this, but he needed to know if this attraction was one-sided.

He caught her eye and looked at her squarely. 'Do you *want* me to stay around?'

Chapter 29

Reggie held Tim's searching gaze and felt her breath catch at the question. *Do I want him to stay?*

Yes.

The thought of him leaving actually made her chest hurt. In here, snug and surprisingly warm, she felt protected from the outside world, and it had nothing to do with the stupid tent and everything to do with the man beside her. He'd saved her from serious injury—if not worse—today, and she knew he'd do it again without hesitation. She'd been fighting a losing battle trying not to think about him, but the damn man was everywhere, and their kiss kept replaying in her head at night. She had almost convinced herself that she'd been exaggerating how good it was, until their kiss moments ago had proved beyond a doubt that she *hadn't* been imagining it.

'Yes,' she finally said. What was the point in denying it? Her heart gave another little skip when she saw his lips twitch into a smile, but then it stopped completely as he drew her into the warmth of his kiss. She caught the tangy scent of something he wore—deodorant maybe, as she doubted Tim was the type to wear cologne—mixed with the fresh smell of rain and a musky maleness of his skin as she pressed herself against him.

He shrugged off his jacket and arranged it beneath them, then gently eased her onto it, following her down as he deepened their kiss. Never before had she connected so intensely with another person. She wanted to kiss him forever, but suddenly there was a more urgent need to be fulfilled, and kissing wasn't enough anymore. Her impatient fingers went to his shirt and she helped him out of it before fumbling with her own and swearing as she got tangled in her coat, thrashing about like a crazed octopus as she tried to dislodge her elbow from the arm of one sleeve. The thought flashed through her mind that this was probably how that calf had felt the other day. She shook the image from her head, trying not to panic as she realised she was really stuck.

'Stop pulling it for a minute,' Tim said, trying to ease away enough to help.

'Oh, for God's sake,' Reggie muttered, then yelped as Tim tried to push her arm backwards. 'It won't go any further, it's stuck.'

There was a mix of grunts and heavy breathing as they both struggled to manoeuvre their bodies inside the cramped confines of the tent. With a final tug, her arm came free of her sleeve, punching Tim in the face in the process, and extracting a harsh curse.

'Sorry!' she gasped.

'Bloody hell. Who would have thought two grown adults could make getting undressed so freaking difficult.'

'Well I don't think either of us is a contortionist,' Reggie muttered, lying back puffed but finally free of her shirt. 'Holy shit, it's cold,' she said as the freezing air touched her near-naked skin.

Tim lowered himself on top of her and the sudden touch of his warm skin sent a bolt of electricity through her. She instantly forgot about the cold. 'Better?' he asked, his breathing a little unsteady as she instinctively ran her hands along his back and arched against him.

'So much better,' she sighed as he bent his head and ran his lips along the side of her neck.

The rain had stopped and the cloud cover seemed to be clearing. Tim could see a few twinkling stars that hadn't been there earlier. It was still freezing outside, but it was warm tucked inside the cocoon of coats and the survival blanket. Metalized polyethylene mightn't be the cosiest material for a blanket, but it sure as hell was doing its job of reflecting their body heat—and they'd just produced a ton of that.

As he lay there now, with one arm tucked under his head and the other under Reggie's, who lay on her side snuggled into him with one leg threaded between his, he found himself struggling to make sense of his good fortune. The difference a few weeks had made to his life was nothing short of miraculous.

He'd left his life behind and hit the road with no plan other than to try to make peace with the nightmares and guilt he carried inside him, and here he was now . . .

He allowed a long, slow breath to fill his lungs as he tried to sort out the jumble of emotions flowing through him. He'd gone from a loner with no real connection to anyone to suddenly finding a part of him that had been lying dormant for years being slowly woken up. He was caring about things again—about people and, in particular, the MacLeods. They'd welcomed him into their home and shown him what a family looked like. For that experience alone, he'd been humbled, but now, with Reggie . . . He felt his throat tighten. He hadn't been expecting to find a partner, and certainly not one like Reggie, but here she was, lying asleep in his arms. Part of him wanted to wake her and tell her all this crazy stuff he was thinking so he could make sense of it, but another part warned him not to act like some weird psycho. He decided to keep his mouth shut and enjoy the moment while he could. He wasn't about to risk doing anything stupid that might upset this delicate tightrope he was balancing on. Everything was perfect right now. He just hoped it could stay that way.

Several days later, Reggie stared up at the ceiling in the shed and listened to the quiet of the early morning, her body warm and snuggly under the blankets. Beside her she could feel Tim sleeping, one arm slung across her hip keeping her in place. It had been so long since she'd woken up with someone next to her in bed. She'd forgotten how nice it could be.

Her parents would be back this afternoon, which would put an end to this strange honeymoon-like arrangement—well, if your honeymoon revolved around running a farm, she supposed. It hadn't exactly been real life. For instance, she'd never had someone tag along while she checked cattle, filled up water troughs and slashed walking tracks, who then made love with her at lunch time down by the fairy glen in the middle of the day! That wasn't real life—that was living because there was no one else around to catch them! She wasn't sure how things would work once her parents were home.

Reggie was still worried about how this was going to work out. Tim might say he was happy to stick around, but what if he changed his mind in a few months when the novelty wore off? The building work would come to an end shortly, and then he'd be doing odd jobs and farm work to fill his day. He was a builder—not a farmer—and his talents would be wasted hanging around here.

She let her eyes wander around the little flat that had once been her brother's and felt the funny pressure on her chest that started whenever she thought about Brent. She wondered if that was what people meant when they said they could feel their loved ones around them. Usually whenever she thought about Brent it was followed by a pang of sadness and grief, but lately she'd been feeling a weird . . . awareness? Presence? She wasn't sure what to call it, but she did know it was different. She still had moments when she felt an overwhelming emptiness and missed him so damn much, but those moments were slowly becoming a little less crippling in their intensity.

Maybe this new phase was simply a coping mechanism to deal with the grief. Besides, she was pretty sure if Brent knew she was sleeping in his bed with someone, he'd have taken any opportunity to make things awkward for her, simply for his own amusement.

The dogs started barking, cutting into her thoughts, and then their bark changed to excited yelping and Reggie swore loudly. She launched herself upright and threw off the blankets as she scrambled out of bed.

'What the fu—' Tim grunted as the cold air hit his still-sleeping, warm, naked body.

'Mum and Dad are back,' she shouted, pushing her bed hair out of her face as she dropped to her knees, reaching under the bed to find her bra and underwear. She hauled them on and shoved her legs into her jeans, jumping up and down and wriggling herself into them, snagging her shirt from the end of the bed as she went. *Not funny, Brent, not funny at all!*

Tim watched the whole thing unfold with a dazed kind of bemusement, looking far too bloody sexy, all bare-chested and tousled as he leaned back on his elbows in the bed. *Why the hell isn't he panicking?* She searched the floor for her socks but gave up as she heard the car roll to a stop on the gravel outside. She let out another profanity, tugging on one boot before pulling the place apart to find the other one.

'Where the hell is my other boot?'

Tim gave a soft whistle and she glanced up to find him holding it and wearing a lopsided grin.

'How did my boot end up in the bed? Never mind, I don't have time,' she said irritably, taking the shoe and hopping around the room as she tugged it on.

'Geez, Reggie, will you calm down before you do yourself damage?' he said, shaking his head as he watched on.

'Calm down?' she exploded, turning on him. 'My parents are home!'

'So? I'm sure they're old enough to accept that their daughter's having sex.'

Reggie squeezed her eyes shut tightly, before opening them to glare at him across the room. '*Never* use the word sex, and my parents, in the same sentence, ever again.'

His deep chuckle followed her as she crossed to the door, mentally trying to prepare herself to face her mum and dad and outright lie to the pair of them. They were going to see right through her—they always had whenever she tried to fib.

She reefed open the door and felt a satisfied smirk on her lips when she heard Tim yelp at the even colder air rushing in. Then she gathered her nerves to put on a bright smile and greet her parents at the house.

Tim dropped back down on his pillows and grinned as he thought about Reggie's hissy fit as she'd left. He figured she'd be a bit antsy when it came to telling her parents about them, but he'd been planning to talk to her about it today, before they came home. He didn't really understand why she was so worked up about how they were going to handle the news—it wasn't like they were a pair of sixteen-year-olds. Maybe country people were a bit more old-fashioned—but, although they were older, he didn't get the feeling that Ray and Peggy were *that* old-fashioned. Reggie had said her brother and his fiancé had practically lived together on and off over the years, so he didn't see what the big deal was. But for some reason it was to Reggie, and he tried to ignore the niggling concern that everything might fall apart before it even had a chance to really start.

Technically it was Sunday and he didn't need to be working on the cabin, but with Reggie gone the bed seemed lonely, and he wasn't tired, so he dragged himself up and got dressed, stoking the fire to take the bitter sting of cold out of the air.

It was colder today than it had been since he'd arrived and he looked out the window expecting to see snow, but there wasn't any; it just *felt* cold enough for it. He'd never been much of a fan of winter before—the jury was still out on whether he was fully converted—but up here there was a certain beauty to the cold. The bare trees and dull paddocks in their whisky and straw colours should look depressing, yet they were anything but. The landscape was vivid in its striking extremes. On the days when the sky was an endless blue, the colours lit up, and when the clouds came over all ominous and dark, the landscape changed again to something mysterious and powerfully beautiful. He'd never seen a place like this before, and it had captured his heart in ways he'd never imagined possible.

He knew Reggie still had her doubts about how long he'd stay, and he'd tried his best to convince her that he had meant what he'd said. But in the end it would have to be something he proved to her. He wanted a fresh start somewhere without the memories—the memories of Dean and the boys. He knew in his heart this was the place.

He'd meant it when he'd told her he was happy to move to Armaglen or somewhere else in the area to work—he'd have to in order to make a new life for himself, and the thought gave him a sense of purpose he hadn't felt in a long time.

But first, he needed to prove to Reggie that he was serious about giving this thing between them a fighting chance, and he wasn't quite sure how that was going to play out now that their time alone had come to an abrupt halt. For now, though, he'd work on the cabin and keep his head down. He'd just have to let Reggie take the lead on where they went from here and hope he'd become important enough for her to realise that they were worth fighting for.

Chapter 30

Reggie paused outside the front door and took a deep breath before pushing it open and walking inside, a sunny smile plastered on her face.

'You're home,' she said, leaning down to kiss her mother and then turning to hug her father. 'I'm so glad the doctor's report was good,' she added, putting the kettle on and taking down some cups. She'd spoken to them two nights earlier and they'd told her what the doctor had said. Skipping on to a new topic, she said, 'The calves are all a fair size and looking good. There's still one cow who hasn't dropped, but she looks like she should any day. I haven't checked on her this morning, yet.' Reggie realised she was babbling. *Stop talking, you fool.* 'How was Sydney? Bet you're glad to be out of the traffic.' She was smiling like an idiot as she noticed her parents exchange a look. They knew. Somehow, they knew she was hiding something. *Maybe because you haven't shut up since you walked through the bloody door. Shut. Up!* But she couldn't. The more nervous she got, the more verbal insanity fell from her mouth. 'Coffee?' she asked extra cheerily.

'Darling, is everything all right?' her mother asked.

'Did you back the tractor into the side of the shed again?' her father asked.

One time. She'd done it one time and ever since it was the first thing he always asked her if he thought there was a problem. 'The shed's fine,' she told him. 'Everything's fine. I've just missed you.' She looked back at her mother, and then hastily lowered her gaze, positive there was a big sign in bold writing hanging over her head saying, 'I slept with Tim . . . and I liked it!'

As she spooned some coffee granules into the cups, her mother asked, 'How's Tim?'

Reggie swore under her breath as her hand jumped and the coffee missed the cup. *Shit.* She reached for a cloth and swept the mess into her hand, heading across to the sink to dispose of it, then swore quietly again as she caught sight of Tim through the kitchen window, heading towards the house. 'Ah, he's fine. I think. I'm not sure—I haven't really seen him around much.'

'Really?' Peggy said. 'Don't tell me you didn't even invite him over for dinner while we were gone?'

'That's your job to spoil him, Mum,' Reggie said, turning away from the window and schooling her face into a smile once more.

A knock at the door drew her parents' attention away from her momentarily, and they broke into smiles when Tim appeared seconds later.

'Welcome home,' he said, shaking her father's hand and nodding across at her mother.

'How's the cabin coming along?' Ray asked.

'Yeah, good. Actually, that's what I came over for. Do you mind if I borrow the tractor for a minute? I've got to move some stuff.'

'Course you can,' Ray said, taking his coffee from Reggie. 'Just don't back it into the side of the shed,' he added, winking at Reggie as she rolled her eyes.

One. Freaking. Time.

'You don't need it for anything this morning?' Tim asked, forcing her to look up at him. Her heart tripped slightly as she felt the zap of electricity he managed to set off whenever he looked at her.

'Nope. I've got nothing planned that I need the tractor for . . . not that I can think of . . . If I do, I know where to find it,' she stammered, like an idiot. *A simple no would have sufficed.*

'Darling, are you *sure* you're all right?' her mother asked, looking a little concerned now.

Reggie noticed the slight lift of Tim's eyebrow and bit down on the inside of her lip to keep her mouth shut.

'Pull up a stump,' Ray said to Tim, moving a chair out from the table. 'Grab another cup for Tim, love,' he instructed as Reggie contemplated sticking her head in the oven.

'Ah, I probably should get to work,' Tim said hesitantly.

'Rubbish. It's flamin' Sunday. You're not even supposed to be working on the weekends.'

'Although, we figured you weren't sleeping in,' Peg added with a smile. 'We heard a lot of commotion coming from the shed when we arrived. Sounded like you had a herd of elephants in there.'

Kill. Me. Now.

'Yeah, I was chasing a mouse,' Tim mumbled, rubbing a hand across the back of his neck.

Reggie reluctantly took down another cup and went through the process of making Tim's coffee, adding the dash of milk and leaving out the sugar, as he liked it, before carrying it across to him.

'So, what's been happening around here?' Ray asked when Reggie eventually came across to join them at the table.

'I guess Reggie told you about the dog,' Tim said, sipping his coffee.

'No. What?' Ray turned to face his daughter.

Reggie sent Tim a quick glance. 'I haven't had a chance yet. I just walked in the door.'

'What's happened now? Did it get more cattle?'

'No. It's dead,' she said, placing both hands around her mug.

'What happened?'

'Apparently it was over at the Parson's place and Simon managed to stuff up a shot and wound it. He let us know it came over here and Tim and I went out to look for it.'

'Take it you found it,' Ray grunted.

Or it found us, she added silently, as she nodded and lifted her mug.

'You bring it back? I'd have liked to get a good look at the mongrel.'

Reggie suppressed a shiver as she recalled just how close a look she'd gotten. She could still see those sharp fangs and hear the bone chilling growl as it prepared to launch itself at her.

'No. We left it up there,' Tim said.

'Must have been when we tried to call you—couldn't get onto anyone. Was pretty late. You didn't go after it in the dark, did you?' Ray asked, switching his gaze between the two of them.

'We didn't find out about it until late,' Reggie said, trying for a dismissive shrug.

'You should have left it until the next day.'

'It was injured.'

'Too bad. That bloody thing was dangerous. I thought you had more common sense than that.'

'Now, Ray,' Peg cut in gently.

'Well, for God's sake. You know that animal tried to attack me, and in broad daylight. Why would you deliberately go lookin' for it in the dark?'

'It wasn't dark when we left,' Tim said calmly.

'And you went along with it?'

'It wasn't Tim's decision.'

'Clearly he had to go to make sure you didn't get yourself killed.'

The fact she almost had died did nothing to take the sting out of her father's displeasure. 'Well, it's done now,' Reggie said, getting to her feet and taking her cup to the sink to tip out the remainder of the coffee with a flick of her wrist.

'Sometimes I worry about you, my girl.'

'You don't need to now. You're home and I'll just go back to doing as I'm told.'

'What's that supposed to mean?'

'Nothing,' she snapped.

'I think you better explain.'

'What's to explain? You just made it perfectly obvious that I'm not to be trusted alone to run this place. Fine. Clearly I'm no Brent. He never did anything reckless or impulsive,' she said sarcastically.

'What are you talking about?'

She was about to say 'nothing' once more but then stopped. She didn't know why she felt this overwhelming urge to provoke an argument—she was usually the first to avoid any kind of conflict—but her father's rebuke over something still so fresh hurt more than she'd anticipated. Deep down she knew it probably came from fear, the thought of what could have gone wrong and her own reaction to how close it had come to being a disaster. But logic took a back seat to her heightened emotions right now.

'The fact that Brent's mistakes are always swept under the rug and mine are the source of endless entertainment. I backed the tractor into the side of the shed *once* . . . What about Brent almost setting fire to the hay shed with a full year's worth of hay inside when he and his mates were drunk and making explosives? Or the time he crashed his car and wrote it off because he was speeding? But heaven forbid *I* do something wrong—I'm stupid and a disappointment.'

'Your father didn't say that.'

Reggie swung around to face her mother and saw her let out a small sigh. 'He was only worried,' Peg said gently. 'Tell her, Ray.'

''Course I was,' he said gruffly.

'Let's all sit down and start again, shall we?' Peg said with a cheerful smile.

'I've got to check on that cow in the yards,' Reggie muttered, heading towards the back door.

She was halfway across the gravel drive when she heard heavy footfalls jogging behind her. 'Wait up,' Tim said, catching her arm and making her stop and look at him. 'What was all that about?'

She gave an impatient huff, feeling tears beginning to gather in her eyes.

'Hey,' his voice softened and he stepped closer, gathering her into him. 'What's going on?'

'I don't know,' she said, shaking her head. 'I mean, he wasn't wrong—it *was* stupid going out there late in the afternoon the way I did, and you even warned me not to do it, but he doesn't get it. I'm still that sooky tender-heart who hates the thought of something hurting. I can't shake that—I try, but I'll never be able to farm the way Brent and Dad did. Deep down I know I'm not cut out to run this place and it kills me,' she said, swiping at the tears that had started to fall. 'I don't want to be a disappointment to him, but I think that's what he sees.'

'That's not true—I haven't been here that long, but even I can tell how proud your dad is of you. He knows as well as anyone else that you've been keeping this place going—single-handedly most of the time.'

'I don't know what's wrong with me,' Reggie said miserably. 'I never speak to my dad that way.'

'Maybe you've been stressing about the whole *us* situation too much.'

'Maybe.' She had been pretty on edge already and they had surprised her by coming home early. But that was no excuse. 'I feel really crappy for dragging Brent into it the way I did.'

Tim shrugged. 'I didn't know him, but from what I've gathered, he probably would have said all his stuff-ups were fair game. He seemed like a pretty easy-going fella.'

'He was . . . but still.'

'Come on, let's go check on that cow and then you can teach me how to drive a tractor. I'll even run into the shed if you want, just so you won't be the only one who's done it.'

'Teach you to drive—you were going to borrow the tractor and you've never driven one before?' she said, staring at him.

'I figured if I've driven a light armoured vehicle I should be able to figure out a tractor.'

'It was good you didn't use that to lead into the conversation. I . . . guess we should tell them about us.'

'I kind of think they already know,' he said, easing back so she could turn around in his arms to spot her parents on the verandah finishing their coffee. She spun back to look up at him with an accusing glare.

'Why didn't you tell me they were there?'

'I only just saw them myself.'

'Crap.'

'At least it's done now,' he said unhelpfully.

'No, now we're going to have to endure all the questions at dinner tonight. Mum's probably heading to the phone to start ringing everyone.'

'I can handle it. Don't worry.'

'That's what I do,' Reggie said miserably. 'I worry and then I bluff my way out of situations.'

'Good luck bluffing your way out of this one,' Tim said, leaning down to kiss her.

She meant to protest—she really did—but it felt too good to have his arms around her, and his kiss cleared her mind of everything else except the intoxicating high of being with him.

She didn't look back to see if her parents were still outside—she'd be hearing about it soon enough. For now, she was just going to stay outside as long as she could and cross that bridge when she came to it.

Chapter 31

Reggie kept herself busy outside for most of the day. After checking on a cow and finding no calf yet, she went with Tim to oversee the tractor work, which he of course picked up like a natural within five minutes.

When she took over some feed for the cattle in the late afternoon, she glanced up and realised her luck was no longer holding out. Glenda was heading down the track towards her with her dad on board.

Focusing on throwing out the hay and keeping her eyes firmly on the cow in front of her, Reggie felt stupid tears threaten once more.

'How's she going?' Ray asked gruffly as he pulled up.

'Earlier she was off on her own, doing a lot of walking and bellowing. It hasn't seemed to progress much though. She should have started calving by now, surely.'

'Leave her be. She'll calve in her own time. A watched pot and all that,' her dad said in his usual, unflappable way. He could always be relied upon to be a calm voice of reason, no matter the situation.

'I'm sorry about earlier,' Reggie said, the words rushing out in a hurry. 'I shouldn't have said all that.'

'Yeah, well, I didn't mean to come across the way I did either. All I could think of was that dog the day he almost had me . . . I don't scare easily—you know that—but there was something about that one. He was testing me. Getting way too brave for a wild dog. They usually avoid human contact, but that one . . .' Her father stopped and glanced across at her seriously. 'We should have shot that mongrel years ago, but we couldn't find him. If anything had happened to you, I'd never have forgiven myself.'

'You were right, I was stupid for going so late.'

'It was just a bit . . . spontaneous,' her father said with a twist of his mouth.

'I had Tim with me—I knew I was safe.'

'Hmm,' her father murmured, and the silence stretched out between them.

'I thought you liked him?'

'I do. Your mother thinks he's the bee's bloody knees,' he added. 'We just want you to be happy. And if that takes you off this place—then so be it.'

'I'm not leaving,' Reggie said, looking confused. 'Why would you think that?'

'You sounded pretty fed up with it all earlier . . . and I guess I should have been a bit more forthcoming with the encouragement . . . I just figured you already knew how proud I am of you,' he said, and Reggie felt a lump in her throat.

'I do . . . I mean I know you have been in the past with other things in my life—school and uni and work—I just . . .' She stopped and looked around, trying to find the right words. 'I love this place so much,' she said. She felt the burn of tears filling her eyes and swore silently. She didn't want her dad to see her cry like a baby—Brent wouldn't be crying. 'I know I can never be the farmer Brent was . . . or you are, but I want to learn. I want to be better and understand more. I don't want to disappoint you. I've had to learn how to do all the basic stuff and I've made mistakes, but I'm really trying, Dad, and I want to eventually learn how to do *everything*—not just be the farmhand forever. I don't want you to hire a farm manager. I want you to teach *me* how to run the place. The way you taught Brent.'

'I never meant to make you feel like you weren't doin' enough. You *have* been runnin' the place. You're way more than a farmhand. I guess I was wanted to make sure you weren't tied down forever. I wanted you to have options. If someone was managin' the farm, you could do more things you wanted to do. But I see now that you *have* been doing the things you wanted. You're bloody good with the livestock—I've been watchin' you. You've got a gentle way about you that calms the cattle. They respond to you better than they've ever done to me, or Brent for that matter. I can see you've been listening to everythin' I've told you and you want to learn . . . I don't know how much more I can teach you, but if you want to sit and listen to an old codger talk about boring farm stuff, then I'm happy to do it. That's how I learned from my old man, and how Brent learned from me. The rest is just getting out there and doin' it, and you do that already.'

'Thanks Dad,' Reggie said quietly. 'I'd really like that.'

She heard him give a quick sniff and turn away slightly, before straightening once more and adjusting his hat. 'I've had a word with young Tim, just so you know . . . I've said my piece and it's all I'll say on the matter.'

'You did *what?*'

'He knows where I stand on the situation,' Ray said and gave her a firm nod. 'Now, your mother sent me down to tell you dinner won't be long, so you better hurry up and finish out here or she'll skin us both alive.'

'Dad . . . what did you say to Tim?'

He didn't stop walking, just lifted a hand and waved before climbing into Glenda and heading back to the house.

The mood around the table at dinner was vastly different to how it had been that morning. It was good to have the air cleared and it felt like life was going back to normal—only it wasn't quite normal, now she was sitting at the table with Tim, the man she was sleeping with, not Tim, the guest, or Tim, the guy building the cabin . . . Now it was Tim, the man with the power to make her melt with one look, like a packet of Tim Tams left in the car on a hot summer's day.

As he was doing at this very minute.

He wasn't even trying to be sexy—in fact he was just talking to her father—and yet, as she watched him, running her gaze over the width of his shoulders and the expanse of his bare forearms as he cradled his beer in his hand, Reggie found herself remembering the salty, woodsmoke scent that had surrounded her as she'd kissed the side of his neck earlier; the way she'd nipped his collarbone gently then traced his warm skin with her tongue; the way he'd softly encouraged her with a low moan followed by a sharply indrawn breath. A shiver of longing ran through her at the memory.

'Reggie?' her mother prodded.

'Sorry?'

'I said, you and Tim should take a drive to the falls and have a picnic or something tomorrow. He hasn't seen them yet.'

'Oh. Yeah. Sure. We should,' she said quickly. She noticed Tim's raised eyebrow from across the table. God, even that was sexy.

As far as dinners with her parents went, this one was surprisingly normal, considering it had the awkward my-parents-now-know-I'm-sleeping-with-him thing. There were no embarrassing childhood stories brought up or photo albums dragged out from the hall cupboard—in fact it was remarkably civilised.

Talk eventually turned to the cabin, and Tim pulled out his phone to show her parents the recent photos of the interior.

'Oh Tim, this is looking wonderful,' her mother said excitedly.

'Yeah, it's come up pretty good.'

Reggie heard Tim's nonchalant reply but knew her mother's reaction had pleased him. She liked that quiet dignity of his. He paid attention to detail and took pride in his work—she'd seen that in the last few weeks of the renovation. He had every reason to be proud of the job he'd been doing, but he just took it all in his stride and went about his business.

'I'll drop those colour samples in tomorrow and let you have a look. Should be ready for painting in the next few weeks.'

'How exciting.' Peggy beamed. 'We should do something to celebrate the grand opening,' she said, clasping her hands together. 'We haven't done anything fun around here for far too long.'

There hadn't been much worth celebrating for the last few years, in fact there'd only been heartache over anniversaries and birthdays missed. Maybe it *was* time to start emerging from all the gloom and try to find some sun.

'What about an open day or something?' Reggie suggested tentatively. 'I've been thinking about the fly-fishing angle a bit, lately.' She looked across at her father. 'Dad I really think this is an area you could do a lot with.'

'Me? How'd you figure that?'

'Look how helpful you were to Tim when he first got here— he couldn't catch a cold before you showed him a few tricks,' she said, grinning at the indignant look Tim shot across at her.

'Hey!'

'Sorry, but you seriously had no idea,' she said with a chuckle.

'True . . . I guess.'

'But in all seriousness, sometimes it's not really about the fishing, is it?' she said more gently, and saw her father lower his gaze to the table before grunting in agreement. Tim also averted his eyes and fiddled with his spoon. 'There's all kinds of great incentives going on—there's men's shed and social golf and tennis days. I think trying to organise a group where men—or anyone really, can come and relax and maybe find some head space would really appeal to people.'

'I think that's a fantastic idea, darling,' Peggy said, nodding eagerly.

'We could maybe launch it with an open day out here—it would be a chance to show off the cabins as well as giving people a taste of fly fishing. We could even host a competition during trout season—make it an annual district drawcard.'

'Well I think that's getting a bit ambitious for right now,' her father said, sending Peggy a concerned look. Reggie realised she may have gotten a little bit carried away there. She didn't want to scare off her father before he'd even agreed to the social club thing.

'Maybe that's something we can look at down the track?' her mother suggested with a nod at her daughter. 'But it's a good idea,' she added.

'Okay. Fair enough. For now, we can just focus on an open day?' Reggie looked hopefully at parents in turn.

'Yeah. I suppose it can't hurt. But I don't know if anyone would turn up.'

'They will. Leave that bit to me,' Reggie said confidently. She already had an idea about where she was going to advertise and a plan to get her mother involved as well. It was the first time in ages that she'd witnessed a stirring of excitement from her parents, or at least from her mother, and Reggie began to feel hopeful that maybe this was the beginning of something great.

Chapter 32

'That went better than I was expecting,' Reggie said, picking at the tablecloth after her parents had said good night and left her and Tim alone at the table.

'You had doubts that it would?' he asked, sounding surprised.

'No, not really, I guess . . . I mean they both think you're amazing.' She shook her head. 'I just expected it to be a bit awkward now that they know . . . we're together, I suppose.'

'As much as I'm grateful your parents like me—it's kind of their daughter that I'm really hoping to win over.'

'I'm pretty sure you've won her over, too.'

He reached out and snagged her hand, holding it in his. His large thumb rubbed across the inside of her palm, sending a little shiver through her as he held her gaze. 'Then my plan worked,' he said, narrowing his eyes. 'Win over the parents and the daughter will follow.'

'You poor fool—you don't even realise you've just dug yourself a hole. You're stuck with them now.'

'I can think of worse fates, to be honest,' he said. His voice turned serious. 'Your dad came to see me earlier.'

'Oh God,' Reggie groaned.

'No, it was fine . . . it wasn't like that,' he said, then grinned. 'I mean, at first I was a bit worried—he can be intimidating, your father,' he added dryly. 'And he did give me the talk about what would happen if I hurt his little girl,' he said, wincing slightly, which made Reggie shut her eyes in dismay. 'Then he shook my hand.' Reggie opened her eyes and watched as a myriad of emotions seemed to race across his face.

For a long moment he didn't speak, but when he did, his eyes met hers and she saw a sheen in them and had to blink quickly to keep the tears from her own.

'He shook my hand and he said, "Welcome to the family, son."'

Reggie understood the significance of the gesture to a man who didn't have a family of his own or a father to help him through the tough times. Wordlessly she stood up and slid onto his lap, hugging him tightly. She wasn't sure how long they sat there, but eventually the old clock on the mantle struck the hour and Reggie realised how late it was.

'Come on,' she said, holding out her hand as she stood up.

'Your bed or mine?' he asked, pulling her back against him.

'Yeah, I'm not ready to have sex under my parents' roof just yet.'

'Good point. Mine it is.'

Later, as Reggie was snuggled under the blankets and tucked into Tim's body, she woke up and gave a reluctant sigh as she prepared to get out of bed.

'Where are you going?' Tim murmured drowsily against her hair as she tried to slide away without disturbing him.

'I've got to go and check on the cow.'

'Now?' he protested. 'It's like three in the morning?'

'Go back to sleep, I won't be long,' she said, kissing him softly.

'I'll come with you,' he said, throwing back the covers and feeling about for his clothes.

'You don't have to.'

'I know. I want to.'

'Are you going to do this every time I have to check on a cow?' she asked, amused by his tousled hair and sleepy-eyed expression.

'Depends how often you check on a cow.'

She chuckled as she pulled on her clothes and shrugged into her warm coat, making a note to leave her gumboots at Tim's place in future as she pulled on a pair of good boots and hoped she didn't get them too dirty. 'Please let this be an unassisted delivery,' she whispered to herself. She seriously didn't want to ruin her boots tonight.

'I love a moonlit night,' Reggie said as they walked through the gate and along the track that led to the top paddock where she'd put the cattle.

Tim blew into his cupped hands. 'I love it a bit more when I look at it from under a warm doona.'

'Oh, come on, big, tough army guy. I would have thought you'd be in your element.'

'Seriously—no one likes freezing their nuts off out in the cold.'

'I'm feeling a little disillusioned right now.'

'I promise I'll show you how big and manly I am once we get back inside where it's warm.'

'I think the damage has already been done,' Reggie said in a haughty tone, before reaching another gate and shining the high-powered torch around the paddock, looking for any sign of an animal in distress. Bright eyes glowed back at her, followed by a few low moos.

'How can you tell which one you're looking for?' Tim asked dubiously, standing beside her.

'She's the only one without a calf,' Reggie replied, swinging the torch a little wider and getting excited when she found her away from the main herd. 'Yes.'

'What?'

'She's off on her own, which usually means she's about to deliver,' she said, narrowing her eyes as she moved the torch over the animal, '. . . or she's already had it!' she finished victoriously, spotting four tiny legs huddled behind the bigger cow. 'Good girl.'

'Thank God for that,' Tim said. 'I was *not* looking forward to another experience like last time.'

'To be honest, neither was I. But it's funny,' she said, as they turned away from the fence to head back, 'I've always been so terrified of having to assist in a delivery—so scared of stuffing it up. And now, after last time, I feel different.'

'You were impressive.' Tim slid his arm around her waist as they walked. 'It was one of the most awesome but *seriously disgusting* things I've ever witnessed.'

Reggie chuckled and rested her head against his shoulder as they ambled along. The sky was clear and cold and the moon shone down brightly, covering everything in a silvery, luminous blanket. There hadn't been a wild dog sighting since the pack leader had been shot. Her father thought they'd most likely moved on. It would be nice not to have to worry about every new birth being a potential kill for a while.

'Your idea about the fishing thing,' Tim said after a few moments, 'with your dad . . . I think it's a really good idea. Especially for blokes. When you have to be still and quiet, it gives you room to think. I know loads of guys this would be good for.'

'As in military guys?'

'Yea, others like me . . . and Deano and the boys. I don't know if it would have made a difference to them or not, but I know it helped me process a lot of stuff I'd been struggling with. I reckon there's a market for this kind of stuff, if you ever wanted to go down that track.'

'Like a wellness retreat for returned service personnel?' she asked. The idea definitely appealed to her.

'Yeah, I don't know anything about all the wellness mumbo jumbo, but having a place where you can come and stay in a cabin and fish with a bunch of other blokes who've been through the same kind of stuff—a chance to decompress or something—I reckon that would be helpful to a lot of people.'

Reggie stayed awake for a long time after they returned to their warm blankets, mulling over Tim's idea and listening to his breathing even out.

The next few weeks flew by in a blur of painting with oddly named shades like Salty Tears and Divine Pleasure and adding last minute finishing touches to the little cabin.

It was hard to believe it was done.

Tim had mixed feelings about the whole thing. He'd felt nervous—after all, Brent MacLeod had left some pretty big shoes to fill and this had been his baby. He hoped Ray and Peggy would be happy with the end result. The project had become special to him, too. He'd never met Brent, but he'd developed a lot of respect for him professionally after picking up where he'd left off. He admired Brent's craftsmanship, and also him personally, as the brother of the woman he was developing serious feelings for. He wondered if it should feel a bit creepy that he'd taken over parts of the guy's life. He lived in his shed, shared meals with his family and was now finishing his building job . . . but, somehow, he didn't think Brent would hold a grudge. He liked to think that he and Brent would have got on well if he'd still been alive. Tim cared about Reggie and thought he was making her happy, so surely that would have been enough to cement a friendship.

Which brought him to his next problem: what happens next?

As the job drew closer to completion, he'd felt himself becoming anxious about what he'd do once it was done. He'd been telling the truth when he'd told Reggie he didn't really need much to live on. He had a tidy nest egg from his army payout and owned two investment properties he'd bought over the years—if growing up in poverty had a silver lining it was that from a young age he'd vowed not to end up like his mother, living hand to mouth and owning nothing. He'd studied investing once he was earning his own money and realised he was actually good at it.

He didn't have to worry about his future. He was happy working for whomever he wanted, when he wanted, knowing the whole time that he had the means to retire early if he felt like it. But he also knew that he wouldn't. He'd go crazy with nothing to do.

He'd been toying with the idea of starting his own business up here once he finished the cabin, maybe contracting himself out around the district. He couldn't live in the MacLeods' shed forever—he wanted to have his own place, something to be proud of that he could share with Reggie. Maybe he'd buy a small bit of land somewhere nearby so Reggie could still be close enough to her parents and help out with the accommodation side of the business but take it a bit easier. He knew Ray wanted to hire a manager so she wouldn't have to work so hard on her own and, if he had his own place, then that would free up Reggie to move in with him.

The thought made him feel a bit giddy. He'd never met anyone he could honestly see any kind of future with before he met Reggie. At one point he wasn't so sure he even *had* a future; things had been pretty dark there for a bit. But now, whenever he thought about Reggie and a future . . . it just made sense. *She* made it make sense.

He knew it was all happening fast, but even when he tried to slow down and think rationally it always came back to the same thing—he wanted to be with Reggie. Today, next week, next year . . . twenty years from now. *He* knew what he wanted. The only problem was, he had no idea if Reggie wanted the same thing.

He'd been too chicken to bring it up with her directly and she never really had either—they rarely spoke about what would happen after the cabin was finished. Now, they'd have to start talking about it. His work here had run out and there was no way he was going to become some kind of freeloader.

Things would be very hectic for the next little while. Preparation was in full swing for the open day, so he probably wouldn't get a chance to bring the subject up for a few more weeks. Maybe by the time everything settled back down he'd have come up with a plan. He hoped so—he'd been putting out a few feelers locally with the trade places he'd been frequenting during the renovation, and there were a few promising nibbles. He felt confident that he'd be able to pick something up. If not, he'd just have to try harder.

Tim resisted the urge to wipe his hands on his thighs as he felt them go clammy. Get a grip, he told himself firmly.

He'd finished the cabin days ago but had put off making the announcement as long as he could. Each time he went to tell Reggie, he found himself hesitating and then would find some small, irrelevant thing that he needed to touch up or redo to make sure everything was perfect. However, the time had come to reveal the finished project, and for the first time ever he was completely petrified of disappointing the clients. Of course, these weren't just any old clients, these were the people who had come to matter to him the most. The woman he loved and her parents, who'd welcomed him into their family and helped heal some of the broken pieces inside him. This mattered.

What if they hated what he'd done? What if they thought he hadn't done as good a job as Brent would have done? The what-ifs had been keeping him awake at night more than he cared to admit.

He glanced over at Reggie as he stood with her and her parents outside the finished cabin. He felt her squeeze his hand reassuringly and managed a weak smile in return. At her silent prod, he forced himself to look over at her parents and clear his throat. 'Well, the moment of truth,' he said, stepping aside to unveil the timber plaque he'd put up next to the front door. Unlike the other cabins, this one had no specific tree planted nearby. But since it overlooked the tree-lined glen nearby it had been decided that it should be named Fairy Glen cabin, and inside it were small nods to mythical creatures and a subtle print of a Scottish landscape.

'I hope you don't mind, but I also added a second plaque,' Tim said, his nerves kicking back in with renewed vigour. He should have run it past Reggie first. Why hadn't he? Because at the time it felt like the right thing to do. He took a step towards the timber bench he'd specially built, revealing a brass plate attached to the backrest, and he held his breath as three sets of eyes locked onto the words.

'In memory of Brent MacLeod: son, brother, friend and visionary.'

No one spoke. Tim's heart sank as they stared at the bench in silence. Eventually Ray cleared his throat and looked up at him.

'That's a fine tribute,' he said gruffly.

'It's beautiful, Tim,' Peg said, reaching her arms up to him. 'Thank you.'

As her hug tightened around his neck, Tim felt his chest squeeze in response.

'Let's get a look at the inside,' Ray said, taking the handles of his wife's wheelchair and thankfully ending the emotional moment.

He felt Reggie's arms slip around his waist and turned to encircle her with his own.

'I wasn't sure if it was a good idea or not—' he started, falling quiet as he saw her head shaking as she looked up at him.

'It was perfect. Thank you. It means the world to Mum and Dad . . . and to me too. I know you were nervous about taking this on.'

'I just hope they like it.'

Reggie smiled as they heard her mother's small gasp of delight. 'I don't think you've got anything to worry about on that front.'

She kissed him gently before taking his hand and leading him inside.

Chapter 33

Reggie wondered, not for the first time in the last few weeks, what the hell she'd been thinking, planning this stupid open day.

Maybe if it had just stayed as the original plan of a family-friendly, come-along-and-have-a-fish kind of event, everything would have been fine, but it had gone from a little do to a full-fledged event.

They now had a baby farm animal display, with her mother sourcing a few dairy poddy calves from one of the CWA ladies who owned a dairy down the road, as well as an assortment of rabbits, guinea pigs and ducks. Even Henny Penny the chook had been roped in, and Reggie had given up trying to talk her mother into seeing reason about the whole thing. 'What if we get sued because some kid gets bitten?' she asked, feeling exasperated after finding out she would have to find yet *another* enclosure for the delivery of two goats and a sheep that had just turned up.

'Jenny Crawford has all the insurance organised,' Peg answered cheerfully, waving her daughter's concerns off without batting an eyelid.

'Well is Jenny Crawford coming to clean any of these enclosures before the event?' Reggie muttered. The open-ended shed had become a livestock pavilion with enough animals to put Noah to shame.

'Stop being such a grump. You're sounding more and more like your father. The kids will love it.'

'It was supposed to be about the cabins,' Reggie reminded her.

'And it will be, but we have to get people out here—we need to draw out the grandparents and parents and we can do that through the kids,' her mother said. 'Oh, which reminds me, the jumping castle man will be here early in the morning to set up.'

'The *what?*'

'Kids love jumping castles.'

Dear God. It was turning into a bloody sideshow alley.

'So, we'll set up the marquees for the great bake-off over here,' her mother continued, pointing from the verandah towards the open area. 'And the jumping castle over there near the petting zoo,' she said, consulting her clipboard.

As frustrated as Reggie was over the expansion of the whole event, she was happy to see her mother blossoming back into her old self. Peg had got in touch with Birdie Nelson the day after they'd talked about doing something and suddenly there were open day meetings and cake-stall baking days—CWA women coming and going and an endless number of phone calls. Through it all, Peggy was back in her absolute element.

Maybe she *had* been hanging around her father too much, Reggie thought as she bit back a groan after her mother mentioned yet another thing before heading inside to make a phone call.

She'd wanted her parents to be more involved, Reggie reminded herself. *Just go with the flow*, she told herself, doing her best to ignore her twitchy inner eye.

Reggie spotted her father driving Glenda towards her, noted the cheerful grin on his face and bit back another groan. *What now?* The last time her father looked this happy with himself he'd just bought a horse from a breeder and discovered it was in foal, getting a two-for-the-price-of-one deal.

'I've just released the new stock of trout into the dam,' he said, turning off the engine.

Okay, well that wasn't too bad, she thought, preparing to release the breath she'd been holding. *Wait a sec. . .* 'But we released the tagged ones yesterday,' Reggie said, frowning.

'Yeah.' Her father nodded and chuckled. *He was chuckling!* 'But I had a thought this morning, we've got the five numbered ones that win the prizes, but I reckon we need a couple of runner-up prizes—something that'll give people a bit of a laugh.'

Sirens started shrieking in her head. 'Dad. What did you do?'

'As an added bonus, there are now two extra chances to win with what I like to call the Cranky Women's Association tags . . . Instead of numbers, they each have the name of a cranky local woman.'

'Dad!' Reggie stared at him. 'You can't do that—the whole day is being pretty much run by the CWA.'

'Nah, they'll get a laugh out of it—trust me, I can't wait to see Big Bertha and Mad Marge get pulled outta the dam.' He chortled at the thought.

Reggie stared at her father in horror. 'Tell me you *didn't* put that on the actual tags . . .'

'It's all in fun.'

Reggie was trying to envisage Bertha Cravet and Marge Biswell chuckling as they had photos taken for the newspaper alongside fish named in their honour . . . She wasn't sure she'd ever seen the two women do more than complain about how hot it was or shake their heads about the youth of today. She was pretty sure they wouldn't be seeing the funny side of it—at all.

'Dad, Mum is going to kill you if she finds out what you've done, you know that right?'

'Nah, she'll be apples.'

This was so *not* going to be apples. She watched her father drive off still laughing to himself, and tried counting to ten while taking deep breaths.

'Tell me again why we're out here in the middle of the night, sneaking around like undercover agents?' Tim grumbled.

'If only undercover agents fished for trout! We have to catch those last two tagged fish Dad put in before anyone does tomorrow,' Reggie said, casting again into the dam.

'Got one,' Tim announced, and at any other time she'd be congratulating him, but not tonight. She was on a mission. Holding the torch and wielding a net, she scooped the slippery, thrashing fish out of the freezing water, swearing when she couldn't find a tag of any sort.

'Seriously?' he complained. 'That's the third one I've caught and it's not the right one?'

'You'll just have to fish harder,' she snapped.

'Is it even possible to fish harder?'

This was ridiculous. She knew that, only she didn't know what else to do. Her mother was going to be mortified if those fish were caught tomorrow. She could cheerfully strangle her father right now if he were here.

'Get the net,' Tim said soon after, and she shone the torch on the water and readied the net. The slithering, splashing trout flailed about, but Reggie's spirits rose when she caught sight of a red tag. 'Big Bertha'. Yes! They quickly removed the tag and released the fish, who vanished immediately back into the depths of the dam.

Reggie's fingers were numb from the cold water and she could smell trout on herself. She looked across at Tim, wearing a beanie and huddled into his thick waterproof jacket, and felt a sudden surge of . . . She blinked uncertainly as the truth of what she'd just discovered ran through her, making her fingertips tingle. *No, that had to be frostbite*, she thought, shoving her hands into her pockets and scrunching them into fists. Surely she couldn't really be in love with him? It had barely been a few months. Maybe it was just gratitude—pure and simple. This man had done so much for her family and they were definitely growing closer with every day they spent together, but surely calling it love was jumping the gun?

Reggie tried to shake out all the jumbled thoughts running through her head, crouching down to pour two steaming mugs of coffee from a thermos. Her hands gratefully circled the enamel mug, soaking up the warmth as she sat beside Tim.

'This is kind of romantic,' he announced after a while.

'Oh yeah. The stink of trout and onset of hypothermia is a real turn-on,' she said.

'Okay, Debbie Downer,' he said. 'I meant most guys would be pretty chuffed to be out fishing with their woman.'

'Their *woman*?' she repeated.

'Their Sheila?'

'Their significant other?'

'Well, okay, if you want to get all fancy about it, I suppose.'

The sounds of the night echoed around them for a few moments. Frogs croaked and the occasional bird called out amid crickets and insects singing their shrill little serenades.

'So, what exactly *are* we?' Reggie asked, breaking the silence.

'What do you want us to be?' he countered.

'That's what I'm asking you,' she said, her fingers tightening around her mug.

'I guess I want us to be something . . . serious.'

Slowly her grip loosened a little.

'I wasn't looking for someone,' Tim continued. 'I kind of figured I'd end up being that cranky old geezer living by himself in the backwoods somewhere.'

She grinned at the image, but found herself waiting for his next words.

'Then I found you,' he said simply.

'Will you still be a cranky old geezer?'

'Probably. But hopefully I won't be living by myself.'

She'd been trying to imagine what life here would be like once Tim left, and it'd been too depressing. She knew she could go on as before if he did leave—after all, she'd gone on without her brother. It hurt, every single day, but she'd proven she could continue living even with a broken heart. She had no choice but to live without Brent, but she could *choose* whether or not to have a future with Tim.

'Catch me that second fish and you've got yourself a deal,' she said, shrugging.

'Oh sure—no pressure. Like the bloody things just jump on your hook—' he started, just as his line tugged and he snapped his hand back quickly.

For a moment she just stood there and stared, then his urgent, 'Grab the net!' jolted her into action. *There is no way this is going to be the other fish*, she told herself as she shone the torch down on the fish that was flipping and twisting in the net in the shallows at her feet. A red tag caught in the beam of light and Tim gave a low chuckle. 'What are the chances?'

Reggie shook her head slowly and sent a brief glance up at the blanket of stars above them. This had Brent written all over it. 'Well, I guess that's decided then.'

Tim was still chuckling as they packed up their gear and headed home.

Chapter 34

The morning of the open day dawned clear and blue and the wind had all but disappeared. It was an omen, Reggie decided as she finished her chores and fed the extra mouths in the petting zoo, which now consisted of an alpaca, three baby goats, two sheep, three poddy calves, a duck and seven ducklings, a miniature Shetland, three piglets and Henny Penny. All that was missing was a partridge in the pear tree.

CWA ladies began filtering in early and they dragged along their ever-compliant husbands, who were put to work erecting borrowed marquees and setting up cake stalls. It felt like set-up day at the local show, especially when the jumping castle guy started up his generators.

'Your mum sure knows how to throw a party,' Tim said, coming up beside her.

'Yep. No such thing as half-hearted around here. What have you been roped into doing?' Reggie asked, looking over at him.

'I'm helping out with the trout tag competition,' he said, nodding over at the dam where there was a tent for the officials. 'To be honest, after last night I really don't feel like looking at another damn trout today. I think my fingers still have frostbite.'

'You did a great job. I'm proud of you,' she said, giving him a kiss.

'Are you talking about catching the fish or . . . later?' he asked.

'Both. You had an extremely manly night all around,' she assured him.

'Reggie, dear!'

Reggie groaned as she looked over her shoulder to find Bertha Cravet marching towards her.

'I just remembered I have something to do,' Tim murmured. He was already several steps away before Reggie could even attempt to grab hold of him.

'Morning,' Reggie said, bracing herself for whatever was to come. From experience, she wasn't expecting it to be anything fun.

'So, I see you and the young man have become an item?' Bertha said.

'Ah, yes,' Reggie replied, caught off guard by the question.

'What did you say his name was again, dear?'

Bertha knew damn well that Reggie hadn't introduced them earlier. For very good reason. 'Tim,' Reggie said, desperately trying to think of a way out of this interrogation. 'Tim Warbois,' she added hastily, knowing that would be the next question from the woman's pursed lips.

'I see,' Bertha said tapping a pudgy finger against her lips, 'I can't place the family—not from around here then?'

'No, he's up from the city. Was there something I can help you with, Mrs Cravet?'

The nosey woman blinked, before seeming to remember why she'd called out to Reggie in the first place. 'I'm trying to find your father,' she said. 'I know he's avoiding me. I have a list of jobs I need him to do.'

'Oh. Well, I'm sure he's around here . . .' Reggie said, as a movement at the side of the machinery shed caught her eye and she spotted her father making his way around to the back, 'somewhere.'

'When you see him, tell him I need him immediately.'

'I most definitely will,' Reggie assured the woman, who sent one final irritated glance around before huffing away. 'Not,' Reggie tacked on the end under her breath.

People began to arrive and the area set aside for parking soon filled. Reggie had to open the gate to another paddock. She'd decided to take advantage of the occasion and had ordered some new signage for the stud, hurrying to have them hung on the yards nearby and out the front, advertising River Styx True Blue Southern Cross Stud. Last night she'd decided to bring a few of the cows and calves, along with Big Wally, into the yards to show them off. It wouldn't hurt to have them on display for some of the local farmers who'd be dragged along for a family day out.

Her father's voice boomed from the borrowed speaker system the CWA ladies had managed to secure, and Reggie found herself grinning as she listened to her dad getting into his role as MC for the day, or, as Reggie liked to think of it, considering this whole thing had become more like a three ring circus, the ring master.

'There's still plenty of time to enter the great River Styx bake-off—a hotly contested competition,' Ray announced. 'It looks like there are lots of entries in already—nice to see the CWA won't be having a clean sweep. And I have to say, judging by the quality of the items so far, I do believe we might be giving Birdie Nelson a run for her money.' He chuckled as the woman in question shook her fist good-naturedly from her position inside the bake-off tent.

Glancing down at his clipboard, Ray went on, 'And the trout tag will be kicking off shortly and running all day. Try your luck at catching a tagged trout and win a prize. We've got some pretty snazzy fishing gear up for grabs, as well as a couple of nights' accommodation right here on River Styx.'

'Your father sounds like he's really getting into it,' Peg said, placing two containers she'd carried on her lap up onto the table.

It was unexpectedly wonderful to see her mother out of the house and venturing into the growing crowd with her new all-terrain wheelchair. Her mother had been restricted with how far she could venture across gravel and grass and her father had just yesterday solved the problem, proudly unveiling the new wheelchair he'd hired for the occasion.

'It looks rather impressive, doesn't it,' Peg had said, after staring at it in surprise. The rugged wheels and sturdier frame were vastly different to her current chair.

'Think of it as a four-wheel drive for outside,' Ray had suggested, patting the handles of the chair fondly.

Reggie found herself needing to blink back the sting in her eyes as she looked at her mum now. 'Yeah, I think he's found his calling.'

'Let's just hope he took my advice on ditching the dad jokes. Well, I better keep rolling,' she said, sending Reggie a cheeky grin, something she hadn't seen in forever from her mother.

Reggie made her way into the animal pavilion, took in the chaos that only a bunch of baby animals and a shed full of excited children can produce, and decided going in there was a big nope. As she did an about-turn, she almost ran into someone and automatically apologised, her polite smile widening into a genuine one as she realised who it was. 'Sarah?'

'I was hoping I'd bump into you today.' The tall, red-haired woman grinned. On her hip she carried a toddler with wide brown eyes, and holding her hand was another little girl, about four years old, who was staring up at Reggie curiously with the biggest bluest eyes she'd ever seen.

'I can't believe you're a mum,' Reggie said, dragging her gaze from the two children and back to the woman who'd been one of her best friends in high school. 'How have you been? What are you even doing here?' As far as Reggie knew, Sarah's parents had left the district years ago.

'We're at Tamworth now. I saw the ad in the newspaper and decided to come for a drive. I've been meaning to get in touch for ages, but . . .' She sighed, nodding at the two children. 'Half the time I don't even know what day it is,' she said, shrugging a shoulder.

'It's so good to see you,' Reggie said. 'Tell me everything. What have you been doing?'

'Well, having babies lately,' Sarah said, then pulled the toddler on her hip away to show Reggie her baby bump.

'Oh my goodness!' Reggie gasped excitedly. 'You're going to have your hands full.'

'Tell me about it. Josh and I both wanted a big family, but I'm starting to question the wisdom of having them all so close together now. What about you? Do you have any kids yet?'

Reggie shook her head. 'No. I haven't got around to that bit yet,' she said with a smile. Her gaze wandered the crowd over near the dam and found Tim, a head taller than everyone else around him. She wondered what his thoughts would be on starting a family. *Talk about the cart in front of the horse,* she thought. Nearby she watched a man kneeling down beside a small child, helping him cast his line. She felt a small tug at her heartstrings, picturing Tim doing the same someday in the future, then shut that line of thought down, filing it away for another time.

Sarah's smile wobbled a little. 'I'm so sorry about Brent. Mum and Dad told me about it—and your parents' accident. I guess you've had your hands pretty full too.'

Reggie didn't want to dwell on the sadness today—not when this had been the first time things had begun to feel optimistic. 'So, three kids,' Reggie prompted, changing the subject back to something happier.

'Four, actually,' Sarah corrected. 'Our eldest, Byron, is over at the fishing comp with Josh. They're both mad fishermen, so it was pretty easy to convince them both to come along today.'

'You'll have to book a weekend up here during trout season, they'd love it.'

'That sounds like a great idea. We were admiring the cabins earlier.'

'Give me a call if you decide to book and I'll give you mates' rates,' Reggie said with a wink.

'I'll do that. It'll give us a chance to catch up some more.'

Reggie left her friend at the petting zoo with a promise to join her later when she was called away to help out at the bake-off stall.

'Well, ladies and gentlemen,' her father's voiced boomed over the loudspeakers, 'it's time to see who our bake-off winners are. The judges have spent a considerable amount of time deliberating over the entries,' he said, wiping at the corners of his mouth. 'Apparently we had to leave some for everyone else to buy after the judging . . . Make sure you stop by the bake-off stand before you head home today. There will be cake and tea or coffee available until sold out. All money raised is going to the CWA's Disaster Relief Fund, with which these ladies provide assistance during fires, floods and drought—they do a truly amazing job.'

A round of applause followed as the crowd swelled around the bake-off tent. 'Now, let's put everyone out of their misery and announce the winners,' Ray said, shaking open the sheet of folded paper he'd been handed and holding it at arm's length to read it. 'The winner of the inaugural River Styx Great Bake-off is entry number four,' he announced, turning the page to find a corresponding name, and then glanced up with a stunned look. 'Tim Warbois!'

Chapter 35

Reggie's head snapped around to see Tim making his way from the back of the crowd, wearing a sheepish grin as he stopped in front of the bake-off stall and shook her father's hand.

'Well, this is a first! Well done son, you out-baked some of this district's best cake makers,' Ray chuckled, before glancing back down at the page. 'Tim's entry was a moist chocolate mud cake. Just so you know—you lost a point for having the word "moist" in the title. Rookie mistake, kid,' Ray said, before handing over an envelope. 'Second place, with an apple tea cake, is Marge Jenson, and third place is Birdie Nelson with her famous jam and cream sponge cake.'

The winners came forward, all beaming as the local newspaper journo, whom Reggie had invited along, snapped a photo and jotted down a few notes. Reggie swapped a glance with her mother and shook her head as they helped cut the huge array of cakes into single serves and prepared for the onslaught of customers ready for their morning tea.

'Did you know Tim was entering the bake-off?' she asked her mother, passing her a slice of cake to cover.

'I had no idea. He was dropping off entries from people arriving earlier this morning—he didn't mention one of them was his own. A man of many talents,' Peggy said, raising her eyebrow suggestively. Reggie did her best to ignore her.

Reggie and the two other ladies serving were kept too busy to dwell on anything for the next hour as all the bake-off cakes, plus the extras her mother and the CWA ladies had supplied, flew off the table. Once it quietened down, she made two coffees and headed down to the fishing tent to find Tim. Reaching up on her tiptoes, she placed a kiss on his lips before handing him his cup. 'Congratulations Mr Bake-off Champ.'

'You didn't know I could bake, did ya,' he said, looking more smug than she'd ever seen him before.

'I have to say, I did not see that coming. The only person more surprised than me was probably Bertha Cravet. She did *not* look happy,' Reggie said, wincing.

'Yeah, I've kind of been avoiding her, I did hear a rumour there might be an appeal launched—apparently sleeping with a judge's daughter could be a conflict of interest,' he said dryly.

Reggie grinned then shook her head. 'But seriously, I have to say it is kind of sexy—a man who can bake, catch trout under pressure *and* wrap parents around their little finger. Is there no end to your talents?'

'Should I be worried that you haven't mentioned my skills in the bedroom yet?' he murmured, lowering his head closer to her ear.

'I didn't want to give you a big head.' She shrugged. 'I am bummed that I didn't get to taste this award-winning mud cake though. It went within the first few minutes.'

'Good thing I made two then,' Tim said with a cocky grin.

'Of course you did.'

'Always have a plan B,' he said, tapping his temple.

'Well don't let Mum know, she'll make you bring it out. The cafe has sold out of practically everything and they still have the afternoon tea trade to do.' It seemed impossible considering the amount of baked goods the women had delivered during set-up.

'Which reminds me, your dad wants me on the barbeque, so I'd better head up there. I'll save you a sausage,' Tim said with a wink, handing over the clipboard so she could take over his place at the trout tag table.

The afternoon flew past and the people continued to roll in. As one wave left, another seemed to take its place, and Reggie began taking notes for the next open day—what they'd need more of, what worked, what didn't—to go over later.

As she headed up to the house from the dam at the end of the day, she spotted her parents sitting at a small table under the shaggy willow tree inside the house yard with a third person she didn't recognise. As she drew closer, her steps faltered a little and her stomach dropped. Felicity.

Reggie forced herself to move again after being frozen to the spot. As she got closer still, she saw her mother dabbing at her eyes, and her dad looked visibly shaken. *Oh, hell no,*

Reggie thought, anger replacing her shock. No one upset her parents—especially not someone like Felicity.

'What are you doing here?' Reggie demanded as she reached the table.

'Reggie—' her mother began.

'Hello, Reggie,' Felicity said quietly. 'I came to see Peg and Ray.'

'I think you should leave.'

'Reggie,' her father said in a warning tone, 'Felicity's been through just as much as we have. It's time we all moved past what happened.'

'Are you serious? She ignores us for almost two years then just shows up out of the blue and you're going to just forgive everything?'

'There's nothing to forgive,' her mother said softly. 'We all lost Brent.'

Reggie shook her head. '*We* lost him—Felicity left him.'

'There was more to it than that, Reggie,' her mother said, but Felicity stood up and smiled sadly.

'It's all right, Peg. Reggie's right. I should have come by sooner and tried to explain. I was too ashamed to face any of you. I've regretted how everything ended every day. I just wanted to say how sorry I am for leaving the way I did. I've wanted to check in on you both for so long, I just didn't want to cause anyone any more grief.'

Reggie watched her mother lean across and gently wipe away the tears that were falling from the other woman's face. She felt a sharp stab of something that felt a lot like betrayal. How could her mother be taken in so easily? Did she seriously think that spilling a few tears was all it took to erase all the hurt? Didn't they remember how heartbroken Brent had been?

'You don't owe us any apologies. What happened was between you and Brent,' Peg said, and she looked up at Reggie before focusing once more on Felicity. 'It was just a terrible shock to us all. You were part of our family and that's not something that simply goes away. We've missed you.'

Reggie watched Felicity's face crumple and Peg's hands clasp hers tightly on the table. Fighting a wave of emotion, which only confused her more, Reggie looked away. She didn't want to forgive and forget—it felt like a betrayal to her brother.

'I've missed you too,' Felicity said, drawing her hands away to search for a tissue in her handbag. 'I stayed away so I wouldn't cause you any more pain, but I should have done this much sooner. I'm sorry it took me so long.'

'You'll always be welcome here,' Ray said.

'Reggie?' Felicity said, looking up at her now. 'Do you think we—'

It was too much. 'I have to get back,' Reggie cut in abruptly. Her parents might be ready to forgive, but she wasn't. She wouldn't forget how this woman left her brother and ran straight into the arms Simon Parson. Reggie ignored the frown on her father's face and the almost pleading look her mother gave her as she turned away.

Her throat tightened and she squeezed her eyes closed. She was not going to cry. What was she even crying about? This whole thing was stupid. God, she was so tired of it all. Every time she thought she was getting a handle on all the pain and grief, something always came up to bring it all back again. Felicity was part of that pain and she belonged in the past. She didn't belong here anymore and she sure as hell did not deserve to be welcomed back by her parents like nothing had changed. Everything had bloody changed and none of it was fine.

Chapter 36

Reggie headed down to the stock yards and greeted a few people she knew. She felt the earlier tension slowly leaving her as she chatted about the cattle and answered questions from a few people who seemed keen to know more.

Some of the older farmers asked where her father was, wanting to talk cattle with him, and she'd briefly felt her confidence waver, but after calmly telling them he was tied up with something else, she jumped in to answer their questions. She knew all the facts and figures—she'd been the one keeping the records, after all—and she found herself gaining more and more confidence with each conversation.

She knew what she was talking about.

It stunned her a little bit when this realisation hit, then filled her with a quiet pride as she scratched Wally's massive head through the yard rails.

'Well there ya go, Wal,' she said softly after a farmer she had been talking to waved farewell and ambled away. 'We might be able to muddle our way through this thing after all, buddy.'

'So, this is the wonder bull?' a voice called out from behind her, instantly making Reggie clench her teeth.

It was bad enough that Felicity had decided to make an appearance—what the hell was Simon Parson doing here?

'Can't say I see what all the fuss is about,' he said, stopping a short distance away as he studied the bull in front of him.

'Doesn't surprise me,' Reggie sniffed. 'You never did have as good an eye for cattle as Brent.'

Just as she'd intended, the comment hit a nerve. For the briefest of moments, she saw a flicker of something mean cross his face and her mind flashed back to another occasion when she'd seen that look.

They'd been at a community fundraiser at the old hall when she was fifteen. She'd gone to the car to get her jumper when she'd overheard an argument between Simon and his father. She'd managed to stay out of sight until Mr Parson left, but the cold way he'd spoken to his son, and the way he'd pushed Simon into the side of the car as he'd berated him for something that had happened in the moments before she'd arrived, had stuck with her. She'd never seen Simon look so terrified, and she'd felt sorry for him. Fred Parson was infamous for his temper and most people dreaded dealing with him. On the way back inside, she'd spotted Simon sitting on the back steps of the hall by himself. At any other time she wouldn't have stopped but, after witnessing his father's wrath, that stupid soft spot of hers had pushed her to check on him.

In school he'd been the bully who never seemed to get detention. Simon always managed to worm his way out of trouble—lying if he had to, or using his father as some kind of threat if that didn't work. In that moment, though, he looked vulnerable.

'Are you all right?' Reggie asked quietly, and Simon snapped his head up—she caught the surprise and then embarrassment on his face, even in the shadows, before he smudged a fist across his cheeks and wiped the tears away. 'Your dad looked pretty angry,' she added, feeling helpless under his hard glare.

'What the hell would you know about anything?'

'Nothing. I just thought . . . never mind,' she said, backing up and regretting the decision to talk to him.

'You're MacLeod's little sister,' he said, slowly standing and walking down the steps towards her. 'Didn't anyone tell you little girls shouldn't be out in dark carparks alone at night?'

Reggie felt fear for the first time in her life that night. Never before had she ever been scared about going anywhere—not in their community. But all of a sudden she was terrified. Gone was the sad, lost look of a boy who'd been terrorised by his father and in its place was a cold mask with a snake-like smile.

He lunged forward faster than she'd anticipated and his hands gripped her arms as he pushed her roughly against the wall behind her, smashing his mouth against hers in a brutal kiss. Before he could do much else, the shock that had initially paralysed her suddenly dissipated and she lifted her knee straight up, hard, making him stagger backwards, wheezing as he clutched at his groin.

Reggie didn't look back, she just ran into the hall, straight into Brent, who'd come looking for her. One glance at her face and he immediately knew something was wrong, but Reggie was too scared of what might happen if Brent went after Simon, so she made him promise not to do anything. Two days later, Brent was suspended from school for fighting and refused to tell his parents why. But Reggie knew.

Knowing Simon had not only been kneed in the balls but also knocked out by her brother had been enough to wipe away any lingering fear she'd felt from that night. But, while she'd never dwelled on it, now and again when she saw his smug face she remembered how he'd tried to hurt her simply because she'd witnessed him looking weak.

Looking Wally up and down now, Simon's face was a picture of contempt. 'I think I'll stick with our Angus. Now that's *real* quality.'

'Yeah, I think you should stick with them too,' Reggie said, leaving childhood memories in the past and pushing away from the rails. 'Stay with safe and steady.'

'You're not your brother, you know, Reggie,' Simon called out. 'You really think you'll be able to handle all this?'

Reggie felt her earlier buoyant mood begin to deflate.

'Dad's willing to make an offer on River Styx whenever you're ready to admit this place is too much to manage. Tell your old man, all he's gotta do is ask.'

'We will die of exhaustion before Dad would ever agree to sell this place to a Parson,' Reggie told him darkly.

'Word around town is your parents aren't feeling very confident about you being in charge. Heard they were thinking of replacing you with a manager.' He shrugged before shooting her a sly grin. 'Tell your dad to think it over.'

Reggie held his look, refusing to give him the satisfaction of losing her temper, until he finally turned and walked away.

Jerk.

He was just trying to get a rise out of her; to hit her where he knew it would hurt. She knew that. Logically. But it still stung, and a tiny part of her worried that maybe it was true.

With only a few straggler guests left wandering about, the open day team started pulling everything down. The trout tag had been a huge success, and Reggie was happy that the local reporter managed to get photos of the winners, which would give the open day and the cabins a plug as well, even though her father was scratching his head, wondering what happened to the elusive CWA fish. 'I was looking forward to that presentation,' he mumbled as they said goodbye to the reporter.

Reggie avoided Tim's gaze, certain she'd never manage to look suitably innocent, and hurried to help carry tables and folding chairs to the waiting cars and trailers parked nearby. Animals went home with their owners, and Reggie was relieved she wouldn't have as many feed buckets to make up in the morning. Though it crossed her mind that she might miss the alpaca. Maybe down the track she could add a couple for the visitors to feed . . .

Stop it, she told herself firmly. *One mess at a time.* They were in the middle of getting a stud up and running—she wasn't going to have time to add more farm animals to the mix anytime soon. She wasn't insane.

Chapter 37

A few days later, Reggie stood on the verandah after waving off Matt, the stock agent. He'd left her with a lot to ponder. The meeting her father had mentioned a while ago had finally come around, and it had brought up quite a lot of things to discuss. Brent's plan of buying, registering and breeding the cattle had been momentous enough, but it turned out that was only the beginning.

'How'd the meeting go?' Tim asked when she came inside for lunch.

'Not bad.'

'You don't sound excited by it?'

'It was all very positive—actually the stock agent was pretty excited. Brent was on to a good thing,' she said, then sighed.

'But?'

'But it all takes money.'

To meet the growing demand for the buyers the agent had lined up, they'd need to rapidly increase their breeding numbers. One way to do that would be to implant embryos from the True Blue cows into recipient cows, which they would need to purchase.

'So you just buy any old cow?' Tim asked.

'Well, any breed, as long as they're healthy.'

'Sort of like surrogate cows?'

'Exactly like surrogate cows,' she said, smiling. 'We give our girls hormone injections to stimulate superovulation so they release lots of eggs, inseminate them with Wally's bull juice and then flush out those eggs and implant them into our surrogate mums. That way we can get multiple births from all those eggs out of different cows and keep the bloodline, which in this case is the True Blue Southern Cross genes.'

'So, you basically have to buy a herd of healthy cows? That doesn't sound too bad, financially.'

'Well, it's not the best time to be buying, with prices so high, but it's more than that. We'd need to have a purpose-built undercover vet yard set up and be able to do on-farm flushing and transfer of embryos, but that requires specialised equipment and facilities. Then there's the vet fees,' she continued with a sinking heart, 'and the list goes on. And all this hinges on how well the steers we've been growing since last season perform. Ideally, we'll get a few competition wins in things like the Royal Easter Show or the Brisbane Exhibition grass-fed performance comp to get the stud name out there.'

'But the stock agent seemed positive?'

'Yeah. He's keen as to get behind it all. It's just going to take time. I think we're too far in not to take the plunge and breed like there's no tomorrow,' Reggie said. 'But I'd like to make sure we aren't getting any further into debt without some kind of safety net. I'd feel better if we waited for a bit to see what happens with the steers first.'

'What does your dad think about it?'

'He's not as impulsive as Brent, thank goodness,' Reggie said dryly. 'Dad's happy to wait and see. There's just so much riding on all this.' She looked up at Tim with a worried frown.

Tim slipped his arm around her and hugged her against him. 'I know it must seem like a lot to deal with, but you've got your parents . . . and me,' he added. 'You're not alone.'

She smiled, grateful for the faith he seemed to have in her ability, but the worry didn't budge.

'I got you something in town,' Tim said, leaning over to lift a large paper bag from beside the lounge and handing it to her.

She looked at him quizzically as she opened the bag and pulled out a long rectangle box. The kind of box she'd seen before. Reggie's eyes widened as she glanced up at him again, but other than grinning he gave her no explanation. Carefully, she lifted the lid and the heady fragrance of leather filled her nostrils as she stared down at the pale green boots with yellow sunflowers embroidered on them that Carol had tried to convince her to buy months ago.

'Do you like them?' Tim asked, sounding a little unsure of himself.

'They're gorgeous,' she whispered, touching them almost reverently. 'But I can't accept these. I know how much they cost.'

'I used the voucher I won for the bake-off.'

'But you should have used it for something you wanted to buy,' Reggie protested.

'It was something I wanted. Ever since that day Carol showed you them, I've wanted to go back in and buy them—I just hadn't gotten around to it till today.'

Reggie bit her lip as she reached in and pulled one of the boots out of the box. 'They're absolutely beautiful,' she told him, looking up and feeling as though her heart was actually going to burst with something that felt a lot like—dare she say it—love. For a moment she thought she might have said it out loud, as she saw his face soften and he leaned in closer to kiss her. Surely it was just the boots talking—that new-boot high she always felt. She pushed the thought away to consider later. Right now, she had some serious thank yous to deliver.

When they sat with her parents at dinner that night, Peggy passed Ray the potatoes, smiling across at Tim. 'We've heard enough about cows today, what did you get up to today, Tim?'

Reggie hadn't seen him since lunch and only now realised she had no idea what he'd been doing all afternoon.

'I went to see a bloke about a job,' he announced, and Reggie looked up from her plate to stare at him in surprise.

'Oh?' Peggy said. 'I didn't know you were looking for one.'

That makes two of us, Reggie thought. Well, technically that wasn't true. He had briefly mentioned finding work nearby, but she hadn't heard him say anything about it since—he certainly hadn't brought it up at lunchtime.

'Now that I've finished the cabin, I need something to keep me busy,' Tim said, and Reggie detected the slightest tone of something she couldn't quite put her finger on.

'Where? Doing what?' Ray asked.

'With a bloke from Armaglen who does a bit of maintenance and some renovation stuff. Just casual for now, but it's a bit of work.'

'We've got plenty work around here,' Ray pointed out.

'I'll still do whatever you need me to do around this place,' Tim assured him.

'If it's the money, I'm sure we can find a way to pay you. You shouldn't be working for nothing anyway,' Ray said, looking at Reggie.

'It's not that. You're already giving me board and most meals,' he said, pointing at his near empty plate. 'It's more to keep my hand in on the trade, really,' Tim added, looking like he wished he'd never mentioned it in the first place. 'Nothing's been decided yet.'

'Well, a man needs a job, I guess,' Ray muttered.

'I made a cake, so we can celebrate with dessert,' Peggy said.

'When do you *not* have a cake on hand, Mum?'

'You don't need a special occasion to have cake. Every day should be special and today just so happens to be Tim's special day.'

Reggie shook her head as she finished eating but her heart warmed at the happiness on her mother's face. It was nice to see her able to fuss over and dote on everyone again. It had been a long time since there'd been any coddling in the house.

❖

The crackle and occasional pop of the fire in the wood heater created a peaceful soundtrack to the pinkish-red hue thrown across the room by the flames dancing behind the heater's glass. Reggie's thoughts had been weighing heavily on her mind. Now that the cabin was finished, everything was going to change.

'What are you thinking about?' Tim asked quietly as they sat together on the couch.

Reggie hesitated. 'Why didn't you mention you were talking to someone about a job?'

'I didn't see much point until I found out if it was going to happen.'

'Is that what the boots were for? To distract me from the fact you hadn't mentioned finding another job?'

'No. I was just looking at some options.'

'Are you're going to take it?'

'I can't sit around here doing nothing all day now the cabin's finished.'

'You heard Dad, there's always plenty you can keep busy with.'

'Reg, I'm not a farmer. I need something to do that makes me feel . . . useful. Half the time I have no idea what you and your old man are talking about.'

Reggie pulled away to look up at him. 'If you don't want to do stuff around here, you don't have to. You can say no.'

'I don't mind helping out—all I'm saying is, to do it full time . . . I can't do all the stuff you do. I mean, I'm happy to lend a hand with the labouring side of things, but, honestly,' he said in a serious tone that made Reggie hold her breath, 'I really don't like cattle,' he finished in a rush, wincing as he held her searching gaze.

For a moment Reggie wasn't sure what to say. 'You don't like cattle?'

'At the risk of you losing all respect for me, I gotta come clean. Cattle kind of freak me out.'

Reggie continued to stare at him.

'I knew I should have kept my mouth shut,' he mumbled.

'They freak you out?' she parroted slowly.

'They have this weird way of looking through you while they chew—like they're sizing you up as they stare at you. I keep thinking they're trying to figure out the best way to mess me up.'

Reggie giggled as she pictured the scenario in her head. 'Seriously?'

'I know. It's pathetic, but there you are. You know my deepest, darkest secret.'

Good grief. 'Why didn't you say something sooner? You don't have to do any cattle work.'

'I don't mind helping out with the cattle work, all I'm saying is'—he gave an impatient huff '—I think your dad pictures me out there, working this place beside you. That's not what I want to do. Farming isn't something I want to do *full time*. Around here I just feel like the sidekick—like I don't really know what I'm doing most of the time. Getting a job I'm good at will hopefully make me feel less like some work experience kid and more like a functioning adult.'

'I didn't know you were feeling that way.'

He shrugged and said, 'I didn't know myself until recently. I was a bit lost there for a bit, but now I think I'm ready to get back into a routine again and I'd rather be doing something I know.'

'I get that,' she said, and she did. He was a builder—he'd learned a trade, it made sense that he'd want to be doing that rather than fencing and digging trenches and lugging feed bags around all day.

'I got used to you being around all the time. Everything's going to change.'

'It's only a bit of contract work—I'll still be around to help out around here,' he pointed out.

'I don't want you to feel like you have to work here.'

'Your parents refuse to let me pay any kind of rent, and I'm not about to become a freeloader,' he told her. 'So, I'm happy to pull my weight around the place in whatever capacity you all need.'

'I don't want to take advantage of you.'

'You can take advantage of me anytime you like.'

'I'm being serious,' Reggie said, biting back a smile.

'If I didn't want to do it, I wouldn't be staying.'

That niggling sensation stirred inside her again. She'd be lying if she said she hadn't been falling for him a little more every day, but where were they going? It was something she knew they'd both been putting off talking about but putting it off wasn't going to solve anything in the long run. If anything, it would only make it harder.

'Where do you see us a year from now?' she asked suddenly.

'This sounds like a job interview.'

'You're making decisions about some pretty big things—finding work in a new place, living here . . . being with me. I think it's only sensible that we be honest about what kind of future we have . . . if any.'

'If any?' He frowned, his face losing its earlier playfulness.

'It's something that's been playing on my mind a bit lately. How is this going to work? Picking up work here and there doesn't sound particularly fulfilling for a guy who's had an impressive army career and has a trade up his sleeve. What do you see in your future?'

For a moment he studied her face silently. 'I guess, honestly, when I think about a future, I see us together. Maybe I'll start a business and we'll buy our own place, where you don't have as much work to do. Somewhere with a couple of acres to put a few cows and horses without the pressure of all this,' he said, nodding his head towards the window.

Reggie felt her stomach drop.

'That's not what you see?' he asked when she didn't respond straightaway.

'Not really, no. It's what I've been butting heads with Dad about all this time. I'm exactly where I want to be. Doing what I want to do. I want to run *this* place. I want to be taken seriously.'

'I didn't say I didn't take what you do here seriously,' he said. 'I'd just like a place of our own. I don't want to be some bloke who snagged the daughter of a landowner and ended up living on their property.'

'You just admitted farming isn't what you want to do,' she said.

281

'I'll do whatever it is you need me to do—I just want to feel like I've contributed to something. I don't want anyone thinking I'm some kind of, I don't know, opportunist,' he said, grasping for the right word.

'No one thinks that,' Reggie said calmly, 'but you have to work out if this is really what *you* want. I don't think I could ever leave this place or my parents. I'm not saying I'd live under the same roof forever, but, until recently, this is where I needed to be to help care for them—I'm not moving away. They're getting older and I won't see them sell up and move somewhere they don't want to be just because this place is getting too much for them.'

Tim was quiet for a while. Reggie couldn't tell what he was thinking, which worried her.

'All I know is, I've never felt this way about anyone before,' he said eventually. 'Before I came here, before I met you, I was in a really dark place and now, for the first time in . . . I don't know, maybe ever,' he said in his deep, gravelly voice, 'I'm content. I'm excited about the future—hell, I can actually *see* a future. All I care about is that you're in it. With me. That's it.' He shrugged. 'I don't care what I have to do or give up, as long as you're there.'

Reggie felt a little bit of the doubt and worry in her heart melt away. She still worried that one day he would discover he'd sacrificed more than he'd bargained for and regret it, but, seeing the honesty in his face now, she knew he meant what he said. How could she ask for more than that? They both knew better than most that you couldn't always count on a future, so maybe there was no point in worrying about it.

When she leaned in to kiss him her lips were gentle—just a slow connection meant to reassure and comfort—but, as the kiss deepened, it soon built into something more, a fire that flared and began to burn out of control.

Clothes were removed and discarded without conscious thought, and their bodies soon found each other, fitting in a perfect gasp of pleasure. As the flames threatened to overtake her, Tim placed his hands on either side of her face and paused—she slowly opened her eyes, fighting the wave of yearning that surged inside her.

'This is what I want. *You*,' he said, in a deep tone that sent a cascade of longing through to her very core.

Later that night Reggie woke up, blinked and took a minute to orient herself. She wasn't sure what had disturbed her but she could hear the sound of an engine fading into the distance. Maybe it was the fact that there was never traffic heading from the national park through the middle of the night that had roused her from her sleep, but the dogs weren't barking so she snuggled deeper into the blankets and felt Tim's body immediately readjust behind her, holding her against him. 'What's wrong?' he murmured.

'Nothing, go back to sleep,' she said with a yawn, before feeling herself drifting off too.

Chapter 38

The next morning she opened her eyes to a dreary, grey-looking day and heard the sound of rain on the roof. It would have been the perfect day to lie in bed and listen to it, only she was a farmer and there was no such thing as a lazy morning.

She heard Tim groan as she slid out of bed then tucked the blankets back around him.

'Come back.'

'I can't. I have to move the cattle up this morning to get them ready for vaccinating and tagging tomorrow.'

'Fine,' he sighed, before pushing himself up in bed to watch her slipping on her jeans.

'You don't have to come. I don't need any help.'

'Yeah, but it's no fun staying in bed all by myself. Besides, there's method to my madness,' he said, reaching across when she sat down on the edge of the bed to pull her boots on.

'If you have help, the job'll get done faster and we can come back here and hide out for the rest of the day.'

'Oh, you poor, deluded city slicker,' Reggie said, shaking her head slowly at him.

'What? It's raining. You can't do much out there in the rain.'

'Maybe, if you're a tradie,' she said. 'Rainy days are for maintenance. There's a whole list of things Dad's got ready for this very occasion.'

'Aw man,' Tim said, lying back against the pillows, disheartened.

'Cheer up, at least we always go to bed early, so there's that.'

When Reggie came back into the shed leading her mare, Tim was up and dressed. He walked out with a mug of coffee and a vegemite toast sandwich for her to eat while she tacked up her horse.

'Are you sure you want to ride in the rain?' he asked doubtfully, eyeing the now saddled horse.

'It's not my favourite weather to be riding in, but horseback is the best way to bring the cattle in from where they are,' she said, then downed her coffee.

'Well, I'm drawing the line at riding a horse, but if it's any help I can ride a quad and lend a hand,' he said, taking her empty cup back from her.

'There's not much point in both of us getting wet.' She was touched he'd made the offer.

'If you think for one minute that I'm sitting in here, dry and warm, while you're out there working, you've got another think coming, lady. I thought we'd already established this earlier?'

'The wood chopping thing?' she asked, then grinned when he nodded. 'Okay, I admit, you earned yourself some brownie points that day, but you still didn't need to do it. You were a guest.'

'And now I'm an unqualified but extremely willing-to-learn farmhand who has a thing for the farmer's daughter and is pretty much keen to do anything to get to spend more time alone with her.'

'You really do have it bad,' she commiserated, shaking her head in mock sympathy.

'You have no idea,' he replied, grabbing her around the waist and pulling her against him.

'How can I say no to an offer like that?' she said after they shared a kiss that threatened to delay her preparations.

After handing Tim a radio, she whistled for the dogs as they headed outside, giving each of them a pat while she waited for Tim to get the quad bike out, then they headed off into the gloomy, grey-sky morning.

As she rode, Reggie thought back over the conversation they'd had last night about the future. While she was certain Tim knew what he was getting himself into, she wasn't convinced that the reality of their situation wouldn't cause problems once the novelty of their relationship began to settle into a routine.

How were you supposed to know?

You're not, a voice sounding suspiciously like her brother's whispered in her ear, and for a moment she almost thought someone was riding alongside her. It was true, no one could predict what was going to happen in the future—look at Brent and Felicity, she thought. They'd been together since high school and they were always supposed to end up married with a ute-load of kids. No one saw that break-up coming. She supposed that was the gamble you took when you fell in love. It was a pretty big gamble.

She watched Tim get off his bike up ahead to open the gate and felt that familiar glow start to radiate inside her once more. Maybe this was the one time she needed to ignore that cautious streak of hers and take a chance. *Attagirl,* the voice said, and this time she smiled.

They continued making their way through the paddocks towards the fresh pasture that Reggie had put the new mums and their calves into a few weeks earlier. Now that the threat of wild dogs seemed to have eased, she'd felt better about putting them back out this way where they had proper feed and she didn't need to throw out hay every day like she had been.

The rain had eased into an annoying drizzle, and she was glad of her trusty old oilskin coat that kept the rain from seeping into her clothes. The rain dripped off the brim of her Akubra and ran in little streams down her coat onto the ground. She hoped it wouldn't get any heavier until after they were back home. As they approached the gate for the last paddock, she waited for Tim to get back on his bike, her gaze searching for the cattle. Then she frowned.

That's weird, she thought, nudging her horse forward. It was a decent-sized herd, they shouldn't be hard to spot, and yet . . . *where the hell were they?*

'Where to now?' Tim asked as he pulled up a short distance away.

'They're supposed to be here,' she said, surveying the empty paddock. 'Can you head over that side and check the fences? I'll do over this way.'

They turned in opposite directions and headed along the fence line. It didn't make sense—these fences were in good shape and it hadn't been that long ago she'd checked them. Even though it had been raining, there shouldn't have been any storm damage with no wind about. Still, maybe a tree could have dropped a branch somewhere and created an opportunity for the cattle to escape. She just hoped they hadn't gotten too far or this was going to turn into a very long day.

The radio in her pocket crackled to life and she dug it out quickly.

'I found the hole, you better come over and take a look,' Tim said, and she turned her horse around and quickly crossed over to where she had spotted him on the other side of the paddock.

As she neared, her frustrated frown deepened. She swung down from the horse and stood beside Tim where he was crouched, touching the ground with his fingers. 'I don't think this fence broke . . . I think it was cut,' he said, looking up at her. 'There are boot prints on the ground.'

Reggie leaned down and stared at the indentations on the muddy ground, taking in the straight edge of the clipped barbed wire fence that lay sagging at her feet. Tim was right. This fence hadn't come down in any storm—it had been deliberately cut. She straightened and stared out at the clearing on the other side of the fence. A small area had been trampled and churned up, as if the cattle had been contained somehow in a square area marked out on the wet ground, but then there was nothing . . . no more cattle tracks, no more stomped vegetation. It was as though they'd vanished.

'Tyre marks,' Tim pointed out from beside her.

'Bastards!' Reggie snapped as she stared at the evidence before her eyes. 'They loaded them in a truck.'

'Is there access to this paddock from the road?'

'Yeah. This is national park. That's our corner boundary fence. There's a track that leads to the road that runs past the front of our place not far that way,' she said as they faced the direction the cattle must have been taken.

Reggie pulled out her phone and searched for the local police number, putting in a call and explaining the situation.

'This can't be happening,' she said as they waited for the police to turn up. 'They were our breeding stock—our whole breeding program is gone.' Then she suddenly gasped. 'Oh God . . . the bull. They took him too.'

'Hey,' Tim said, wrapping his arms around her. 'It's going to be okay.'

'It's not,' she said, feeling hollow. 'Brent paid a fortune for that bloody bull, money we didn't have. Everything depended this year on selling those calves. And now, not only do we not have the calves to sell, we don't even have the bull and breeders to start again.'

'Let's wait and see what the police say. Maybe they'll be able to track them down before they get too far.'

'Last night,' she said suddenly, pulling away slightly to look up at him. 'I woke up last night and heard a truck.' It had to be the noise that had woken her. They'd be hours away by now.

❖

A police four-wheel-drive came into view followed by her father's old ute, and Reggie's stomach turned. The call to the house after she'd phoned the police had been a hard one, and she dreaded the look of disappointment she was about to see on her father's face.

Two rather formidable-looking men in a dark blue shirts and jeans stopped in front of them and the older of the two put out his hand to Reggie and Tim. 'Hi. I'm Detective Senior Constable Pete Hume of the Rural Crime Squad and this is Constable Darrel Fisher. We'll be handling the investigation.'

Reggie shook their hands then switched her gaze to her father, who limped across to join them.

'Dad,' she started, but stopped when he shook his head and put an arm around her briefly.

'Bunch of thieving bastards.'

The two officers took a look at the fence and asked a number of questions before heading back to their vehicle to retrieve their equipment. They photographed the area, and then spent considerable time measuring and recording all the evidence they gathered at the scene and taking Reggie's statement. When the policemen told the three of them there was nothing else for them to do, they headed back towards the house to get the paperwork side of things organised to assist in identifying the cattle.

'I feel responsible,' Reggie groaned, dropping her head into her hands as they sat with coffees in her parents' living room.

'None of this is your fault, darling,' her mother said.

But it was. No matter what they said, the cattle were stolen while she was supposed to be in charge. They'd been her responsibility and now her parents would be struggling to make the repayments on the overdraft they'd had to take on to tide them over until they sold the cattle.

'That bloody bull!' her father said suddenly, making everyone start. 'I knew it was cursed from the day it got here.'

'The bull is not cursed,' her mother said wearily.

'It bloody well is. Look where it came from. Jock went broke and flogged it off to Brent and then his whole place got repossessed. Then *we* end up with it and look—everything went pear-shaped after that.'

Reggie had to agree that the bull had caused *her* a number of sleepless nights over the last year or so, but that had been Brent's fault, not the bull's. Brent was the one who'd made the decision to buy it without any thought about how they'd be able to afford it.

'Other than being tied up in all the history with your brother, what's so important about this bull? Can't you just buy another one?' Tim asked later, when her parents had gone to bed.

'No. He's the product of twenty years of breeding and the only one of his line in Australia.'

'Who's this Jock bloke they talked about?'

'The breeder who used to own a property up the road. He'd been building his bloodline for two decades before he got sick. Brent had always been fascinated by the process of creating a new breed and had been talking about doing it on River Styx for years but could never get Dad on board.

When old Jock offered the herd and bull to Brent, he made an executive decision and did the deal without talking to Dad.'

'I can't imagine your father taking that well.'

'He didn't know about it for a few months, it was just after the accident. When he found out it was too late. The only thing that won him over was the fact that Brent had heard the Parsons had made an offer for the cattle and he'd managed to get Jock to sell them to him, stealing them from right under Parson's nose.'

'So, it was a big deal then.'

'It was huge. Jock had spent all this time doing the hard work and breeding the bloodline up but never got around to taking the new breed line to stud registration, which Brent did in Jock's honour. So yeah, the bull is kind of a big deal—big enough to risk bankruptcy for, apparently.'

'That should at least make it easier for the cops to track them down. They'll be harder to offload, right?'

'I hope so. Unless whoever stole them had no idea what they were stealing and sent them all to the meatworks.' The thought made her feel ill—all those years of breeding for it to end like that. In the current market, with cattle prices going through the roof, thieves would be willing to grab anything to cash in on high beef prices. They wouldn't be worrying about bloodlines and sacrifice, just how much they could pocket at a sale. This could bring River Styx to its knees.

Chapter 39

The pub was busy as usual, with a mix of locals and tourists who'd stopped for the night either on their way down the mountain or on the way up. From the cluster of motorbikes parked out the front, Tim assumed the majority of the unfamiliar faces were part of a group on a weekend ride.

After stopping in at the Armaglen police station to get an update from Detective Hume, who unfortunately hadn't given them anything promising, he and Reggie had decided to stop and have a meal at the pub before heading back to River Styx.

They found a table and Tim went to the bar to order drinks. As he waited for the bartender to finish serving a couple of weekend bikers, he took the time to observe the other patrons. There were the obligatory older regulars on their customary bar stools, looking settled in for the evening; a few tables of tourists, poring over road maps and flicking through the local activity brochures, and a couple of rough-looking young blokes who'd clearly dropped by after work, still in their dusty work shirts and jeans, their hats tipped back on their heads and already four or five beers in by the volume of their conversation.

Tim frowned as he overheard a couple of their comments and shook his head silently. He wondered how long it would be until the bar staff got sick of them and stopped selling them drinks. For the sake of local tourism, Tim hoped it would be sooner rather than later.

The young blokes gave a loud cheer as a third man entered the pub and ambled slowly across to the bar.

'Here he is! The walkin' wounded.'

'It's not funny,' Tim heard the man say as his mates laughed loudly.

'It was hilarious,' the bloke in the dirty baseball cap snickered. 'Your testicles swelled up to almost the same size as that fuckin' crazy bull's. Christ, did you ever see a set of nuts as big as that on a bull before?'

'Only on Robbo,' the other man chuckled, raising his beer in a mock toast to the newcomer.

Robbo frowned and shot off a long string of profanities that had a few nearby tables sending disapproving glances at them. 'Wasn't expectin' the fuckin' bull to go psycho on me,' he complained in a whiny, nasal voice.

'Yeah, gotta admit, it didn't seem that crazy till we hit those lights.'

'You weren't wearin' hi-vis shirts were ya?' one of the old regulars from the end of the bar suddenly asked, causing the three younger workers to look over at him.

'What?' Robbo grunted.

'Knew a bull once that had an aversion to hi-vis shirts. All the local drivers knew not to load him at night or the glow strip on ya shirt would send him crazy once it lit up.'

The men looked at him as if he was speaking a different language and turned back to their beers and rowdiness with shrugs. A few minutes later the door of the pub closed behind them, and several people sighed in relief as the overall volume of the pub dropped considerably.

Reggie heard the boisterous laughing mixed with swearing and name-calling, and immediately recognised the three men making the row. They weren't from around here but had been staying and working in the area for the last few years, and at least one of them had had a run-in with Brent. A pub fight over something or other, but even if she hadn't known them because of that she still wouldn't have liked them. She detested loud, obnoxious men who swore with no regard for anyone around them. Including the family with three small children seated across the room.

Her gaze found Tim, waiting at the bar, and she felt her irritation wash away, allowing that light-headed, tingly feeling he sparked to fill her up. A movement at the dining room door drew her attention to some newcomers walking in, and instantly the feeling evaporated as her gaze clashed with theirs.

Great. Simon and Felicity and, worse still, the only spare table was beside theirs. Reggie stifled a groan and forced a polite, impersonal smile to her lips.

She saw Felicity stiffen slightly as she sat down and caught sight of her dining neighbour, realising it was too late to turn around and leave.

'I'll go and get our drinks,' Simon said, and Reggie saw Felicity shoot him a frantic glance. 'I can get them,' she said, moving to stand.

'Don't be ridiculous. I don't date a barmaid,' he snapped. 'I'll order while I'm up there. What do you want?'

'Maybe the pasta?'

'You sure? Michelle's wedding isn't far away. You don't want to be the chubby bridesmaid, do you?'

'The Caesar salad's fine,' Felicity murmured in barely more than a whisper.

Reggie was torn between dismay and disgust. Why the hell would anyone put up with that? Then she remembered that Felicity had made her choice. She was the one who had swapped a decent bloke for a rich knobhead, and Reggie squashed down any sympathy she might have felt.

'He wasn't always like that,' Felicity said quietly after a few moments.

Reggie glanced up from the menu and found Felicity watching her warily.

'It's none of my business,' she said, shrugging, but she couldn't quite shake the lingering indignation she still felt at the way Simon had spoken to his partner in public.

'I know I made a mistake. Leaving Brent,' Felicity added.

Reggie looked back down at her menu. She had no desire whatsoever to get dragged into Felicity's drama.

'You seem happy,' Felicity said after yet another uncomfortable silence, and Reggie fought to keep a neutral expression. Why couldn't this woman understand that she had no desire to talk to her—ever again? She was sick of the tension that hung in the air every time she saw her. Added to the sleepless nights she'd been having ever since losing the cattle, Reggie was pushed to the limits of her politeness.

'Look, Felicity. You don't have to keep trying. Just let it go. What happened is in the past. Mum and Dad forgive you, so just . . . let it go.'

'We used to be friends,' Felicity said softly, toying with the cutlery on the table before her.

'We used to be. Then you dumped my brother when he needed you most and we stopped being anything.'

'It wasn't like that,' she said urgently, looking up and holding Reggie's glare. 'You don't know how it was. I wanted to explain it all to you the other day at your parents' place.'

'How was it then, Felicity? Please, tell me—clearly you feel a need, so go ahead and get it off your chest once and for all.'

She saw Felicity swallow hard before lifting her chin slightly. 'Brent and I hadn't been happy for a long time. We were going through the motions. I'd tried to talk to him about it, I'd even thought maybe it was just me and that, if I gave it time, those feelings we had as teenagers would come back again. So, I kept pushing the wedding date back to give us a chance . . . but it didn't help.'

'You didn't think to just do the grown-up thing and end it when you knew it was over?'

'I tried . . . You know how Brent was,' Felicity said, biting the inside of her bottom lip as though to keep it from trembling. Her voice wavered. 'If he didn't want to hear something, he just ignored it.'

Reggie opened her mouth and then closed it, realising that what Felicity had said actually held some truth. She'd tried unsuccessfully to make Brent listen to her warnings about the books and spending, but he'd always either brushed it off or dodged her requests to sit down and go through it all with her. That was different, though. 'There was no excuse for the way you left. Or the timing.'

'I know,' Felicity said, lowering her head. 'I can't take any of that back, but I'd been going to break up with him the night we got the call about your parents' accident. I'd come over to tell him, and suddenly we were racing out the door and heading for the hospital . . . I couldn't do it then, and afterwards I barely saw him between the hospital visits and working the farm. Then when he went in for all those tests, I couldn't do it anymore. I couldn't take on any more. I knew I'd fallen out of love with him—we were kids when we started going out, and I wanted different things by the time we became adults . . . Brent just wouldn't see it.'

'You wanted a rich farmer, not one in debt?' Reggie asked coldly.

'Simon was there for me.'

'Simon didn't have two parents almost die in a car accident and have to run the entire property and business on his own!' Reggie snapped. 'It wasn't all about *you*, at the time.'

'It hadn't been for a long time,' Felicity said sadly. 'In the beginning it was. He couldn't keep his hands off me, and he'd look at me as though I was the only woman in the world. Then it somehow all changed. Simon came in and swept me off my feet,' she said, giving a little dejected shrug. 'He made me feel special again.'

Reggie looked dubious. 'How he speaks to you is what you call special?'

'No,' she sighed. 'But maybe that's my punishment for treating Brent the way I did.'

Reggie considered the other woman silently for a while. It didn't sit well to hear someone say they deserved to be treated badly in a relationship. That was just wrong. 'Felicity, no one should put up with that kind of behaviour. It has nothing to do with anything you did in the past. If Brent were here now, he'd tell you to get the hell out of this relationship and find someone who treats you with respect.'

She saw a small smile tug at Felicity's lips before it wobbled and she sniffed. 'That sounds exactly like something Brent would say. I really miss him,' she said, wiping a stray tear from her eye. 'I know you must think I'm a horrible person, but even though I wasn't *in* love with him anymore, I still loved him . . . He was a big part of my life. I know you must miss him too.'

Reggie felt her throat close up and she struggled to force out any kind of response. She was glad when Tim chose that moment to walk across the room carrying two drinks. He did a double-take when he saw who was seated next to them.

'You remember Felicity?' Reggie asked, clearing her throat as Tim placed a glass in front of her and nodded at the woman who was wiping her eyes quickly.

'So, did you work out what you wanted to order yet?' Tim asked tactfully, taking his seat.

Before she could answer, Simon returned to the adjacent table and Reggie gave a weary sigh.

'Heard about your trouble,' he said, settling into his seat and handing a glass of wine to Felicity. 'Can't imagine how badly that must suck. Losing not only your dad's prize bull but the entire herd. Bet he's not happy about that.'

Reggie felt her teeth clench and she made a conscious effort to relax her jaw. 'Since when did you start drinking wine?' she asked Felicity.

Before Felicity could answer, Simon jumped in. 'She acquired a taste for the finer things in life, didn't you, hun?' he said with a smug little smile. 'And not only in wine.'

Tim reached for Reggie's hand—she hadn't realised it was clenched on the tabletop—and drew her angry gaze across to his. 'How about we skip dinner?'

'Good idea.' Reggie nodded. 'I've lost my appetite anyway.'

They both stood up from the table and wove their way out of the dining room. The cold air hit Reggie's face as they stepped outside and she took a deep breath.

'You okay?' Tim asked.

'I didn't believe it was possible to despise a person as much as I do him. He was a jerk in school, and he hasn't changed now.'

'He's certainly something,' Tim agreed. 'I couldn't see dinner being much fun.'

'No,' she said, then added mournfully, 'But it was schnitty night and they do *the best* chicken schnitzels.'

'We can find something else?' Tim said hopefully.

Reggie gave him a doleful look. 'Have you taken any notice of where we live? The pub's the only place within a hundred kays to get a feed.'

'We could go back in and order takeaway?' he suggested.

'No, let's just go. I'm sure we can rustle up something to eat back at home.'

As they stopped beside the car, he stepped closer and tugged her against him. 'I like the sound of that.'

'Of what?' she asked, tilting her head back to look up at him.

'Home,' he said simply.

'Me too,' she admitted, relaxing against him. 'Let's get out of here.'

The encounter with Simon had left a vibrating tension in the pit of her stomach, and his jeer about the cattle had stung more than she cared to admit. She couldn't even argue with him—it was true, she *had* lost the cattle. They were stolen when she was supposed to be in charge. Why didn't they have better security around the place? Especially with a damn bull worth as much as he was.

She hadn't really thought it was needed. They had good fencing and it was always checked for the safety of all their cattle, not just the bull. Plus, he was out in the paddocks doing his job—running with the females and making babies—and it wasn't like she could have locked him in a pen or a cage when he wasn't in use. He was an animal, not the royal jewels—even if he *had* cost almost as much to buy. No, she thought determinedly, there was nothing she could have done differently. It wasn't as though they came through the front gate and drove off with him. They cut fences and had an escape route planned—there was no way she could have predicted that.

And yet, she did feel responsible. This whole thing was a nightmare.

Chapter 40

Tim shut the fridge in the shed and gave a disheartened sigh. Grocery shopping hadn't been high on their list of priorities since the cattle had been stolen, and he was starving after being in the pub and smelling that damn bistro cooking.

'I'm going back in to buy a couple of those schnitties,' he announced as Reggie kicked her boots off and sank wearily onto the lounge.

'We just got home—you're not seriously going to head back into town now?'

'It's, like, twenty minutes up the road. I used to drive an hour and a half to work most days,' he told her cheerfully. They'd had this conversation before, and it still baffled him how she could think he was crazy for driving a couple of hours to get to places, and yet out here it took a of couple of hours to reach the closest big town and amenities. He supposed the difference was distance. He sat in traffic for almost two hours to travel only a handful of kilometres, which was, when he thought about it, pretty crazy. Now he really wanted a schnitty, and he was willing to drive back along the potholed dirt road into town just to get one.

'Go have a bath and relax. I'll be back soon,' he said, dropping a kiss on her head. She looked like she was ready to fall asleep where she sat.

The dark road stretched out before him in the bright headlights like a long narrow ribbon. He kept a sharp eye out for the occasional dark shape hunched over at the side of the road and let some sharp expletives fly when he narrowly missed a few roos that seemed intent on inspecting the undercarriage of his four-wheel-drive.

The pub was a lot quieter when he walked inside after parking, and he was glad he'd called to place their order before coming in.

'Won't be long,' the cheerful bartender announced. 'Can I get you a beer while you wait?'

'Sure. Better just make it a middy though thanks, mate.' His last beer had left a bad taste in his mouth, and he hadn't even finished it when he'd found Simon Parson sitting by their table.

Tim paid for the meals and the drink and looked sideways, noticing that the old bloke who'd been there before was still seated at the end.

'G'day,' Tim said when the old fella glanced over at him. Something that had been niggling at him surfaced in his mind. 'I couldn't help but overhear your conversation with those young blokes earlier,' Tim said. 'Just out of curiosity, who owned that bull you used to know?'

'Old bloke, gone now,' the man said. 'Jock Wallace.'

Tim felt his gut clench. Could it just be a coincidence? Common sense told him yes, and yet . . .

'Bloody thing used to go crazy around anything hi-vis. You could never load the bugger at night or early morning.'

'Do you know much about those young guys who were here earlier?' he asked as casually as he could while his mind raced with a thousand questions.

'Don't know them personally. Blow-ins from out west. I think they're camped out on a property somewhere doin' some seasonal work.'

Tim collected the two meals from the counter, giving the bartender and the old man a nod. In his gut he knew it wasn't a coincidence that the men had been talking about a bull just like Wally. He dug his phone out of his pocket and scrolled through the list of numbers until he reached the one for Detective Hume and hit call.

Reggie stared at Tim as he leaned against the kitchen bench and told her what he'd discovered at the pub, the meals suddenly forgotten on the bench between them.

'And Pete's looking into it?'

'Yeah. He said he was.'

'I can't believe they were *right there*,' she said with a ferocious glint in her eye.

'There's no actual evidence at the moment,' Tim pointed out cautiously.

Her loud scoff suggested exactly what she thought of his comment. 'We should have confronted them in the pub. Detained them until the police got there to question them.'

'It would only have scared them off—if they *are* involved, there's no way we could have held them until the cops arrived, and they'd have disappeared and then we'd never have had a hope of finding them.'

Reggie gave a frustrated grunt. She knew Tim was right, but it still irked her that those idiots had. Been. Right. There! It had to be them.

Tim lay awake that evening, listening to the steady rise and fall of Reggie's breathing. He was glad she was finally getting some sleep—he'd been listening to her tossing and turning every night since the theft had happened and wished he could do something more to help. It wasn't in his nature to sit on the sidelines and wait for someone else to solve a problem.

His thoughts turned to the men from the pub once again and he pondered the information. His gut was telling him this wasn't some random coincidence, but was it enough for the police to go on?

He didn't want to get Reggie's hopes up only to have them dashed. He felt his mood darken as his mind turned to the encounter with Simon Parson. The guy was a slimebag, barely even *trying* to cover up his amusement about the MacLeods' loss. Who even did that? Some bloody neighbour. Tim had been itching to smack the smirk off his face there and then but figured the fallout would probably ruin the brief moment of satisfaction. Still, someone needed to straighten that guy out. Tim would simply bide his time and wait for the opportunity—it'd come along, he just had to be patient.

For now, though, he'd lie here and make sure Reggie got her sleep and, in the morning, hopefully the cops would turn up something interesting on those blokes.

Chapter 41

Reggie tried not to feel deflated as she headed home from yet another ride through the national park. She'd been coming out daily on the off-chance she could find some sign of the herd, maybe even a couple who might have escaped the thieves and run off into the park. She knew it was a long shot, but it was better than sitting around twiddling her thumbs waiting for the phone to ring. The police were remaining tight-lipped and had given them nothing concrete about the men from the pub so far. She was growing increasingly frustrated by their 'we're looking into it' assurance that was no assurance at all.

A car slowed down then pulled off to the side of the road ahead and Reggie pulled Banjo to a stop at the driver's side window, masking her surprise as she recognised the person who looked up at her.

'Felicity,' Reggie greeted her curiously. She was probably the last person Reggie would ever expect to be driving out along this road since it only really led to her parents' place or the national park.

'I thought that was Banjo,' Felicity said and gave a wavering smile. 'Brent loved that horse.'

The usual urge to snap at the woman was no longer there. Reggie wasn't sure if it was because she'd been thinking the same thing about Banjo as she'd saddled him or if, after her exchange with Felicity two nights ago, she'd finally managed to let go of her anger and disappointment at a friend who'd practically been her sister-in-law. 'He did,' Reggie heard herself say, giving the horse a pat. As she straightened, she glanced into the back seat of the sedan and noticed it was packed high with boxes and suitcases. 'You going on a holiday?'

Felicity cleared her throat before dragging her gaze away from the grey gelding. 'No. I'm leaving,' she said, summoning a bright smile—a little brighter than she felt, if the glisten of tears in her eyes was any indication. 'I've been thinking about what you said the other night and you were right. I don't deserve to be treated the way Simon treats me. I don't want losing Brent to be in vain. I want to do something with my life.'

Reggie blinked quickly. This was not at all what she'd been expecting, but she didn't have any time to process it as Felicity continued, 'The thing is . . . at first, I didn't know Simon was into party drugs.' She shrugged. 'He was always so angry with his Dad and he was under a lot of pressure, and then on weekends he was different. He was fun and happier. It was never really an issue, he always managed to function okay, but lately he's gone from being a recreational user on a weekend to doing it a lot more often. The way you saw him the other night. He wasn't like that before.'

Reggie had heard talk that Simon and some other local guys had over-the-top parties on occasion. Personally, Reggie thought he should have outgrown all that by now, but apparently he hadn't. 'I'm not judging you.'

'Yes, you are,' Felicity said with a grim smile. 'And in your shoes, I probably would have too. But I thought you should know: the police came by yesterday asking questions about your cattle. They said they were following a new lead and Simon told them he was home with me the night they were stolen, but he wasn't. He went out. I got up during the night to get a drink and I saw him coming home from somewhere. He wouldn't say anything about it the next day, but the police visit really rattled him.'

'Why would they think he had anything to do with it?'

'I don't know, but . . .' Felicity paused. 'He was really angry after that open day. Like, crazy furious. He kept raving on about Brent stealing the deal out from under him.'

'Why didn't you go to the police about it?'

Felicity shook her head quickly. 'I can't get involved in all this—he scares me, Reggie.'

'But the police might need you to testify,' Reggie said, feeling desperate.

'They'll be able to find me if they need me. But I honestly don't know anything else. I just wanted to tell you. I have to go. Thank you, Reggie,' she said softly.

Reggie felt unexpectedly emotional as she watched Felicity pull out onto the road and drive away. Her brother may not have been a saint—but he hadn't deserved to be abandoned the way he was by the woman he loved either. Felicity would have to live with that. Reggie would miss the girl she'd grown up with who she'd once loved like a sister. She felt a sharp stab of pain for the past that was now gone, but it was time to let it go.

As she prodded Banjo onwards, she tried to process the information Felicity had passed on. Could Simon have been involved in the cattle theft? Sure, the Parsons had always been sore about missing out on buying Wally, but were they capable of actually stealing? Was Fred involved in this as well? She found it hard to believe. Despite his faults, Fred Parson didn't seem the type to lower himself to cattle stealing. Simon, on the other hand . . . But what was he planning to do with them? Surely he knew they'd be far too easy to recognise if he tried to sell them?

This bit of intel from Felicity could be the thing the police needed to move forward. She urged Banjo on faster, eager to get back to the house to call Hume. 'Please let this be the lead that helps find them,' she murmured. They couldn't lose everything now, after all their hard work.

Tim tapped a finger on the top of the steering wheel in time to Jimmy Barnes as he drove along the highway, turning off at the intersection to head back to River Styx. He'd jumped at the opportunity to go into town and pick up a part for the tractor, needing something to do. Reggie had left for a horse ride without telling him, and he was still a little annoyed. He knew he shouldn't be—she probably just needed some time alone to clear her head, but still, it would have been nice to have been asked to go along.

A large B-double cattle truck passed him, taking up a considerable part of the road. He glanced in his mirror to see it slow down and turn onto the highway. His thoughts turned once more to Reggie's missing herd and he felt his frustration growing. So far they had no new information. He was sure those guys had been connected somehow. In fairness, the cops did have to make sure everything was above board before they made any moves, so maybe things were happening quietly in the background. He had to be patient and hope that there was something useful in the information he'd given them. It was hard, though, with Reggie and her parents looking so gutted by the whole thing. He just wanted to fix it. That's what he did—he fixed things, got the job done. He needed to make things right for the people who'd changed his life; they deserved it after everything they'd been through over the last few years.

A car overtook him, speeding and blasting its horn. He swore under his breath, suddenly feeling like a grumpy old man as he frowned at the blaring music and reckless driving, then did a double-take as he caught sight of who was in the vehicle. It was them—the guys from the bar.

Just as that was sinking in, he saw them turn off onto a dirt road up ahead. Without stopping to think, he followed them, although the dust they'd thrown up covered their tracks and blocked his view. When it settled, he spotted their white, souped-up LandCruiser adorned with a bull-bar big enough to stop a rhinoceros, multiple six-foot radio antennas swaying crazily in the air and several 'Deni Ute Muster' stickers on the back.

He didn't know what he was going to do once he caught up with them—he hadn't really thought that bit through—but he knew he couldn't just let them go by without doing something.

The road curved in a long sweep through the bushland and he slowed down to take the bend. When he came out onto the straight, they'd disappeared. There was no dust plume in the distance, and for a concerning moment he thought he'd lost them, before a driveway appeared on his left and he realised they must have turned into it. Pulling into the gateway and peering through the trees, he saw a white vehicle stop in front of what looked like a building. Now that he'd actually caught up to them, he supposed he really should think his next move through. For starters, there were three of them and one of him, not to mention how many more mates they might have inside, so rushing in like a bull at the gate was probably not the smartest move. It also wasn't what he was trained to do, and the thought pulled him up. He needed to get his head back in the game and stop thinking like some wannabe hero. If Deano were here he'd tell him to smart the fuck up. And he'd be right. *You're a professional mate, start bloody actin' like one.*

Tim reversed back out of the driveway and drove a little further up the road, parking his car in the bush beside the quiet road and taking out his backpack. He'd walk in on foot and do a recce of the situation before he made a decision about what to do next.

Tim cautiously made his way through the scrub, approaching the building at an angle until he had a clear line of sight. He lay down on the ground, satisfied no one would spot him at this distance. Ignoring the chill in the air, he took out the compact binoculars from his pack and focused them on the cars parked outside a large farm shed. The sound of cattle bellowing broke through the still air. He could see the dirty LandCruiser and a fancy Land Rover but there was no sign of anyone outside. He'd need to move in closer to get a look at who else was there. When he'd repositioned himself closer to the shed, he could hear voices coming from inside.

He crept slowly towards the vehicles and crouched behind the one he'd been following earlier. With his back braced against the side of the four-wheel-drive, he eased himself up and peered through the back windows to see if he could get a clear view of anyone inside the shed, but his attention was snagged by what he saw inside the car. He eased open the back door, keeping a wary eye on the shed for anyone coming out, and reached inside to throw back the tarp covering something inside. He saw a number of boxes and opened one, surprised to discover prepacked little plastic bags of pills. It seemed these blokes were doing a little drug dealing on the side.

Tugging the cover back in place, he quietly closed the door and bent low, then made his way to the shed behind the vehicles.

He spotted the three men from the bar immediately. As usual they were mucking around and hurling insults, this time at something in the yards in the centre of the huge shed. Something that let out a loud bellow that Tim immediately recognised. Wally, in all his enormous-scrotum glory. Tim wasn't sure if he was more excited about seeing the bull alive and well or the fact that his gut had been correct about the wankers at the bar. A shout from another man drew Tim's gaze to the newcomer, and he bit back a curse as soon as he saw who it was.

Chapter 42

Simon Parson.

What the actual hell. *Parson* had been involved in all this? The urge to wrap his hands around the guy's throat sent a red-hot rage through his body. *The bloody nerve of this bastard,* Tim thought, remembering the night at the pub when he'd offered the backhand slap to Reggie about losing her father's cattle. It had been him behind the whole thing.

Now Tim knew exactly why Simon Parson was acting smug. And now Tim had this arrogant prick exactly where he wanted him.

As Parson started snapping orders like a wannabe general, Tim decided to put his plan into action.

He made his way around the rear of the shed and waited for the first guy to come around the corner, then grabbed him, covered his mouth and pushed him up against the shed. 'If you want to stay alive, you keep your mouth shut, understand?' Tim whispered harshly. He had the guy's wrist in a lock, applying just enough pressure to receive a muffled squeal of pain in compliance. He covered the man's mouth with tape he'd taken from his pack moments earlier, then secured his wrists, dropping him to the ground before stealthily moving on to the next target. In quick succession, Tim managed to disable each of the men without incident, grateful for his years of experience in close combat techniques. With all three men bound and gagged, he left stealth behind, taking out his phone and finding the app he needed before walking calmly into the shed.

Parson glanced up from where he stood at the edge of the yards watching the bull, and noticeably jumped, startled by Tim's sudden appearance. His gaze darted around anxiously, no doubt searching for his mates. 'They aren't coming to help you,' Tim informed him.

Parson scoffed. 'You think you're some kind of Rambo or something?'

'Or something.' Tim shrugged, undeterred by the dismissive tone.

'Okay, tough guy,' Parson said. 'Do yourself a favour and get out of here before I press charges.'

'You're in possession of a stolen bull, dickhead, but by all means, go ahead and call the cops.'

'I'll just say I came out here to check on my property and found those idiots keeping this bull here without my knowledge. No one can prove I stole it.'

'The way those guys out there were squealing, I wouldn't be so sure of that. Once the cops get hold of them they'll be ready to tell them everything.'

'They won't say a thing.'

'Wouldn't be too sure about that. They've been running their mouths off in front of everyone. I overheard them at the pub the other night—won't be too long before the cops put it all together and they're hardly going to take the fall for you. The way I see it, you're pretty much screwed.'

'Much like Reggie. Tell me, is she really as crazy in bed as they say?'

Tim's eyes narrowed. 'Sounds like something a man who got rejected would say. Turn around,' Tim ordered, refusing to react to the bait.

'Lay one finger on me and my father will sue you for everything you have—which clearly isn't much, so we'll then go after the MacLeods and take them for everything *they've* got, which will be sad for you seeing as you were clearly hoping to bag the daughter and take the land for yourself. I wonder what the male term for a gold-digger is,' he mused, tilting his head to the side slightly.

Until that point, Tim thought he could restrain himself from doing too much harm to the guy, but after scoring that hit, all bets were off.

'Ah, I see that's a sore point,' Parson chuckled.

Tim took a threatening step closer and grabbed the front of his shirt, before pushing him to the ground to tie his hands. *Don't listen to him,* a voice told him firmly. *He's just playing on your weakness.* And it *was* a fear he had. The last thing he'd wanted was for the MacLeods to think he was taking advantage of their generosity.

'For a guy who thinks he's so damn smart, why would you do something so stupid as to steal cattle that were so easily traceable?'

'Because I could.' Parson shrugged, no longer struggling as he lay on the ground with his hands tied.

'Reggie threatens your manhood that much, huh?' Tim said.

Instantly the smug expression vanished, replaced by something that looked almost feral. 'That bitch has always thought she was better than me. Her and her bogan brother. Thankfully I have some standards, though.'

'Oh yeah, you're all class, mate. Drug dealing is such a respectable occupation.'

Parson shrugged again. 'Profitable though.'

'Seriously? You're one of the richest families in the district and you risk throwing it all away dealing drugs?'

'The perfect Parsons with their perfect life and their perfect children,' he said, then let out a giggle.

Tim raised an eyebrow. It seemed like Parson had been sampling his own product. The guy was sounding a little unhinged.

'The mighty Fred Parson. Maybe it's time everyone learned the truth.'

'That his son is a cattle thief and drug pusher?'

'If it wasn't for me, we'd have lost everything. My father almost sent us bankrupt, but did I get any thanks? Of course not,' Parson snarled. 'I'm still the loser he can't trust to take over running the property. I'm too irresponsible. Well, he wasn't too proud to accept me bailing him out of trouble with drug money, was he? It might be interesting to see how Fred tries to spin this one.'

Parson started laughing, and Tim eyed him with caution. There was definitely something not right with this guy, but he didn't have the time or inclination to delve any deeper.

'But this will all get buried, like everything else. Nothing will happen.'

'Mate, how delusional are you? There are drugs in the car outside and a stolen bull in here. Even Daddy won't be able to get you out of this mess.'

'The drugs aren't in *my* car. You think I'm stupid enough to risk being caught with them *on* me? All I have to say is that I don't know these men, I just came here and found them.'

Tim pulled his phone from where it sat poking just out of his shirt pocket and stopped the video recording, watching as Parson's face lost colour. 'I think you're all kinds of stupid, but you're not my problem now,' he said, then called the police.

Tim hung up after passing the information along and then texted the video. Pocketing his phone, he glanced around, suddenly realising something was missing. He'd been so relieved to find the bull he'd forgotten all about the cows. 'Where's the rest of the cattle?'

Parson let out a snort and turned his face away.

Tim dropped down on one knee and grabbed the back of the guy's head. 'Where are the others?' he said in a cold, dangerous tone, and watched as a flash of uncertainty crossed Parson's face.

'It's too late,' Parson sneered. 'They're already gone. You missed them by that much,' he said, letting out a harsh laugh, and Tim was more convinced than ever that the guy was on something.

Pushing himself to his feet, Tim ran outside to look around. There were tyre marks on the ground leading from an outdoor set of yards. He examined them carefully and quickly deduced they were from a truck—a big one. Instantly, the image of the cattle truck he'd passed just before spotting the LandCruiser flashed through his mind. Just missed it? It had to be that one. It was on its way to the meat works and all those years of breeding would be gone in a split second.

Tim made a call to the detective and filled him in on what he'd found as he ran for his car.

Chapter 43

Tim had given the police a description of the cattle truck but he was kicking himself for not paying better attention to the number plate, other than the fact it had been from Queensland. He wasn't sure where it was headed, but he was now certain it wouldn't be Armaglen. Now that he knew Simon Parson was involved, he realised this wasn't a random theft to cash in on high cattle prices. It was too close to home, and someone would surely recognise them since everyone knew everyone else's business in the area. No, they wouldn't risk selling them anywhere in the district.

Once he was on the road, Tim called Detective Hume back.

'I have a feeling it'll be making a run for the Queensland border. It had Queensland number plates,' Tim said.

'Unfortunately, that doesn't narrow it down much. Trucks can be registered anywhere and do pick-ups along the way.'

Tim swore. God, he'd been so bloody close. He could have stopped the truck.

'We'll do our best to pull up any truck within a fifty-kilometre radius. Let us handle it.'

'I'm not going to give up now,' Tim said, shaking his head. 'I'm going to keep going north. If I find anything, I'll let you know.'

'If you *do* find anything,' the detective said in a voice that didn't allow any room for argument, 'you'll let us know and do nothing. You hear me? I don't want to come across any more hog-tied perpetrators.'

'I don't know what you're talking about,' Tim said calmly.

'Uh-huh. I mean it, Warbois. If you want to help, you call it in. There are too many things that could get this case thrown out of court if everything isn't done by the book and that won't help anyone. Least of all the MacLeods.'

'Okay,' Tim snapped. 'I'll call it in if I find anything.' He let out an impatient sigh as he nudged the speedometer higher on the long, empty road. He needed to cover as many kilometres as he could to try to catch up with that truck.

As the hours ticked over, Tim realised that maybe this was a wild goose chase after all. But he'd already committed to it, so he may as well keep going. In truth, some of the adrenalin had worn off and was being replaced by niggling doubt as he went back over some of the things Parson had said.

Parson's gold-digger comment niggled at him. He'd felt people's curious gazes and imagined it *could* look odd that a stranger had suddenly started living at River Styx and then was suddenly in a relationship with Reggie. It didn't bother *him* what people thought, but he did worry that the MacLeods might suddenly have their doubts.

Today, for the first time in a long while, he had felt something he hadn't felt since leaving the army. Strong. In control. It felt good to be back in that place. But Alicia's words echoed in his head from the funeral. *You're all addicted to that rush that danger gives you.* Maybe it *was* an addiction. There was definitely something about slipping back into that mode that had felt good. There'd been a surge of something powerful, and it had momentarily quietened the unrest that had been there before.

He knew without a doubt that settling for being a farm labourer and a part-time tradesman was never going to make him feel the way today had. Suddenly everything he'd been so certain of before now felt like a stupid dream. He knew he wanted a life with Reggie, but could he push away this thing inside him that continued to crave something more than what he'd been doing? He wasn't sure what he was going to do, but he knew he had to figure it out.

Everything had moved fast after Reggie had called the police to pass on Felicity's information. Within the hour, Detective Hume had called to say they had suspects in custody.

She hadn't been able to get hold of Tim. Her father had told her he'd gone into town, and she was too busy working out what was going on to give much thought to Tim's whereabouts, but after her fifth phone call went unanswered, she began to worry. It wasn't like him to not return her phone calls, and after ringing the spare parts place she knew it had been hours since he'd left.

It wasn't until later that afternoon, when the police arrived to fill them in on what was happening, that Tim was mentioned and real fear set in.

'What do you mean he's gone after the truck?' Reggie said, alarm in her voice.

'I know,' the detective sighed, 'I tried to reason with him.'

'What if these people are dangerous?'

She saw his lips twitch slightly before he asked, 'How much of Warbois' army career do you know about?' he asked.

'Not much . . . I mean, just the basics. He's been out of the army for a while.'

'Well, after today, I can safely assure you that if there's trouble, he's better equipped to deal with it than most. However, he has promised me he won't be getting involved and his job is to call it in if he finds the truck.'

'Do you think he'll find it?' she asked hesitantly. There was a lot riding on locating the missing animals—twenty-odd years of breeding, to be exact. The police had already told her that the men who'd stolen Wally thought there was no interest in the cows and calves, which meant they'd been sent off to slaughter to get rid of the evidence. These men didn't care about the devastation they were leaving behind. But Simon knew. Just thinking about him made her want to scream. How could he do that to them? Sure, there had never been any love lost between the neighbours, but to do this? When he, *a fellow farmer,* understood the work that had gone into building up a bloodline like this. 'What'll happen to Simon?' she asked.

'He's up on some pretty serious charges. We managed to uncover a lot more he was involved in, which we're not at liberty to talk about yet, so the case just got a whole lot more complicated. There'll be a number of people lining up to get information out of Mr Parson.'

'But he won't get off on the cattle stealing charges, will he?' Reggie asked, frowning. 'They won't give him a plea bargain or something, will they?' The last thing she wanted was for that jerk to be released just because he dobbed in someone else—which she knew beyond a doubt he absolutely would, given half a chance.

'No, we've got enough on him to make sure he does some pretty serious time.'

'Poor Fred and Julie,' her mother said, dabbing at her eyes.

'Are you serious, Mum?' Reggie said, staring at her mother.

'No matter what Simon's done, they'll be devastated. He's their son.'

Reggie supposed her mum had a point, although she secretly suspected the Parsons would be more devastated that their reputation was being ruined. Maybe that was being unfair, she conceded reluctantly. She was sure they would be worried about how much trouble their son was now in and what his future would hold, and yet she still couldn't quite bring herself to feel sorry for him. She was just glad that Felicity had found the strength to leave him when she did.

When she walked the police to their car and waved them off, Reggie pulled out her phone and called Tim again. What the hell was he trying to prove?

❖

Tim saw the petrol station up ahead and gratefully pulled in. His eyes felt gritty and sore and his head had begun pounding with a headache he hadn't been able to shake. He'd lost track of how many truck stops he'd pulled into, looking for the truck and asking truckies and servo attendants if they'd seen anything matching the description he had—which was pretty vague and bugger-all help. A B-double carrying cattle around here was pretty much every second vehicle, and he had no real identifying marks other than Queensland number plates he'd vaguely remembered from earlier and photos of the cattle he had on his phone. Even that wasn't any help considering you couldn't even see what stock most trucks carried anyway.

He'd taken a gamble on following the back way up to the Queensland border, based on the assumption that if you were transporting stolen cattle you'd probably want to avoid as much traffic and police presence as possible and stay off the main highway. But it was only a guess. For all he knew, the truck could be heading west . . . or south, or pretty much any-bloody-where.

As he pushed open the glass door, he squinted against the bright fluorescent light inside the shop.

He searched the shelves for a box of paracetamol and took a cold bottle of water out of the fridge, placing them on the counter and waiting for the tired-looking servo attendant to finish talking to a customer up the other end.

'Righto, safe trip. Take care of ya family jewels,' the attendant called, sniggering as the man hobbled away.

Tim glanced up as the attendant wandered over and began scanning his items. 'You had many cattle trucks through this afternoon?' he asked as he tapped his card and reached for his water and tablets.

'Yeah. Couple,' the man said, rubbing his prickly chin. 'There's one just there,' he said, nodding his head at the window as a semi started its engine and warmed up.

Tim's head snapped around and a memory of the truck he passed earlier instantly came to mind. His eyes widened. Now the details were coming back to him: the red letters on the side, partially hidden under dust, and the Queensland number plates. That was it. It had to be. He raced for the door and heaved it open, running past the petrol bowsers and climbing up the side steps of the big truck as it idled in the parking bay.

The driver turned his head and gaped in alarm as Tim banged on the window. It was him! The guy from the pub who must have been kicked by Wally.

'Get out of the cab!' Tim yelled.

'Piss off,' the man yelled back through the closed window, shoving the truck in gear, releasing the brake and revving the engine. As the truck lurched forward, Tim jumped down. The driver, obviously panicking, ground the gears as he tried to get the big vehicle moving.

Tim raced to his car, then took off and swerved around the truck as it headed for the driveway of the servo, pulling his car up in front of it sideways to block the truck's exit. There was a loud screech as the truckie slammed on the air brakes and blasted the horn.

Inside the servo, Tim could see the attendant on the phone, hopefully to the cops, but he pulled out his phone and made a call to the detective, just in case things turned ugly.

'I've got him,' Tim said as soon as the policeman answered the phone, and told him where he was. 'You might get a call from some local coppers in a minute though . . . Do me a favour and explain who I am, will you?'

'What the hell have you done, Warbois?' the policeman groaned.

'Nothing. I haven't laid a hand on him. But I'm not letting this bastard leave, so you better call it in that they need to arrest this guy.'

'I'm on it. Don't do anything. Leave it to the police.'

He hung up and watched the guy rant and rave inside the cabin of the truck. Tim almost wished he'd get out and try to run, but clearly whatever was making him limp had hampered any hope that he could flee on foot. He just hoped the cattle were still okay in the back. He wasn't even sure they were the right cattle yet, but, considering how flighty the driver was, Tim was willing to bet they were. Within minutes, the sound of sirens filled the darkening sky and Tim stepped away from the car and put his hands up. He hoped to God that Hume had managed to get through to these guys or he was going to have to do some pretty fast talking.

Chapter 44

'Are you out of your mind?' Reggie yelled into the phone as soon as Tim answered. 'I cannot believe this is what you were doing all this time. Why the hell would you go after these guys on your own?'

'I'm fine, by the way.'

'I'm so angry right now, Tim,' Reggie snapped. 'This isn't a joke. You could have gotten yourself killed.'

'I didn't have time to stop and think it through, and when I did I'd already gone too far to stop. I didn't mean to worry you.'

'Well, you did! You could have at least answered your phone.'

'I've been in and out of crappy reception,' he said, knowing that none of his reasons would justify his actions to her.

'You took on Simon and those guys all by yourself?' Reggie said after a moment of silence.

'Is that what the police told you?' he asked slowly.

'They wouldn't comment officially, but it's pretty clear they know you did.'

'Look, I honestly wasn't planning on doing any of it. I spotted the guys I saw in the pub the other night and I followed them to see where they lived. I was going to call the cops, but it all moved pretty fast and there wasn't time. I was in a situation I was trained to be in, and it just happened. I know it must seem a bit reckless—'

'You think?'

'I don't expect you to understand—' he started before Reggie cut him off.

'Only because you've never explained anything to me.'

'What?' He was confused by her angry tone.

'I don't know anything about your past. You don't talk about it.'

'I've told you stuff,' he protested.

'Not about your time in the army—except for a few funny stories. But nothing about what you used to do or how taking on a bunch of criminals is somehow supposed to be a *normal* situation for you.' After talking to Detective Hume, Reggie had suddenly realised she barely knew this man she was preparing to start a life with. Somehow what he had done in the army had played a vital part in what he did at that shed.

'I was in the Special Air Services Regiment.'

'What is that? Like Special Forces?'

'Yeah,' he said. 'It's just not something I'm used to talking about with people.'

'Don't you think *I* should know this kind of stuff—we're supposed to be in a relationship!'

'To be honest—no. It's got nothing to do with who I am now, or who we are.'

His frank answer momentarily stunned her. 'I disagree, considering your past just decided to put you in a really dangerous position.'

She heard his drawn-out sigh on the other end of the line and fought back a growing sense of unease. Tim had a whole other life he'd led before they'd met—one that she knew had caused him a great deal of grief and had been part of the reason he'd lost so many of his mates. Sure, for now he seemed like a new person, like he'd made peace with whatever demons he'd arrived here with, but what if they came back someday? If he wouldn't talk about his past, how was she supposed to help him?

'It's been a long day,' Tim said finally, jolting her back to the present. 'I'll head home first thing in the morning and we can talk more then.'

Reggie bit the inside of her lip anxiously. It didn't sit well with her to leave their call on such a cool tone, and the conversation had done nothing to put her mind at ease. 'Okay. See you tomorrow.'

Reggie hung up and swiped at a stray tear that was tumbling down her cheek. She was stressed and tired and Tim was right—it *had* been a long day. Maybe it was just pent-up worry that had found its way into their phone call. After a good sleep, they'd both be in a better place to have this conversation again.

But why did everything suddenly feel as though it had changed for the worse?

❖

All he wanted to do was hold Reggie and fall asleep with her wrapped in his arms. Not spend the night in a roadside donga with a rattling reverse-cycle air-conditioning unit over the bed.

This had been the longest-arse day ever, he thought as he lay down on the uncomfortable mattress in the small room. Try as he might, though, he couldn't get the conversation with Reggie out of his mind.

Maybe he was just tired, and so it all seemed worse than it really was, but Reggie's attack about his past had caught him off guard. *Was it an attack though?* a little voice asked. He pinched the bridge of his nose and closed his eyes. The headache from earlier had returned. He had to admit, with the return of his dormant military training, the unwanted memories he'd thought he'd managed to lay to rest had come back as well.

Rationally, he knew he hadn't been on an operation—it was just that his body and its automatic reaction didn't know the difference, and with the surge of adrenalin came the eventual, plummeting low. A wave of darkness threatened to envelop him, and he fought hard against letting it take over. He didn't want to return to that kind of existence—trapped beneath bad memories that weighed him down.

He sat up slowly and reached for the tablets he'd retrieved from the counter after they'd cleared up everything with the police, and he searched for a glass. His gaze fell onto his phone, and he fought the urge to call Reggie and try to explain. In their current state, it stood a fair chance of backfiring since they were both tired and worked up. He hadn't meant to hurt her feelings by saying she wouldn't understand—and he'd instantly realised his mistake as he said it. But how could she? She wasn't the wife or girlfriend of a serviceman. She didn't understand that there were some things that just weren't spoken about. His work had been dangerous and mostly done covertly. They weren't permitted to discuss what they did or where they went with anyone, even those they were closest to. Today hadn't been about that, but his past—the things Reggie wanted him to talk to her about—was still wrapped up in secrecy and he knew he'd never really be able to share a large part of himself with her.

A text popped up on his phone. He reached for it and peered down at the screen. Alicia. Immediately he clicked on the message.

Have been thinking about you lately. Check in with me when you can. I need to know you're okay.

Of all the times she could have sent a text, she chose right now? Was this some kind of cosmic sign that he needed to pay attention to, or was it just a fluke? It didn't matter, because all of a sudden, he knew there was someone who he could talk to about everything that had been happening; someone who would hopefully have some good advice.

Chapter 45

'You're not coming back today?' Reggie asked slowly, feeling her heart drop. She'd woken up that morning excited about seeing him, only for him to call and tell her he needed to make a detour on the way home and would be gone for a few days.

'I had a message from an old friend last night. We went through a lot of stuff together and I . . . I need to make sure everything's okay. Do you mind?'

'Of course not,' she said, trying to keep the disappointment out of her voice. 'It sounds important.'

'It is, or I wouldn't be going. I miss you.'

'I miss you too. I'm sorry about last night,' she said, wishing she could wait till he got home before they spoke about it and feeling like her hand was forced now that he wasn't coming back for a few days.

'I'm sorry too,' Tim replied. 'I didn't mean for it to come across the way it did. But listen, I need to go. We'll talk about it when I get back, okay?'

His abrupt end to the conversation left her staring at the wall in her bedroom uncertainly. Had she somehow managed to annoy him all over again? 'Okay,' she said warily. 'I'll let you go.'

'I'll be back in a couple of days.'

'Bye,' she managed eventually, but he'd already hung up.

'When's Tim due?' Peggy asked as Reggie came out of her room a few moments later.

'He's not. He's visiting an old friend on his way home.'

'Oh?' Peggy eyed her daughter carefully. 'Is everything okay?'

'Of course,' Reggie said, trying for a smile. 'I mean we had a bit of a weird phone call last night, but I don't think his not coming back has anything to do with that . . . something just came up unexpectedly.'

'Well, every couple fights now and again and you've been through a lot over the last few days. A bit of a break might help things settle down.'

'It wasn't a fight exactly,' Reggie hedged. 'It's just that I suddenly realised there's a large part of his life I don't know anything about.'

'That's not entirely unexpected though, is it? I mean, you're not a pair of teenagers—you both had lives before you met. I'm sure there's a lot he doesn't know about your past too.'

'There's nothing to know about my life, and it's not that. I mean, we've spoken about our lives growing up and our families and he knows all about Brent and that I lived in London, but he never talks about his life in the army. Don't you think that's strange?'

'Not necessarily,' Peg said calmly. 'From what you said about his friends who'd passed away, it seems like that part of his life is extremely painful to relive. I think that kind of pain is something that might never really get spoken about. When your Uncle Ted came back from the war, he would never speak of it—it was as though it hadn't happened. Maybe you should be prepared to face the possibility that Tim may never tell you about the things he's been through— or done.'

'But if you were going to start a life with someone, surely that person has a right to know? To understand why they're like that? How am I supposed to help him?'

'I think you've already helped Tim—it's not really about knowing what to say or do, it's about being there for them.'

The sound of tyres on gravel alerted them to an approaching car.

'That'll be the girls,' Peg said, and Reggie crossed to the window to find a people-mover pulling up outside. 'There's a meeting on today over in Springsvale. Birdie's cousin has a vehicle fitted out for a wheelchair, so they've borrowed it for the day. Isn't that nice of them?'

'Peg, your ride's here,' Ray called out from the verandah.

'I know, I see them,' Peg called back, rolling her eyes at her daughter.

'Wait,' Reggie said. 'You're going to a meeting?'

'I am,' Peggy said decisively. 'It's time I got back out there. Everyone was so lovely at the open day, it reminded me that I'm very lucky to still be here and I'm not going to let fear stop me enjoying things from now on.'

'Oh, Mum,' Reggie said, leaning down and hugging her tightly. 'I'm so proud of you.'

'I'm proud of me too. Now, I don't want to keep them waiting,' she said with a smile, heading for the door.

Reggie followed her mother down the ramp and over to where Birdie and another woman stood at the rear of the vehicle. A hydraulic ramp was lowered and her mother positioned her chair then grinned once she was locked into place. 'See you this afternoon.'

'We'll take good care of her,' Birdie said, patting Reggie's arm as she walked past.

'She looks so happy,' Reggie said as she stood beside her father and waved them off.

'She does, doesn't she.' Ray watched the van drive away with a satisfied look on his face. 'I think we might finally be turning a corner, Reg.'

Reggie remained where she was after her father ambled back to his newspaper and the sunny spot on the verandah. Things were changing again. Her mother's newfound independence was exciting, and it signalled the end of another era. One more step towards returning to a somewhat normal existence. But Reggie couldn't say the same about her own life. Something had changed between her and Tim since yesterday and she wasn't sure what it would mean for them.

❖

Tim parked outside a modest brick house in a quiet cul-de-sac but didn't get out. Memories invaded the silence. How many times had he been here over the years? The kids' trampoline sat in the front yard, a thin layer of leaves covering the top, a signal that maybe they'd outgrown it. He remembered the Christmas Eve they'd put the damn thing together—the four of them, Simmo, Fitzy, Dean and himself. They'd been drunk, tired and not long back from their last tour. He could picture them right there in the yard. The playful insults being hurled, the *unhelpful* advice, the laughter and every now and again, Alicia hissing at them from the front door to keep it down or they'd wake the kids. The pain in his chest was still there as he remembered his mates, but it wasn't the same crippling pain that had made him want to erase it with too much alcohol and try his best to outrun it. It was just there—a dull, sad ache that he knew would stay with him forever.

The front door opened and he looked up at the dark-haired woman standing in the doorway. Another pang went through him. The last time he had seen her was at the funeral.

He opened the door slowly and climbed out. Wordlessly, Alicia stepped forward and they hugged. She felt like a fragile, tiny bird in his arms, but there was a fierceness in her hold on him.

'I'm glad you decided to come,' she said when she finally released him and led him inside to sit at the kitchen bench. 'The kids will be home from school soon. They'll be excited to see you.'

He gave a small smile. He'd really missed being part of all this.

'You look better.'

'I did a lot of soul searching,' he admitted as he watched her move around the kitchen making coffee.

'Where have you been? You just vanished.'

'I needed to go bush for a bit. I ended up in this place in the New England Tableland—it's amazing. The rivers and the fishing; the *quiet*. I stayed on and finished building one of their cabins. It's like I found *home*,' he said softly.

'It sounds great. It's been good for you. You look . . . happier,' she decided, nodding to herself.

'I met someone,' he blurted out.

'You did?' Alicia tipped her head sideways like a curious owl as she studied him. 'She must be pretty special if she managed to get through that wall you built up.'

Tim reached for the mug she handed him and stared into it for a moment before replying. 'It just happened. I don't think either of us expected it. But I'm not sure where to go from here.'

'How do you mean?'

Tim placed the cup on the bench and shook his head irritably. He really needed a shower and a few hours' sleep, but this was important. The need to come back—to talk everything over with someone who knew the real him—had been like a magnet pulling him here. He needed contact with someone who knew who he was, knew what he'd been through, knew *him*.

'It's gonna sound crazy,' he said, smiling self-deprecatingly as he looked at her, then dropping his gaze once more. 'I don't know what happened to me out there, but it was like I was able to talk to Deano and the others—really talk. To tell them everything I was angry at them for and how hard it is here, without them—stuff I'd been carrying inside me for a long time,' he said quietly. 'It helped. It changed things. After that I just felt . . . freer. It was like I could suddenly see things around me for the first time in I don't know how long. And I've got this need inside me to do something *more* with my life. But I have no idea what that is.'

'Is it something to do with this someone you've met?' Alicia asked.

'Reggie. Her name's Reggie,' he said with a small smile. 'We've got some obstacles in our way. She's a farmer and she doesn't want to leave her family farm, so the location can't change. I can pick up some local work contracting, which is fine. It's just that there was this incident,' he said, then paused. 'I fell back into ops mode like it was second nature, you know? It reminded me that I had this whole other life. I was doing something important. Something that mattered. I can't find that in just being a tradie anymore.'

'You know that job only had a limited shelf life,' Alicia said after a few moments.

'Yeah, I know. It burns you out.'

'It burnt all of you out,' Alicia reminded him softly with a sigh. 'But that's the reason none of you could ever settle back into civilian life once you left. There's nothing else out there that really compares. I don't think any of you really understood that until it happened. Dean filled that gap with drugs in the end,' she said sadly. 'I used to blame myself. I used to think we weren't enough for him. Then I'd get angry, because we *should* have been enough.' She looked up and the sorrow in her eyes almost killed him. 'That's why I was so worried about you. I don't have the answers, I don't know if I could have said or done anything differently that would have stopped Dean taking his own life, but I do know the reason he did it was because he could never find anything that felt as good as being in the SAS did.' She reached for Tim's hand and held it tightly. 'You *need* to find that one thing that makes you feel worthy again. I know you can do it. I think deep down you must already know what that one thing is, but promise me you'll keep trying to find what it is,' she said, holding his gaze as firmly as she held his hand. 'Promise you won't give up until you find it.'

'I promise,' he said, his voice hoarse with emotion. But was she right? Did he already know what that one thing was? He wasn't so sure, but Alicia's belief in him—her gritty determination to make him believe in himself—was a powerful thing and, for the first time since this uncertainty had begun to plague him again, he felt a glimmer of hope shining through.

Chapter 46

Reggie finished cleaning the last cabin and closed the door behind her, stopping to look out over the paddocks as the sun sank low and turned the sky into a riot of deep orange and red. 'Red sky at night, shepherd's delight,' she murmured to herself. She could use a nice day of sun to dry out some of the mud left behind from the last lot of rain. She leaned her arms on the rail of the verandah and watched four big roos graze near the dam.

She missed Tim. All day she'd tried to put him out of her mind and failed miserably. She took her phone out of her back pocket and stared at his number on the screen for a moment before giving in to the urge she'd been fighting all day and pressing the call button.

The phone rang in her ear and continued to ring until she decided he must be busy or didn't have it on him.

'Hello? Tim's phone,' a voice answered as she was about to hang up. A very female voice. When Reggie was too shocked to speak there came a second, 'Hello?'

Reggie swallowed back her surprise. 'Hi. I was looking for Tim,' she managed weakly. *Why is a woman answering Tim's phone?*

'He's just in the shower,' the woman explained, and Reggie felt herself gape, before panicking and hanging up as the woman was mid-way through speaking.

Oh my God. Who the hell was that woman? Why had she answered Tim's phone if he was in the shower? A little voice did try to point out that had she not acted like a moron and hung up then she could have asked these questions. But she'd been flustered and it had caught her off guard. Surely there was a logical explanation. Tim wouldn't . . . She let out a small groan. Now she had to act like she wasn't some jealous, neurotic girlfriend checking up on him. Then anger begin to stir. *Was* she being neurotic if a woman unexpectedly answered her boyfriend's phone? What the hell was going on?

Part of her wanted to call back and demand to know who the woman was, and yet another part—the cowardly part— decided the best course of action was to turn off her phone and shove it back into her pocket. *Very mature,* the voice taunted her. Instead of confronting Tim when he eventually found out she'd called, she was going to ignore it. *Because putting it off is such a great way of handling the situation,* the voice pointed out.

'Oh, shut up!' Reggie snapped, leaving the verandah.

❖

Tim walked out of the spare room feeling more optimistic than he'd been when he'd arrived. It was amazing what the combination of sleep, a shower and talking with a close friend could do for the soul. But with one look at Alicia's face, his hopeful mood dropped. 'What is it?'

Alicia gave a small wince. 'I think I just majorly stuffed up. I answered your phone—it was just sitting here on the kitchen bench and I thought it might be something important . . .'

'Is that all?' he said, instantly feeling relieved and taking a step into the room.

'I think it was your *someone*,' she said.

'Reggie?' he asked, confused.

'She hung up before I could explain. I think you better call her back and tell her who I am.'

It then dawned on him *why* Alicia was so concerned. Reggie wouldn't have expected a woman to answer his phone. *Shit*. 'It'll be fine. Reggie's not like that. She'll understand.'

'Call her back *now*,' Alicia said firmly.

He did. It went straight to voicemail. 'She's probably busy feeding animals or something,' he assured Alicia as she stood across from him, anxiously watching his face. 'I'm telling you, it's fine.' But by the fifth time he tried calling and still had no answer, doubts were beginning to creep in.

'I have to go,' he told Alicia, who was nodding in agreement. He said goodbye to the kids, and having fallen back into the favourite uncle role once more he felt that old tug of wistfulness he remembered occasionally feeling whenever he'd spent time with Dean and his kids in the past. Maybe it wasn't too late to have a kid of his own. He could see Reggie teaching a toddler how to ride and her dad teaching the kid to fish, and a sudden flare of hope rose in his chest.

'Thanks for everything,' he said, turning once more to Alicia.

She hugged him tightly before stepping back. 'Keep in touch. I hope everything works out the way you want it to.'

Tim glanced in his rear-view mirror as he drove away and felt a bittersweet mix of emotions. Things would never be the same now that Dean and the others were gone but Alicia and the kids were still important, and they'd all promised each other to take care of their families. In his grief he'd run from that responsibility—but never again. Somehow Reggie would understand, once he explained it all. Deep down he knew she would. It was something he couldn't walk away from.

There were still people he cared about here—and people who cared about him—and that helped ease some of the pain of losing Dean. Now he just had to work out the rest of his life and try to salvage the most important part: Reggie.

Reggie forced herself to turn her phone back on and braced for the notification bing to indicate a missed call. Her phone connected then went crazy as bing after bing chimed, sounding like a poker machine going off on a big win. Crap. She'd underestimated Tim's concern.

As she went to dial his number her screen lit up with a number she didn't recognise.

'Hello?' she answered cautiously.

'Is this Reggie?'

'Yes,' she acknowledged slowly.

'Reggie, we spoke briefly on the phone yesterday. My name's Alicia Johnson. I answered Tim's phone and spoke without thinking. I wanted to explain . . .'

'No. It's okay. I'm sorry I hung up like that, you just surprised me.'

'I can imagine. But I don't want you to get the wrong idea. Tim's a good friend, he's more like family really. He stopped by because he needed to talk to someone. That's all.'

He needed to talk? *That's why he'd made the detour home? To talk to* her? *What was Reggie? Chopped liver? Why couldn't he talk to his girlfriend?*

'Reggie?'

'I'm here. I knew he was visiting an old friend. I just assumed it was an old army friend or something.'

'Well, it kind of was. I was married to Dean,' Alicia said softly, and instantly Reggie let out a slow breath.

'I'm so sorry for your loss,' Reggie finally said after a brief pause. 'Tim told me about Dean . . . and his other friends.'

'They were all close. Like family. I also wanted to call so I could thank you.'

'Thank me?' Reggie said, puzzled by the comment. 'For what?'

'For somehow bringing back the old Tim. The last time I saw him,' she said, and Reggie felt the hesitation that briefly followed, 'was at my husband's funeral. To be honest, Reggie,

I was expecting a call one day to say he'd also taken his own life. He was in a terrible state at the time, and I couldn't help him. I had nothing left to give anyone at that point. I'd just lost my husband—my whole world really,' she said, and Reggie heard the waver in her voice and felt an echoing sadness. 'Seeing Tim yesterday made me so happy. I saw a man who had come out the other side and, according to Tim, you're responsible for that.'

'I think he just found the peace he needed to sort himself out here. At least, I thought he had. Then everything changed. Something's wrong and he won't talk to me about it.'

'I know,' Alicia said gently. 'I can see how you'd be wondering why he'd come here and talk to me and not you.'

'He seemed so happy before.'

'He still is. I think everything about the other day just stirred up some old feelings in him that he needed to talk about with someone who understood his past.'

'Well, that's the point,' Reggie said, feeling exasperated. 'He won't tell me about his old life. He's told me stories about Dean and the others, but he refuses to tell me anything about what he used to do. I have no idea who he was before he arrived here.'

The line went quiet for a moment before Alicia spoke. 'Reggie, the guys did a very dangerous job. They operated under complete secrecy, even most of the people they worked with didn't know what they were doing or where they went—I sure as hell was never told. They would be called out at a moment's notice and gone for months on end. Dean never talked about it with me.'

'How did you live like that? With a family?' Reggie asked.

'We learned to cope. It was part of the deal when I married him—I went into it knowing the demands his job would put on our relationship. I was warned about it many times,' she said, and Reggie could hear a smile in her voice. 'But I was young and stubborn and determined that we could make a marriage work no matter how tough it was. And we did, for a while. But it wasn't easy.

'I know it must be scary—going into a relationship with someone who has secrets, a part of themselves that they'll never share with you—but if it helps, I was married to one and lived with him through that entire time and I still have no idea what they did or where they've been. There are years of my husband's life missing. Gaps I'll never be able to fill. He came home to me and we lived our life but, unfortunately, after Dean left the job, he could never find the peace that Tim obviously has now, and there's a piece of me that's angry about that. I don't know why he couldn't. But please don't let this thing drive a wedge between you. The past that Tim is keeping from you has no bearing on your relationship. It's not personal. It was just something that went along with the job. A job in his past,' she added firmly. 'He needs you, Reggie. He's trying to find his way forward and he will. He'll figure out whatever it is that's niggling at him, but he needs you there alongside him. Don't give up on him yet.'

'Thanks Alicia,' Reggie said, clearing her throat slightly. 'I'm really glad you called.'

'I hope we get to meet in person really soon.'

They said their goodbyes and hung up. For a long while Reggie turned their conversation over in her mind. Surely if Alicia could live with not knowing parts of her husband's life, then she could too?

Chapter 47

Reggie heard the car pull up outside and walked across to the door. Ever since Alicia's call she'd had butterflies in her stomach thinking about when he would arrive, and now that he was here she was bubbling with emotion. As he reached the door, she saw him search her face warily, as though unsure of his welcome. The vulnerable look she saw in his eye pulled at her heartstrings and she stepped into his arms, holding him tightly.

'I'm sorry,' he said against her hair as they held each other.

'No, I am . . . I hated everything about that damn phone call the other night. Can we just pretend it didn't happen?'

'Fine by me,' he said and smiled, pulling away just enough to kiss her. 'But can we move inside and shut the door? It's bloody freezing out here.'

Tim sat on the lounge inside the shed and tugged her into his lap and Reggie burrowed into his arms, savouring the warmth of his chest and his strong arms around her. 'I missed you.'

'I missed you too. But I wasn't sure if I would get a hug or a slap when I turned up. You weren't answering my calls. I need to explain about the woman who answered the phone . . .'

'It's okay. I know all about it. Alicia called.'

'She did?'

'Yeah. Why didn't you just tell me who you were going to see?'

'I wasn't thinking too clearly, I guess. It didn't occur to me that you'd think I was seeing another woman—in that way,' he added.

'It was good you went to find someone to talk to . . . I guess I was a little put out that you didn't think you could talk to me. But I understand it now . . . I get why you'd want to see Alicia. She's your connection to Dean and the others.'

'She is.' Tim nodded slowly, watching her. 'Alicia pointed out that maybe you'd feel like I was shutting you out. That wasn't my intention.'

Reggie nodded back. 'I know. There are parts of your life I wasn't there for. I know Alicia will always be someone you care about.'

'She and the kids are like family—my only family left, really. It's my responsibility to look out for them. Deano'd do the same for me.'

'She's part of your life,' Reggie agreed. 'I hope one day she can be part of mine too.'

His smile, full of relief and something else—a tenderness she hadn't expected—filled his face as he leaned in to kiss her. 'I love you, Reggie,' he said, and Reggie felt her heart skip a beat at his husky tone—emotion making the words sound as though they were being pulled from his chest.

'I love you too.' Her own voice sounded breathless as she fought back a wave of tears, and he gathered her into his arms.

For a long time they simply enjoyed the feeling of holding each other, but eventually they began to remember how long it had been since they'd last eaten.

'I still can't believe you went after those guys,' she said as they rose and began preparing a meal in the small kitchen.

'I wasn't going to let everything you and your family worked so hard for slip through my fingers when I could do something to stop it.'

'Nothing is worth taking the risk you took. They found weapons and drugs in that car, Tim. Those guys were bad. You were lucky you caught them off guard.'

'I don't think luck had anything to do with it,' he objected with a scoff, before seeing her eyes narrow. He decided to set aside his dinted ego for the moment. 'I'm glad they got them off the street.'

She reached up to put a hand to the side of his face. '*You* got them off the street.'

'I'll feel better once I know Parson's father isn't going to get him off on some lame excuse.'

'Doesn't seem much chance of that. I'd say Simon will be out of action for quite a number of years.'

'Never liked that prick anyway,' Tim said, sliding his arms around her waist.

She'd missed him so much and it'd only been two nights. If ever she'd needed confirmation about how serious this thing was between them, she'd just gotten it. 'We better go in and see Mum and Dad. I had to talk them out of a marching band and a ticker-tape parade for when you arrived home,' she said dryly. 'Mum's made a cake to celebrate the return of the mighty hero.'

'I wasn't trying to be a hero,' Tim muttered, then winced. 'That's not what any of this was about. That's what I'm trying to tell you, Reggie. That stuff is just what I do . . . did . . . once upon a time.'

'I know,' she said, and this time she didn't feel the same stab of unease about his past. This was who he was. And she could accept that. He was with her now, and that was all that mattered.

Reggie paced the verandah three days later, checking the road every time she heard a car engine. 'Would you sit down?' her father asked wearily after the third time she got up to check. 'You'll wear a hole in the boards.'

'They should be here by now,' she muttered.

'They'll get here when they get here.'

Once the truck and stock had been impounded, they'd had to wait for the DNA results to come back before the police could release the livestock, and now finally they were on their way home.

Wally was eating contentedly in the paddock near the house, no worse for wear after his little adventure. Reggie let out a shaky breath as the memory of discovering him gone replayed in her mind. *It's over now,* she told herself firmly. *He's back and safe.* It had been a very close call.

Tim came outside carrying a tray of coffees Peggy had gone inside to make. He placed them on the table. 'Still no sign?'

'No, maybe I should give them a call to make sure everything's al—' Her words were cut short by the sound of a truck engine slowing down and within moments a vehicle came into sight. 'They're here!' Reggie rushed out the gate and down towards the cattle yards where the big truck was preparing to back up to the loading ramp.

Inside, she could hear the jostling of anxious cattle waiting to be unloaded and nervously bit the inside of her lip as she waited for the doors to open.

There was a series of bangs and bumps as cattle shuffled and manoeuvred themselves, bellowing and calling out to one another amid the chaos of barking dogs and men yelling. But after a few minutes the large beasts made their way out of the truck, down the ramp and into the yards.

Reggie watched on as the cattle were unloaded, her eyes scanning each animal as they lurched into the yards, enjoying their sudden freedom after the confinement of the truck. A vet had given them a health check before loading, but Reggie still checked them over with her own eyes, needing to make sure for her own peace of mind that they were all okay.

She shaded her eyes against the sun as she did a head count and was finally able to release the last of the tension she'd been holding onto. While her dad talked to the truck driver, Reggie glanced up to see Detective Hume walking towards her.

'All there?' he asked, wearing a gentle smile.

'Yep. All accounted for.' She grinned back. 'I can't thank you enough.' To her dismay, she felt the sharp sting of tears threatening.

'We can't take all the credit,' Hume said, lifting his chin in greeting as Tim came across to her side. 'But I have to say, it makes this job worthwhile when we have a win like this. I'm just glad it all worked out.'

'Me too.' Reggie turned her gaze back to the cattle and heard Wally bellowing excitedly at the sudden reunion with his girls. 'I think Wally even more so,' she added.

For the rest of the day, Reggie, her father and Tim finished the vaccinations and retagging they'd been planning on doing before near disaster had struck, and once they'd finished— tired, dirty and sore—Reggie had never felt more complete.

'I've been thinking a lot about things . . . about us,' Tim said late that night as they lay in bed.

'What about us?' she asked, sounding sleepy.

'What we talked about a little while ago. About what I planned on doing. I don't think I want to start up my own business, at least not in building.'

'So, what do you want to do then?' He heard the slight hesitation in her voice and swallowed.

'That's the million-dollar question,' he sighed. 'Parson said the whole district thinks I'm some kind of gold-digger,' he told her.

'Simon Parson was just ousted as a drug dealer and cattle thief. Do you really think you should be listening to anything he said?'

'But it's true, isn't it,' Tim said dully. 'You must have picked up on it? Noticed how people looked at me when you introduced me. You're supposed to be with someone who's in the cattle industry—someone they consider your equal. Not some tradie blow-in from Sydney.'

'Since when has anyone else's opinion ever bothered me? I don't care what people think. We know the truth. Mum and Dad know the truth. And I can guarantee you, if anyone was stupid enough to actually voice any of that, my parents would be the first to pull them up on it. You don't have to worry about that stuff. Besides, it'll be old news now—the Parsons' fall from grace will be all anyone is talking about for the next couple of months.'

Tim sighed. 'What if one day you realise you don't have a farmer by your side and you feel let down or something?'

'Are you breaking up with me?' Reggie asked after a moment.

'What? No,' he said, shifting in the bed so that he was looking down at her. 'I'm just pointing out that, at the moment, I guess I don't feel like your equal in this whole thing, and it freaks me out a bit,' he said, before dropping back onto his pillow and staring up at the ceiling. 'It took losing Dean to make me realise I'd just been existing after I left the army.

I feel like I need to be doing something *more* with my life—something important. Something that gives me the same satisfaction as farming gives you. I just have no idea what it is.'

'Your building doesn't do that?' she asked.

'I used to think it did, but after the other day—using my training and realising it was like second nature—it brought back how much the army meant to me. I don't think anything else really compares with that. I'm not sure anything else ever will.'

'Are you thinking about re-enlisting?'

'No,' he said with a shake of his head. 'I don't think I can go back—not now with all the boys gone. It just felt good, *doing* something. Something I was good at.'

'Maybe you're good at other things you don't even realise you're good at yet,' Reggie said thoughtfully.

'What do you mean?'

'What about what you were saying once, about the fishing thing. What if you put together a program to help people who might be struggling like Deano and the others? You'd be the perfect person to do it. You understand what they're going through. You have the contacts and the background. You have the place to do it—right here.'

'Here?'

'You said yourself it helped *you* heal.'

'I don't know, Reg, I'm not a counsellor or anything. I don't actually *know* how to help people,' Tim said doubtfully.

'So, go research it. Find out how to set it all up.'

Suddenly a thousand things began running through his head at once. What if he really did create a program that could help others like him? What if he *could* save just one Deano or one Simmo? But surely this was a crazy idea. He didn't even know where to start.

'Sleep on it,' he heard Reggie say as she kissed his cheek and rolled over. For a long time he lay there listening to the sound of her breathing as ideas continued to roll through his brain. It was early morning before he finally felt himself begin to drift off to sleep.

Chapter 48

Tim sat in his four-wheel-drive in the driveway at River Styx and let out a slow breath. It'd been a long week. He'd started working on the job in Armaglen, trying to take his mind off everything else going around inside his head. He didn't mind the casual work—the blokes he worked with were easy to get along with and the job was interesting without being too challenging, but something was lacking. He'd lost the drive he usually had for his job. Somehow everything seemed different.

He looked up from where he'd been staring at the dash of his car and spotted a lone figure down by the dam.

The sun was sinking low in the sky as he headed down to the water's edge. 'Catch anything?' Tim asked Ray as he sank to his haunches. They looked over the water as it gently rippled in the light breeze.

'A few. Not long till we don't have to throw 'em back. Trout season is just around the corner,' he announced happily. A silence settled between them as the two men soaked in the quiet surrounding them. 'Got somethin' on your mind?' Ray prodded a few minutes later.

Tim pulled at some grass beside him and twisted it through his fingers. 'This program thing . . . Reggie said she spoke to you about it?'

'Yep. She did.'

'You think it's a good idea?' Tim asked hesitantly.

'I think there's a real need for it. Has been for a long time. For too long we've turned our backs on blokes comin' back from war. Saw it with my brother in the seventies and my father talked about it with men from his generation and the one before that too.' Ray shook his head. 'I reckon it's past time all this stuff was dragged out in the open and dealt with. There's been too much bloody pain.'

Ray's words made Tim swallow over a lump in his throat. 'I don't know if I'm the right one to do it. I don't have the answers. I couldn't even save my own mates,' he said, and to his horror heard his voice crack with emotion. Tim clamped his lips shut and tossed the grass away, staring down at the dirt between his boots.

'Son, no one said you had to have the answers. If it was that simple, we'd have worked out how to fix it by now. Seems to me you just have to find a way to open some of those doors. Men don't like to sit and pour their guts out to their mates like women do—it's just the way it is—but in our own time, and in a place that lets us breathe and quietens the noise . . .

well, that's when some of the pressure comes off. I reckon your job is to be here to listen. You don't have to fix anythin'.'

Ray's words eased some of his doubts. It sounded simple, but he wasn't dumb enough to believe it would be. Then again, maybe it didn't have to be complicated. He'd spoken to a lot of people over the last few weeks and a number of services were keen to jump on board. The idea had become a full-blown mission—one he couldn't stop thinking about.

'So,' Ray drawled slowly. 'I guess the question is, are you gonna do it?'

Tim felt his uncertainty disappear and he stood up, looking across at the man who'd quietly stepped in and opened a few doors of his own. 'Yeah. If you'll be around to give me a hand?'

He caught the flicker of surprise in the older man's eyes before Ray cleared his throat and gave a nod. 'Yeah. I reckon I'll be around.'

'There's one more thing I wanted to talk to you about,' Tim said as Ray started packing up his fishing gear.

Life went back to a kind of normal in the weeks that followed the great cattle heist, as her father liked to refer it to. They could make the odd joke about it, but there'd be no forgetting it had almost ruined them.

For Reggie, it brought home the importance of her brother's breeding program. This was Brent's legacy. He'd taken on Jock's vision of registering and creating this new breed and now it was Reggie's turn to carry on that dream. It was a huge responsibility, but she finally felt up to the challenge.

She soaked up as much knowledge as she could, reading till midnight in bed and picking her father's brains. At last, she'd found her calling as a farmer.

She noticed the dogs' ears prick up and followed their gaze to spot Tim coming towards her. She kissed him lightly, then rested her head against his shoulder as they stood side by side and watched the cattle grazing in the paddock before them.

'Thought I'd find you down here,' he said.

'Yeah, I've just been plotting my dream breeding plans.'

'The embryo thing?' he asked.

'It's a long way off yet, but with our herd back everything's still on track to keep going that way.'

'What if it wasn't a long way off?' he asked.

'What do you mean?'

'What if you could buy the surrogate cows and set up the mad-scientist-embryo-lab you needed, now?'

Reggie gave a small snort. 'Yeah, 'cause that's doable last time I checked with the accountant.'

'I want to invest.'

Reggie turned her head and stared at him.

'I sold an investment property. Sydney house prices have gone through the roof lately and I figured I'd cash in while I stood to make a decent profit.'

Reggie looked at him, speechless.

'I spoke to your dad about starting up the retreat thing.'

'That's good . . . What did he say?' she asked slowly, still not sure what this had to do with anything.

'He told me to go ahead and do it,' he said. He stared out at the cattle calmly, but she detected the slight waver of emotion beneath his words.

'That's awesome,' she said softly. 'You know Dad always thought it was a great idea.' She'd been talking about it with her parents for a while and knew they were both interested in seeing where Tim's idea would go.

'The thing is, it means a lot to me to have their support, and to have your support too, but if I go ahead with it, I have a condition,' he said, stepping back to look down at her earnestly. 'I want to use the money from the house sale to buy the extra cattle you need and build a proper shed and yard system to do all the embryo hocus-pocus stuff on the farm.'

Reggie blinked and opened her mouth, but he hurried on.

'I don't want to be a farmer,' he said. 'I still have no idea what you're talking about when you rattle off words like genetic gain and flushing versus IVF and oocytes and follicles,' he said, 'and I'd seriously rather poke a fucking stick in my eye than learn about it. But I *do* want to be involved as a silent investor and a farmhand. Hell, I'll even be an assistant midwife, but you and your dad will continue to run the cattle side of things.'

'Tim, that's a lot of money. It's your savings. Your investment.'

'I'm investing it.' He shrugged. 'You've been talking about nothing else, so I know you're eventually going to get a return back on it.'

'Yeah, *eventually* being the key word. We won't be seeing any profits for a good couple of seasons yet. It could take years to pay you back.'

'It's an investment, not a loan,' he told her pointedly. 'And I don't care how long it takes to see a return, I intend to be around for a while,' he said, sliding his hand into his jacket pocket. 'In fact, and this isn't just to keep an eye on my invest- ment, if you'll have me, I'll guarantee I'll stick around,' he said, opening a small grey box to reveal a sparkling diamond ring.

Reggie felt her mouth drop open. 'What. The. Actual. *Hell?*' she whispered, staring at the bedazzling glitter of the diamond in its box.

'Not the exact response I was hoping for,' Tim said. Her gaze shot to his to find him watching her warily.

'You surprised me . . . I wasn't expecting . . . Yes!' she said quickly. 'Hell yes!'

'Yes?' he asked, still looking at her cautiously.

'Yes! I'll keep you around.'

She saw the relief flood across his face and his tense expression fell into a wide smile as he picked her up, twirling her in a circle.

'So, just to be clear, by keeping me around . . . you get that I'm asking you to marry me, right?' he said, letting her slide down to set her back on the ground.

'Yes, I got that,' she said and smiled, shaking her head. 'But just so *you* know, investor or not—that doesn't mean I'm going to start taking orders from you.'

'What?' He feigned shock. 'I'm pretty sure that'll be some- where in the fine print.'

'You have a lot to learn, grasshopper,' she said, patting his cheek before she reached up to kiss him.

'And I can't wait to start,' he said, pulling her close.

Acknowledgements

Lyn for the constant read-throughs and occasional brainstorming sessions (which now happen via phone instead of over a cuppa on the verandah). Keith McArdle, fellow Aussie author, and David Ross. Annette Barlow, publisher extraordinaire. Renae Haley, for always being happy to supply gruesome medical info in the name of research—complete with photos! Glenda Grey for the inspiration behind our Blue Bull and countless messages back and forth answering my questions. True Blue Southern Cross Stud is as much yours, my friend, as it is mine!

My son Rourke, for his helpful brainstorming assistance over Tim's rifle and the amazing backstory that would have needed an entire book of its own.

Sue from Onward Murray Greys for the insightful and always educational posts on farming. If you're interested in getting a real-life glimpse into the struggles and triumphs of a cattle producer, head over to their Facebook page. Sue is a shining example of how passionate our farmers are about their livestock and the process of producing these amazing animals.

A big thank you to Russ, who patiently answered lots of my questions, from the beautiful Two Styx cottage in Ebor—a gorgeous property where you can stay and explore the spectacular New England region. We truly are blessed to have so much of nature's wonderland on our doorstep—the waterfall trail and national parks in this area are well worth a long weekend visit to explore.

Also, a big thank you to my long-time reader and friend Steve Grant, the best truckie I know, and to all my readers and Facebook friends who constantly support me. Without you, I'd just be some crazy person listening to voices in my head instead of having the legitimate job description of writer!

If you loved *Wish You Were Here*, read on for a sneak peek into Karly Lane's new book . . .

For Once In My Life

Jenny Hayward cannot believe that she's fifty years old and a grandmother with adult children! When did that happen? Not that long ago her three daughters were in school and Jenny was following her dream of becoming a nurse.

In the two years since her husband walked out, Jenny has been absorbed in her family and work, until her daughters and her best friend secretly set her up with a profile on a dating app and she is thrust unexpectedly into the world of dating.

However, as the dates keep coming, Jenny wonders how the people she loves the most in the world have managed so impressively to pick the wrong men for her.

The annoying barman watching on is much more enjoyable company. The barman who is more than a decade younger than her. Yet Nick doesn't seem to notice her age at all . . .

Is Jenny's next date the date of her dreams?

One

Jenny Hayward flopped down on the lounge chair, kicked off her shoes and closed her eyes as she let out a slow breath. Home. The silence of the house was like a soothing balm to the hectic pace of the hospital. It'd been a long day—a long *two years*, if she were being honest. That was when her husband of twenty-seven years had announced he was moving out.

Lost in the shock and pain of his betrayal, Jenny had turned the house into her sanctuary, doing a clean-out of anything she didn't find comforting or calming. Her best friend, Beth—dark-haired, Italian-Maltese—became a slightly more intimidating version of the decluttering queen, Marie Kondo, as she held open a garbage bag and barked, 'Does it bring you joy? No? Well chuck it!' In a couple of days, they'd transformed the house. It had been nothing short of a miracle.

Jenny had never been a big believer in the whole crystals and energy hocus-pocus the way Beth was, but weary and heartsick, she couldn't have summoned the strength to protest even if she'd wanted to when Beth had told her to 'leave everything to me'.

As far as makeovers went, there hadn't been anyone better qualified for the job. Beth had always had a knack for decorating and had done a course, intending to one day turn her talent into a business. She'd filled Jenny's house with soft furnishings, scattered soothing colours about the rooms and added little touches—a plant here, a Buddha statue there and, of course, her signature crystal-infused candles, which she'd begun making during Covid and had become a booming success.

'When you've been knocked down, bloodstone will pick you back up,' she'd said, then had placed little pottery bowls of tourmaline near the front and back doors and lit a candle, carrying it through the house like a priest performing an exorcism. 'This will flush out all the negative vibes and allow the good stuff back in,' she'd explained as a delicious scent of sage, black tea and bergamot filled the room. In Jenny's bedroom, she'd scattered amethyst, informing her that it would relieve stress and anxiety and promote a chill vibe for sleeping.

And there'd been more. Beth had placed her candles infused with their healing crystals in every nook and cranny, and as much as Jenny—a level-headed, science-based nurse—wanted to scoff at the ridiculousness of the idea, she'd found herself noticeably calmer and the house, which had always been full of the eggshells she'd been walking on, suddenly felt like a *home*. Of course, the candles smelled gorgeous, but maybe there *was* something in the whole crystal thing, because now her house was a haven and she loved coming home to it at the end of a long shift.

Sometimes it seemed hard to believe the split had been that long ago. Austin had been her life for so long. They'd had a reasonably happy marriage, getting married young and starting a family. Jenny had always wanted a brood of children, but Austin—ever practical—had declared that two kids were all they could afford. Deep down, she'd known he was right. After all, she'd had her hands full with an almost-two-year-old and a newborn. As the girls grew older, she'd learned to ignore the little whimper inside whenever they passed by a baby in the shopping centre. It was silly—she was far too busy for any more children, she'd remind herself.

After Brittany started school and she only had Savannah at home, Austin began to hint at Jenny going back to work. His income as a salesman in a white goods store wasn't stretching all that far and raising two children on a single wage was never going to get them where they were hoping to go. The only job she'd ever had was as a check-out chick in a grocery store from when she'd left school up until going on maternity leave with Brittany, and as much as she'd enjoyed the job and the people she'd worked with, it had been almost five years and everyone she'd known had moved on. She wanted to do something different, only she wasn't sure *what* exactly. Austin hadn't been overly sympathetic when she'd brought up her concerns. 'It's not like you've had any burning ambitions to have a career or anything. We just need something that brings in a pay cheque.' Which she had to grudgingly admit was true, but it did nothing to still that growing restlessness she was noticing inside. All she was any good at was having babies. She loved being a mother, but unfortunately, you didn't get paid for that, so she knew she needed to start thinking seriously about what did pay—and what she'd enjoy doing.

In the end, the answer had arrived in the form of her aunty, who'd commented on how short-staffed the hospital system was and that Jenny should think about becoming a nurse.

'But I didn't even finish high school,' Jenny had said.

'You can go in as a mature student. Do a bridging course and enrol in university. You'd make a great nurse.'

Jenny had chewed the idea over in her head for a while. It hadn't crossed her mind before. She wasn't sure why; her aunty was a nurse and she had multiple cousins who were nurses, but she'd always considered herself not quite smart enough to do anything that would require getting a degree.

She'd brought it up with Austin, who'd laughed, then sobered at the look on her face. 'How would we afford university? That's a lot of money for something you didn't even want to do before today.'

'I wasn't planning on enrolling right now,' she snapped, hurt by his lack of encouragement, which immediately caused all her insecurities to resurface. 'It was just an idea.'

She handed her resume to the local supermarket the next day and managed to pick up a few hours a week. She put Savannah into day care for the days she worked, hating every minute of it. Guilt became Jenny's constant companion. She felt guilty that she was putting her child in day care when she should be at home looking after her. She felt guilty that she resented her husband for making her go back to work so early when she knew the money would help out enormously. She felt guilty for hating a job she was lucky to have when there were people who didn't have one. The guilt went on and on, draining her energy and making her miserable.

Eventually, she'd brought up the nursing idea over coffee with Beth, who'd encouraged her to enrol in a bridging course so she could think about university in the future if she still wanted to. Jenny didn't tell Austin. What if she failed? What if she couldn't even get over this first hurdle?

What if you can? her little voice of reason piped up helpfully.

Jenny studied and submitted her assignments and, to her surprise, she was passing—not only passing, but doing better than she'd ever done at school. She discovered she was enjoying it. *Her! Enjoying* study? It was crazy. Managing to keep her newly acquired diploma a secret, by the end of the year she'd worked up the courage to apply to university to see what happened. To her shock, Jenny was accepted into a nursing degree.

Telling Austin hadn't been as bad as she'd been anticipating, at least not once she'd assured him she could get a student loan to cover her fees, and so there she was, sitting in a lecture room, surrounded by other people like her—some older, most younger—but other people excited to be taking this next step and forging themselves a bright path into a new career. She'd never felt more alive.

It'd been a crazy time, juggling two small children and study, but she'd managed with Beth lending a hand to babysit and cheer her on. Her graduation had been the proudest day of her life, with her family travelling to be there and Austin accepting all the congratulations and admiration about how difficult it must have been for them all to have taken such a huge thing on. She'd put aside her irritation, deciding not to bring up the countless arguments they'd had over the time, when he'd occasionally had to cook his own dinner or heaven forbid, find his work clothes in the folding when she'd been struggling to meet a deadline.

Jenny gave a small smile. Back then she'd had so many big plans.

After that, life finally started to get easier. The girls were a little older and both in school. She loved her job and the people she worked with and the extra income—nothing outrageously wonderful—but enough to allow them to move into a bigger house with a backyard and room to grow. Austin had scored a job with a large firm and had his sights set a lot higher than being a salesman. He seemed happier than he'd been in a long time.

Then one day she found herself staring down at two red lines on a pregnancy test.

It wasn't that she didn't *want* another baby, it was just that their lives had moved on from nappies and toilet training. Brittany was eight and Savannah was six and now she'd be going back to breastfeeding and sleepless nights after taking for granted the fact that she'd finally got both children sleeping in their own beds.

If she hadn't been so caught up in everything going on, she probably would have realised that it was at this very point in time that her marriage had begun its downhill slide.

'You can't be pregnant. Take another test,' Austin had said after staring at her for what seemed an eternity.

'I took two,' she told him dully. But at his insistence, she did a third test and watched his face fall as the twin stripes appeared in the window.

'I knew I should have got that bloody vasectomy years ago!' he growled, getting to his feet to pace the room.

'I didn't stop you,' she pointed out.

'You didn't make the appointment though, did you?'

It wasn't her place to do it, she thought irritably. He was a grown man more than capable of booking his own doctor's appointment and yet maybe he had a point. Had she been the one who'd wanted him to have the vasectomy, she would have definitely booked it in and seen to all the arrangements, but she was beginning to suspect that perhaps she hadn't felt entirely comfortable with their options being so . . . final, despite the fact she wasn't exactly over the moon about the news either.

'We should never have trusted the pill. How did it even happen?'

'I don't know,' she said, sinking to the edge of their bed. 'It was probably when the kids were sick a few weeks ago. I had a touch of it—an upset stomach,' she said.

'You're supposed to be a bloody nurse. How did you not realise you wouldn't be protected?'

'I don't know!' she snapped irritably. He was right, she should have suspected that diarrhoea, even a slight case of it, could have affected the pill's protection. It hadn't helped that they'd also had sex unexpectedly. Their sex life had been as dismal as their budget over the last few years, with her exhausted from shift work most of the time, and him travelling with his new job so much. She simply hadn't thought about any consequences—hadn't for so long that she'd almost forgotten about sex being linked to babies and stretch marks!

Eventually, shock had turned into acceptance and Jenny found herself becoming excited about baby number three. Everything would be fine. They'd manage—they always had in the past, they would again.

Chloe had been the perfect baby—adored by her two older sisters and managing to wrap her father around her little finger from the very first moment he'd laid eyes on her. The initial concerns about having another baby seemed to have been forgotten and life settled into a new rhythm. Everything *seemed* to be fine-ish. But she'd felt Austin pulling away. At first it hadn't been that noticeable—his work took him away on conferences and training seminars, so it was normal that when he was getting home she was heading out on a night shift, like ships passing in the night. Then it was *her* job causing issues. She needed to do casual shifts after her maternity leave in order to keep her registration, so she was often stressed and tired, looking after a young baby on top of the odd work hours. Intimacy had naturally taken a back seat for a while. She noticed, of course, but she wasn't too concerned—in a year or two things would settle down and they'd reconnect and get back on track . . . Only they hadn't. Nothing went back to any kind of old normal. Instead, they settled into some *new* normal that was only ever supposed to be temporary.

Over the next ten years or so, the investment apartment in Sydney they'd bought so Austin didn't have to pay for accommodation on his numerous trips eventually became his full-time residence—for work. Then he'd dropped his bombshell on her: he'd been seeing someone down there for two months. He'd seemed surprised when Jenny had been shocked.

'You barely even notice I'm gone,' he'd accused when he'd come home to announce he wanted out of their marriage.

'That's because you're never here,' she'd thrown back.

'Because I was working. To give you and the kids a better life.'

'And I haven't been?'

'My career has always been the one that allowed us to live the lifestyle we have. Do you honestly think you'd be living in this house or that the girls would have got a new car for their birthdays if it wasn't for my job? Your pay cheque wouldn't cover half of this stuff.'

She'd been stunned, truly shocked by his remarks. She shouldn't have been—she'd always known Austin was ambitious. When they were first married, he'd lay awake at night and tell her all about his plans for making his first million. She'd always let him dream big without trying to pop his bubble—she'd never cared about the money side of things, she had everything she'd ever wanted: healthy children, a stable marriage and a house to live in. But Austin had never been satisfied with what they had for long, always striving for more. And she took offence at his belittling her career. She hadn't become a nurse to make a fortune. She loved her job, despite the fact it was stressful and nurses were underpaid and often under appreciated. She did it because she cared about people and wanted to look after them. And she was good at it.

She still loved her job, Jenny thought as she pushed herself up off the lounge and headed for the black tourmaline candle on the sideboard, lighting it with a decisive strike of a match.

There was no room in this house for bad energy anymore. She took a long breath in and let the spicy citrus scent fill her senses.

She wasn't sure why she'd felt a need to let the past intrude on her thoughts like this. She'd spent the last few years learning how to be herself and she had to admit this newfound independence thing could be quite exhilarating. It was time to stop looking back and focus on the future.

Two

The sound of the front door opening and voices chatting drew Jenny's gaze to the living room entryway. She smiled as a small human cyclone came running across the room towards her.

'Nanna!'

'Sophie!' Jenny gathered the grinning toddler in her arms and hugged her until she squirmed and wriggled to be put down. It was hard to believe that in, three short months, her only grandchild was going to be two.

Brittany, Jenny's eldest daughter, had moved back home six months earlier when rental prices skyrocketed in the area after Covid sent the real-estate market through the roof. As a single mother who worked as a teacher's aide in a small school, it had become impossible for Brittany to afford rent. While most of Jenny's friends looked forward to their children moving out so they could redecorate their empty nest, Jenny was happy to have hers living at home again. The house had been quiet with only herself and her youngest, Chloe, living there.

Shortly after Brittany and Sophie had moved in, Savannah had come home from backpacking overseas to pick up a bit of work before meeting up with some travel friends. The six weeks had turned into an open-ended kind of arrangement. Now, with her three grown daughters back home, it felt like a bunch of flatmates living together, only Jenny still had to play referee and break up arguments over who was hogging the bathroom in the morning. But most of the time she enjoyed this new adult companionship.

'Leave the cat alone!' Brittany called after the toddler, who was gleefully chasing the cranky old tabby that simply wouldn't die. The damn thing had to be close to twelve and was still going strong.

'How was your day?' Jenny asked as Brittany dropped a bright pink Bluey backpack on the table followed by her own huge tote bag. She often wondered where her girls had gotten their height from—certainly not from her. Brittany, dressed in a flowy maxidress that would have bunched on the ground if Jenny was wearing it, her long black hair pulled back in a thick ponytail, always looked so graceful—something Jenny had never been able to pull off.

'Long. How about yours?'

'Yep. Same.'

'One more day to go till Friday,' Brittany said, coming to a stop beside her as Jenny stretched her arm out and fist-bumped her.

'We got this,' she said with a determined nod.

'You'd better go and get ready,' Brittany said.

Jenny fought back a sigh. Damn it. She'd forgotten.

Once a month, they went down to the markets. Jenny loved the night markets—they were breathing fresh life into Barkley and always had such a great vibe—but she was finding it difficult to summon up the energy to get dressed and leave the house again. Once upon a time, between kids' activities, work and sport, she'd barely stayed at home. Nowadays, however, nothing gave her more pleasure than an early night curled up in her pjs, watching a chick flick with a glass of wine. But that was not going to happen tonight.

Jenny got out of the shower and wrapped the towel around herself as she walked into her bedroom, noticing Savannah sitting on the end of her bed, curly blonde hair cascading over her shoulder, wide blue eyes studying her mother thoughtfully. Her middle child was the most outgoing of her three children. She was Jenny's little adventurer. And the one she seemed to worry the most about. She'd left university—or rather, 'put it on hold for a bit', as Savannah described it—to go and travel for a year. That had been about five years ago and, other than the compulsory return home after her visas ran out, she'd pretty much been working and backpacking the entire time.

'What were you planning on wearing tonight?' Savannah asked as she leaned back on her arms.

Jenny raised her eyebrows at her daughter's sudden interest in her fashion choices but shrugged nonchalantly. 'Jeans and a top, I suppose.'

'That's what you always wear,' Savannah said dismissively, then pushed herself up and walked across to her wardrobe. 'How about this?' She held up a teal and brown dress. 'With those tan boots you bought. And maybe a belt.'

'Don't you think that's a little dressy for the night markets?'

'You should start dressing up more. You don't want to become one of those women who let themselves go.' Savannah draped the garment on the bed and bent down to place the boots on the carpet beneath it, giving it a firm nod of approval.

'I hardly think my seventy-odd dollar jeans and the ninety-nine-dollar blouse I just purchased is letting myself go.' She'd recently found an online boutique she loved and had been splurging a little more than usual on new outfits.

'Oooh,' Savannah said, her eyes brightening as she ducked into her mother's walk-in wardrobe and produced a garment. 'This denim jacket you got would look awesome over the top.'

Jenny shook her head wearily, giving up trying to protest. Part of her wanted to see what the outfit looked like. She'd had no idea what she was going to wear the jacket with, wasn't even sure why she'd bought it in the first place, only that it had looked too nice *not* to buy. Maybe she did need to cut back a bit with the online shopping.

'Okay, fine. Get out and let me get dressed,' she mumbled, snatching up the clothing from the bed.

'And do your make-up,' Savannah threw over her shoulder.

'Make-up? It's just us and Beth going to the damn night markets,' she said, exasperated by this sudden bossiness. They tried to do something with Beth every few weeks when her husband, Garry, a fly in, fly out worker, was away.

'Will it kill you to wear some make-up once in a while? Seriously, Mother.'

I'll give you seriously, Mother *in a minute*, Jenny thought, but eyed her reflection in the mirror critically. Lately she'd been ignoring the faint crinkles in the corner of her eyes. They were laugh lines, she reminded herself, before reaching for the foundation she hardly ever bothered wearing. Maybe she could go and get her eyelashes and brows tinted again soon. It seemed like a waste of time and money when she rarely went anywhere, but if the kids were beginning to notice she was giving up on the maintenance, did that mean her age was starting to show?

She was fifty. Fifty! When the hell had that happened? When she was a kid, fifty had been ancient—incomprehensible, really. Suddenly, though, she was staring down a very confronting barrel. She was a fifty-year-old divorced woman with adult children . . . and a grandchild, she reminded herself. Crap! *She was a divorced grandmother!* God, that sounded even worse. *Stop it*, she told herself firmly as she applied eyeliner and eyeshadow. *You're being ridiculous.*

When she headed downstairs to the living room a few moments later, she found the others waiting and it crossed her mind that it was a little odd that she wasn't the one calling to her three daughters to hurry up and get ready. Even Beth had already arrived.

'Are we ready, then?' Jenny asked after she'd kissed Beth's cheek. But she paused when she realised no one else was following her to the door.

'What's going on?' she asked.

'Okay, so don't be mad,' Brittany started, and dread filled Jenny. Nothing good *ever* started with that phrase.

'The thing is, Mum,' Savannah said, picking up from her sister, 'we kind of *did* something.'

'Did what?' Jenny asked as real panic began to set in.

'We're not going to the markets,' Beth said. 'Well, *we are*,' she corrected, glancing at the other girls, 'but *you're* not.'

'What Beth's trying to say'—Brittany once again took the baton and ran with it—'is that we've organised a date for you.'

'You've *what*?'

'There's this app—a dating app—and we kind of set you up on it,' Chloe said excitedly.

Jenny had a million questions racing through her head but not a single one of them would come out as she stared with growing horror at her children and best friend.

'We thought it might take a while to get a response so we didn't say anything, but the notifications have been going off all day, so we accepted,' Chloe continued with a small squeal and clap of her hands. Her honey-blonde hair was pulled back in a high ponytail that was swinging like a cheerleader's.

'You accepted a date *for* me? Without asking if I even wanted to go on it?'

'You would have said no,' Savannah said.

'Of course I would have. This is insane.'

'Jen,' Beth started in the calm, let's-talk-the-crazy-woman-down voice she'd had plenty of practice using on Jenny over the years. 'The girls just thought this would be something fun for you to do . . . you know, get out of the house a bit.'

'You thought it was too,' Savannah reminded Beth, clearly not about to be thrown under the bus alone.

'Well, you can just go and *un*-accept and explain what happened.'

'We can't,' Brittany said with a slight wince. 'He's on his way over.'

'What!'

'It'll be fine,' Savannah said, airily. 'We checked him out; it's not like we'd set you up with some weirdo.'

'*How* did you check him out?' Jenny asked, suddenly concerned.

'We've been chatting online to him,' Chloe said.

'So, he's perfectly happy to be set up on a date with someone's mother? This doesn't scream *weird* at all?' Jenny asked, searching their faces frantically.

'Well, technically, he thought he was chatting to *you*,' Brittany admitted.

Jenny opened her mouth to yell, but nothing came out. She couldn't seem to manage a single coherent word as she stared at her best friend and daughters, lined up like a football team's front row, staring her down determinedly.

'You can't be serious.'

'We are. It's all been arranged.'

'But I don't *want* to go on a date.'

'We've waited patiently for you to take the first step back out into life again, and you haven't done it. We can't sit by any longer and watch you wither away,' Brittany said.

'You're too young to be an old, lonely woman,' Savannah said with a shrug.

'An old, lonely . . .' Jenny let the sentence fade away as she stared at her daughter in shock. 'I'm *not* old!'

'Well, you're not getting any younger, either, Mum,' Chloe pointed out.

'Now hold on a minute—'

'Jen, it's all right to acknowledge that you're not as *fun* as you once used to be,' Beth soothed.

Okay, that one hurt. She was still fun, damn it! 'I am *not* ready to be sat down in a rocking chair with my knitting just yet, thank you very much,' she informed them bluntly, then narrowed her eyes as all four of them displayed sporting, smug smiles. Too late, she realised she'd walked into a trap. Maybe she *was* losing her edge a bit—once upon a time she'd have never fallen for something that obvious.

Brittany nodded. 'So you agree, then, that you're not ready to give up and you should be out there enjoying life.'

'I don't see why dating has to be the thing that's going to save me from a life of dreary boredom,' Jenny shot back.

'Because you're still young and attractive and you need to get back out there and find someone to have fun with again,' Savannah said.

'Among other things,' Beth added with a wink.

'Eww,' Chloe said, with a dramatic shudder.

'Well, what did you expect was going to happen if you set your mother up on a date with a man?' Beth asked, seeming genuinely confused by the reaction.

'I was trying to *not* think about it, that's all,' Chloe answered.

'Would you two stop?' Brittany cut in before turning back to Jenny. 'Ignore them. Look, you don't have to rush into anything—'

'Good. So, I don't have to go out tonight then,' Jenny said.

'You do. That bit's already been arranged. But you don't have to feel *pressured* into doing anything more than going out to dinner, if that's what you're worried about.'

Until that point, she hadn't even thought about what more could be involved than going out for dinner and now she *was* worried. Considerably. Surely this person wasn't going to expect *sex? Tonight?* She hadn't even shaved her legs, for goodness' sake!

'Uh-oh . . . I think we're losing her,' Beth murmured.

'Nope. I'm not ready for all this.' Jenny shook her head and backed away.

'You are. At least, you will be,' Brittany assured her. 'You're never going to feel ready unless you get out there and do it. Remember what you always told us? Whenever we were nervous about doing anything new, you used to tell us to just wing it. Get in there and just do it.'

Well, that seemed like stupid advice now.

'Yeah,' Chloe piped up, nodding encouragingly at her older sister. 'When I had that meltdown about a class presentation I had to do in year seven, you made me go in and do it . . . Actually, you pretty much dragged me into school that day, when all I wanted to do was hide in bed.'

'This isn't the same thing . . . that was school and you *had* to do it,' Jenny said, sensing a touch of malicious revenge in her daughters' pep talk.

'Think of this as something just as important. You can't hide in bed every time something scary happens and you don't want to face it,' Savannah replied.

This time, Jenny was positive her children were enjoying the opportunity to fling their mother's advice back in her face. No one told you what to do when your great and wise parental advice came back to bite you on the arse years later. She'd brought this on herself by being such a brilliant mother. 'Oh, for goodness' sake,' she muttered.

'Mum, if you can't do it for yourself, then do it for us. Be the role model you've always been and show us what a brave, independent woman looks like,' Brittany said, using a motivational tone that Tony Robbins would have been proud of.

Fuck. There was no getting out of this—not unless she wanted to admit that everything she'd used in the past to try and mould these kids into responsible, well-adjusted humans could be ignored once you were an adult.

'Fine,' she said tightly. 'But this is the one and only time. You take me off that stupid dating app and *never* do this again.'

'So, about that . . .' Brittany winced—actually winced, as though in great pain. 'You've kind of got a few more dates for the rest of the weekend.'

Jenny stared at her eldest daughter. She thought she'd already been shocked as deeply as a person *could* possibly be shocked . . . but nope, now she was shocked into speechlessness.

'There's *more* men I'm supposed to be seeing?' she finally managed. Who the hell did that, lined up multiple dates with different people all weekend?

'Well, they all responded to your profile and we didn't want to risk turning any of them away in case they were, you know, "the one",' Savannah told her, making little quotation marks in the air.

'"The one" . . .' Jenny shook her head, trying to dislodge the absolute insanity she was hearing. 'This stops now. I'm not some piece of . . . meat you get to hold out as bait to catch a bunch of crocodiles with.'

'Seriously, Mum,' Savannah said, eyeing her pityingly. 'This is why you needed a push. You have no idea how the world of dating works. You'll thank us for stepping in and navigating all this for you so you didn't stuff it up.'

A knock on the door cut short her scathing reply, which was partially a relief since she wasn't sure she could keep to the 'no swearing out loud' rule, as panic quickly settled in.

'It'll be fine. His name's Derrick and he's an accountant,' Beth said in a pacifying tone as she walked—or rather frog-marched—Jenny to the front door. 'He lives in Hamwell. And smile,' Beth ordered in a sugary sweet tone, as Brittany opened the door to a man who looked to be in his late fifties. He was dressed in a pair of impeccably ironed navy trousers and a crisp white shirt.

'Jenny?' he asked, as his gaze shifted between the five women smiling at him—well, four smiling and one frozen in a terrified, caught-in-the-headlights kind of expression.

'This is Jenny,' Beth said, thrusting her forward so that she almost staggered into the poor man's chest.

His face did a quick change from surprise to delight before he stuck out his hand. 'Derrick,' he said, as Jenny automatically shook it. They stood there staring at each other awkwardly until Beth stepped in again.

'Well, you two kids have a great time,' she chirped, pointedly ignoring Jenny's dangerous glare.